Death in the Borderlands

Simon Phelps

Published by Forward Thinking Publishing

First published 2025

Published by Forward Thinking Publishing

Text © Simon Phelps 2025

A catalogue record for this book is available from the British Library.

ISBN: 978-1-916764-06-4

Place Names

I have used spellings as close to the time the novel is set as far as possible to create a flavour of the times. My sources are various and spelling at the time varied from writer to writer so accuracy is impossible. Regions and Earldoms, even nations, had different boundaries from today so names that sound similar to modern ears do not necessarily correspond to present day mapping. Towns are usually where they were a thousand years ago.

Afon Guoy	River Wye
Cirenceaster	Cirencester
Colecestra	Colchester
Brecheniauic	Brecon, Aberhonddu
Afon Dyfrdwy/Deva River	River Dee
Deverdoeu	Chester
Dyflin	Dublin
Elwistonet	Pontrilas
Fforest Glud	Radnor Forest
Fleet Holm	Flat Holm island
Glowecestre	Gloucester
Gipeswic	Ipswich
Hereford	Hereford
Hope	Hope Mansell
Ircingafeld	Archenfield
Jorvik	York

Llandaf	Llandaff
Lundenburh	London
Roskilde	Roskilde, Denmark
Rwydin	Ruardean
Safearn Sea	Severn Estuary/Bristol Channel
Talgart	Talgarth
Y Clas	Glasbury on Wye

Death in the Borderlands

The year of 1055 had been a challenging one for the people of western England. Gruffud ap Llewellyn had united the Welsh into one kingdom under his banner with the help of an English Earl and Irish mercenaries. To recoup his expenses Gruffud had unleashed his combined forces to capture the city of Hereford. To the country's horror the Minster at Hereford was burnt and its priests murdered.

Our young protagonist, Sar, now reunited with his sworn Earl, Harold Godwinson, is once again caught up in the turmoil raging along the borders between England and Wales.

Simon Phelps

Chapter One

I'm standing at the back of the King's Hall in Glowecestre on a broad wooden platform. Here too, sitting around a sturdy plain table, there is Earl Harold alongside some of the kingdom's most powerful notables who are picking over the remains of a meal. In the hall below long trestles are lined by all the lesser thegns, reeves and aldermen from the surrounding shires. There is no merriment. No minstrels entertain. No young women are serving wines or ales. The mood is sombre. The purpose of this meeting? War.

All the men here will soon leave to levy the fyrd. Every man available will have to take his war spear, his helmet and whatever mail he owns or is issued and converge on Glowecestre. The majority will be armed peasant freemen, but every landowner will have some trained warriors to steady the rest. Chief amongst them are the elite housecarls of the Earls. Men like my friend Gyric. But not, ignobly born, me. The reason for all this tumult? A combined force of Welshmen under King Gruffud ap Llewelyn, the army of the English Earl Aelfgar and Irish Viking mercenaries have captured the borderlands up to and including the great city of Hereford. They have burnt down its minster, stolen its riches and enslaved many of its inhabitants. Not long ago I had been one of those mercenaries.

It is cold, the shutters are down letting in what little winter light there is along with a steady chilling wind. The ochre-stained walls are bare of tapestries, the rusting heavy iron hooks to bear them jut out at intervals, grim reminders of the King's absence.

I cast a bored and weary eye at my Earl's company. There's Earl Ralph, the King's French nephew, his tall, once elegant, figure slumped in shame at one end of the table. It was his forces that ran before the Welsh, abandoning Hereford to its fate. Assisted by a young priest, Bishop Athelstan of Hereford, trembles as he searches around with sightless eyes. No longer active in the church, he is here because his deputy, Tremerig, died soon after the minster burnt. Athelstan doesn't look far away from his heavenly reward himself. Ralph the Staller is here too, a formidable presence, representing the King. Earl Tostig, my Earl, Harold's brother, ruler under the King of Northumbria is not here. His huge restless Earldom of Northumbria keeps him busy and the Scots at bay. Also notable by his absence is Earl Leofric, although his lands border Wales to the north, Aelfgar, who is his son, fights with the Welsh. Should he have to fight against his own son? Can he be trusted? Aelfgar fights alongside Gruffud ap Llewellyn, now King of all Wales. Yet in the distant past, Gruffud killed Leofric's brother. One of England's most powerful Earls; nobody is certain where Leofric stands.

Harold's brother Gyrth is here, as too is Thurkill, commander of Harold's housecarls, a Dane by birth. Next to Harold sits his chaplain, Leofgar, a priest, but one who sports the moustaches of a warrior as well as the tonsure and robes of a religious man. All I know about him is his name. Thegn Scalpi is also at the table, Gyric's father, half Danish like Harold himself. All the other great men are strangers to me.

My guts rumble noisily, God, am I hungry. My mind wanders to visions of bowls of curds, fresh baked rolls.......

'Sar, here!' Thurkill's voice booms in my direction. 'Here, your Earl wants your views.'

I leap upright, my pale face blushing, 'I'm here sir.'

'Yes, I know you are there, now get over here.'

I walk over to the table and stand behind Thurkill's shoulder, between him and my Earl. Harold half turns and looks at me kindly.

For now, I have his approval, it is our secret that I have avenged the death of his cousin Beorn.

'Sar,' he says, 'Tell these men how you and your friends captured Hereford.'

'Jesu Mawr.' I muttered under my breath as twenty odd pairs of malevolent eyes glared at me.

Ralph the Staller half rose, his left hand on the table, his right, finger pointed in my face, his mouth twisted in fury, 'Harold, are you saying this stripling is one of the men who pillaged and burnt an English city, our King's city?'

Earl Harold grinned good humouredly and nodded.

'You fought with foreigners against your own country,' spluttered Ralph sitting back down in astonishment.

'I was hardly the only Englishman there, was I,' I retorted. 'Aelfgar had an army of his own.'

'He was serving with my friend Faelen,' said Harold.

'Faelen, that Irish adventurer who you used to threaten your King not that long ago.'

'Ralph, my father and I were negotiating with the King, nothing personal.'

The other Ralph stuck his oar in here. 'And now instead of being executed for your temerity you have become the most powerful man in the Kingdom after my uncle the King.'

It was now his turn to be stared at by the Staller. 'You might be the King's nephew but I am the King's man. You would do better to stay quiet,' he bellowed.

Earl Ralph reddened and shrunk in his chair, torn between his authority as an Earl and his recent disgrace as a warrior. 'It's not so important how they got into the town but how we're going to get them out,' he muttered.

'You would say that,' said the Staller, 'Though, to be fair, you are right.'

'Sirs, Lords, may I speak?' Again, those malevolent eyes. 'I don't think they'll want to stay anyway.'

'Go on.'

'Speak up young man.'

'Tell your boy to shut up Harold.'

'No,' said my Earl. 'Let's hear him out.'

Now I wished I'd kept my mouth shut. 'Two things; first everyone has got what they wanted. Second, the Irish are to sail round Wales to Deverdoeu to get paid, but I don't know when.'

Harold spoke first. 'So the Irish will want to leave and they will want Gruffud in Deverdoeu to meet them.'

I nodded.

'That leaves your first point,' said the Staller, 'Explain.'

Diw Sant, these are the people that run the country, I thought, 'Gruffud, is now King of all Wales. He's conquered the southern Waelas and united them all by beating the English. A thing every Welshman loves. He'll claim everything beyond the Afon Guoy as his own.'

'And Aelfgar?'

'Aelfgar has Hereford to bargain back for his Earldom.'

'And the Irish and their Dyflin Viking friends?'

'They'll get their pay, any loot they've kept and very many slaves.'

'You think we'll be offered Hereford and peace in exchange for Aelfgar's Earldom?'

'And the King's acknowledging Gruffud's as the King of all Wales. He's a brute but he's not stupid. He'll know he won't be able to hold onto the town forever but he'll get himself recognised as the Welsh king and at very little cost.'

Most of the malevolent eyes turned back to Earl Ralph.

Harold rapped his cup on the table. 'Now Sar, show us how Hereford was taken. The river goes down the western side as I remember.' He dipped his finger in his wine and drew a line on the table top.

I leant forward to add to the picture when my heavy bag of coins hidden behind my short cloak bumped into Harold's upper arm. He drew his elbow back and for a moment weighed the leather bag in his hand. He looked at me with narrowed eyes.

'Carry on Sar, use this wine.'

I dipped my finger in the cup and sketched the rough half-circle of the town, and a wavy line from each end of the crescent to show the river. 'All the town on the landward side was walled. Stone and timber. There was a gatehouse, here, on the town end of the bridge. Along the riverbank the wall was much lower and made of rammed earth.'

'But protected by the river?' said the Staller.

'Yes, fine for an attack by the Waelas, but we had ships full of warriors. The wall was lightly manned. They threw a few spears at us but the wall was low enough for us to throw them back alongside a barrage of our own spears and darts.'

'Darts?'

'Like short spears but with leather flights like arrows have feathers. Some of the Irish favour them. So, we're assaulting the walls while Aelfgar rams his huge longship into the bridge and his men climb straight up on to it. We're on the wall. Then after a short fight we attack the gatehouse from the flank. Aelfgar's men are facing both ways on the bridge. A wall of spears facing the routed horsemen forced them to go north and ride through the ford.'

The Staller, clearly eager to understand asked. 'Then they couldn't get back into the town?'

Earl Ralph was shifting uncomfortably.

'Not the way they went out. They could, those that survived, have gone in one of the landward gates.'

'So why didn't they?'

'I don't know sir. Mostly we worked all this out later. I was one of those who scaled the wall and attacked the gatehouse.' I shuddered as I remembered stabbing a young man in the face before tumbling him into the waiting warriors below.

'And then?

'And then we were in the town where nobody was there to defend.'

A tremulous voice came from further down the table. 'You were with the Irish?'

It was the blind old bishop.

'Yes, with the Irish and the Dyflin Vikings.'

'First into the city.'

I wondered where this was going.

'Yes.'

'At the minster.'

The penny dropped. 'And everywhere else.' I answered evasively.

'Where my priests were hacked down in cold blood?'

'I did hear something about that.' I lied. 'But I didn't see anything.' Truth was his priests had acted like idiots and brought their martyrdom upon themselves.

'Hmmm, I can't see you boy, but your tone tells me you're lying.'

'No, your worship, I'm not.' I lied again.

'You burnt the minster down.'

'Not me, I think that was an accident. Aelfgar was furious.'

'I should hope he was. And you stole all the vestments and all the gold crosses and chalices. Your sacrilege brought on my Bishop Tremerig's death. He was a Welshman did you know that?'

'No Father, I'm just an ignorant foot soldier, sir.'

The Bishop's blind eyes started to weep. His aide tried to comfort him.

Good luck to him, I thought as I became conscious that Leofgar had been staring at me for quite some time.

'That's a very fine sword you're carrying. Did you steal it?' he asked aggressively.

'No.' I shot back just as hard, 'I killed an Englishman for it.'

'You what?'

'Aelfgar's men were English. Your enemies. Still are, Father.'

'Sar, behave yourself. This man is my personal chaplain. If you can't respect his priest-hood you can, and will, respect that. We will speak later,' said Harold, forcefully.

It was clear that I was dismissed so I resumed my hungry wait at the back of the hall. Not long after more wine was brought in and along with it the bard. It was my old friend Candalo, whose fingers, broken by Oslaf, could no longer play the harp. Morwid, his beautiful daughter played for him while he sang. There she was, her long black curls, her brilliant blue eyes. My heart thumped. I felt weak at the knees, and, although she hadn't even seen me, I knew my face burned bright red.

Eventually, all the powerful men got up and, taking their musicians with them, went, leaving the housecarls and other retainers to sit at the boards and eat. Not curds but a filling barley and root stew with a wheaten bannock. No sooner had we started to eat when Thurkill came in and called Gyric and I out.

We followed him into a small house behind the cathedral. I'm still trying to stuff the bannock into my mouth as we walk when we came face to face with the Earls, Harold and Gyrth, Ralph the Staller and Leofgar. Father Leofgar as I suppose I was to call him.

The three of them are sat on stools around an upturned barrel. Thurkill walks to take his accustomed spot behind Harold's right shoulder. Gyric and I, after leaving our weapons by the door, stand, side by side in front of them.

It was Ralph who spoke first. 'You two were at the battle of the Seven Sleepers, yes?'

We both nodded and shuddered. It had been a truly horrific day. Many great men had died and many, many more ordinary people too. The lucky ones violently in the battle, the unlucky in fever and delirium from black and stinking fly-blown wounds in the days that followed.

'Why do you think you won? There were as many, if not more enemies arrayed against you on ground of their choosing and in their own country.'

'Earl Siward was a great commander, Sir.' I said. I knew no one would be unhappy with that answer.

Gyric, after pausing for thought spoke up. 'I think it was Burgric's planning.'

'How so?' asked Ralph.

'We were well supplied, sir. Even in Alba, so we didn't have to raid for food and there were always spare shields and other weapons, like the angons.'

'Angons, what are they?'

The others exchanged glances, equally mystified.

'Sar, knows best. He had to throw them,' said Gyric.

I was surprised they didn't know. 'They were throwing spears with a thin metal shaft behind the head. When they stuck in a shield or hit the ground they bent, sirs.'

Earl Harold asked, 'To what purpose?'

Always hard to explain to your betters what to you seems bleeding obvious. I squirmed a bit and said. 'Cos they were bent, they couldn't be thrown back and if they stuck in a shield, it became unusable.'

Burgric told me that they used them in the old days,' added Gyric.

'Your foster father isn't he, Burgric, I mean,' asked Harold.

Gyric nodded assent.

'Clever man. Liked his history, eh?'

I wasn't so sure. The horror of standing out in front of our army to throw those cursed weapons and my companion's foul death was still strong in my mind.

'A terrible number of fine men died that day.' I chipped in, sharply.

'Heroes, all of them,' said Father Leofgar.

Sibhyrt wasn't a hero. Didn't want to be one either. Just wanted to look after his oxen, not to die in a foreign country. I glared at Leofgar but held my tongue.

'They fought long and hard, all day long. It was horrific,' said Gyric. 'Horrific.'

I could see he was starting to shake. Gyric had been deeply affected by the events of that day. He'd fought in the front line of the shield wall for hours.

'As for me,' said Leofgar, 'I'm surprised it took quite so long to beat a bunch of savages.'

I nudged Gyric with my elbow and spoke up. 'Sir, some of them were very savage, sir. Fierce warriors fighting on their own ground.'

Leofgar's grey eyes turned to mine. 'You look like a savage yourself. I've seen you strutting around with a targe, throwing spear, your long hair. And you speak with a Welsh accent. So, what have you done? Just run around on the edges throwing things?'

Harold laughed. 'You should be careful here Leofgar my friend. This lad killed the shipmaster Eardwulf while he was still a pup.'

'Ah, this is the boy, I heard about that. A freak moment when you attacked a distracted warrior,' said Leofric.

'I killed his son too. It is his fine sword I carry.' I retorted; suddenly aware I might have said too much.

Harold saw this and said, 'Don't worry Sar. Leofgar is my chaplain. He hears my confession and Thurkill is privy to all such matters.'

'This, then, is the young man who avenged your cousin's murder. No doubt you had allies.'

'Come, come, you both serve in my household, put aside this squabble,' said Harold. 'Here, Sar, show him your scars and he'll know you for a fighting man.'

Now, don't get me wrong. Harold is my master. I'm sworn to serve him, I owe my life to him and have fought for him more than once but asking this of me I did not like. Reluctantly I started to strip off as if the marks on my face and my missing finger weren't enough. I tried to conceal my bag of coins in my short cloak as I took it off but it thumped as it hit the floor. My body is covered in scars. Old ones, a large one along my right side, and new ones. Barely healed leg and shoulder wounds that still made me hunch and limp at times. I already had the lattice of small scars up my forearms that all seasoned fighters carry.

Even Harold was shocked and he quickly bid me to get my clothes back on. Leofgar grudgingly conceded that I'd been beaten a few times. I was growing to hate that man, who had never fought a battle, but I could see it mattered to Harold to believe we'd get along so I bit my tongue and hurriedly dressed. For the second time that day my face was burning red.

Then Harold asked me about the bag. 'I noticed you carry a lot of coins Sar, let me see.'

I was very reluctant, although the original hoard had been split in four and much of it spent, it was still a sizable sum. I just didn't know what to do with it. I picked it up and took it to my Earl.

He tipped it out. 'By the Holy Cross! There are gold mancuses here, and a fortune in silver.'

'You stole this from the church in Hereford, didn't you?' said Father Leofgar.

I glowered at this priest with his tonsure and his warrior moustache. 'No, Father, I did not. I swear on the cross I did not.'

Earl Harold sighed loudly, 'You do need to account for this Sar. Where did you get it?'

Reluctantly I told the story. How Maelcolm of the royal line of the Strathwaelas had been sent up to join Earl Siward's army to be set up on the throne of Alba once MacBethadhad been expelled. How he had run away in fear of his life and took all the cash in the treasury with him. I had found him skulking around and we had escaped to Ireland together. I implied that I left him there, which wasn't true. My reward had been this money.

'He's lying,' said Leofgar. 'Maelcolm Canmore is ruling over the Scots in Alba as we speak.'

'Hmm,' said Harold. 'In truth, he's not the same Maelcolm our King first sent north. The original Maelcolm did disappear. We all believed he'd been murdered by another of the Strathwaelan princes, jealous of his success. Tell me Sar, what did he look like? Remember that I knew him from his days as a hostage in the King's court.'

'Well, sir. He liked to joke, at first anyway. He could fight with a sword, but he was soft.' I paused to think. 'Oh, yes, he could still speak his native tongue though he'd been in England since he was a boy.' I thought some more and then laughed, 'He was going bald. He wasn't happy about that because he was still a young man. Said, it proved he was a prince because his grandad was Owain the Bald.'

'It does sound like him,' said Harold.

'Yes, but anyone could know that,' said Leofgar.

I stood silent.

'They could, but the money disappearing was kept secret. Only Siward, Burgric and a select few know otherwise. We swore to the King to keep it in confidence. I'm going to keep this money for now, Sar. We'll talk more later.'

I was aghast, 'Jesu Mawr, I earned that money. I took care of Maelcolm from Alba to Dyflin. I earned every silver penny and gold coin. We made a deal.'

I'd actually left Maelcolm in Wales, but he didn't need to know that. Maelcolm had become my friend. He wasn't so soft now either.

'Don't shout at me Sar. I've said what I've said.'

I ranted on. 'I'm also owed my share of the northern campaign and Gruffud owes me for my part in taking south Wales for him. Don't suppose I'll ever see that. Do I get nothing for all these scars?'

'Get out, Sar. Get out the both of you.'

There was yet another embarrassment to follow. As he escorted us out of that confusing meeting, Thurkill asked me about my sword.

Can you fight with it, Sar?' he asked.

'I'll learn when I have to.' There's no point pretending to Thurkill.

'You'll start learning tomorrow. See me at dawn.'

Chapter Two

I slept badly. Angry as hell with Harold for showing me off and taking my money. Hard for me to be angry with this man. I was not only sworn into his service, I owed him my life. His way of seeing you and his easy charm had gained my loyalty almost from the moment we met. Taking my weapons, I crept out of the hall early. There was not a glimmer of the sunrise as a cold icy dew fell from the starlit sky onto the frozen ground. Over by the gatehouse a couple of guards stood, muttering to each other by a small brazier glowing with the last of the night's firewood. I preferred my chilly solitude to the meagre warmth and the grumblings of tired men. Tucking my throwing spears into the crook of my arm I breathed into my hands and waited for the black shapes of the buildings to turn grey in the fore dawn.

I felt calmer in the cold as I waited. The sky paled, quickly followed by the first twittering of the sparrows then the clarion calls of the local cockerels echoing back and forth around the town. As the first rays of the sun shafted through the chinks in the gates Thurkill strode around the corner of the hall.

'Come with,' he said beckoning. I quickly ran to his side. He gestured at the guards who slid the bar out from the gates and hauled them open. In the sudden burst of light, I saw the shapes of a man, a boy and a horse, black against the rising orb of the winter sun. We walked towards them. As we closed, I could see that the horse was drawing a two wheeled cart, piled high with bundles, boxes and spear shafts. The boy was leading the horse.

Thurkill gestured towards the man, 'Tunglo, Sar, Sar, Tunglo.'

We nodded a greeting, instantly sizing each other up. He was a swarthy man of middling height. A pot belly. Huge shoulders and chest. Shaven head, a long thick moustache and at least a week's worth of stubble on his chin. He was wearing a byrnie, the padded jacket that is worn under a mail coat in battle. Thick and heavy, it's sweaty as hell but very warm on a winter's morning. He was carrying no weapons but stood firm in the icy mud of the road. A wooden staff was loosely held in his right hand.

'I'll leave you with Tunglo,' Thurkill says to me, then turning to Tunglo, 'He's yours until we sail.'

Tunglo nodded, 'Follow.'

'But I thought?' says I.

'You thought Thurkill would be training you? Our Earl's right-hand man?'

Yes, maybe that was a bit dumb of me. I swallowed my disappointment and followed Tunglo through the alley between the King's compound and the buildings of Saint Peter's Abbey. This turned us westward. To our left the tracks all led to the docks while ahead lay the flat meadows of the flood plain grazed by the abbey's flocks and a few cows. The grass was still silver with the frosted dew, now sparkling in the bright sun.

'This'll do,' he said to the boy, a tousled headed kid of about ten.

The boy ran to the cart and threw off a large stone attached to a rope which was in turn attached to the horse's halter. An effective enough tether. Tunglo and I held the shafts and lowered them to the ground as the boy led the horse out.

'Stand in front of me. Take off your top,' said Tunglo.

Bloody hell, not again.

'I heard. Just your top. I need to see how you're built.'

I did as he asked and stood, all goose bumps in the wind coming off the river. I had a sudden vision of what he saw. A tall lad, young man, thin but wiry, too many scars. One, ran from my ear to my chin barely covered by my thin beard put there by Olsaf the day I killed his father. Very, very dark red hair worn longer than even the Danish style worn by the Godwinson's followers. A small shield, a targe, hanging by a rope loop on my back. The two throwing spears I leant against the cart, a seax sheathed across my belly a small throwing axe and a blackjack in my belt. As well as, of course, Oslaf's sword.

'What's that?'

I showed him the blackjack. Made from the foreleg of a deer the hoof and ankle bone made the handle with the first foot of leg skin stuffed with packed sand sewn tight. I was proud of this.

'I can knock a man out with this and not split his skull.' I boasted.

'Hmmmm,' was Tunglo's response. 'You've clearly been in a few fights, but you stand weary.'

This was true. I'd been fighting or campaigning for two years. Even the winter rests had not been long. In Jorvik we'd, Gyric and I, struggled for a living and wintering with Faelen had not been all rest and cheer. I'd never thought about it, but now it had been said, I felt like I could sleep for a month.

'And you're too thin, you need to eat and rest more.'

'Chance would be a fine thing,' I said, remembering last night's broken meal and the breakfast I'd not yet had.

'Hmmmm. Can you throw those things? Show me. See those dead thistles.' He pointed at a clump quite a distance away. 'Don't hit any sheep mind.'

Tunglo was clearly a man of few words, and those were a mixture of English and Danish. I was ready not to like him but I found that I did. His boy seemed very relaxed in his company so a stern man but not a bully was my guess.

I'm very good at throwing spears. I like it. Take someone down before they even get near you. Do it well, you don't get hurt. I threw one of my spears and it landed inches away from the tuft. I swiftly threw another to land it near enough to a sheep to make it jump with surprise. The flock ran off bleating loudly.

The boy laughed out loud and ran off to collect the spears.

Tunglo grunted, 'How do you like to fight?'

'I like to throw things if I can, one spear, then the axe, then I keep the other throwing spear to stab with. If things don't go well, I can either throw it or my opponent will have cut or broken the shaft. Then I rely on my seax and my targe.'

'Show me.'

'How?'

Tunglo shrugged, 'Throw things at me.'

Jesu Mawr, I said to myself as I trotted away, with my left hand through the strap of my targe and a spear in each hand, to make some distance. I can't kill this man.

I turned and threw anyway, not stopping to pause. He took one step sideways and snatched my spear out of the sky. That was a shock. He stood there now, my spear in his right hand and his staff in his left. I threw the axe. People aren't used to this. It was an old style of fighting shown to me by a Friesian pirate. As I threw, I ran towards him moving my other spear from my left to my right. He leant sideways and the axe whistled past his ear and in that instance, he threw my spear back at me. God he was fast. I threw up my targe and pushed it away at the very last moment. The speed of this was such that I lost balance and staggered and let go of my spear. Next thing he'd ran up and knocked me to the ground with his staff. Stunned I tried to draw my seax.

'Don't bother son. You've been bested.'

There was no triumph in his tone. It was matter of fact. I pride myself on my speed and this muscle-bound, pot-bellied man had just taught me a lesson.

He thrust a paw towards me, I grabbed it and he pulled me to my feet.

'You know why I'm here?'

'To teach me to use a sword?'

He scoffed, 'I'm here to help Thurkill turn a bunch of farmers and ploughboys into an army to push the Waelas back into their mountains. And you are going to help me.'

I did, but not straight away. Tunglo, the boy and I had just taken a moment to breakfast. Tunglo was clearly well connected. We were eating cold mutton, wheat bread with honey, all washed down with watered wine. I couldn't stuff it in fast enough, greasy mutton fat, sweet honey, bread that wasn't gritty. While I'm sat there with the boy, Thurkill wanders up with a group of housecarls. He pauses for a quick chat with Tunglo. By the way they talked I could tell I was the subject.

Thurkill strolls over and takes me aside. 'Tunglo says you'll do. I'm now telling you that you do everything he says. Tunglo is only a slave but as far as you are concerned, he's your lord and master.'

My eyes widen in surprise as I'm trying to chew and swallow at the same time.

'Yes, a slave. I found him in the fighting pits in Roskilde.'

I frown, still chewing.

'In Denmark, Sar. From a boy he's fought for his life so do not be deceived or you will be humbled.'

I swallowed, 'Already have been sir,'

Thurkill smiled his quiet wry smile. 'Good, cockiness can get you killed. Now, Tunglo learned to fight in the pits but his battle tactics he learned from me. As did you.'

I smiled as I saw myself on the beach at Porloc barely able to lift a shield and swamped in a mail coat.

'Just a boy you were Sar. Now you can carry a man's shield and learn to wear mail. I need you to be able to fight in the wall as well as skirmish and scout. Time for you to grow up.'

I flinched at this but I respected Thurkill and knew he liked me. I was tempted to protest. I'd been in more fights than any of those fine housecarls but it was true. I needed to learn how to fight like a thegn's son, mailed, with sword, helmet and war spear.

As Thurkill turned to leave I noticed a couple of the housecarls muttering together and scowling at me. One of them, a dark haired handsome young man, stared directly in my eyes and spat on the ground before him. I know a threat when I see one. I shrugged, ignored him, then rejoined Tunglo and the boy.

Tunglo had me dress in a byrnie, mailed coat, and helmet and then he gave me a full-sized shield. It was heavier than any I had lifted before.

'Oak, not lime wood,' he said. 'Strengthens you.'

I went to strap on my sword when he shook his head and gave me a wooden one, ill balanced and heavy, it felt clumsy in my hand.

'Really?' I asked. 'I've got to fight with this?'

He nodded, 'Work it out.'

I stood there with all this weight dragging me to the ground. I felt knackered already and I'd not lifted a finger. I realised then that all those thegn's sons, men like Gyric, had all done this, probably since they were boys. If you could fight carrying all this a real sword and shield must feel light as feathers.

For the rest of the morning Tunglo came at me with his staff. Everything was hard. Used to my small targe I'd keep wildly swinging the heavy shield when a small shift would have worked. Every blow or feint with the sword was so slow Tunglo just danced out of the way and clouted me again. As for a sword having two edges. I couldn't get that at all. I'd fought swordsmen and knew you can cut both ways I still couldn't stop hacking like with a seax or axe. By noon, despite the mail and helmet I was bruised all over and my head was ringing. The boy had laughed himself sick. I was beginning to hate him. Then Tunglo called a break. Once again we ate, cheese, eggs, cold meat, all washed down with more watered wine. He said this is what a fighting man needs. I was happy to agree.

That was the end of my training for the day. By the time we'd finished eating the first fyrd levies started filing onto the floodplain. Got to admit, it was not a hopeful sight. Apart from their aldermen commanders and their housecarls the rest were just a mass of mostly unarmed freemen milling around. Thurkill turned up again with a group of Harold's housecarls. Once again that same young man was glaring at me while laughing with his friends. This time Gyric was with them.

I walked over. 'Hey Gyric, who's that guy there?'

'Hello Gyric, how are you? Are you having a good day?' Gyric said mocking me gently. 'Which one?'

'That dark pretty boy. Gave me the eye earlier.'

'Oh, that's Wulfgeat. Think he's pretty do you?'

'You know what I mean.'

'The girls like him.'

'Yeah, bet they do but he don't like me. Why's that?'

Gyric shifted uncomfortably, his cheeks reddening.

'Come on Gyric, spit it out.'

'He's the son of one of the King's thegns. Thinks, like most of the nobility, that full-time fighting men should only come from noble families. Sons of thegns and above.'

'So, he doesn't know me.'

'Sar, it's clear you're no noble despite speaking your mother's English. The Welsh comes through and you're not a housecarl yet Harold lets you carry weapons even in his household. No one knows who your father is. You don't fit.'

'Like I fucking care. Entitled fuckwits.' I spat out, angry now. 'I suppose the rest of them think the same way.'

'Well, some do. Some were more understanding when I told them about how you came into Harold's service.'

I turned and shoved my fingers hard into Gyric's chest. 'You told them about me? You told them what? That I'd been wearing rags and was herding goats. Is that what you told them?'

Gyric stepped back both angry and defensive. 'I was trying to help you Sar, just trying to stick up for you.'

'Stick up for me you prick. Don't you fucking understand anything, anything at all? Just get the fuck away from me. I'll go where I belong, with the slave and his boy.' I stalked off, angrier than I needed to be, angry, and truth was, hurt.

Chapter Three

I walked back to the milling crowd of freemen angry, sullen and miserable. I was to help Tunglo sort them out into types. Useful in a shield wall, useful as spear throwers and second row men, useful only to fetch and carry. You always need a lot of the last. To keep your fighters fresh, you needed to feed them, water them, carry spare weapons and shields, feed them again, repair shoes, clothes, mail and keep weapons rust free and sharp and then feed them again. Thankfully for Tunglo and I the last group was someone else's problem.

I stripped off the mail coat and byrnie and put them back on Tunglo's cart. The boy helped.

'Tunglo said you was to have this.' He handed me a spear shaft.

'I'll have my throwing spears too.'

He took them down from the cart and handed them to me. 'I have a name you know.'

'What?' I answered irritably.

He stood defiantly in front of me his head no higher than my navel, hands on his hips and his dirty face with its mutton greasy mouth looked me directly in the eyes. 'You think you're better than me, don't you?'

He had a point. Didn't excuse Wulfgeat, or stop Gyric from being a prick but, 'babes and sucklings' as the saying goes. I crouched a little and stuck my hand out. 'My name is Sar, what should I call you?'

The boy laughed then grinned cheekily, 'Sir, perhaps. My name is Aelfric.'

My turn to laugh, 'Aelfric, isn't that a nobleman's name?'

The boy blushed, 'I think my mum had plans.'

Oh yeah, what does she think now?'

Silence. Then, 'My mum died. After me, many still born babies then she wasted away.'

'Oh, I'm sorry. My mum died too. Hard isn't it.'

He nodded, 'Don't remember her.'

I thought of the last time I saw my mother. Her face smashed to a pulp and her murderer standing, crowing, over her corpse. By the end of the day, he was dead. At my hands. That terrible blood-filled day. My village burnt and my twin sister enslaved. Oslaf carving my face. Harold saving my arse. Started the day herding goats and ended it tied to a post by a longship.

'And your Da?'

He nodded toward Tunglo, 'That's my Dad.'

'He seems like a good Dad.'

Aelfric grinned, 'Mostly.'

Suddenly I was laughing. 'Tell you what. I'll leave my spears here. If I need them, I'll shout you, alright?'

He nodded and put them back on the cart. I had a feeling that I'd just made a new friend. I went over to where Tunglo was lining up the men. 'Those with weapons over here. The rest over there. See you met my son. Oy you, got a spear? No? Then over there.'

I chuckled, 'Yeah, I did. He's like you. Sees everything that's going on.'

'Say away from Wulfgeat.'

I grunted.

'Right, you take those without weapons. Strong, heavily built, send them back to me. Too young or too stupid, send them to the reeve and his flunkeys. The rest, turn them into spear throwers.'

'You said,' I grunted.

It was clear from the men we were to train that the general fyrd had been called up. The thegns chosen men would be properly armed and mounted as well as to an extent trained. We had the rest. These, the first to arrive from the surrounding hundreds, were a decidedly mixed bunch but their presence could extend a line so as it could not be outflanked and create an impressive mass to overawe our opponents. Harold was taking no chances.

As we were talking a wealthy looking man and a group of priests had arrived, walking alongside heavy ox carts. Provisions. Good. Spare shields and weapons. Good. Tally sticks and counting. Pain in the arse.

As each thegn's cohort came in we divided them up accordingly. Then we'd take each group up to the carts and equip them all. This took most of the day. By the time dusk fell I had dozens of spear throwers with one spear each. I also had a bag full of split tally sticks and a massive resentment towards the nit picking of officious clerics.

I spent the night with Tunglo and Aelfric under their cart beside a small fire. All over the flood plain were similar fires surrounded by groups of disgruntled men unhappy about being forced to sleep outdoors. My sleep was fretful, dreaming of my mother. Not as she used to come, angry and reproachful, but just her usual wild and haughty self. My sister's name was Moira, meaning bitterness while mine is Sar, meaning pain. You get the idea. She loved us, I guess, in her tough kind of way. I knew it was hard for her to see Moira and I, so like our real father in looks. Moira even down to the amber eyes, while I at least had hers. I pushed all these thoughts into the black, hard stone inside of me and snuck out from under the cart. While I breathed life into the ash pile remaining of last night's fire I thought of the man with the dark red hair and my sister's eyes who seemed to know the blade I carried. My mother's knife. He'd kept it. Gyric thinks he might be my father. Seems unlikely. I remain, no man's son. A bastard, with even my aunt's family wiped out, cousins, retainers, and land all gone. Wiped out because of me.

The sword practice went a bit better that morning. Tunglo grunted his pleasure and I shed the mail and byrnie with a satisfied sigh of relief. After we breakfasted I found my cohort of spear throwers to be all equipped with two spears each. I checked them all. Then I sent Aelfric back to the clerics with the bent and twisted ones to get them replaced. Meanwhile, I started to teach. This felt strange but the simple fact I could throw a spear better than any of them, further and more accurately earned me enough respect for them to listen to me.

Soon enough they were laughing and taking the piss out of each other. I was on a winner. I didn't need them to be that accurate. I needed to get them to be able to be able to throw it over the heads of two or three ranks of men in the shield wall so as to hit the men behind the enemy's front ranks. Not too far and, definitely; not too low. I had visions of our shield wall being struck by a wave of spears in the back of their heads. I set up half their spears in a row upright in the ground and got them to throw their other spear over them. Then to run over, pick them up and throw them back.

'How're we going to do this in a real battle?' one young clod-hopper asked.

I was tempted to laugh at him but caught myself. Until I'd seen my first real fight, I had no idea what went on. 'You'll be picking up the spears that the Welsh have thrown at you. They'll be throwing yours back. It gets nasty. A lot of them use bows as well so keep your eyes up and be ready to move. You have no shields. Not long after most of the spears will be spent and your job changes. You'll be carrying spare shields, if we have any, to the men in the first ranks, giving spent men water and dragging out the wounded, and the dead.'

Uncertainty swept through them as the reality of what they were readying for sunk in. I shouted, 'So come on lads. We just have to get so good at this you kill them all first.'

I wasn't sure how much that helped but they went back to their practice and, overall, they steadily improved. As the morning went on more wagons arrived and our men lined up to replace spears, be given leather caps and jerkins in the case of mine and helmets, byrnies and mail for Tunglo's men.

While they queued up, Tunglo and I looked on. We stood there, side by side, arms crossed, keeping an eye on the clerics and the men to make sure tallies and equipment matched.

'Your boy, nice lad. His English is good.'

'Ay, his Mum was English.'

'He says he doesn't remember her?'

'It's easier than talking about her.'

'Yeah, I can understand that.'

'I'm not really his Dad either.'

'You're not?'

'No, we met soon after I was brought here, three years ago.'

I winced as I realised how recently Aelfric had lost his mother.

Tunglo noticed and nodded, 'Over a year now. I kept him on.'

'Where's his Dad then?'

'Who knows? Slaves don't get a lot of choices.'

I squirmed. Slavery made me uncomfortable. I should've saved my sister. I changed the subject, 'Tunglo, odd name.'

'I'm a Sorb.'

'What's a Sorb?'

'Sorbs are a tribe of the Wends. You English know nothing.'

'Say something in your own language.'

Tunglo made some completely meaningless noises.

I laughed, 'I've heard nothing like that before. So where do Wends live then?'

'Other side of Denmark, on the Baltic Sea.'

'Is that north? Do they have wolverines there?'

'Wolverines?'

'Like giant polecats. Lady Gytha says my sister is where wolverines come from. It's cold, snows a lot and is north.'

'Never heard of them. You've met Lady Gytha?'

'Yeah, scary isn't she?'

We grinned at each other at the memory of the matriarch of the Godwinsons, our Earl's mother. At last, my men finally had everything they needed. Tunglo's much bigger force would take longer. I walked back to the training ground my head full of memories, most of them painful.

I ran them back to the line of spears left upright in the ground and set another row up fifteen paces further.

'Now lads, in between these posts are four or five ranks of warriors, all facing the enemy. If they're moving forward, you will find new spears to throw. If they're being forced backwards, you go and reinforce their lines. For now, you just need to be able to throw over that distance every time. Every time.

This proved a lot harder for some of them. I got impatient and irritated, herding them one way then the other, watching them throw, then herding them back. Often with my staff. While all this was going on Harold's housecarls filed onto the meadows. They'd be practising more complicated actions. The 'boar's snout', an aggressive wedge, it's point tipped with the fiercest warriors. How to do a fake retreat and combine spear and shield warriors with the huge wielders of the bearded axe. The long-bladed battle axe favoured by the strongest warriors. These had come to include Gyric. Another thing to sort out. I owed him an apology. Again.

I carried on wrestling with my men and my memories. Behind me I could hear the horns blowing and the shouted commands followed by Harold's war cry of 'Holy Cross'. The sounds of well-trained warriors preparing for war. Suddenly there was a prickling between my shoulders as I became aware that the sounds behind me had ceased. Someone was watching me.

'You should go back to herding goats, boy. What you were born to do.'

Wulfgeat's voice, informed by Gyric's stupidity. I shook my head, ignored him. I kept my back to him and carried on the training, but a little seed of iciness settled in my guts.

'Now look at you. Think you're a warrior. Born an outcast. Still an outcast.'

His voice again, followed by talk I couldn't make out. A group of men chuckling, laughing, at Wulfgeat's taunts. At me. I walked over to show a man a better hold on his spear and stole a glance behind me. Seven, maybe eight, of the housecarls had separated off with Wulfgeat to jeer at me. All wearing mail, no helmets or shields.

The taunts continued. About goats, about being Waelas, not an Englishman, the colour of my hair. About pissing myself while Oslaf cut my face. Gyric didn't tell him that one. People talk. Some of Harold's older housecarls had been there on that fateful day. I ignored them all. I wasn't that boy on the beach at Porloc anymore. I didn't have to react.

Wulgeat raised his voice, 'Heard your mother had a bad day too.'

'Christ man, that's a bit harsh,' said one of his companions.

'Who cares about some peasant's feelings? Do they even have them?'

The cold spread through my guts and I whirled around to face him, 'Yes, my mother died that day. And I killed the bastard that killed her.'

'Bit of a fluke though, wasn't it?'

That much was true. I looked at him. Certain that he could not be challenged. His status meaning even the wergild for an injury would ruin the common man. Untouchable. I took a step towards him. He drew his sword and beckoned me forward.

'Come and get me boy. Come on if you dare.'

My mind was racing but incredibly clear. I gripped my staff tightly and sprinted towards him. His face blanched with shock. This he hadn't expected. I'm fast. As I ran, I swapped my staff from my right hand to my left. Swung, struck his sword hand reversed the staff and two handedly rammed one end into his gut. Rammed it so hard that it winded him through both his mail and byrnie and threw him onto his back. His sword flew from his hand and he fell, gasping, to the floor. I jumped back and stood square, daring anyone else to come at me. It happened so fast they were all standing there with open mouths. For a moment all was still. I wanted to giggle. I didn't.

Wulfgeat was furious, having no breath he could not curse me but his face told the story. I heard the drubbing of horses cantering up behind me, Then I felt the hot breath of a horse was snorting down the back of my neck.

'Are you two fighting?' It was Thurkill.

'No sir, just part of the training,' Somehow, Tunglo was now standing between Wulfgeat and I. 'Just matching different styles.'

I turned to face Thurkill as my immediate commander. Wulfgeat got back to his feet. I placed my staff on the ground and stepped back while Wulfgeat sheathed his sword and stepped forward. The three of us were now in a row before Thurkill and the thegns who rode with him.

It was clear to me that Thurkill wasn't fooled for a moment. He chose not to see, 'My men train hard and rough but as long as no bones are broken or wounds that need stitching then I'm fine with that.' He dismounted and continued, 'Now Sar here, has had a lot of fighting experience but has had little experience with a sword. Wulfgeat has yet to see a battle but is a fine swordsman. Let's watch them train.'

He had words with Tunglo and while the thegns dismounted and had my spear throwers hold their horses. Tunglo equipped both Wulfgeat and myself. Wulfgeat had to lose his mail until we were both in byrnies and thick leather caps carrying oaken shields and heavy wooden swords. My heart sank. Tunglo came over, and while checking my shoes were strapped tight, muttered, 'Wulfgeat won't have a problem with this. What I taught you isn't enough. You'll need to find your own way through this.'

'Thanks, I think,' I was thinking too, why was Thurkill doing this? Teaching me another lesson? Or just amusing his friends? Maybe he was just finding a way for Wulfgeat to save face. Probably I would never know. I needed to get into the moment. I'd been in a ring of shouting men twice before. Can't really say either went well. I nearly killed Jokul that first time, though we did become friends after. With Oslaf, he nearly killed me, would have if Morwid hadn't saved me.

I was a boy then. I'd killed Oslaf since and scalped his bleeding corpse. Thing is Wulfgeat would have been fighting like this since he was a boy. Even if I got a beating, I would survive. No one was going to die today. Didn't mean I wanted to lose.

I pulled on a pair of hide gloves, hefted my shield, took a firm grip of the heavy wooden sword, and stepped forward.

Wulfgeat came at me straight away with a flurry of blows from different angles. No feints, all real strikes. I was quick enough to shift my shield here and there or push his sword away with mine. Then the feint came. I tried to deflect a blow and was wading into thin air. I felt a hard blow on my right shoulder, for a moment my arm went numb. I nearly dropped the sword. If this had been a real fight, I'd have been bleeding and defenceless.

He hit out again. I turned and deflected with my shield. I think I'd expected more fancy sword work. Maelcolm used to be a bit flash, swinging around, leaping about and showing off. Opportunities there, to get in, take advantage, keep calm and slip in through the showiness but Wulfgeat did none of those things. He stepped back and grinned at me.

'Not so easy fighting a real warrior eh, churl,' he said, setting into a firm fighting stance.

I didn't answer, what was there to say? He'd not seen half of what I'd seen. I knew despite all his confidence; he could crumble as easy as anyone in the random brutality of a real battle. This wasn't a real battle.

He then attacked me with a series of short, sharp, chopping strokes from all directions. I fended them off but found myself stepping backwards. I steadied, taking the blows. He altered his attack to wide swinging blows which thudded hard against my shield or made my wrist ache when I took blows on my blade. He drew back, he didn't need to say a word. He just grinned at me.

We returned to the fight, both breathing heavily. I managed to defend myself but barely got in a single blow, while he kept hacking at me like a woodsman attacks a tree. My limbs grew wearier under the weight of the practice weapons. The crowd got restive and the odd nasty jeer came my way. He feinted high then swung a blow, low under my shield which would have taken my legs out from under me if I'd not jumped back at the last moment. This wasn't a fight anymore. This was my inevitable defeat.

We both paused, breathing hard. I remembered Tunglo's words. I can't fight this man on his own terms. I loosened my hold on the bar inside my shield boss, took a deep breath and ran at him. I raised my sword as if to make a down cut towards is head. He raised his shield. I knew he could counter with his sword and defend himself at the same time. I was wide open. I swung with the sword and pushed away with my shield and let go of both. The shield flew away just catching the tip of his sword while his eyes followed the skyward spinning of mine. I followed them in and grabbed his sword arm with both hands and pulled it close to my side and whipped my right leg behind his left calf. He toppled backwards to the ground. I went with him. He landed hard with a grunt across my right leg. I swung the left one over his body and twisted around, never letting go of his sword arm. I twined my feet around each other. I now had his right arm braced over my thigh, rigid, held close to me with both hands. I could break it if I wanted. I didn't. He thrashed around, tried to push up with his legs. He let go of his shield and braced against the ground with his elbow while the muscles in his right arm twisted and strained in my grip. None of this could move my leg or push himself off the ground. On the ground I was a strong as him but better placed.

'Are you beaten?'

The crowd was roaring. I couldn't hear him or see his face but his body going limp told me that he knew he was. He let go off his sword. I lifted my leg of him. He rolled off my other one which was beginning to go numb. We both leapt to our feet, wary of the other. His eyes narrowed at me. I couldn't tell if this was hatred or respect. The crowd's racket suddenly ceased.

A furious voice came from behind and above me, 'You two, follow me.'

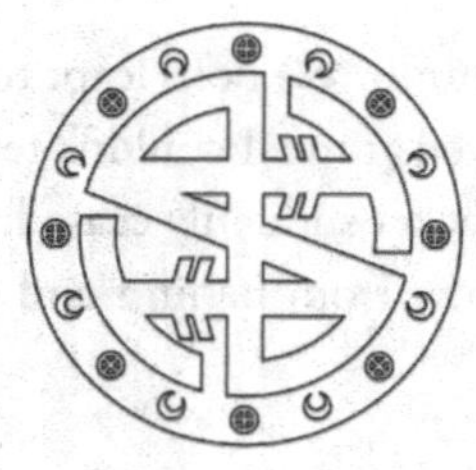

Chapter Four

Harold was furious, 'I never expect to see members of my household rolling around in the dirt. Ever.'

Wulfgeat and I squirmed before him, back in that same small house. Back again in front of Thurkill, Gyrth, Leofgar and my Earl. Harold even turned on Thurkill.

'How could you have let this happen? By the Cross, you of all people know that we do not disgrace ourselves in front of our soldiers. Especially when a week ago they were ploughboys and carpenters.'

Thurkill chuckled, unfazed by Harold's anger, secure in his worth and their long friendship, 'I was curious to see how they'd match up. The rolling in the dirt bit? That was a surprise. Had you though, Wulfgeat, didn't he?'

Wulfgeat stared at the floor while Harold raged on, 'Look at me. See how I dress? All this finery? You know why? To show my status, my place in the world, so people respect it and know their own.'

The Godwinsons, and the other Earls, certainly dressed magnificently. Harold, even in his role as a military commander wore long gowns with borders embroidered with silver wire and semi-precious stones while his hooded long cloak of the finest woven wool was fringed with pearls. Gold and silver long pinned broaches held everything together. His sword pommel too was silver and stones and its sheath equally richly encrusted. On a stand behind him hung a suit of highly polished mail and a gleaming jewelled helmet of unbelievable value.

I'm doing that soldier being bollocked thing. Staring straight ahead but not actually looking my superior in the eye and letting it roll over me.

Harold wasn't having it. He grabbed my face and made me look him in the eye. 'You are a man in my household. You will act like one. You will dress like an Englishman. You will stop looking like some Waelas tribesman. You can still carry the weapons of your choice but you will shave your beard, grow your moustache and cut your hair short. Not Danish short but Saxon short. Do you understand?'

He let go of my face, which was red with anger and shame, 'Yes sir.'

'And, Sar, you will not be sleeping under a cart with Thurkill's slaves but will sleep wherever my housecarls sleep and eat when they eat.'

I said nothing. There was nothing to say.

'Wulfgeat, my household must not only be seen to be united it has to be united. United around me as your Earl and as the King's man. If I choose to have a warrior in my attendance who is not a housecarl that is up to me, not you.'

By now Wulfgeat had stopped staring at the floor and had adopted a similar pose to mine.

Harold, frowning, was striding from side to side of the room, 'You two have wasted enough of my time. For now, Wulfgeat, you will train Sar to use a sword and battle shield every daybreak. And you, Sar, will tell Wulfgeat and any other housecarls at your mess table how the Waelas, and the Irish Norsemen fight.'

As my eyes swivelled to look at Wulfgeat, his eyes swivelled to mine. A fellow feeling flashed between us. Neither of us were happy with these orders.

Harold stopped striding and with his left arm across his body he cradled his right elbow in his left arm while rubbing his chin. He was still thinking. His eyes crinkled with something like amusement, 'Wulgeat, you can help Tunglo train the levies.'

'Sire, is that not beneath me?' Wulfgeat found his voice.

'Fighting a churl wasn't beneath you? No, don't bother arguing. I need a lot of men trained in a short time. You won't be alone. I'm going to ask every thegn to contribute trained men to train the rest. These peasant freemen won't be going home anytime soon,' said Harold, actually grinning now. 'At least some good has come out of this nonsense.'

At that moment several well-dressed men walked into the room. At least a couple of them I recognised as having been at the fight. Among them too, were Earl Leofwine, Harold's younger brother. Wulfnoth, the youngest, was living as a hostage in Normandy. Here too, was Thegn Scalpi, Gyric's father.

Harold turned to them, instantly reverting to his usual genial self, greeting them warmly. Scalpi saw me, raised his eyebrows, and said, 'Might have known. I heard you were back.' Turning to the man next to him, he said, 'Sithric, your son is lucky to be alive. This boy,' he nodded towards me, 'has something missing. He can kill, just like that, no feelings. I saw him do it when he was still a boy.'

Thegn Sithric looked me up and down, 'Doesn't look like much. You lost to this then son?'

Wulfgeat mumbled assent. Sithric huffed scornfully. Thurkill overheard the exchange and decided to shove his oar in, 'You should be more careful now about who you deride Wulfgeat, this lanky streak of piss could pay your wergild and still walk away a rich man.'

Wulfgeat looked at me in surprise. I almost felt sorry for him. Almost. As for me a big smile grew across my face. It looked like I'd be keeping my money after all.

Thurkill spoke again, 'Go on you two, get out. The adults need to talk.'

It's evening now. I'm in one of the Abbey's buildings eating and drinking with about a score of Harold's housecarls. The back of my neck and ears are feeling really fucking chilly and my face is still sore from the barber. We're being served by a few middle-aged men and women from Harold's household, I can hear two of them gossiping behind me.

A woman's voice, 'Do you remember him? That white faced redhaired boy? The Earl brought him from somewhere when his father challenged the King, three years ago.'

'Looking at him now, I do remember. They say his father came out of a burial mound in golden mail. He carries an ancient seax with a gold and garnet handle and can curse you with a look,' a male voice replied.

Not any more he doesn't, I thought. That seax is now in the hands of another white faced redhaired man. Odd to hear that old nonsense again. The golden mail is a nice new touch. Grinning inwardly, I dunked a chunk of bread into my broth and gazed around the room. Gyric was here, we'd not talked yet, just nodded at each other. He was pleased to see me here, I knew. I knew too, that he would want me to say sorry to him. He liked things put right. I just found it awkward. Friendship is hard. It's easier not to like anyone.

Harold wasn't here but Thurkill, as our commander, was. 'Right Sar, your moment has arrived.'

Diw Sant, I thought as all eyes turned to me. I reddened; easier to fight than to talk in front of this lot. My tongue felt thick in my dry mouth.

'Come on, stand up, what can you tell us about the Waelas?'

I stood up, took a swig of ale, and looked around at the eyes looking at me. 'They fight a lot.'

'Tell us something we don't know,' shouted someone, followed by other men laughing.

I faltered, drank again, wishing this weak ale stronger, 'They like to fight each other but most of all they like to fight the English.'

'And then we kill them,' another voice, more laughter.

I waded on, 'They are not a wealthy people, few have mail, they are lightly armed and they move fast and quietly. Many of them carry bows.'

'Coward's weapons. Arrows are easily stopped by our broad shields,' said another over confidant idiot. They were losing interest now and talking amongst themselves. How could I get them to understand the terror of arrows flying from the trees shot by unseen enemies. The sudden ambush at the end of a weary day. The nightly screaming of captured stragglers.

I got angry, 'You're a bunch of fucking idiots, dreaming of great deeds in the shield wall under the banners of your Earls. It won't be like that. The Waelas can win a war without ever fighting a battle.'

That didn't go down well. Now men were shouting at me. Thurkill, smiling wryly, was quietly watching things play out. I'd failed it seems.

Then, to my great surprise, Wulfgeat stood up and started banging loudly on the table. 'Quiet you fools. If you can't listen to him, then listen to me.'

Stunned silence.

Wulfgeat was liked by some and respected by many. The room stayed quiet. 'This morning, I was beaten by a disarmed peasant. I still had my sword and shield yet was bested by speed and the unexpected. I was shamed, not by this man here. I was shamed by my own arrogance,'

I fidgeted, not knowing what to do. I looked at Thurkill, he was no help. Then another man stood up. It was Gyric.

'I want to speak. I'm the youngest of us housecarls but I've seen a lot. Some of you here were at the battle of Porloc and fought the Cornwaelas with our Earl. I was there too. So was Sar. He was at the fight at Lundenburh gate and he and I were at the battle of the Seven Sleepers. Since then, he has fought the Manxmen at sea and he has fought the Waelas for other Waelas. Has anyone else here seen that much action? Any of you?

I looked at him, tall, broad and muscley but I was remembering that chubby boy who helped me on Fleet Holm beach. My eyes prickled with tears. Still my friend. Still saving my arse. Gyric flushed, smiled his crooked smile, and sat back down.

Wulfgeat nodded at me and returned to his bench. The room stayed quiet. I began to speak and once I'd started it was hard to stop. I told them how any time we arrayed in a large force they would disappear into the woods and hills. That when we marched, they would take stragglers, leaving them gutted and hanging from trees to be found later. How they would fire arrows at our horses making them panic dropping riders or packs. How they gave orders through shrill trumpets that confused men and startled horses. How when we camped at night, men would creep in silently and deal sudden death. We could take ground in the hills but when we left, they would steal back in.

Wulfgeat tapped his cup on the table before him. I turned and he said, 'Are you saying that we've lost before we've even begun?'

'No, I'm saying that unless we were to conquer all of Wales they will always come back. I'm saying that when we fight, we have to stay together. If you need a shit, shit by your friends, if you go to a stream or a well, never go alone. They are now a nation under Gruffud ap Llewelyn. They are not united by love for him but by hatred of us. Like us, sooner or later they will want to go home. To plant crops, to see their children and make love to their wives. We'll have to stick it out longer than they do.'

I ran out of words and sat down drained. I'd done what I needed to do. These men at least would not under estimate their enemy. After a short, thoughtful, pause they began to talk amongst themselves.

Thurkill came over, 'Get up lad. Now you've got to say all that again, to Harold.'

By the time I was done the night was nearly gone. It wasn't just Harold and his brothers; I spoke in front of a room full of thegns and a priest or three.

At the end Harold came over to me as I sat slumped on a stool. He put a gentle hand on my shoulder. 'You've served me well Sar. Tomorrow, you come with me.'

I never had my lessons, apart from the fight, with Wulfgeat nor did I get to say goodbye to Aelfric and Tunglo. I continued to wear the sword anyway. The next morning, I was at the dock with my spears and my targe, but still not my purse. I had all my other things, except the horse I'd taken, with me. I'd forgotten about the horse. Sod the horse, I didn't like it anyway. There were several ships moored against the quays. One, a fine longship, was flying the White Dragon banner of Wessex. This would be Harold's ship. I boarded to join a busy company of soldiers, priests, noblemen and bussecarls and, of course, Harold's household.

'Haia Sar,' a woman's voice spoke to me from behind in Welsh. I instantly knew who it was by the Cornwaelas accent. I turned to find myself looking straight into Morwid's startling blue eyes.

For a moment I faltered, tongue tied and weak while she smiled gently at me. Then I came to myself and all those difficult feelings just went away. Calmly we both sat down on a long chest. One among many placed down the length of the deck, each side of the sail spar. This wouldn't be raised today. The ship would be rowing upstream, slowly, fully laden on these quiet waters.

'You've been a long-time away Sar?' she said continuing to speak in Welsh.

'Yes, I've missed you, you know.'

One hand came out from behind her blue cloak to wave those words away revealing a yellow dress and an embroidered sleeve. She was very finely dressed. Rings on her fingers, fur around the edge of her hood. Her hair loose underneath it showed she was still unwed.

'I see Harold is treating you well. And Candalo, how is he?'

Candalo was her father. After Oslaf broke all his fingers Morwid played his harp while he sang. He'd been the skald at Conor's court in Kernow before we'd burnt them out. That's why they spoke Welsh, English was their second tongue.

'He is well. He will want to hear about your adventures. He'll be around Harold at the stern, earwigging for the latest news or inspiration for a new song.'

'I'll always have time for your Da. I owe my life to you and him.'

She laid a hand on my forearm, 'Our debts to each other are long cleared, Sar. You owe us nothing.'

My eyes welled with tears. My life had never felt quite my own since the day she had saved me from my death blow at Oslaf's hand.

'I killed him you know,' I whispered.

'I suspected as much. Harold does not guard his tongue as well as he should around his household. He's a trustworthy man so he thinks others are too.' She paused, 'I'm glad Oslaf is dead. I hated him for what he did to my father.'

I thought of my murdered aunt and my little cousins, and my mentor Toki, all murdered by Oslaf's family because of his hatred of me. Guilt twisted inside of me. The darkness still hard and black as jet deep in my heart.

I changed the subject, 'You're not married or betrothed then,' I asked hesitantly.

'I've told you before. I'll share no man's bed.'

I knew why this was. Just thought time might have changed things. Her answer pleased and dismayed me. Too many feelings. Then a horn blew and the ship was all activity as we cast off, the bussecarls leant into the oars and we pulled into the stream.

We chatted off and on about nothing in particular until we reached our destination. Then as we stood waiting to disembark, she turned and once again putting her hand on my forearm said, 'Just be a friend to me Sar, be my friend.'

I looked into her eyes and nodded, 'I can do that.'

Just then Candalo pushed his way through the throng and, embracing me, whispered in my ear 'I heard what you did. Well done my boy. One day I will make you a song.'

'As long as you never sing it. What I did is meant to be a secret.'

'For now. For now,' he said thoughtfully.

I looked at him with great fondness. He was back in his prime. Little gold bells in his long, now slightly greying, hair and jewelled rings on his twisted fingers that contrasted with his dark clothes. Quite how Morwid and he reconciled themselves to serving in

Harold's court after what had happened at the hands of Harold's force I never really understood. I guess for a while they shared the same enemy. But now that enemy was dead?

For the rest of the journey, I mulled over Morwid's words. Did she really need me as a friend or was she just letting me down gently?

It wasn't far up the river but in that time the weather worsened. The relatively fine morning was now blowing in blustery squalls from the west. When we disembarked, we had to slop through the mud towards a walled enclosure on an island of higher ground. Still, it beat trudging miles through the countryside over rutted roads behind hundreds of other men slipping and sliding their way ahead of you.

The river ruled this land. The river ruled and moved where it willed. The remains of old causeways and jetties, banks of mud, broken trees and muddy, water scoured, ditches littered the flood plain.

It was a relief to get out of the wind as we passed under the arch of a substantial gatehouse. Within the walls was a stone church, a large priory, many animal sheds full of lowing cattle and long stable blocks as well as a fine timber house, built around a great hall as befitted an English Earl.

We were greeted courteously by a finely dressed elderly noblewoman who turned out to be Ealdgyth, Earl Odda's sister. As our party made themselves at home, she took Harold aside and said, 'That Odda is not here to greet you is not an insult. Since our brother Aelfric died two years ago, he's declined and his thoughts turn more and more towards the afterlife. He's not the man he used to be.'

'With respect, Ealdgyth, I need Odda's help to regain our King's lands. I come on his orders.'

'Go back through the gatehouse and take the causeway going south. You'll hear where you have to go.'

At all times four of Harold's housecarls escort him. One of them today was Gyric. I decided to tag along, hoping to get a chance to talk. Thurkill and Harold led the way. It wasn't far before we heard the sound of monks chanting. Before us stood a small chapel built of newly cut, warm yellow stone. Harold went in. I caught a glimpse of kneeling monks and gleaming gold crosses in front of tapestried walls lit by beeswax candles whose flames guttered in the sudden gust of wind. Almost as soon as the door shut it opened again and Harold came out with Odda by his side. His appearance shocked me. Since I'd last seen him looking more like a prosperous farmer than a great Earl he'd lost his paunch, his chubby face and double chins. He was dressed in a monk's robe but his short grey hair was not yet tonsured. It was clear he would soon be taking holy orders.

Harold waved us away and, with Odda, walked round behind the chapel to get out of the wind. I sidled up to Gyric.

'Thanks for sticking up for me, Gyric.'

'Again.'

'What?'

'Thanks for sticking up for me again.'

'Fucking hell, Gyric, why do you always have to make things awkward?'

He turned on me angrily. 'Maybe because my oldest friend forgets that's what he is.'

'Ah, that's it,' I squirmed, why was it so hard?

I'm staring at the floor. I can hear Gyric laughing.

'Go on then, say it.'

'I'm fucking sorry Gyric, alright. I'm sorry. I know you were trying to help.'

'Yeah, I maybe said a bit too much.'

I remembered the servants talk. 'Rather think everybody knows anyway. What is this place anyway?'

'It's a chantry for his brother Aelfric. They sing masses to speed his passage into heaven.'

'They do? Fucking hell, the rich even get to heaven quicker than the rest of us. No one would be singing masses for Tunglo's Aelfric. Or me for that matter.'

'Thought you were a rich man now.'

'Oh yeah. When I get my money back, I'm going to spend it on horses and fine mail. Maybe a longship and sail north to find my sister. Heaven can fucking wait.'

'You still don't know where she is though do you?' said Gyric in his kind voice.

Suddenly I felt hollow. I didn't. Maybe I never would.

Chapter Five

The next morning saw Harold, Thurkill, Leofgar, myself and the four housecarls riding hard across country to Harold's estate at Much Marcle. We'd taken the last seven horses in Odda's stable. He'd handed over control of his men to Harold. Harold had immediately sent messengers out in all directions to inform Odda's thegns to levy their fyrd and gather supplies. With Earl Ralph's Earldom in chaos after the capture of Hereford, Odda's realm was vital to feeding and resting the army that was to assemble at Much Marcle before the final push on Hereford.

The estate was set in rolling meadows and woods on rich red soil. Like everything Harold owns, the buildings were well looked after as were the fields and fences. If I had an estate, I would want it run like this. We entered the main house to find people already running around trying to get the place in order and some food cooked, so at least one messenger had arrived before us. Before we got to eat Harold had us outside setting up horse lines while Leofgar had found another priest and had started setting up an area for the clerics to come with their lists and tally sticks.

That night we enjoyed the comfort of sleeping indoors. Over the next few days thegns and their servants would occupy all the best spaces and we'd be out sleeping under the clouds. More house-carls rode in during the day, ate and then were immediately set to organise a hunt for the following day. Not a fun hunt as is usual for the rich. We had to spread out with all the people of the estate to sweep the whole area and drive every living beast into nets and traps where they were slaughtered. It was bloody work but by the end we had enough deer, hare and wild pig meat hanging to provide meat for the first cohorts that would be marching in. A couple of people had broken bones and one man's leg was badly ripped by an angry boar's tusk but a good day all in all. That night we feasted magnificently on fresh bread and mixed livers while the farm people happily butchered all the beasts.

This time it felt good to share with the housecarls. Gyric and I could sit together with no one giving us stick. Wulfgeat and I didn't talk unless we had to and the following morning, we both ignored our orders. Who would notice?

From then on troops of horsemen rode in behind their thegns, followed days later by their foot soldiers. Then pack ponies, then ox carts and of course, tribes of priests and last of all, herds of cattle with their drovers and their dogs. The once well-kept estate was now a muddy wreck reeking of shit, both human and animal. A couple of men had been hung for assaulting dairy girls and the whole army was getting foul tempered and moody.

Then Harold gave an order and the whole mass of men seemed to shake itself like a dog shedding fleas and began to march. The vanguard reached Hereford by the evening to find the city empty of invaders. Seems I was wrong about Aelfgar's bargaining piece.

The city had been left undefendable. Every gate was slighted. The minster was unrecognisable. It must have burnt for days. Many of the houses and stalls were also reduced to ashes. The population was perhaps half of what it had been. The young, the fit and the skilled were all gone leaving only the old, the very young and the useless behind. It seems that the invaders had only just gone as the streets were filled with the sounds of wailing and weeping. I rode through the town down to the riverside, foolishly hoping I might get to see Faelen and Sahb Hosvir one last time. I supposed that they were resting in their ships while their newfound slaves pulled on the oars, setting out for the long haul around the entire coastline of Wales. I saw myself with them, happy and looking forward to my share of the monies owed us by Gruffud and Aelfgar.

'Do you miss them, Sar?' It was Harold's voice. I'd not heard him riding up behind me. I must have been miles away.

He skilfully sidled his horse next to mine, 'Why did you come back?'

Good question. I looked behind to make sure we couldn't be overheard and shrugged, 'My revenge was your revenge.'

'Oslaf? You didn't have to come back to tell me that? Did you want a reward?'

I pursed my lips, feeling insulted, 'I had a fortune on me sir. You took it from me.'

'So why?'

'Why? My mother always said we were English and not to forget it. Saxon was how she put it but it seems to be much the same. Maybe that's why.'

Harold said nothing, quietly staying put.

'I swore an oath to you, sir. I swore to serve you on Fleet Holm.'

'You had little choice.'

'You'd saved my life.' Truth was that was only part of it. Harold was a man who inspired loyalty. I'd felt seen and befriended by him. Me a nobody, him an Earl.

'You served Faelen. Did you swear him an oath?'

'I served Faelen until I could get back to you. It was no secret.' I turned to face Harold, the horse under me stirred restlessly, 'I am your man sir. I am loyal to you.'

'Does that mean you won't be riding off to tell your Waelas friends about our dispositions and plans?

I was shocked, 'Jesu Mawr, sir,'

'You swear at me in Welsh,' he interrupted, 'Is that what you are?'

He was staring at me intently, 'Why did you come back, Sar.'

'I don't know. I never questioned it till now. I needed to know how Gyric was doing.'

I heard Harold breathe out, 'Now that I can believe of you Sar, your loyalty to your friend.'

I was puzzled, 'But I am loyal to you sir.'

Harold ignored me, 'Where was it then that you killed Oslaf?'

We were facing west. 'See those hills, that cleft to the left of centre. Up through there for a while then up a long side valley and further up into the hills. Up there.'

'Shame those hills are full of Waelas. When we've cleared them out you can take me there.'

With that he turned his horse's head and rode back into the town.

By the end of November the whole army was quartered in or around Hereford. Then, to the sounds of drums and horns, Harold led the whole force through the ford above the town and towards the Welsh hills.

Maybe I'd over egged the pudding when I told them all about the Waelas way of fighting or maybe Harold had his plan all along. He was very cautious, keeping the whole army together, pushing into the foothills and valleys while the Waelas melted away. If we found a village or a farmstead it would be deserted. We'd burn it, then that night arrows would fly into our camps and we'd suffer a few casualties. Our supply trains never moved far from Hereford and were always escorted by large troops of horsemen. We barely saw a Waelas but we wore ourselves out marching back and forth. Every morning. while breakfast was got ready. we'd be training the men. Me, the light fast spear throwers who were also the army's messengers, horse holders and general dogsbodies. The housecarls, the main body of the troops. Even though there were no battles the men were kept busy. On top of that whenever there was any spare time Thurkill made sure that Wulfgeat gave me sword fighting lessons. He certainly taught me lessons, bruising ones, but my skill improved until I was becoming a decent swordsman.

I can't say we became friends but we were no longer enemies. Gyric and I ate together and slept side by side in the cold nights.

'We're all worn out Gyric. Harold gives us no rest. If it wasn't for the long nights I'd be spent.'

'Can you imagine what it would be like if we had time to moan? All these men campaigning through the winter? Harold knows what he's doing.'

'How do you mean? If we got into a fight now, I could barely lift a weapon.'

'We're not going to have a real battle with the Waelas. It's just like you said, but we got to stay here. Show them we won't give up. Harold's biggest problem is keeping the army together not the fighting.'

'Worn out men have no time to grumble and get rebellious.'

'You've got it.'

This was true. It was cold, wet and the days were short. Idle soldiers will complain about everything given half a chance. Even the long nights weren't restful. Mud, washed out fires coupled with arrows and the braying of trumpets from the dark meant that not only our bodies were tired.

Chapter Six

It was deep into winter when Harold decided to make one last push into the hills. He called me over.

'This is when you show me where you killed my cousin's murderer. You will lead and direct a group of scouts always within shouting distance of our army.'

'You'll be hard put to fit an army up that valley, sir. It's narrow and wooded.'

'What valley in Wales isn't,' he chuckled, half to himself. 'We'll get as close as we can and go from there.'

Scouting was pleasing to me. I gathered up a group of my dogs-bodies. Armed them with two throwing spear each and paired them off.

'Look men,' I said, 'So far no one has had to move separate from the army. The valley we're going up today is too narrow and too wooded so we have to go ahead and find out if any Waelas are in there setting up an ambush. We may not have seen any but you can bet your life they've seen us.

They looked at each other nervously. I wasn't too sure either. These lads had never done anything like this but I was sure most of them had sneaked up on hare or deer before. They would know how to move quietly.

'You all know how to move without a sound, right?'

They exchanged looks.

'Well, that's the main thing,' I said. 'So, you move in pairs. If you see the enemy, one of you runs back to me. You two,' I pointed,

'Dearsige and Eanraed, will stay with me. I'll be in the centre of the valley and if I need you, I will send you to Thurkill. No one calls out unless we are being attacked. They don't need to know they've been seen. Now if you get to the ridge at the valley sides, do not stand showing on the skyline. Crawl if you need to, to see over, or crouch behind bushes. A man shape against the sky can be seen for miles.' I looked around at them, they were keen enough but I was trying to give them the learning that I'd learned in Ireland and used during the following campaign in one short talk.

'You will be armed with two throwing spears each, muddy the points, don't want sunlight flashing off them. There'll be no leaves on the trees which means you can see quite a distance but you can also be seen. Stay low, move quietly when you can be hidden…' I could see their eyes glazing over. 'If you get seen move back to me, not the main force. If we are really being attacked, yell like crazy and head for the main force. They might not know you so yell out Harold's war cry, "Holy Cross, Holy Cross." Then they should open the ranks and let you in.'

'What if they don't,' asked Eanraed.

I remembered Sibhyrt being cut down between the two armies in Alba and lied, 'They will, don't worry, just shout out in English.'

The main army rode and marched up into the wide valley that led to Abergafenni. I'd taken off my mail coat and the padded byrnie and dressed in dark clothes. I'd kept my targe and a couple of throwing spears and ran alongside Harold's stallion feeling much more my usual self. We came to the side valley.

'We can't ride far into there before the sides will force us into a line either up or one side or the other of the stream. An easy ambush, sir,' I said.

'I'm not happy about this, Harold,' said Thurkill. 'There's no military reason to do this.'

'I want to see where the man who killed Beorn , my cousin died,' said Harold. 'It matters to me to see his corpse.'

'It was your dead brother, Sweyn, gave the order.'

'I don't need reminding,' said Harold with an unusual chill in his voice.

Thurkill knew when a line had been drawn. He ordered all the housecarls to dismount and leave their horses with the bulk of the army at the mouth of the valley. They formed up in a tight wedge formation around Harold's banner.

'Sir,' I piped up hesitantly, 'Why take the banner? Why let the enemy know that you are here?' I knew I was overstepping but this was crazy.

'Don't question me Sar. Besides I won't be with the banner. I'm coming up the valley with you.' With these words he took off his helmet and ordered one of his men to help him pull his mail off.

Byrnies are woven from undyed wool, not as dark as I would have liked but I could hardly ask him to take it off. I crouched and dirtied my hand, wiped mud on my own face then took a brief pleasure in wiping it on to Harold's, to Thurkill's audible disgust. My troop of scouts followed suit and muddied their own faces. I waved at them to fan out up the sides of the valley. No time to teach them hand signals but they moved without a shouted order. Dearsige, Eanraed, Harold and I set off along the faint path alongside the stream. I could already hear the wedge splitting as they tried to keep formation in the trees. We loped off ahead putting leaving the housecarls a decent distance behind until we couldn't hear them anymore.

We came to the remains of the camp where Bruni and I had killed the first of our pursuers. A rusting pile of mail and bones marked his death. Then the scattered bones of a horse and the black patch of the campfire. A few hundred paces further two more scavenged corpses mouldered before the now deserted beaver dam. I guess the rotting horse carcass had poisoned the water in their pond. The rusting mail and rotting harness showed that no men had found and plundered the remains. If the Waelas were about they'd not moved ahead of us. There were no footprints in the muddy ground. I scanned around, here and there I caught glimpses of my scouts through the bare trees. I waved us forward up the steepening path towards where the alders and hazels thinned and dead clumps of nettles and bramble patches joined windswept thickets of hawthorn. I held up my arm and was pleased to see all the visible scouts come to a halt. The world was still, the odd crow, a buzzard on the wind, nothing moved out there. No dark shapes flitted between the bushes.

We were now at the steepest stretch beside the waterfall I remembered. This was below the natural platform where the last fight had taken place. Oslaf's body had tumbled over the edge after I'd scalped him. It had to be somewhere here or lower down the stream. I spoke quietly with Harold trying to explain why I was looking where I was looking.

'Let's see where the fight took place and work back,' he said.

We climbed on up. The arena we had fought in was on the spring line so still below the ridge. I asked Dearsige and Eanraed to instruct the scouts to move up to the skyline and try to see over it without showing themselves and to return. One pair went up ahead of Harold and I while I described the strange windswept fight.

The two other bodies were still here, empty eye sockets stared sightlessly at the sky, rotted limbs tugged out from under the mail amid wolf paw prints. Rusty weapons and broken shields lay among the dead tufts of grass.

I shuddered as saw Bruni's unconscious body in my mind's eye. We were so close to losing that fight. I shuddered as I remembered the horror and weariness of the aftermath of the trap I'd set, and so nearly ensnared myself and my companions.

Harold was pacing around, trying to read the ground. 'His body fell over here,' he asked.

'Yes, I scalped him in this pool and the water built up behind his floating body, then pushed it over the edge.'

He half walked, half slid down the track beside the waterfall, 'It would have come over here, maybe tumbled down steam a little but even if the wolves had found it, they wouldn't have dragged it far.'

I was as puzzled as he was. I poked around with one of my spears in the bushes getting more and more frantic. Thrashing about and swearing as my clothes caught on dead brambles. No mail, no body, nothing. His helmet lay rusting above the fall but no sign of him lay below.

'I don't know what to say, sir. I scalped his bleeding head. You saw it. His long white, blond hair. I gave it you. You handed it back. It was Oslaf's scalp, I swear.'

'Where's his body then, Sar, where is it?'

I had no answer. Then Dearsige ran up to me and I had to pull myself together.

'Goda has seen someone running away,' he said breathing heavily.

I didn't recognise the name, 'Where is he?'

'He's on the other side of the valley, I sent his runner back to him.'

'Good man,' I said, 'Now catch your breath. Are you fit to run back?'

'Yes sir.'

Sir, I thought, that's a first for me, 'I want you to run to Goda and send his runner to the next pair along. You tell Goda to look over the ridge, remembering to stay hidden. You send his runner on to the next pair, sunwise round the valley. You run the other way until every pair knows. If you see the enemy coming, try to assess their number then send your runner back to Thurkill. The other scout goes round the valley to inform the rest. Tell them to fall back quietly. You never know, we might be able to ambush the ambushers. Have you got all that?'

Dearsige nodded vigorously, still panting. Then Eanraed ran up, 'No one has seen anything along this side of the valley.'

'Slight change, Dearsige. I want all the scouts on the west side of the valley to fall back to Thurkill. Eanraed you will tell the scouts on the east side to fall back below the ridge and circle round to get here. They must find their Earl and me. Got it.'

They ran off, no longer so quietly but by now I suppose that didn't matter. The man they'd seen would be off to tell his friends. Only question left, how many of them are there?

I turned to Harold, to find him staring straight at me, 'Where did you learn all that? The scouting I mean.'

Faelen sir, we worked like this with the Dyflin Vikings. We, the Irish I mean, scouted with the Norse types acting as the heavy troops.'

He nodded, 'So what happens now?'

'Depends on how big their force is. They'll want to attack your men in the woods because they can't form a tight shield wall. Being light troops, they'll be able to rain down missiles from the steep sides of the valley where mailed men cannot easily climb.' I thought for a bit, 'They won't have had time to plan, else they'd be sending men around the valley to attack from this side. It's a long way round, I think we are safe on this side for a while.'

'And what about us?'

'Well sir, you are here. We should fall back as a group as fast as we can back to rejoin Thurkill and make a fighting retreat. He won't go without you and the Waelas will attack with fury believing you are with your banner.'

I was surprised to see that Harold was grinning at me, 'And if I wasn't here?'

I felt like my mind was being read, 'First, I'd go to the top of the ridge above us to make sure no one was coming from over there.' I paused.

'And then?' Harold urged.

'If it's clear, I'd gather as many men as I could, cut across the neck of the valley and, if possible, attack them from the flank.'

'Then that's what we'll do.'

'What, Christ Almighty sir. I've got a few untrained lads with throwing spears and an Earl. No way, no way.' I backed off, holding my palms up in front of me, to be rewarded by being drenched with spray from the waterfall and a soaked foot.

I jumped forward to find Harold laughing at me. This was all getting confusing. Just now I was being quizzed about the absence of Oslaf's body. Now I'm being laughed at while planning to ambush the enemy with the most powerful man after the king and a few ploughboys.

'Get on with it then,' he says.

So I did. I climbed up to the pair at the ridge above us. They were doing exactly as they were told. I felt proud. I crept up and peered over. Everything looked clear. No obvious disturbance. No unusual sounds or sudden eruptions of birds. Always a good sign as they flocked together over the winter. Dark clouds to the north east.

'It's going to rain soon,' I said as I got back to Harold. My men were gathering now. About sixteen of us. Despite huge misgivings I told them what was planned finishing with, 'Above all, we stick together. We do not attack unless it's in our favour. You wait for orders and we move as quietly as speed allows.'

'Who gives the orders,' I was asked.

I stopped, uncertain, until Harold spoke up, 'You Sar, you are in charge.'

No pressure there then, I thought, I don't even think this is a great idea. If the Earl gets killed, they'll probably hang me. I kept my mouth shut.

I lead my men down to the edge of the woodland, 'We stay just inside the wood and follow it round. Eanraed will lead, I will be behind him. You, sir, will stay in the middle of the column. When I'm ready, I will stop and we all gather. If you see any unusual movement, tap the man ahead of you on the shoulder point to the movement and crouch. Do this until we are all crouched. Stay still and silent. Leave it to me to check it out.'

They all nodded, we went to just inside the tree line. It's sometimes clearer there once you've passed through the thicker shrubs at the edge. We all started loping along, a spear in each hand. I realised Harold didn't have one, paused, and gave him one of mine. We waded the stream and started to climb. Eanraed stopped and crouched, pointing up and to the side. I turned to find everyone crouched and looking about. Good men. I crept up to Eanraed and then beyond with my spear held up ready to throw. Eanraed was right, a small group was struggling through the brambles above us. I watched. If I could I'd let them go. We had other fish to fry.

Then I smiled, held a hand up behind me to halt everyone and crept out. It was Dearsige with five other men. I whistled quietly and slowly stood up, showing my hands. I was recognised. Releasing my pent-up breath, I hissed, 'This isn't what I ordered, why are you here?'

'Goda and three others went to Thurkill, I thought we might be more useful finding you.'

'You were right, Dearsige, as it happens,' I said and explained what our plan was. 'And remember, if it all goes wrong, we must get the Earl out of here.'

Soon we were two thirds the way up the west side of the valley. If the enemy had extended along the ridge. We were screwed. My hope was that they would head directly to attack the main force. I spread us out along the valley side. As we were doing this there was an eruption of shouts and war cries. This time I lead, creeping forward, I held up my hand. I'd seen the first movement. There was a bowman, wild haired and bearded, firing downhill, concentrating hard on missing the trees. I slithered towards him. He wore no helmet, long hair tied back, a few arrows stuck in the ground before him. I placed my spear on the ground and pulled my blackjack from my belt and gripped my targe behind its boss in my left hand. At the last moment he heard me, his mouth opened in shock and I whacked him hard with the blackjack. He collapsed, not out cold but close. I hit him again and again with the boss until his face was a bloody pulp. He'd made no sound but the crunching of his bones. I turned back to see Eanraed white faced with shock and disgust. I paused, steadying him with my gaze, and then crept on. The bowman had been an outlier, maybe a careless picket. His friends wouldn't expect us to be here without having heard from him. I picked up my spear.

We followed the noise, staying high up on the valley side. Then we saw them. A large mob of tribesmen were throwing rocks, spears and firing arrows down onto Thurkill's men in the valley floor.

They were encouraging each other to throw at the Harold's banner of The Fighting Man, instantly recognisable even to those who'd never seen it. I knew the Waelas would not want to close in, they had neither the numbers nor the equipment to fight heavily armed housecarls man to man. They would harry them, trying to force them into retreat. Preferably leaving dead and wounded behind to be looted and worse.

The problem for the English was that they could not form a solid shield wall amongst the trees and the men along the stream banks were slipping in the mud. The problem for the Waelas was that the valley sides were so steep they were inexorably getting closer and closer to their enemy. There was probably a couple of hundred now flowing over the hillside pushing the ones below them down keen to get their own chance to attack. Some of them had the sense to start circling around the fringes of the English below us. I had a decision to make.

If we attacked those below us, my inexperienced men might hit the housecarls beyond. It had to be the flank of those still far up the hillside. My force, about a score of men, forty spears to throw. Then they'd be left with the seaxes in their belts, not a shield or a targe between them.

Chapter Seven

I felt stuck, unable to move or think. I'd never commanded men before. I knew the worst thing a leader could be was indecisive. A squall blew in, gusting cold rain from the north east. I saw a Waelas turn, disturbed by the rustling in the trees. His eyes widened as he saw me. I felt too far away but threw my spear anyway.

'Close in lads, close in and throw,' I yelled. 'One spear each.' My spear had caught the man in his left upper thigh. He screamed just as burst of icy rain hammered through the branches. I could see the odd spear thrumming in the side of a tree but a number had struck the unsuspecting attackers. Some of them turned to face us, a couple raised bows.

'Get behind the trees, lads, get behind the trees,' Some heard me and ducked behind nearby trunks. These were hazel, birch and hawthorn, un-coppiced with narrow trunks but they offered some cover and confused the aim. I turned and was relieved to see Harold scrunch down as an arrow flew over his head. I reached for the bow of the archer I had killed and tried to nock an arrow. I have no skill with a bow and fumbled. The string seemed slack.

'It's got wet Sar, the bowstring is wet,' shouted Harold, 'Their bows will soon be useless.'

This was good news. The rain was now drenching us all and the slope getting slick with wet land slippery leaves. I looked around and saw that most of my men still had one spear each. One or two had panicked and thrown both, while one was writhing around on the floor with a spear in his guts.

Along the valley side I could see a helmeted Waelas trying to get his men into some kind of order. Most of them had no spears, they'd already thrown them down the hill. A spear or two of our own was thrown back. A gash appeared in Eanraed's left arm but the spear sailed on. Another caught against a tree and flew off its mark. My lads quickly picked them up and rearmed those with empty hands. Except mine. Now what.

'Holy Cross, Holy Cross,' a voice yelled out from behind me. Harold ran past me straight towards the Waelas in front of us. We all started screaming like banshees and followed him. I drew my little axe from my belt. It was chaos. Everybody slipping and sliding. Using one hand to fight and one to hold onto a tree. Mayhem. Below came back more loud battle cries and the noise grew deafening. Thurkill could be heard yelling, 'Thrust, shield, thrust,' as he encouraged the housecarls into redoubled effort. I saw Harold attack the man with the helmet with his spear but lose his footing. My heart sank, the Waelas carried some kind of club. He turned and stood over Harold who had now managed to swivel onto his back and was holding his spear in both hands across his body. His adversary was lifting the club high above his head with two hands. As the club came down Harold pushed up with the spear. Even amongst all the racket I heard the shaft snap. Harold frantically tried to reverse the pointed end of his spear as the club was raised again.

I threw my axe. My grip was soft because my palm had slid down the moss-covered side of a tree. The shaft slipped a moment too soon and it was the handle that connected with the side of the clubman's head. Enough though. His head turned and, in that moment, he was lost. Harold gripped the broken shaft below the head and shoved the point into the man's inner thigh and pushed away at the same time. Cloth and flesh ripped. The man screamed. I was upon him. I grabbed his club as he dropped it. He was groping at the agony in his leg with both hands so I smacked him round the head, hard. He fell, Harold pulled out the spear point and pushed it into the fallen man's right eye. He was dead.

I felt movement behind me, flailed around, slipped, fell to my knees to find Dearsige stood above me. 'Oh fuck, it's you. I thought I was about to meet my maker.'

Dearsige helped me to my feet. I noticed his hand was shaking and his face white, eyes wide, 'Eanraed is meeting his.'

I held him firmly, 'Later, Dearsige, later.'

The Waelas in front of us were wavering, unsure after seeing the fate of their leader. My men too, were pulling back, the now thundering rain chilling their excitement. Below us we could see enemy figures trying to get back up the hill. Beyond those we could see the mailed housecarls struggling to advance with shields and war spears. They were getting nowhere. The gap between the two sides was growing rapidly.

Those before us with no idea of the size of our force were pulling away and heading for the ridge. We drew together and let them go Another of ours had been wounded, two men pulling him back. The other wounded man had stopped moving. Harold, now with his sword drawn, a near useless weapon in the trees, was calling them together. I found my axe and rubbing my hand on my tunic took a firm grip.

We now lined up facing downhill. It dawned on me what Harold had in mind. He was going to charge down into those coming up. Our wounded man was leant against a tree. Many of us were bleeding but otherwise mobile. A few still had spears. The Waelas climbing up below us seemed unaware of our identity. Dearsige was crying quietly, another lad was retching repeatedly, we were all panting heavily.

I yelled, loud as I could, 'Take out your seaxes. Throw your spears and follow Harold.'

While Harold roused them all into chanting his war cry our last volley of spears flew into the climbing Waelas. Then our men charged down on them. I turned to our wounded man. There was a hole in his chest and he'd bled heavily. I looked him in the eye.

'We won't be able to come back for you,' I said, putting my axe down and pulling my eating knife from my belt.'

He gasped as my words sank in and his eyes filled. He tried to speak but couldn't.

'I'll not leave you to the tender mercies of our enemies,' I said letting go of my targe. I cradled the back of his head and pulled him into me. 'You fought bravely,' I whispered, stupidly, into his ear as I pushed the knife under his ribs.

I felt furious and, after snatching up my weapons, I charged, raging, down the hill behind the others. They were passing through the enemy rather than fighting with them. One of the enemies appeared before me, climbing on all fours up the slippery hillside. I swiped him across the face with my axe and took pleasure as his face opened split into a gaping red gash. I was past him and hacking down on another. The axe stuck briefly in his head as I flew past. My body was moving faster than my legs and I sprawled in the mud. Hands grabbed me. I thrashed around then realised I was surrounded by English voices and was safe within our ranks.

We made a slow fighting retreat to the main force. Exhausted men wearily lifted their shields to defend against the few spears the Waelas could find to throw. As their bows were now useless the last of them called it a day. Dusk fell and that night the only sounds were the wind, the rain, and the hooting of owls.

Chapter Eight

Earl Harold took the whole army back to Elwistonet where he gave orders to set up camp for the rest of the winter.

'The men are worn out. I'm taking one fourth of them back to Hereford. Thurkill will command while I'm gone. The remaining three fourths of the army will patrol the east bank of the Monnow and the Dore. For now, this will be our border. Any Waelas cross the water, slaughter them. Any questions?'

Earl Gyrth stepped forward, 'We haven't beaten Gruffud. Or even depleted his forces.'

'They melt away, Gyrth, then we wear ourselves out marching up and down achieving nothing.'

'Does that mean he's beaten us? What are we? A whipped dog?' This was Scalpi.

'Whipped? No. But we are like a gazehound that's chased too many hares in a day. Trembling, blown, willing, but a good master knows, run that dog once more and it'll never work again. Our army is that dog. I am that master,' said Harold.

All the commanders present were hunting men. They shuffled and nodded at each other with their left hands on their sword pommels, their right ones stroking their chins.

'Look at all the wise men,' I whispered to Gyric.

Gyric always struggled when I mocked the gentry, 'Shut up,' he said, stifling a laugh which came out as a snort.

Harold whirled round, 'You. Why is it always you?

He was talking to me. 'Father Leofgar is in that house,' he pointed, 'Go there and wait for me.'

I went in to find him sat there on a stool next to a little bodged table, warmed by a small fire and reading by a rush light.

'Oh, it's you. Sar, isn't it? Did the Earl send you in?'

I nodded, unbuckled my sword belt, and squatted before the fire, 'Yeah, I've annoyed him again.'

'You're his pet, you know that?' he said, spite in his voice. 'Why is that? What does he see in you?'

'I'm not his pet.'

'You don't think?'

I was silent, maybe there was truth in what he said, but I'd only been back a few weeks.

'I heard your walk in the woods was a mixed blessing. Couldn't find Oslaf's body? I think you made it all up. Then you curry his favour by attacking the Waelas, risk his life, and lose the lives of a few fine young men.'

Jesu Mawr, every arrow went home. I stared into the fire to hide my face. Those men had died. Dearsige had been inconsolable, to the point where other men cast shame on him. Maybe he and Eanraed had been more than friends. It happens. Either way their families had me to blame.

'While I've been managing the diocese for our poor blind bishop, you've been sneaking around the Earl trying to get noticed.'

I frowned, why was this powerful churchman bothering with me?

I rose and faced him, 'What's your problem? You with your tonsure and your sword. Foot in both camps. Dream you're a warrior, do you? Dream on.'

He stood, shaking with anger, 'Not just a warrior, a leader of warriors.'

I twigged, 'You're jealous, you pathetic twat. Fucking hell.'

'And you? You are upstart scum.'

At that moment the door swung open, Thurkill strode in closely followed by Harold. Leofgar and I both greeted them with false smiles.

'Ah, good to see you two getting on,' said Harold, seeing what he wanted to see.

Leofgar resumed his role as the muscular, good-humoured, churchman like a snake shedding its skin, 'Yes, he's been telling me of your adventures.'

A villager pushed through a door from the back with an armful of firewood, placed a couple of branches on the fire and set the rest by the hearth. Confused by the presence of these powerful men he stammered something and held out a handful of rush lights. Everyone ignored him so I took the lights from him and shepherded him back out. Leofgar's light was fizzling out so I lit a new one and placed it in the holder and left the rest on the table.

By now Harold and Thurkill were sitting on the remaining stools. I couldn't squat back where I was between the fire and them so leant awkwardly against the wall.

'Stand up Sar,' said Thurkill, sternly.

I stepped away from the wall to where I could fully stand.

Harold spoke, quietly, 'Two things Sar. First Oslaf's body or rather lack of it. How do you explain that?'

I wished I could, 'I have no idea sir. Maybe someone took the body. His family?'

As soon as I said that I knew it was nonsense. What was left of his family lived in the east of England.

'You sure he was dead?' asked Thurkill.

'I scalped him. He was bleeding from many wounds,' I said.

'Could you see the wounds? A death wound?' it was Harold.

I turned slightly, 'Not as such. He'd been stabbed through his mail many times. When I scalped him, his body barely twitched.'

'But twitch it did?'

'The recently dead do twitch sir. Sometimes a lot.'

Harold nodded.

'Or the whole thing is just a story,' this, of course, was Leofgar.

'No Father,' said Harold, 'Everything else we saw fitted the boy's story.'

I'm a boy again now it seemed. 'You held his scalp in your hand sir,' I said, sulking.

'Some blond locks on a shrivelled bit of skin, could have been anyone's. Banish this boy and give his money to the church,' said the priest.

'No sir. I took that scalp from Oslaf's head and left him in the freezing water.' I was pleading now while another part of me thought; it's the money he's after. That's why he undermines me.

Thurkill spoke in his deep firm voice, 'To sum up. No certain fatal wound. No body. You carry his sword but not his sheath. It's very likely you won that. Oslaf would never have given that up lightly. Why did you not take the sheath?'

I thought back trying to picture the scene, 'He'd dropped the sword before I scalped him in the water. It lay in the edge of the pool. I didn't think about the sheath until we were heading off and by then his body had gone over the fall.'

'You could have sought it out on the way down,' said Harold.

'I'd pushed the sword through my belt, sir. Then we were helping each other down the hillside. I remember even thinking about the sheath until the next day by which time I was alone and trying to find where you were sir.'

Thurkill again, 'Was there anyone who knew where you were, or where Oslaf's party had gone?'

'No one could have known where he was going sir, because he was following us.' Then I remembered something, 'Two of his men deserted him before the final fight.'

All three made sounds of disgust. This was the worst thing a sworn man could do. If this gets known, such a man lives lordless and disgraced.

'Scum, they could have gone back. Second thoughts or just to loot the bodies,' said Thurkill.

'Maybe sir. Oslaf was a cruel leader,' I said, 'His men feared him.'

'Like you fear me, Sar?' said Harold.

'No, not like that,' I said, quietly.

'They could have gone back. Found Oslaf, dead or alive, and taken him away.'

'I can't believe he was alive. He was bleeding heavily, scalped and face down in icy water when I last saw him. Then he tumbled over the fall. He had to be dead.'

'Look at it through my eyes Sar. I believe you believe what you saw. I, though, don't know for certain that my cousin, Beorn , is avenged. Until proved otherwise, I'm going to believe that Oslaf has survived,' said Harold. 'Though Sar, this means that you have been away from my service for the best part of two years with nothing to show for it.'

I felt wronged by this. I'd fought for our King in Alba and followed Oslaf with the one intent of killing him. Though for my own revenge, not Harold's. If he was still alive, I wanted him dead more than anything else.

Harold stood so did everyone else did likewise, 'I say nothing Sar, but clearly you learnt ways to fight from the Irish. Might be useful. Where are those lads now?'

'They've rejoined the men from the hundreds that they came from,' said Thurkill.

Harold nodded thoughtfully while pulling back on his fur lined gloves. 'By the way Sar, I won't keep your money. For now, it is being kept in the treasury of my mother, the Lady Gytha, it will be safe there. Meanwhile Thurkill has a purse for you.'

He turned to the door. Leofgar rushed to open it scooping up his book as he did so. Thurkill handed me a small purse of coin. Then the three of them walked out. As they left, I heard Harold say, 'He rescued me from a tight spot in that wood,' and Leofgar reply, 'That boy got you in that spot in the first place.'

Harold was there, you prick, I thought. You weren't.

And that was how it was left. Gruffud stayed in the hills and we stayed on the plain. Harold, with his housecarls and I went back to Hereford.

When we got there the town seemed to be full of monks and their lay people. They were trying to rebuild the burnt monastery and shore up the Minster which was now lacking all its riches. These included the relics of Saint Ethelbert who was much loved in this town and had attracted hundreds of pilgrims every year. They also tried to look after the old and orphaned who slowly disappeared from their begging spots around the town.

Harold had other concerns. He recruited another small army of those too young or too old to fight to dig a ditch around the entire town. Then he had another small force of carpenters and masons build a new bridge above the ford and outside the city walls. He'd left Thurkill with the main army but the fourth he brought back weren't left to their own devices. Although we slept indoors and had regular meals, we still had little rest. He had us tearing down the old bridge and dragging every useful beam up to the new one.

'No one will be ramming ships into that again,' he said.

My hair was getting a bit longer and I'd carried on dressing as I had when I was scouting. I always carried a throwing spear with my targe slung across my back. Harold chose not to see, or probably more like, what he'd seen in the woods had changed how he saw me. It wasn't long before I came to regret that decision.

One morning the Earl, the housecarls, Father Leofgar and myself had been riding round the city inspecting the new ditch. As noon approached, we rode into the town and began dismounting in the square before the ruined Minster. I was showing off by standing the butt of my spear on the ground and using it to vault out of the saddle. I'd landed on two feet and bounced, turning to hold my horse's halter in my left hand. I stood there, smugly pleased with myself, when a woman's voice screeched out.

'That one, that red-haired devil. He was here. He killed the priests. Just here. About where he's standing now.'

I turned my head to see a small group of elderly people surrounding a priest who was handing out loaves. All of them,

and the priest, were staring straight at me, following the finger of
a stout woman, better dressed than those around her.

'But Bebbe this is the Earl's army. He can't be one of them,' said
one of the men, 'and some of the Danes had red hair too.'

'Not red like that. That dark, you ever seen that before? I'll never
forget that white faced demon.

Briefly I saw myself lifting my spear and throwing it into her.
In one swift movement she could be shut up forever. Then, a few
moments after that, so would I.

I looked around to find every pair of eyes, except those of
the horses, staring at me. More townsfolk, black robed monks
and priests were gathering, arguing, then angrily shouting at me.
The housecarls were quiet, waiting on Harold to command the
situation.

'Sir, I don't know what she is talking about,' my voice was a
little shrill. I coughed, and in a lower tone said, 'I wasn't even
here.'

Harold, still mounted, looked down on me, and speaking quietly
said, 'You do know what she is talking about, Sar, you do.'

A chill went down my spine as he raised his hand for calm.
Thurkill bellowed out to the crowd to shut up. They did.

Harold pointed to the woman and beckoned her over. She handed
the loaf she was carrying to her neighbour, walked up to the Earl
and curtseyed.

'Ale-wife Bebbe sir,' she said, trying to smile at the Earl and glare
at me at the same time.

An ale-wife, that explained her confidence. Mistress of her own
fortune. She'd be well known and respected and believed.

'You are accusing my man of killing priests are you not?

'If it was not him, sir, as he was with fierce Viking types and wild
Irishmen, it was his twin.'

Father Leofgar spoke up, 'He was with those men, Harold.'

Harold raised his hand, 'And where were you when you saw
this, Ale-wife.'

'We were stood behind the lower stone part of the Minster sir. You can see it there. All above was burnt since and has tumbled, but that corner there is just as it was.'

'How come you to be there?'

'I was running into the town. Those wild men had come over the ramparts by the river. I had a tavern there for the merchants near the gatehouse. A good business it was too before they ransacked it. As good as ruined me, I had to grab my purse and run. They killed my barman and took my maid as a slave, Terrible it was,' her voice tailed away, and her face flushed as Harold raised his hand again.

'You saw this man kill the priests?'

'Him, not on his own mind. There was a bunch of them. Big man with an axe, gold chains and furs. He started it, then the rest piled on. Him, I saw him stab with a spear. See that little shield, got a kind of whorl on the boss. I'll never forget that.'

Whatever Harold was thinking, the crowd was hanging on every word she said. Word must have been getting around. More and more monks and priests were turning up. The townsfolk moved aside to let them through until before me I had a circle of hostile churchmen and behind me, a wall of housecarls. No one loved a priest killer.

Harold spoke, 'Gyric take your friend's weapons.'

Gyric handed his horses reins to another housecarl and walked over to me, 'Not a word Sar, not a word.'

I silently handed him my spear. He passed that on, then I pulled my blackjack and axe from my belt and gave them to him. He calmly thrust them into his own belt. I then unbuckled my sword belt and handed it over with the sword. All the time we looked into each other's eyes. Gyric's, usually so easy to read, were like stones.

'Take his eating knife as well, son. I've seen that one kill,' called out Scalpi.

Gyric looked up at Harold who nodded. I handed over my eating knife. I felt naked, disgraced, gutted, and scared for my life.

'Sir, I did not do this. She is mistaken. I wasn't here when the priests were killed.' I pleaded.

Harold ignored me, 'Wulfgeat, Ketil, find the shire-reeve. I know he has returned.'

They both remounted and rode off into the town. Harold, Thurkill and that fucking priest dismounted and stood, muttering to each other. There was a stirring in the crowd. Lead by his helper Bishop Athelstan walked into the square. He had the ale-wife repeat everything she had said. She added some more unwelcome details. How I'd told the big Norseman what the priest was saying. How my hair had been longer and plaited. Gyric had seen me do that before a fight even if no one else here had. He'd hate me if he believed I'd killed those priests.

The crowd was getting restive. Those who'd survived the capture of their city had lost a lot. Many of their friends and families had gone along with the relics of their Saint, their Minster lay in ruins and their priests had been slaughtered, their misery was turning to anger and there I was. To this day I think the bishop saved me from being stoned to death. The first clods of mud had been thrown when he stepped blindly between me and the angry crowd.

'He may be a murderer,' he said in a surprisingly firm voice, 'but we are not. He shall face God's mercy. He shall be tried by ordeal.'

The crowd roared their approval and the housecarls seemed to agree. Just then the shire-reeve arrived with a group of his own soldiers.

'Athelnoth,' said Harold, 'I give my man into your custody.'

Chapter Nine

Faces, faces of dead men. Men who are dead because I killed them. They float below me around the man I drowned in the Irish Sea, the oar still holding him under. They whirl slowly round the oar. They stare at me. They reproach me. The horse thief, once I knew his name. Osric, his face pale. The young man on the wall at Hereford. There are more. Eardwulf, the first, the bowman, the latest. I'm losing count. They go under the dark water, they rise again, whirl again, staring at me, accusing me.

'Yes, son, but who is missing? You didn't finish the job. Christ, boy, you can't be trusted with anything.'

It's my mother's voice. Where is she? 'Oslaf is missing. That's who's missing.'

'You had one job son, avenge my sister and her children, avenge your own enslaved twin. Avenge me. I want them dead to every generation. Did you do that? Looks like you didn't. Useless child.'

Now, I'm on the beach at Caer Dydd. Small, a child. I stare miserably at the wide muddy waters of the Safearn Sea. A small hand slips into mine. I turn to see my twin, my sister Moira. I feel warm, instantly safer. We put our heads together. Our long dark locks combine.

I open my mouth to speak. Then I'm awake. I'm crying. I'm sweating. I'm alone, in a cell in the foundations of the unbuilt castle. A faint glimmer from a grill at ceiling height lit the room, it was not long after dawn. I shuddered. Oh God, it's been a long time since had one of those dreams. I puked emptily onto the earth floor, as I moved from one nightmare to another. The door rattled and a monk came in carrying a wooden bowl and cup.

'Water and barley gruel for the priest killer,' he said, then pointedly spat into the bowl and put them both on the floor. I managed to grab the cup as it began to topple. I raised it to my lips. It smelt alright. Probably river water but I'd drank worse. I stared up at the monk, he stared at me, spat again, on the floor this time, and walked out. The door was slammed shut. A bolt rattled. I left the gruel, took a piss in front of the door, and waited for the monk to come back and tread in it.

It must have been following Terce they came to get me. The winter sun was still low in the sky. The day was fine, bright even, with long dark shadows cast from the sunlit wooden framework that stood, gallows like, waiting for their castle walls. Earl Ralph's folly they call it. I saw it differently. We'd never have been able to take the whole town with a fortified building full of soldiers. Partly in the city but guarding the river too.

I was led, hands tied in front of me, across the castle grounds to the Abbey of Saint Guthlac, famous for fighting demons, and only drinking water. I would bet that his monks found a way round that one. Guthlac was a warrior before he was a priest. I know all this because Gyric admired him, I could guess why.

I was still daydreaming, when I was pushed into a long hall, the refectory probably, emptied of tables and benches but full of monks and priests. The priests were all formally dressed, albs, green and purple chusables, dalmatics, the full quiver, lining one side of the hall. Down the other, rows of black robed monks, their hoods up, were crossing themselves to ward off the evil of my arrival. At the end of the room, enthroned, was the blind Bishop, mitre on his head and a gleaming, jewelled, gold headed crozier in his hand. His guide sat at his feet. The Abbot, and Father Leofgar stood behind him and each side of them the temporal lords, Earls Harold and

Gyrth, the shire-reeve Athelnoth, Scalpi and a few other thegns. In this space, the churchmen ruled.

I was pushed roughly into a wide space running down the centre of the flag-stoned floor. I stood upright and stared around the room to see more frantic crossings and hear muttered prayers to ward off evil. They can believe what they want of me but they don't have to see my fear.

The Abbot took the lead, 'The accused must state his name.'

Something poked me hard in the back, 'Speak, boy.'

'My name is Sar Nomansson.'

A scandalised buzz of conversation rose around me. For these churchmen there was only one being who did not have a man for a father. Not only that, most peasants only had a first name and at most a trade. I'd been given that name in jest the day I entered into Harold's service. I liked it.

The Abbot spoke again, 'Yes, I've been told some think you are the child of a demon who rose from the burials of the pagan dead.'

I smirked and said nothing while everyone in the room crossed themselves again.

'You have been credibly accused of the heinous sin of murdering churchmen in front of their own Minster. What do you have to say?'

'I wasn't there.'

Harold's voice cut sharply across the room, 'I wasn't there, Reverend Father. If there's any time for a bit of humility Sar, it is now.'

'I wasn't there, Reverend Father,' I said, begrudgingly. Just as if I was falsely accused.

'Yet you were part of the attack on our town.'

'Yes, Reverend Father.'

'Did you steal the relics of our Saint?' came another voice. It was Bishop Athelstan.

I shook my head, forgetting that he couldn't see. Another rough poke in the back.

'No,' I thought hard, 'No, Your Excellency.'

'Come forward, boy. Come forward and kiss my ring.'

Two more prods in the back. I stumbled forward and was then pushed to my knees before the Bishop, who was waving his hand around vaguely in the air. I raised my tied hands, caught hold of his fingers and kissed the amethyst embedded in the heavy gold ring. He then felt around some more until his hand lay of the top of my head.

Gently he spoke to me, 'Can you swear to me that you don't know where the relics of Saint Ethelbert are?'

'No, Excellency, I don't,' I answered truthfully. I then decided to play it safe, 'I was nowhere near the Minster,' I lied.

'I'm a tired and sick old man, Sar. I'm not willing to spend the day here while everyone has an opinion. I can't tell if you are a liar but God can. You shall be tried by ordeal.' He felt around my face and, cupping his hand around my chin, lifted it until I was looking into his sightless eyes.

'If you are innocent God will save you during your trial. If he doesn't, then we will know your guilt and you will be put to death for the crime of priest killing. I cannot second guess the Lord, but I suspect you will burn for all eternity,' he said, sitting back wearily.

I shuddered, stayed kneeling, and prayed silently to myself. Trial by ordeal. I was doomed.

'I ask for corsned,' said Harold, 'if my warrior is innocent, he needs to be fit to fight.'

The high clergy started whispering among themselves. From where I was knelt, I could hear Leofgar objecting. I didn't know why. I could feel my mouth drying up and my throat closing just at the thought of eating the accursed morsel.

They came to some agreement. The Abbot spoke, partly to Harold but also to the room. 'We jointly agree that this is too serious a crime for corsned.'

Harold spoke again, 'I thought the trial was to determine If he was lying, whether he killed the priests. He certainly didn't do it alone.'

I certainly didn't, I thought, remembering Ulf's first blow decapitating the leading priest before we all piled in. Honestly, it was all a bit of a blur from the moment we broke through the town's defenders until I'm drunk inside the Minster.

'Sir,' said Leofgar, 'It amounts to the same thing.'

Harold grunted unhappily; it was rare he didn't get his way.

'We prefer to reserve corsned for the clergy,' said the Abbot.

'Yet those of you who disliked my father claimed he died because he choked on the accursed morsel when denying the murder of the King's brother. Isn't that right?'

I hadn't heard this but I'd been there when Godwin died and that wasn't true at all. Harold sounded angry. He was very devoted to the church and constantly granted it money and lands but clearly there was some bad blood here.

I looked up to see all the clergy looking everywhere but at Harold, while Leofgar was making placating gestures with his hands.

'Trial by combat then. Let the church find a champion. My man is a warrior, he deserves a warrior's fate,' said Harold forcefully.

His words were music to my ears, calling me a warrior and offering a proud man's fate, not a grubby one at the end of a rope. This started another series of arguments between the clergy and the secular lords. Then their dispute was cut short.

'It will be ordeal by hot iron and it will take place this afternoon in the place where the crime was committed. The square in front of the Minster. Now help me to my room,' pronounced Bishop Athelstan, struggling to his feet. His assistant jumped to his aid and, amid a great hubbub, he and the bishop left the room. No one was going to argue with this, obviously dying, holy man. I was hauled to my feet, dragged backwards from the room and across the courtyard then thrown back into my cell.

I gave in. I rolled in a ball and sobbed. I lay there in despair. By the end of the week, I'd be dead. God would judge me and I'd be found wanting. Between now and the end, a world of pain. Well, one hand, three days, then what? It was better not to think about it.

I wasn't given long to wallow in my misery. The cell door burst open and five burly monks crashed in. Three of them held me down. I don't know why. I wasn't resisting. The other two pulled off my boots and leggings and foot cloths. Then my hands were unbound and they pulled my tunic off over my head. I was left barefoot in my shirt and loincloth. They weren't gentle. Then they retied my hands.

I was hauled to my feet then, half carried, half dragged to the courtyard gate where a group of the shire-reeve's men were waiting for me. Next, I was lead through the town to the square in front of the ruined Minster. The crowd that lined the streets had already judged me. The foulness of the street floor was picked up and thrown at me, until all of me was as filthy as my feet. The horse, frightened by this, reared and bucked, nearly unseating its rider and causing me to fight to stay on my feet. Luckily, we didn't have far to go.

When we got to the square a ring of armed men, none of them Harold's, were holding their spears horizontally to make a railing which kept the crowd back. Behind one of them I spied Gyric, dressed in ordinary clothes looking at me. God knows what he thought of me. If he believed I killed unarmed priests he'd wash his hands of me. In three days, he would know that I had. Inside the ring were groups of clergymen and once again the leading men of the town. In front of where the Minster doors had been there was a fiery brazier of charcoal. Beside it, two hooded men. One carrying a bellows which was rendered pointless by the brisk chilly wind. The other carried a long pair of tongs. Then beside these two a stone with a short iron bar on the top.

As I was untied from the horse a great racket of prayers and curses rose into the air. A group of priests huddled around the stone, either praying over or cursing the iron, I couldn't tell. I stood, shivering miserably while a priest explained to me that I had to mark out nine lengths of my own feet. I'm a bit lanky so my feet are long. I marked the distance from the brazier into where the priests were murdered. I was shaking, scared but also cold as I was taken back to the brazier. The praying increased as the iron was put into the fire, more charcoal was put on top, the wind quickly breathed fierce life into the coals. I watched sickened when the bar appeared as the coals were riddled. It was already beginning to glow a dull red.

I couldn't take my eyes off the iron while I was told that I would be given the red-hot rod and have to walk the distance I had marked out. Then I could drop the iron. Did I understand? I nodded. My mouth was too dry to speak. The iron was glowing a dark red, then a bit brighter, black flecks appearing on its surface then melting away. A short argument between a priest and the first hooded man ensued.

'It's hot enough,' said the hooded man as he grabbed the end of the rod with his tongs and turned it about.

'No, we need to be sure. Use the bellows.'

'The wind is strong enough,' he answered.

'Use the bellows.'

The other man pumped the bellows into the base of the brazier. The fire got a little fiercer. Maybe the iron got a little brighter.

'See,' said the priest, 'Now it is ready.' He turned to me, 'Hold out your right hand and open your palm.'

I did as I was told. The hooded man raised the dully glowing bar with the tongs and held it in front of me.

'Take hold of it now. Take hold.'

Every part of my being didn't want to do this. I watched my hand reach out and grasp the glowing rod. Jesu Mawr, the pain. I think I screamed out loud. My knees buckled and I couldn't think what I was meant to do. As I'd taken the rod the crowd had fallen silent. One voice cried out.

'Walk, Sar, walk to the mark.'

It was Gyric. I took the first step, then the second. My hand hurt so much I could barely see. I took one last, very long step, crossed the mark, and dropped the iron. It stuck before it left my hand taking charred skin with it. I fell to my knees and only just managed to pull my hand up before I used it to brace myself against the ground. I snatched it back to my waist and made a fist and fell hard. I was hauled to my feet and then, among more prayers, had my hand forced open and a cloth wrapped around my wrist and hand in an intricate folding pattern.

Now I was in the hands of God. The monks seemed to think so too. I was walked gently back to my cell, given watered wine with bread and soup. At first the pain in my hand was so bad I couldn't eat or drink. I just rolled onto my back and howled. A while later I pulled myself together drank and eat as well as I could with my left hand.

The light from the grill shifted around the room. At one point it jumped. I must have dozed off. Shock, exhaustion, food and the weak wine must have dulled the pain. Didn't feel like that when I woke up. Still hurt like fuck.

Time passed and the light dimmed to darkness. I could hear chattering not far from my cell but no one came to check on me. I tried to fall back to sleep but to no avail. I stared into the darkness.

'Sar, Sar, are you in there?'

It wasn't my mother's voice. I bit my lip. My hand hurt. I was awake.

'Sar, wake up. You need to wake up.'

I realised with a jolt that the voice was speaking Welsh. Welsh with a Cornwaelas accent, a soft, mellow, deep voice for a woman. Morwid?

'I am awake.'

'Up here Sar. Outside the grill.'

I stood and turned towards the faint glimmer half an arm above head height.

'How come you are here?'

'The Earl has brought some of his household to Hereford while he is based here.'

'It's good to hear your voice, Morwid, but why are you here?' I too was speaking in Welsh.

'I've come to save your sorry fate, you dumb bastard.'

I almost laughed, 'No need to be rude. Look Morwid, there's nothing you can do. I did kill those priests. My hand is bound to fester then they will hang me.'

'If you really believed that you could have told them the truth and not gone through this.'

Duh, I thought, that hadn't even occurred to me. I said it out loud. 'I didn't even think of that.'

'You believe that shit then. Sometimes you're not that smart. Here can you get your hand out of the window. Maybe there's enough moonlight I can see how it's bound.'

'We'll get caught. They're sure to check on me soon.'

'Not likely, my Da is entertaining the guards right now. Like all monks they have a taste for honey cakes and mead.'

I reached up and put my hand through the window. 'You can't take it off. They'll know and kill me anyway.'

'So what? It'll only be a day or two earlier,' She was laughing, quietly. 'Don't worry I can work this out.'

'It won't change anything, Morwid.'

'Saxon nonsense Sar, Saxon nonsense. Just Churchmen's drivel. If I can heal your palm, I can save your life.'

I chuckled, wincing as she peeled off the cloth binding my hand. 'Again.'

'I might need a favour from you some day.'

'Like what?'

'Never mind, truth is Sar, I'd do it anyway. Just don't forget me.'

This maybe wasn't the time to confess that I spent a good part of everyday thinking about her. She gently turned my hand about. I felt her smear something on it. I tried to pull back but she held it firmly and carried on.

'What are you doing?'

'Honey, I've kept it warm and soft. It can help healing.'

I felt doubtful. Balms are made with a mixture of lots of things and are prayed over and left by church altar and you need to chant the right words.

'Do you know the words, Morwid?'

'Just trust me Sar. You have nothing to lose. The words are different in different places and tongues. Some things work and some don't. You've nothing to lose.'

The last statement was true. I'd forgotten how different Morwid could be.

'There it's done.'

'Morwid?' I said, but she was already gone. I brought my arm back in but it was too dark to see. It still hurt. I cradled my right arm in my left and tried to sleep.

Chapter Ten

Dawn came and with it enough light to peer at the binding around my hand. The strip of linen looked the same as I remembered but I couldn't be sure. I felt torn, how could Morwid be right? God would know and you can't trick God.

I didn't have to worry about the binding the first day. No one looked at it. I was fed again twice. I pissed in the corner that day and took a shit there too. I stank, the cell stank and the day felt longer than any ever had before. Then as night fell, I heard her voice again.

'Sar, be quick. Father wouldn't risk the same ruse a second time.'

'No one comes except to feed me.'

'Even so, be quick.'

I saw the darker shape of her head against the dark of the night. Cloudy, windy, in our favour. I stuck my arm up through the grid, wincing, it hurt less now. More a constant throbbing than the searing pain in had been.

'Christ, it stinks in there,' said Morwid, retching slightly, 'Are you feverish?'

'Not so far,' I answered, 'bit shaky.'

I swore quietly as she unwrapped the binding then washed my palm. I smelt wine. She smeared something sticky on it, honey again I supposed,

'Here drink this, it'll help you sleep, then give me back the flask.'

I did as she said, wanting her to stay. She quickly rebound my hand.

'I'm doing it by feel Sar, don't worry.'

That worried me, I felt lonely and scared. 'Stay a while.'

I saw the dark shape of her head shake, and she was gone.

I did sleep, deep and dreamless. I felt groggy most of the next day. Not so bad. It made it harder to think about the mess I was in. She came again that night and wiped my hand clean before rebinding it once again. She gave me the contents of another flask. I drank it but it didn't work so well. The night passed slowly as in my mind's eye I saw them unbind my hand a thousand times. And every time, just before I could see my palm, the vision began again.

Just before dawn they took me outside. While one monk held my arm to one side, two others cut off my filthy clothes and threw buckets of water over me. I felt limp and hopeless and just let them do what they wanted. They pulled a clean shirt over my head and stood about while I shivered in the cold wind.

'Enjoy the cold, boy. When they unbind your hand, it'll be festering. Then cold will be the least of your worries because by tonight you'll be burning in hell. For eternity.'

They chuckled together. I didn't even have the fight to even swear at them. I believed every word they said. I'd seen the fanged demons pitchforking sinners into the flames painted on church walls. I knew where I was going.

Then all the monks filed out and formed two rows with me between. This time I was allowed to walk into the town while they paced each side of me chanting. Everything felt unbelievably clear and bright. Crows and kites fought the wind in the sky between the roofs of the town and the scudding clouds above. For a moment I was up there with them, escaping, flying away in my mind. Then I became aware of the sounds of drums and horns. We had arrived back in the square.

The monks filed to one side. In front of the ruined Minster stood a group of priests. This time it was Harold's housecarls managing the crowds. I saw Gyric, staring unhappily towards me. Wulfgeat too, glared at me from Harold's side among a group of powerful men. The bishop was there seated on a chair before a trestle table. I guessed that the housecarls were there so there would be no questions from them about the justice that was to follow.

I was led to the table feeling strangely calm. My Earl, the bishop's assistant, Athelnoth, the Abbot of Saint Guthlac's and Father Leofgar gathered around as the hooded man unbound my hand and laid it, palm up, on the table top. It was still very sore. I didn't want to look at it.

I stared into the air while they poked and prodded my hand, muttering amongst themselves. Why was it taking so long?

'It's clearly not festering. Anyone can see that healing has begun,' said Harold above the clamour of the crowd.

'The skin has gone. What is underneath is clean and pink,' said the Abbot, 'This young man is innocent.'

Shocked, I took a quick look at my hand. He was right. It was pink, a was lot of skin gone, some blackened bits at the edges, clearly not festering, and no puss. Suddenly Leofgar was holding my hand, bending over it, and peering intently.

'It's true,' he said, angrily, 'It is healing. The Abbot is right. God has given us a sign. The boy is innocent.'

Harold grabs hold of me as the crowds in the square erupt.

'Hold your hand out and walk around the square. Show your companions first. Here, I'll walk with you.'

I showed the housecarls, who encouraged by Harold, cheered me. I caught Gyric's eyes and winced inwardly us his face lit up with joy. The crowd behind were less easily convinced. While the housecarls held them back I was made to show different people my hand. Then the Ale-wife pushed her way to the front and, staring at me, demanded a look. She was so dismayed I felt sorry for her. She'd never be allowed to live this down.

My Earl formed a squad of housecarls around me and marched us out of the city to the south. Just outside of the gate was a boy holding two riding horses and a pack pony.

Harold turned to me, 'I arranged this on the small chance you were found innocent. Have to be honest, Sar, I thought you looked guilty as hell. Shifty. That said, you passed the trial.'

I shuffled my feet uncomfortably.

'On that pony you will find your clothes, your weapons, byrnie, helmet and a suit of mail. See those two riding horses?'

I nodded assent.

'That dubious looking one is yours. The powerful stallion is Wulfgeat's. I'm sending you back to Much Marcle, you will do what my mother tells you. Wulfgeat has a package for her. He also has orders to chase you down and kill you should you run.'

That got my attention. 'Why would I run, sire?'

'Why do you do anything, Sar? You ended up in the land of the Scots, then the Irish, then the Welsh all for me? Not really was it Sar? You wanted Oslaf dead and you wanted to see that Gyric was alright.' He paused, then looked me straight in the eyes, 'Or you could be a spy. That walk up the valley could have been a trap.'

'You saw me kill a Welshman. I helped you.'

'That is what it seemed like at the time. I went over it with my chaplain, moment by moment. Your hand slipped when you threw that axe. Maybe it was me you were aiming for. Or maybe you wanted to gain my trust even further by sacrificing one Waelas. Who knows?'

'Maybe I didn't want to see you killed. Maybe I was serving my lord.'

That fucking cunt Leofgar has been whispering in his ear, I thought. I'll get that fucker someday.

'Harold hadn't finished, 'People say I favour you. Perhaps I have. I can see you two ways. The very loyal boy whose life I saved and trust I earned. Or a tricky, lying, two-faced spy. You left with nothing. You come back with a fortune. You make friends with England's enemies.'

I butted in, 'Faelen was your friend first.'

'You then fight alongside those enemies and though you didn't kill those priests, I think you were there.'

I went to speak. He held up his hand.

'Hereford needs time to lick its wounds and grieve. Your death might have helped. Alive, you're salt in the wound. If anyone can work you out it's my mother. You'll go there until I send for you.'

Wulfgeat pointedly tied the pack pony to my horse while I dressed. A sign that he didn't trust me. Even harder to bolt dragging the pony along. I had no desire to bolt though I was beginning to think I'd be better off back in Ireland. I mounted, wincing, my hand might not be festering but it hurt like hell. I grabbed the reins in my left hand and left my weapons on the pony. I kicked with my heels and set off. Wulfgeat followed me, his eyes like daggers in my back.

The journey is not long but the days were short. It was truly dark when we roused the gatehouse. As the estate was within raiding distance from Wales the stockade was manned day and night. Myself, I'd rather fight an army than face the Lady Gytha. That pleasure was to be delayed. Wulfgeat handed his messages to a cleric and I found myself locked in a storeroom for another long dark cold night.

It was late morning when a couple of Gytha's warriors came to get me. Her men were generally older than Harold's. They'd been her husband's, Godwin's, housecarls, thegns in their own right. Men of property and experience. Their sons would all be in the service of one or the other of Gytha's many children, four of them Earls and one, the Queen.

I was taken into the hall, despite the cold most of the shutters were open, the day being dry so far. Gytha was sat in a chair among a semi-circle of her ladies at the top of the hall.

'Come, boy. Or are you afraid of us women,' she said.

I walked up the side of the long hearth down the centre of the floor. My stomach rumbled, loudly, as I passed the remains of many breakfasts being collected by the serving girls.

'Give the boy a full bowl of leftovers.'

A pretty, young woman did as she'd been asked, grinning at me. I blushed, apart from Morwid and the Ale-wife, I'd not been near a woman for many weeks.

'Feed him, girl, don't flirt with, him,' said Gytha loudly, though with a chuckle in her voice.

I took the bowl and a spoon and wolfed down the odd mixture of meat scraps, barley porridge, bits of hard cheese and breadcrusts. Another girl came over with a large cup of weak, morning ale, she'd drawn from a barrel on trestles at the side of the hall. My right hand was still sore so I ate clumsily with the left.

'Long enough, bring your ale with you.'

I put the bowl down, picked up the ale and turned towards Gytha. There was a low stool on the floor in front of the semi-circle. Gytha nodded towards it. I sat down.

For a while I was ignored as Gytha and her ladies talked among themselves. Most of them were embroidering linen strips, one of them was reading from a psalter, only Gytha had nothing in her heavily bejewelled hands. I remembered that Gytha had a fondness for furs. She still had the wolverine pelt around her neck that she'd been wearing when we last met. She caught my glance.

'You remember this?'

I nodded.

'You can speak.'

'Yes, Lady Gytha.'

'Because of your sister.' A statement, not a question.

'You remember?' I said, surprised.

'I remember everything Sar.'

'Yes, because of my sister.'

'I heard you call yourself Nomansson.'

I nodded.

She laughed, 'Aren't you meant to be the son of a ghost.'

'Some say so.'

All the women started making signs of the cross to avert the evil eye or some such. Gytha scoffed at them, 'Tssk, ladies, just the silly talk of serving folk.'

'I saw my sister,' I said. 'She was on a cart, in the snow.'

'She's not in Alba, Ireland or Wales, boy. So how could you have seen her?'

Again, I was surprised, how would she know where I'd been?

'Ladies, give me the room. And the rest of you, get out.'

Everyone left, even her warriors, without a word.

'I know because Harold and I talk to each other. Did you know that Beorn was my brother's son? You revealed Oslaf's part in his death. I also want him avenged.'

'I think I did. I really think I did. I'd fought him, stabbed him many times and scalped him in the water. How could he have lived?'

'Hmm, so what was his mortal wound?'

'He was bleeding all over through his mail.'

'He was dead when you scalped him?'

'Yes.'

'When you scalped him, did he bleed a lot?'

'Heads do, my lady. Heads do.'

'When the heart no longer beats?'

I paused, feeling the first real sense of doubt, before answering, 'It had been beating a moments before.'

'You're not so sure now, boy, are you?'

I shook my head.

'And then you left him in the cold water?'

'Icy cold.'

'And then?'

'I crawled out of the water and went to look for my dog.'

'Not you, Oslaf's body.'

'It rolled over the fall.'

'You took Harold there. Nearly got him killed.'

'He wanted to come with me,' I protested. 'The whole thing was his idea.'

'Come here.'

I got up and walked to her.

'Kneel.'

She leant forward, took my face in her right hand, and stared into my eyes.

'You're older but still the same boy.'

She let go of my face and leant back.

'Harold doesn't know if he can trust you. He thinks you might be a Welsh spy, or an Irish one. He says you and Faelen are close. Get off your knees.'

I sat on the stool, 'I was loyal to Faelen while I served him. He knew I was Harold's man and he knew I would leave. I am loyal to your son. I swore my oath to him and I meant it.'

'What did you mean you saw your sister?'

My mind swirled as she changed tack. I tried to tell her about the people I stayed with, in the hollow hill. How I'd flown and seen my sister through the eyes of a bird.

'She was on a cart?'

'Yes, well a wagon, four wheels. She was with two other women, one old and one much older.'

'Anything else?'

'They were in a clearing in a wood. There were a lot of people. A man was hung from a tree and stabbed in the side. She saw me, Moira, she saw me in the bird. Then I was gone.'

Lost in the memory I forgot where I was. I was sobbing, in grief for my lost sister.

'Maybe it is you that are lost, Sar.'

Christ, can this woman read my mind?

'It seems to me that your sister is doing better than you.'

I snuffled and wiped snot on my sleeve, 'What do you mean?'

'Listen to me boy. My grandmother rode the wagon. She was worshipped and revered because she could talk to the god's and see what is to come.'

I didn't understand. 'I don't understand,' I said, then I remembered something, 'Frejya's wagon?'

'You too have a good memory. You have been Christian here for many centuries. Where I come from there are people alive who remember when we worshipped the old gods. Your sister seems to be somewhere where the old customs are still followed.'

'You believe me?'

She nodded.

'About what I saw?'

'Priests don't know everything,' she said.

Strange I thought, how like Morwid she could be. Morwid's people had been Christians much longer than the Saxons but she too had a dim view of priests.

'So, it was real?'

Did you think it was real?'

'Yes, but I don't talk about it. I don't think people will believe me?'

'That's wise. I think you've been blessed. I also think your sister saved your life.'

'Oslaf told me he used her before he sold her.'

'He might have. He might just have said it to get to you.'

That could easily be true. He was a cruel man. If he is alive, I'll just have to kill him all over again.

'When we first met, I was told you had visions, remember?'

I nodded.

'Do you still?'

'Less so, my mother, not sure she knows everything now. Maybe they are just dreams.'

'Maybe. Maybe your sister has visions too. Maybe hers are more certain than yours. It's more common that women have the sight. If your sister was hurt, she is beyond that now.'

Yeah, maybe this, maybe that, I thought. I knew that however well my twin was doing now; she'd have the same hole in her as I did.

My turn to change the subject, 'So these old gods, what are they?'

Gytha laughed, 'Don't you have enough trouble with the church as it is? That hand? Show it me.'

I got up and did so.

'When I've finished with you go to the weaving shed and ask for Hildifryth. No, don't sit back down. I think people see you as complicated. I see you more clearly. You are no traitor to my son. You're loyalties are absolute, perhaps naïve, your sister, your friend Gyric, Harold,' she paused for a moment, 'hmm and that Candalo and his daughter. Now those two, those two need some thought.'

I looked up surprised.

'It's my business to know things, Sar. Now listen. I trust you. You will serve me here. You won't be watched or followed. If you disappear, well then, I was wrong about you. You sleep and eat in here with my warriors. Now go get that hand seen to.'

I walked to the door.

'One last thing Sar. My son's chaplain, Leofgar. I'll get him promoted out of the way. Once Athelstan dies, I'll pull strings, get him made bishop. Man's a fool.'

I didn't have to be told to keep that to myself.

Chapter Eleven

Weaving sheds can be difficult places for a young man to be. It's a woman's space where they talk among themselves. Can get a bit saucy, step in at the wrong moment and you'll hear worse language than around soldier's cooking pots. You are also likely to be assaulted by remorseless ribald teasing and leave with a bright red face.

So, when I found it, I took a deep breath and braced myself before entering. As I opened the door, I could hear them all talking at once and laughing amongst themselves. Then one of them saw me and nudged her neighbour, slowly one by one, the room fell into silence and the shuttles stopped moving.

All eyes turned to me and then every woman in the room was crossing herself as I asked, 'Is Hildifryth here?'

'That would be me,' said a woman at the end of the room. She stood and handed a skein of wool to a slave girl who was sat on the floor threading clay loom weights with warp yarns and tying them on the ends. 'What do you want?'

She was, tall dressed in fine, but not fancy clothes, as she walked through the shed the other women moved carefully out of her way.

'Lady Gytha said you would see to my hand.' I said holding it out palm up.

She didn't look, 'Gytha seems to be under the illusion that I am her servant.'

I grinned, 'Aren't we all?'

'I'm the steward's wife. He's with Harold at the war. If she wasn't here, I'd be running this place myself. As indeed I was.'

I thought for a moment, 'About my hand?'

She smiled, wryly, 'Not stupid, are you? Let's have a look.'

She took my hand and peered carefully at my sore palm. 'You passed the ordeal of hot iron?'

I nodded.

'It has healed well so far. God has cleared you.'

'It still fucking hurts.'

'Watch your mouth.'

'Sorry, can you help?'

'I have some knowledge. Come.'

I followed her swaying skirts to a small chapel. Inside its humble exterior it was hung with fine tapestries with a gold and silver cross above the altar. Just like Harold to have any chapel of his finely adorned. A priest was on his knees praying as we entered.

'Father Praen, I have a request.'

He got to his feet, a short man with a kindly face. 'A privilege, what do you need?'

'A remedy blessed.'

They went to the altar where bundles of herbs, assorted flasks and pots lay around its base. They knelt together and selected a pot. The priest stood, intoned some prayers, then sprinkled some holy water on the pot. I looked on approvingly, this was the proper way to do things. We then went outside to where a seat had been built around the base of a fine old oak tree.

We sat together. She smeared some poultice on my hand, looked like tallow with lots of herbs in it. It didn't smell great to be honest.

'You have a charm?'

She smiled and began to chant a charm which rhymed and had words I'd never heard before. Clearly powerful words. This felt good to me and I knew my palm would heal much more quickly now. She then produced a strip of cloth and started to wind it around my hand.

I looked up to see her smiling lightly while looking keenly into my face. 'You're not that much more than a boy really, aren't you?'

Her voice was kind. I was shocked to find tears in my eyes. I was about to protest but suddenly felt very childlike, 'Maybe that's so. So why do all your women fall silent and cross themselves when they see me?'

'We've heard stories about you. Killing priests would be one.'

'I passed the ordeal. I was found innocent.'

'And that your father came out of a burial mound fully armoured and stole your mother away.'

Normally I don't tell anyone the truth about this, 'My mother's sister told me that my father was a raider who dug up a rusting richly hilted seax from a king's grave. My mother ran away with him.'

'Where is he now?'

'I don't know. My mother jumped in the sea, pregnant with my sister and I, and washed up on the Welsh coast where we were born.' This was getting painful. I'd said enough. 'So, what do you think?'

'I think you've said enough for now,' she said, patting me gently on my arm. She tore the end of the strip of cloth lengthways, reversed one end and tied a knot, 'There, that's done. Leave that on and see me in a couple of days.'

I leant back against the tree feeling oddly calm. What did I have to do now? Not much, find my weapons? They could wait. I was going to enjoy this moment where no one was telling me to do something and there was nowhere else I was meant to be. Why had I told Hildifryth all that stuff? I felt alright, even a bit better. I just needed a doze.

And doze I must have because I was woken up by a pair of arms wrapping tightly to me and a small tousled head thumping on to my chest. For a moment I felt fear then, quickly realising where I was, I wrapped my own arms around the boy.

'Aelfric, what brings you here?' I asked.

He looked up at me, 'I'm here with me Dad.'

I laughed and, pushing him off me, said, 'I didn't think you'd come here on your own.'

It was a fine winter's day so I just sat there listening to Aelfric chattering excitedly about armies and the other kids here who he mostly wasn't allowed to play with because he was a slave. It was alright because Tunglo was training some older rich boys who were kind to him even though Gytha was their nan and she was only kind to them but when she brought them honey cakes they shared them with him and he thought they were the best thing ever and so on and on.

After a while I stretched and yawned, 'So where's your father now?'

Aelfric squinted at the sky and laughed, 'Look how high it is. Ha, you've missed the midday meal. We slaves eat after. That's where Dad will be. Come with me, we eat well here.'

Jumping up he pulled on my sleeve until I got up, laughing too, and followed him to the slave quarters. This was another place, as a freeman, I might not be welcome, but as it turned out when they found I was easy with them, they were easy with me. The pretty girl from the hall was there, but Tunglo caught me grinning at her and warned me off.

'Hildifryth won't stand for that. Do the girl a favour and stay away.'

There were quite a few people in the slave shed. Being winter, no one was out in the fields and all Harold's stock had been slaughtered so not even any animals to look after.

Tunglo spoke, 'You're wondering what they do all day?'

'Yeah, yeah I was.'

'They'll be clearing ditches, fixing fences and buildings, scraping skins, boiling clothes, scrubbing pots, moving firewood and fetching water. In a few moments this place will be empty. With two mistresses, they're being worked harder than if the steward was here.'

That left me feeling a bit stupid and made me realise how lucky my sister has been to end up where she has. If my vision was true. As time went by, meeting that man at the battle at Dunsinnan and our time with those strange dark people seemed more and more unreal. What if I just wanted to believe those things? After all, I'd thought Oslaf was dead and that I'd helped kill those priests, but now it seemed that neither was true.

Then everyone left leaving an old woman, bent up with rheumatics, to clear up. Aelfric ran around looking in each place for scraps. I don't think that boy could ever get enough to eat.

We left soon after and went to the home field. Being well drained it wasn't too muddy. A couple of grizzled warriors were sparring with each other at one end while three boys were attacking a post with wooden swords.

'There they are, my charges.' he said. 'Oy, boys, come here.'

They ran over and lined up. Three fine looking lads each a head shorter than the other. I guessed the oldest was about twelve or thirteen, he had yellow hair while the other two were russet. It was easy to guess whose boys these were. Harold's, by Edith the Fair.

'Here Earlings, this is Sar. Sar,' he pointed in turn, 'Godwin, Edmund and Magnus. This man can throw a spear, almost as well as me.'

'Hello lads, good to meet you.'

'You're our father's man, is that right?' asked Godwin.

I nodded at this confidant youth, 'That's right.'

'Why, then, aren't you with him?'

I wondered what he knew. 'Because he ordered me here.'

His eyes briefly narrowed at me then he let it go. 'Tunglo, let's get on with it.'

Tunglo turned to Aelfric who was already running off to where their horse and cart were tethered.

'I'll go find my weapons,' I said and ran back up to the hall asked around a bit and soon found them stashed in a corner of the hall. I was soon back at the field to see the little lords practising their sword strokes. I noticed that each of them had shields, swords and helmets all made to suit their size.

Aelfric noticed me watching, 'They've got spears and bows, made to fit, on the cart as well.'

'Does it bother you?'

'Can't let it. Thurkill owns the clothes on my back. I'd have to be jealous of everyone.'

'Wise words from one so young.'

Aelfric gave me a long look, then his face lit up once again, 'Sometimes I fight with the younger two. I'm quite good you know. I can sword fight, wrestle and throw spears. I do have a little wooden sword Dad made me. Sometimes there's a hunter who comes here and teaches them to use a bow. When Gytha's not around Magnus lets me use his.'

'I'm useless with a bow. Perhaps he'll teach me. Here show me how well you can throw a spear.'

For the next couple of weeks, I felt happier than I'd been since my time with my aunt Ealhild and my little cousins, Aebbe and Godric, all of them dead now. On fine days we'd train and run in the woods with Harold's sons, on wet days I'd spend time in the hall with Gytha's housecarls. She'd come and watch the training, proud of her grandsons. She softened up, especially with Godwin, named after her late husband, but could still quell any one of them with a look. The hunter tried to teach me how to fire a bow, but honestly, Aelfric could do better than me. I finally got my daily sword and shield lessons with Tunglo as soon as my hand was sound enough. Wearing gloves helped. I can't throw a spear with gloves on but for sword play, they are the thing.

Then one day around mid-morning a messenger's horn sounded outside the gate. Harold and his entourage were on their way. The whole place burst into frenzied activity. Flitches of bacon and hams were lowered from the smoky rafters while the meat of cattle, deer, sheep and fish was hauled out of salt barrels and set to soak. Ovens were fired up and huge balls of dough were soon being rolled out in wooden troughs. Hildifryth must have completely restocked the whole place after the army went.

When they rode in there were over fifty of them and even more horses. They made a fine sight led by Harold's 'Fighting Man' banner and the snapping tubular white Dragon of Wessex. All of them were clad in gleaming mail with their shields on their backs and a spear in one hand. Something had changed, these men were dressed to impress more than to fight. Not long after we were all crowded into the hall. I managed to sidle up next to Gyric. he grinned at me and I back at him.

Thurkill stood and called for silence as only his bellow could.

Then Harold spoke, 'The fighting is over. A truce has been agreed.'

For a while everyone was talking at once then there was some cheering and calls for ale.

'I know that this winter campaign has been cold and miserable with no conclusive results. We have not got revenge and that will disappoint many of you. The King is on his way to Glowcestre and from there my brothers and Earls Leofric and Odda will, with our housecarls go to meet, peaceably with the self-styled King of all the Waelas.'

Harold sat down to let his words sink in.

Thurkill stood, 'There will be no feasting tonight. You will eat and drink as normal then bed down for the night. Tomorrow the housecarls will breakfast first and be ready to ride very shortly after.'

With that the serving people start pushing everyone about so they can set up the trestle tables and benches. Eventually everyone was jammed in elbow to elbow and food and ale set out. I squeezed in with Gyric.

'How've you been my friend,' I said.

'A lot better since you passed that ordeal. I felt really bad, Sar. I wasn't sure you were telling the truth.'

I shifted uncomfortably, and changed the subject, 'So, what's been going on?'

'We were rotated out of Hereford back to patrolling the river banks. Hard work, riding most of the day. Not fighting, more just making sure the fyrd men didn't run off back to their farms and that supply trains came and the supplies given out fairly. That sort of thing.'

'You didn't see the enemy then?'

'We did. They'd come to the river and shout insults we couldn't understand and we did the same back. Nothing more.'

'So, what changed?'

'Don't know. Suddenly we're sent back to Hereford and are cleaning and oiling mail, leather and our horses and here we are.'

Just then I get a tap on my shoulder and turn to find one of Gytha's men servants there. 'You're to come with me, now.'

I shrugged at Gyric and for a moment struggled to get out because my legs were under the table. We were all jammed in along the bench. I found laughing with one leg on one side of the bench while trying to lift the other one over Gyric's head. For a happy moment we were both the boys we were when we first met.

I'm taken outside from the hall then back into a room adjoining the hall's end. Gytha, Harold and his boys are sat round a table with Hildifryth and a man I didn't recognise. The walls were hung with tapestries and there is another fire in here. A doorway opens into the hall through which I can just see Thurkill's back. There were some serving people standing against the walls. I could see Hildifryth tense as Gytha ordered them to close all the doors.

'Sir?'

'Ah here you are,' said Harold, 'I've spoken with my mother. You've been free to leave but you haven't. How's your hand?'

I held it out before him. It was back in its usual grimy condition.

'You're rebuilding the callous I see. Looks good to me so you're fit to serve again.'

'So I'm coming with you, sir?'

'Um, no, no you're not. Housecarls only.'

'I want to say something sir.'

Harold sighed and walked over to me, 'What is it Sar?'

'I think you should trust me or get rid of me sir.'

'You think I'm not taking you because I don't trust you?'

'It's all happened before remember? Your brother Tostig wanted to kill me.'

'It's true Faelan will be at the meeting with Gruffud and the King.'

'Oh, I thought he'd be long gone,' I interrupted.

'My sources tell me they are going to meet at Deverdoeu. It's the timing you got wrong.'

'I don't want to run off to the Irish.'

'I believe you.'

'So why aren't you taking me?'

'You're a soldier Sar, you shouldn't ask questions.' He stared at me then grinned, 'But you always do.'

I felt confused.

Harold reached out and held my shoulder. 'I'm taking Godwin with me, he's old enough to start learning about affairs of state. My mother too will be coming. You will stay here with Fordraed, my steward, and keep training my younger sons. Trusting enough for you?'

Now I looked shocked.

He laughed, 'Go.'

I went.

Chapter Twelve

Housecarls, being themselves nobles, thegns or the sons thereof, are usually accompanied by older boys who look after their mail, weapons and horses. These boys will come from good families themselves, the foster sons of the housecarl's own family. The leading people having the strange custom of sending their boy children to grow up in other people's households. Gyric explained it all to me once but it still seems cruel to me. Harold and all his housecarls left at first light then, after a quiet day, come sunset, a tribe of boys and various members of Harold's household arrived on ponies or carts. I was delighted to see that among them were Candalo and Morwid.

Keeping an eye on Edmund and Magnus was a nightmare after that. In the daylight it wasn't too bad. All the boys wanted to be warriors. They saw it as their birthright. They were all willing to train with Tunglo, the hunter, Mul the Stealthy they called him, and I, but the nights being so long they'd be up to all sorts of tricks with the housecarl's boys. Christ's Mass came and somehow Fordraed and Hildifryth had again restocked enough for a fine feast in the great hall.

After the main event Gytha had her grandsons, a couple of her oldest warriors, some of her lady companions, Fordraed and Hildifryth, Candalo and Morwid, and to my surprise, myself, join her in the private quarters at the end of the hall. There was a small hearth in there with three proper chairs for Gytha, Fordraed and Hildifryth and some stools set around it. A servant was setting up cups of mulled wine on a table to the side which gave off sweet heady aromas. Gytha settled herself in and pulled her furs around her.

'Sit down all of you,' she said, raising a finger at the servant who gave us all a full cup each, 'smell this before you drink. It contains spices from the Orient. Spices that have travelled thousands of miles before my kinfolk, the Rus, brought them to the Baltic Sea from where traders have brought them here along with fine silks. For this we gave them, gold, silver, falcons and hunting dogs. We also gave them ship loads of wool and grain. All of that is in these cups. Savour it.'

My head swam with the thought of all those riches as I sniffed over the cup. The smells were warm and unlike anything I'd ever breathed in before. Very odd, I thought as I drank some. Wonderful. I could get to like this. I looked around at all the surprised faces and the two giggling boys. I wouldn't be here if Gytha or Harold didn't trust me. Now I was not only here, I was sitting with Gytha and her grandsons drinking wine. Tensions I didn't know I had began to ease. The warmth of acceptance and spiced wine spread through me. I belonged.

'The King will be holding the Witan in Glowcestre today,' said Gytha, 'As you know there is a truce with the Waelas. The great men of the land will meet with the King and discuss what terms will be offered to Gruffud.'

'He'll do well out of it whatever the terms are. He's now ruling all of Wales. We haven't beaten him. He'll keep all the slaves and wealth he's already taken. And there's still the problem of Aelfgar,' said Fordraed.

Candalo laughed, 'Aelfgar will be given back his Earldom. Isn't that what you English do?'

Gytha chuckled, 'Yes, my husband and our sons set a precedent there.'

She was referring to the time Godwin and his sons went into exile then raided England to get their Earldom's back after the King had revoked them. This was when I'd been swept up by Harold's forces.

Here I was, once a dirty skinny boy herding goats in a colony of outcasts, now a man without a family in the household of an Earl.

'The King needs Earl Leofric back on side. Exiling his son while leaving him in post was never going to work,' said Fordraed.

'The King sometimes acts before he thinks,' said Gytha, 'We are fortunate that he has my daughter Eadgyth to give him wise counsel.'

'But not an heir,' said Hildifryth.

Gytha shot her a sharp glance, sighed, and let it go. 'Sadly, that is true, and the Kingdom is left with no successor.'

'Is not Bishop Ealdred in Europe seeking the children of Edmund Ironside?' asked Candalo.

'When I saw the King and Godwin at Wincestre the King told the Earl that he'd told William of Normandy that he could have the throne,' I said.

Whap! Without even looking at me, Gytha had swung out her right arm and knocked me off my stool. I found myself flat on my back in the rushes with a couple of young hounds excitedly licking my face.

I shook myself and after peering into my now empty cup I got, sheepishly, back onto my stool. The conversations carried on as if I was invisible, except for the two young boys who were nudging each other and laughing at me. I shot them a very sharp look and they quickly calmed down. Out of the corner of my eye I could see Morwid's wry smile swiftly hidden as she leant forward and her dark locks covered her face.

'Yes, Ealdred has been in Europe, but the Holy Roman Emperor, Henry the Third does not support our quest,' said Gytha.

Edmund and Magnus were whispering and nudging each other, then Magnus piped up, 'Who was Edmund Ironside, grandmother?'

'Don't you know, Edmund? You should. You were named after him at your grandfather's request,' said Gytha.

Edmund blushed and shook his head.

'Candalo, tell them the story. Short version, leave out the messy bits,' said Gytha.

Candalo smiled wryly. I wondered what at. Morwid reached down beside her and lifted up a bag. She opened it and pulled out a small harp of dark wood inlaid with bright silver. Placing the harp on her lap she leant over it and ran her fingers over then strings. As the beautiful notes sounded all the small talk in the room stopped,

'In your honour Gytha Thorkelsdóttir, wife of the late, great Earl Godwin, mother of the queen, mother of Earls, I, your skald, your tadhg, your minstrel, will tell this tale,' said Candalo, as he adopted the sing song tones of the storyteller.

Morwid struck some dramatic chords and Candalo began, 'In the far-off days when the father of our present king was on the throne, King Aethelred was his name, the country was sore beset by hordes of Danish warriors no longer come to raid but to conquer. To take the land of the Angles, for themselves.' Candalo leant forward towards the boys, 'Their leader was the great warrior king, Sweyn Forkbeard, King of both Denmark and Norway. Not content with ruling two countries, in his ferocious greed he sought to rule a third.'

I looked at the two boys, their eyes were growing larger by the moment.

'King Sweyn was a huge rough man, with massive arms covered in thick arm rings from shoulders to wrists and a long, grizzled beard forked like the tongue of a snake.'

Candalo's voice dropped while Morwid played low notes on her harp.

'Sweyn was greedy but he had another reason to attack this country. Vengeance. Vengeance for the death of his sister who was killed on Saint Brice's Day.' Candalo's voice rose, 'For King Aethelred had committed a mighty sin. Aethelred became king as a boy and for his whole life he had fought the Danes. When that failed, he tried to buy off the Danes with all the riches of his kingdom. Still the Danes came, again and again, in their fleet ships full of bloodthirsty warriors. At that time many Danes already lived here, mostly in peace, content upon their farms. Vengefully King Aethelred ordered the killing of all these Danes, men, women and children.'

Gytha, Danish herself, made an angry grunting sound but held her tongue. Candalo paused, leant back, and took a drink while Morwid stopped her strumming. Everyone relaxed, drank, and nibbled on honey cakes that Gytha's serving girl handed around.

'Enraged by this,' Candaolo's voice boomed, 'King Sweyn brought more armies to England. War raged across the land for ten more terrible years. The English Kings two eldest sons, the Aethelings, Athelstan and Edmund, fought valiantly on their father's behalf but the Danish forces prevailed. Beaten and shamed Aethelred fled to Normandy and his sons went into hiding. Sweyn became King of England. God denied him the pleasure of his conquest because five weeks later he was dead. King Aethelred returned and fought Sweyn's own warrior son, Cnut. Again, fierce fighting raged throughout the land until Cnut retreated to Denmark leaving his allies to be slaughtered as Aethelred took his revenge as well as his realm. During this time the King's eldest son, Athelstan, died leaving Edmund as the true heir to the realm.

Then, just as all seemed settled, Aethelred died and Cnut stormed back into the country with two hundred fine ships, carrying ten thousand hardened warriors. The forces of King Edmund and Cnut clashed in fierce battles from one end of England to the other as Edmund fought to save his kingdom. And, boys, do you know who fought alongside Edmund?'

They spoke in unison, 'Our grandfather, the Earl.'

'That's right. Godwin was a loyal companion to Edmund who was now the rightful king. Due to his fortitude and his courage in battle he became known as Edmund Ironside.'

Here, Candalo paused again and our cups were refilled with the spiced wine. It was clear we were approaching the end of the saga.

'Eight battles were fought, eight battles were won and lost, eight battlefields were strewn with the bodies of valiant men but neither side could get the upper hand. In October of that year Cnut rowed his fleet up the river Thames raiding and pillaging. King Edmund assembled the forces of Wessex and attacked the Danes as they were returning to their ships. He bravely led his men into the battle wielding his bright sword. Cnut, a different kind of leader, did not fight in the ranks. He stayed on his horse, directing his men from the back.'

Morwid made discordant sounds with her harp, to create the fierce noises of battle.

'The King, with his great companion, Godwin son of Wulfnoth Cild, fought hard and long from dawn to dusk. Then, just as they were gaining the upper hand against the angry stubbornness of the Danes, the evil Eadric the Grasper, one of Edmund's Earldormen, betrayed his king and took his men out of the fight. Undeterred Ironside fought on, now outnumbered by his foes, but the tide of the battle turned and Cnut fought the English to a standstill. After this battle Edmund knew he could no longer win and his people would die for no gain. A truce was declared and a treaty was agreed giving Cnut all he had taken of England. This left Edmund with little more than the Earldom of Wessex. Soon after this Edmund died. Was he ill? Did he succumb to wounds? Did Cnut have him poisoned? We will never know the answer. In this way Cnut became king of all England.'

'But grandfather served Cnut, didn't he?' asked Magnus in a puzzled voice.

'He did, Cnut saw that Godwin had served his king loyally in both success and defeat so took him into his service because he knew your grandfather's word was true. Eadric met a different fate. King Cnut knew him to be false to his oath having switched sides more than once. So even though the Grasper's actions had won Cnut the battle, Cnut had him killed on Christmas Day all those years ago. The body was thrown over the walls of Lundenburh and left, unburied, to be eaten by dogs and pigs. Such is the death a traitor deserves.'

'But I thought we were to be told about King Edward's heir,' piped up Edmund.

'Ah, smart lad, that is the last part of the tale. With Edmund dead there was no grown man in England with the right to the throne but his young and defenceless family were left to Cnut's tender mercies.'

Here, Candalo paused again, 'Now boys, did you know that our King Edward was Edmund Ironsides half-brother?'

The two boys looked at each other uncertainly.

'If you didn't, you do now,' boomed Gytha, 'get on with the story.'

Candalo coughed to cover his irritation, 'That means that King Edmund's sons are the present king's nephews. King Edmund had two sons, so young they hadn't left the nursery. Their names, Aethelings Edward and Edmund. Aetheling is the name the English give people who have a right to inherit the throne. Now, what was King Cnut to do with these young princes?'

Now it was Gytha's turn to cough.

'Those who had the ear of the new king advised that he had the boys killed. Cnut, who was a clever man, knew that this would make many of his new subjects very angry, so sent the boys to his step-brother Olof, King of Sweden with a note to have the boys quietly done away with. Cnut had forgotten that Olof had once been a friend of the boy's grandfather Aethelred. Olof couldn't kill his friend's children so he secretly sent them to stay with King Stephen of Hungary, far, far away in the east. After many years our Bishop Ealdred heard rumours of their survival and is now in Aachen trying to get to the boys who will now be men. As our King's natural successors, the hope is that they will return to inherit the realm.'

Morwid continued to play on her harp as the people not in the know absorbed those final words.

'Right then,' said Gytha, before Morwid had rounded off the melody, 'you've all heard the story. I need my bed. All of you. Get out.'

Chapter Thirteen

We all heard the squealing, scuffling and snorting, the first signs of life, apart from crows, after half a morning's walk deep into the woods. Aelfric, Magnus and Edmund looked at each other bursting with excitement. Tunglo and I made suppressing motions with our hands while Mul, living up to his name, moved silently to the ridgeline. We formed a semi-circle and moved up behind him at about ten paces distance. The fallen leaves had laid here long enough to get slimy. The slope was steep so that every step risked one of us slipping. The bare branches rattling above our heads disguised the snapping of the odd twig.

Mul beckoned us forward and we all slunk, careful step by step, up to the ridgeline and lay down before peering over the edge. A small sounder of sows was milling around while two hefty boars were pushing each other up and down a small muddy gully. Every now and again they'd stop, chomp their jaws and face in opposite directions, heads pushed in each other's flanks. Then they'd start grunting and savaging each other again. The darker of the two managed to rake the other across his ribs, who then squealed loudly and pulled away. He stood sideways onto the darker boar, bleeding and shaking, glaring through one mean bloodshot eye at his adversary. After a pause the darker boar barrelled into the wounded rib cage of the bloody pig who then turned and ran.

The triumphant boar strutted up and down the gully checking on his sows. Then he started looking outwards, raising his snout and sniffing the air. Tunglo, Mul and I looked at each other. This was when things could turn nasty. Mul knocked an arrow on the string while Tunglo and I signalled the excited boys backwards down the hill. Once we were some distance away Mul joined us, his finger to his lips.

We followed him further west, weaving through the trunks until we came to a small clearing.

'Well done, boys,' said Mul, and you Sar. You Tunglo don't know your way about the woods at all. I could hear you yards away.'

Tunglo shuffled his feet in the mould looking sheepish. He and Mul had developed a close friendship each admired the abilities of the other. They shared a quick grin and for a moment I missed Gyric and felt alone. We were all carrying bows and now Mul had us string them. We only had one arrow each. Mul said this was good practice because there was five of us and if all five of us missed then we didn't deserve the kill. Not that you get a second chance. Unless the animal is wounded.

We were hunting roe deer. Some bucks had been heard moving back into the area. Deer meat was always good but I was more concerned with improving my scouting skills and keeping the boys busy for yet another day. The truth was, I was getting tired of looking after them and living under Gytha's gaze.

A chilly, slow, mile or so later Magnus stopped, crouched, and put up a hand as he'd been taught. Mul put his palm towards us. We stopped. He beckons us. Silently we move towards Magnus, the wind blowing gently in our faces. We see a two-point roe buck, the velvet still on his antlers. Mul signalled us to nock our arrows.

We're all now in a half crouch, arrows on strings. Mul signals. We rose and loosed. I saw Tunglo's arrow fly over the buck, one of the boy's arrows went into the ground while two hit the beast. I loosed, snatched the string, and my arrow skittered off to the left. Mul's arrow thudded in deep behind the shoulder blade. With a surprised grunt the buck's legs buckled and he slumped to the ground.

Mul runs up, knife ready in his hand but the buck was already dead. The boys started cheering and jumping up and down. Then, a moment later, they are squabbling about whose arrow hit the ground. The argument erupted into a fight until all three of them were rolling around in the mud. Furious, I dive in and separate them. Mul, wise to their ways, congratulated them all for not scaring the beast off, then makes a joke in my direction. The boys resolved their dispute by having a good laugh at my expense. Sulking, I went and found my arrow.

By the time I got back Tunglo, was showing off his strength by heaving the carcass across the back of his shoulders, holding it by the legs each side of his head. We'd all given up on any attempt to keep silent. The boys chattered away happily, re-enacting the morning as we made our way back to the manor. Mul, a cautious man, who had children of his own, had not returned their arrows.

Just as we were coming to the track that divided the ploughed fields from the woods, we heard a horn sounding to the south-east. Someone was travelling in our direction. The horn was to warn locals that a stranger was approaching who meant no harm. Even so Mul had us crouching behind a thicket of dead brambles until they came in sight. First, we heard horses, five according to Mul. I agreed, four or five, a small party. Then they came in sight, four armed and mailed warriors and another younger man swathed in a leather, hooded cloak. One of them held a spear with a small white pennant fixed to it.

'Men of Wessex,' I said, 'Harold's men.' I stepped out onto the track and held up my hand. I was a little nervous in case it was a ruse but I was almost certain the Waelas would only arrive as an army or creeping through the woods.

The horsemen kept coming, then pulled up sharply. The leading stallion, reared, protesting until his rider skilfully settled him. Helmeted men in mail are hard to tell one from another, the nose bar doesn't help. Dark hair, dark eyes, then he spoke, Wulfgeat, of course, looking every inch the warrior he was.

'Sar, you're still here? Alone?'

'Not alone,' I replied, as the others came out onto the track.

Wulfgeat grinned and, leaning his forearm on the pommel of his saddle, said, 'Yes, we'd heard that you'd been promoted to nursemaid.'

What could I say? I felt the same way by now. Being trusted was one thing and at first I'd really enjoyed being with the boys but now it was beginning to sting.

I smiled, trying to make the best of it and with no desire to pull the scabs off the wounds between me and Wulfgeat, said, 'Yes, I feel like one of Gytha's servants while you lot have been with the King. What brings you here?'

'We're escorting this messenger to Gytha,' he answered, dropping his taunting manner. 'I might as well tell you that we're meeting Gruffud and Aelfgar soon to settle peace terms. No one is happy about it except perhaps Aelfgar. Oh, and maybe the King, he likes to see himself as a peaceful man, except when he loses his temper. Harold says it makes sense in public and then tells us that our time will come.'

'So, what does Leofgar say?'

Wulfgeat shot a quick look at the messenger and drops his voice to a whisper. I took a few steps closer. Soldiers love to gossip.

'Harold and Leofgar squabbled behind the scenes. Leofgar still thinks the Waelas are a bunch of savages who will give up if we burn them out. Harold says Gruffud's achievements at uniting the Waelas and successfully attracting allies, Norse, Irish and English, needs respecting.'

'So, what do you think?'

'What do I think? It can't be denied, Gruffud has outwitted us. He's worn us out marching around uselessly for much of the winter. He still has all the plunder from the sack of Hereford so he'll be able to pay his mercenaries. He still has an alliance with a powerful English Earl and a united, on the face of it, country behind him. A draw is a win for Gruffud.'

I nodded in agreement, 'Your fellows are getting restless. You'd better get on. Gytha is not a patient woman.'

'True,' said Wulfgeat, then, with a smile, said, 'I hope we'll see you back with us soon.' He pulled his horse around and set off while I gaped in surprise at their disappearing backs.

We trudged back. As the boy's excitement faded and weariness set in, they became a bit fractious. I pulled Aelfric to my side and told him to stay out of it before the rich boys turned on the slave. These things happen. When we got back Mul made them gralloch the deer, then taught them how to skin it. He was about to get them to clean out the bowels for sausage skins when I stopped him.

'They're the children of an Earl. Take care Mul. Aelfric and I will see to this.'

Mul nodded, stepped away and hung the naked carcass up high in the butcher's shed. While Aelfric and I sorted the offal, Tunglo set a small fire, then went off and came back with a loaf and a jug of weak ale. Mul set off home while Tunglo and I roasted slices of liver and kidney on sticks and then ate them with the boys. Once they were fed their good humour returned and I knew that they'd be no trouble to me for the rest of the day. I breathed a deep sigh of relief. Who knew looking after children could be so tiring.

After we'd eaten, I sent the boys in to find their grandmother and slid away to sit on the blind side of the big oak. I needed some time alone. As I turned around the trunk I saw a mass of black curls, Morwid.

I sat beside her. She acted as if she were expecting me.

'Had enough of people, have you?' she asked.

I nodded, 'Something like that.'

'How's your hand?'

'Pretty much healed. Surprising really. Very fast.'

'It was the cleaning and the honey.'

'I think Hildifryth helped. She knows the right spells.'

'You really believe that?' she said smiling quietly to herself.

'It's what everyone says.'

'Everyone says that ordeals find the truth.'

I picked up a stick and doodled in the dirt. 'Yes, yes they do.'

'But it didn't, did it Sar?'

'No.'

'Why's that then?'

'I guess God must have saved me for something,' I said, feeling very uncomfortable.

Morwid laughed at me, a little unkindly I thought, 'Sar so special. God's favourite boy.'

I sat up straight and tossed the stick away. 'So why then? Why did my hand not fester?'

'Your hand didn't fester because I treated it. Like it or not Sar, I saved your life. Again.'

'So now it's you that's special? You're more powerful than God?' Strangely I felt angry with her.

She spoke quietly, unaffected by my tone, 'Maybe it's nothing to do with God. The whole thing is invented by men.'

I didn't know what to say. Even if it wasn't God he would've know what was going on. I was very confused.

'There were different God's before the one we have now. What about that then?'

I'd heard that too. Gytha even, had said so. My head was reeling. 'Morwid, just shut up, would you?'

She recoiled, 'I was just thinking about things.'

'Well do it quietly,' I snapped at her. Then shocked at myself I tried to take it back. 'Oh no, Morwid, I didn't mean it. I'm sorry. You know that I love you.'

She stood up, looked at me scornfully and said, 'For fuck's sake, Sar.' Then she swept off with an angry swirl of her skirts.

I stared at the floor, clenching my jaw, and pursing my mouth. Why did she treat me like this? What a fucking mess. I choked back tears and nursed my anger. Getting angry was easier. Fuck this, I thought, and standing up abruptly, headed towards the hall.

I'd not got far when I heard Candalo's voice, 'Wait Sar, wait.'

'Fuck off Candalo, leave me alone.'

'Why? What are you thinking?' he said, grabbing me by my left arm with his crooked broken fingers.

I wrenched his hand off, seeing the pain in his eyes, 'Not now Candalo. Do one.'

He grabbed my again, 'No. I won't. What are you going to do? Get drunk. Find your weapons. Pick a fight with someone. Hurt, or worse, someone who doesn't deserve it.'

I scowled at him, 'Yeah, something like that.'

'You could end up dead yourself.'

'So, fucking what.'

'That full of self-pity, are you?' he said, making a scornful face and spitting on the ground, 'Pathetic. Stupid and pathetic.'

I felt like I'd been slapped. I dropped into a squat and held my head in my hands. Oddly I had this passing thought about my hair getting longer again.

'So why, Candalo, won't Morwid have anything to do with me?'

Candalo placed his hand on my shoulder, I tensed, but didn't shrug it off.

'It seems to me Morwid has quite a lot to with you when we are in the same place. Twice now she's come to your aid, possibly saving your life. When she heard that you were jailed by the monks and why, she took a great risk to help you.'

'Yeah, but, you know what I mean.'

He scoffed at me again, 'Yeah but, yeah but. You mean you can't get what you want.'

I sulked some more. My gut was writhing around. I got up and twisted about and squatted again. 'Fuck, fuck, fuck.'

'Got to be honest with you Sar. I wouldn't want you close to my daughter anyway.'

I felt a flash of anger, 'What? Why the fuck not?'

'Don't you have a child somewhere near Gipeswic?'

'Hmm, maybe.' Where was this heading, I thought?

'Does it have a mother?'

'Yes of course. Ymma.'

'End well, did it?'

I squirmed, 'No, it didn't.'

'I heard from Gyric about your time in Jorvik. He never says a word against you but his silences say a lot.'

I squirmed some more and said nothing.

'I bet there's been others too.'

I thought of Bruni, who started really liking me then, well things changed. I was very red-faced by now.

'Alright, alright. I get it.' I felt a strange feeling and recognised it as shame. I know Candalo, I know deep inside I'm not right. I'm not like other people. Scalpi always knew it. Says I'm a cold-blooded killer. He's not keen on my friendship with Gyric. And he's right, I do horrible things and feel nothing. I dream about them.'

Candalo gently pulled me to my feet, 'About Morwid. She doesn't want any man, ever, she says. And you Sar, you're not all bad.'

Tears sprang to my eyes. I had a lump in my throat and couldn't speak.

'I'm getting old Sar. I can't take this cold. I'm going in.'

I nodded and watched him leave. I was getting cold myself. It's very hard in any household to be indoors and alone but I found the shed I was first kept in, curled up, and wept.

The first glimmers of dawn were slipping through the cracks between the boards of the door when the courtyard erupted into hustle. Clearly not a normal morning as a lot of horses were being brought out, groomed, and saddled. My stomach growled as I watched the crowd of busy boys through the gaps. Then Aelfric staggered into view, half carrying, half dragging a bucket of water towards the horses.

I opened the door and took the bucket from him, 'What's going on? Where's everyone going?'

'Oh, hello Sar. You look a mess you've still got deer hair and blood on your face and clothes.'

'Where are you going with this bucket?'

'That black stallion.'

I recognised Wulfgeat's horse from yesterday being held by one of the many boys who was clearly nervous of it. The stallion was restive but not mean. I dropped the bucket under his nose. It snuffled me warily, but probably accustomed as a warhorse is to blood and hunting smells, settled to drinking. Then Wulfgeat himself walked out pulling on his gauntlets.

'What's going on Wulfgeat?'

'Good morning, Wulfgeat, how are you?'

I snorted in frustration, 'Come on man. Tell me.'

'You'd do well to understand these niceties if you're going to spend time among the gentry,' said Wulfgeat. 'But, to answer your question, the King is meeting Gruffud at a place called Billingsly, not that far away. He wants all the available noblemen and mounted warriors to go there to make a show of wealth, might and power. Also, our attendant boys to keep the mail shining and the horse glossy.'

'I'll get my things then.'

'Sar.'

'Yeah.'

'Do you have your own horse? Suit of mail? Orders of any kind?'

'Well, no. Mail, yes, lent me. But I'm sworn to Harold.'

'Not really the point here Sar. The messenger had specific orders. Only those who can put on a good show. Gytha's men are going but she's not invited.' He grinned, 'She's having a right sulk in there.'

I grinned too, picturing her mood.

'Yes, even the most powerful woman in the country has to do the King's bidding,' said Wulfgeat.

'What do you mean? What about the Queen?'

Wulfgeat scoffed, 'The Queen is Gytha's daughter. Most of our Earl's are her sons. Her family run most of England. Truth is, she probably has more power than the King.'

My eyebrow's shot up with surprise.

'Think it through Sar, think it through.' He finished pulling on his gloves. 'Take that bucket away boy,' he says to Aelfric. 'I don't want him drinking too much before we ride.'

With that he mounted up, 'I've got to lead so I'll be off.' He rode to the gate and commanded everyone's attention. They started forming a column readying to leave.

I caught a glimpse of Edmund and Magnus out of the corner of my eye and shot over and, grabbing by the scruffs of their necks pulled them under the eaves of the hall. Last thing I needed now was for one of them to get trampled. I stood with them and watched as all the horsemen rode out. In my mind's eye I had a vision of Gytha as a huge spider in the centre of her web.

Chapter Fourteen

So, that suddenly, everything went quiet again. With all the older boys gone there were only the older girls left and the rest of the younger children. No longer masked by all the adults they seemed to be everywhere. Not my problem though. Tunglo and I carried on training and entertaining Harold's sons. Tunglo and I never got any closer. If anything. he spoke less and less. With Aelfric and I, it was different, I really came to care about that slave boy. His unfailing good humour and his strangely acute child's wisdom touched my gloomy soul.

I got to know Magnus and Edmund quite well. Out of Tunglo and I, I was the easiest to get along with and they knew I'd been with Harold at Porloc and in other battles too. You don't tell children about how horrific it all is, boys love the glory stuff and that's what we give them. It's a violent world and they will have to fight to survive. Sometimes I'd tell them about banners and valiant deeds and, in my mind, I'd see the gore, smell the opened guts, and start to shake. Then I'd turn away until it passed and then I'd get tough on them. They needed to know how to defend themselves. Those nights the dreams would come back, the scorn from my mother, and the faces of the dead.

It got very cold for a spell. Once my duties were over, I'd spend a lot of time hiding, hoping, and shivering, on the blind side of that tree staring into the darkness. Then one evening she came and sat down beside me.

'Sar.'

'Yeah'

'I thought we'd sorted all this out while we were on the river. I told you how it was. You need to listen. I will never be any man's woman. Ever. I will always be your friend. I will always be grateful for what you did for me and my father. Always.'

'I didn't mean for it to burst out like that.'

She put her hand on my arm, 'You don't need to be keeping it inside, you need to be letting it go.'

I nodded though in the dark she probably couldn't see, 'Yeah, I do know that. It's just that ever since you turned up in Wincestre I've clung on to the idea of you through all the difficult times since. It's hard to let that go.'

'I thought it was finding your twin that you clung to.'

'Not the same.'

She sighed, 'No, I suppose not.'

'Besides, Moira's in a far-off land. Out of reach.' I felt that old guilt again, 'I should have saved her.'

'Do you want to talk about it?'

I shook my head and stayed silent.

'I'm in Harold's household. You are his man. Our paths will keep crossing. Let me be like the sister you have lost.'

I looked up at the stars blinking brilliantly in the cold clear sky. There was a kind of comfort in what she was saying but her words still hurt.

'Did you hear that a messenger came in today,' she said, 'Harold will be back tomorrow. We'll all be on the move again soon. Think on what I've said.' With that she touched my arm again and left.

I sat for a while longer thinking and shivering, then I returned to the hall which had been cleared for the night, found my sleeping place, and called it a night.

Early the next morning I was sent instructions to get the boys ready for their father's arrival. This meant dragging Aelfric up to scour their boy size mail suits. This is done by putting the mail in a leather bag with fine sand and shaking it vigorously. It's hard work so Tunglo helped him with that. I guess if I'd thought ahead, I could have had their shields repainted. Hopefully their chipped and battered state would speak to the efforts the brothers had made. Then I became aware of my own state. I'd not given it a thought so my clothes were dirty and tattered, my hair straggling and I was unshaven. My weapons, as always, were clean and sharp.

Then I woke Magnus and Edmund and hassled them into their clothes in time to join their grandmother for breakfast. After that I tried to tidy myself up a bit and grab a bite to calm my growling guts. By then the boys had finished breakfast and I sat them down to burnish and sharpen their swords and spear heads.

Meanwhile Aelfric was rubbing a mixture of tallow and pitch into their boots, while Tunglo gave their helmets a last rubbing. All this effort for two little Earlings who took it all for granted. I looked at them laughing and chatting excitedly together as they waited for their father and realised that I would miss them.

By the time Harold's entourage arrived they were fit for inspection. Gytha stood, with the boys before her, opposite the gatehouse as Harold rode in. The boys strutted before him and I was pleased to see him admire their warrior like appearance. Godwin soon jumped from his horse and joined his brothers. I watched this family scene and felt an acute stab of grief.

Nobody needed me that day so I stayed out of sight and managed to get shaved and my hair cut short. New clothes and boots would have to wait. The following morning, I was back on the training ground with Tunglo and Aelfric when Gytha, Harold and Thurkill came down with all three Haroldsons.

Tunglo and I were ordered to put the boys through their paces with swordplay and spear throwing, followed by them running a few laps around the field. While they puffed and panted in front of their proud father Gytha pulled me aside.

'After the midday meal you are to join us in the back hall to talk over your future.'

I nodded, 'I'll be there.'

Four of us, Gytha, Thurkill, Harold and I sat one side of the hearth.

'You've done a good job with my sons, Sar,' said Harold, 'In a few weeks they've improved faster than they ever have with their sword master in Wincestre.'

'That would be Tunglo's doing, sir,' I said.

'You took them hunting too,' he said, 'on foot.'

'That would be Mul sir,' I said.

'Your decision, your responsibility,' said Harold.

I took a deep breath, 'Yes, sir.'

'You didn't think they might be a bit young for that? Hunting like a poor man, on foot. Wild boar, maybe wolves about.'

'Mul says no one has heard a wolf since he was a boy, but boars yes. We watched them.'

Suddenly Harold's face lit up with that charming, slightly sideways, smile of his, 'Yes, they loved that. Told me all about it. And the deer. They told me you can't shoot a bow to save your life.'

Now I'm rocking from foot to foot and chuckling myself, 'They're right there. If I want to hunt a deer I'll stick to my spears.'

'You did a good job, Sar.' He started pacing, and talking at the same time, 'We have peace with the Waelas. It won't last, before long they'll be raiding us again, and, more than likely Englishmen will be defying their King and raiding them. I'm setting up men loyal to me in estates along or close to the border. They will keep an eye on the Waelas and report to my mother. I want ears along the border. We have found you an estate between the rivers Safearn and the Wye. Rwydin. You can hunt your own deer there.'

'I'd have no idea what to do with an estate sir.'

'I know that Sar, you'll get help from the steward of a nearby manor. I've used some of your money to pay the see of Hereford for it. Now it's yours, you will owe tithes and taxes. You'll also need to provide your own suit of mail, weapons, and two horses, and be ready to come to me whenever I send for you.'

'Does this mean I will be one of your housecarls sir?'

He stopped pacing, 'No Sar. I know that's what you want. You'll be attached at times but I want to keep you independent.'

Then Gytha spoke, 'It's not far from here. We will give you a horse, some more of your money. When you know how to manage it, we'll give you the rest.'

I opened my mouth to argue, but Harold spoke before I could put my foot in it. 'These are orders, Sar. This is your future.'

'Candalo tells us that you might have a child,' said Gytha.

'Did he?'

'Is he wrong?'

'Last time I saw the woman she was pregnant. That's all I know.'

'You will go to your manor. It's not far from here. Contact the steward. Then you will go and find this woman. If she has your child, you will offer them a home. I don't care what your arrangement with her will be but I want you to start a household.'

I didn't like being told what to do like this but she was my Earl's mother. I felt curious. What if Ymma had birthed my child? Many children die in their infancy but what if?

'She's near Gipeswic,' I said.

'Then that's where you shall go. I don't care how you get there but return via Wincestre and leave a report with the head cleric there. Then go to your manor. Make it pay. Messengers will be sent when we need you.'

Harold shouted out and Leofgar and Fordraed walked in. Leofgar carried a scroll with him and rolled it out on a small table. A boy followed him with ink and a quill. Everyone present signed it then I was called to make my mark. I put an S and an N on the paper which was the best I could do.

'You are now responsible for this manor Sar. You own land, you now have status. From now on you must reflect well on me, your sworn Earl,' said Harold. 'This deed will be kept in the Minster at Hereford.'

I dropped to one knee, not sure why, but it felt right. 'Thank you, sir. I won't disappoint.'

'You'd better not,' said Gytha.

'Now go,' said Thurkill, 'we have better things to do.'

Harold stood me up and shook my hand, 'Now, do you understand that I trust you?'

'I do sir,' I said and turned to leave.

Behind him Leofgar coughed into his hand.

That evening, I ate next to Gyric who told me what had happened at Billingsley. Aelfgar got his Earldom back, the border would stay along the banks of the Morrow and the Dore and Gruffud's kingship was recognised by King Edward. He was delighted to hear that I now had my own estate. He'd had one for some time which had never even occurred to me.

'You just need a good steward,' he said.

He'd met Ymma and clearly approved of her. Something else that was a surprise to me.

'Did you know that I'm betrothed, Sar,' he said.

This too was news to me.

'Yes, my parents have found a suitable bride, one of Burgric's nieces,' he went on. 'I'm meeting her as soon as we are released from this campaign.'

'You've never met her?'

He blushed, 'No, but my mother says she's very nice.'

'I hope so, my friend, I hope so. Let's drink to that.'

There was a lot of drinking that night as these tired men looked forward to some home comforts. The fyrd men were already making their way home to their families, to repair their ploughs and ready themselves and their oxen for the ploughing. Many of the housecarls too would return to their estates and families, get their gear repaired, and look to their farms and livestock, and remind the peasants who they were working for.

The next morning, I was prodded awake with a spear shaft and told to report to Thurkill. I found him standing in the yard with Tunglo who held the reins of a stocky little riding mare.

'This horse is yours now,' said Thurkill, 'and this saddle and bags. And here is a purse with more than sufficient funds for now. Your money of course, not a gift. Unless you hear otherwise you will report to me in Wincestre a week before Easter.' He then told a short list of villages I needed to pass through to reach my own and where the steward would be found.

I looked at the horse, it looked like a better animal than the one I'd stolen and left in Glowcestre. 'Thank you Thurkill, for everything.'

Glancing up I was surprised to see Thurkill smiling at me, 'You know Sar, you've come a long way. It's a rare thing that someone with humble origins gets to where you are. You did well in that valley in Wales. You were put in a difficult position, kept your head, and saved nearly all your men, not to speak of your Earl. Leofgar likes to think of himself as a warrior. He isn't, and he wasn't there.'

He then shook my hand and returned to the hall.

'Well, Tunglo, looks like I'm off. Where's Aelfric by the way.'

'I told Thurkill he was ill and left him in the slave quarters.' Tunglo shifted uncomfortably. 'I have a favour to ask.'

Ask away, you've made a swordsman out of me. I owe you.'

'I'm a slave, you owe me nothing. I want you to take Aelfric with you.'

I frowned, 'Why would you want that?'

'He knows a lot for a small boy. He can take care of weapons, horses, tack. With you he will be a person. In Thurkill's world, he's just another slave boy.'

'But with his dad.'

'Two things, if I live for a while, he will replace me. A tool to train arrogant young men how to use weapons. It's dangerous work, Sar. I learned to fight in the slave pens. I don't trust anyone, least of all these lordlings. One day I'll slow down and start getting cut. Then I'm just an old slave past his prime. Aelfric is too trusting, he likes people. I don't. He doesn't know when to shut up. I do. If I die soon, then what? He'll be just another overworked drudge until the day he dies.'

'What will you tell Thurkill?'

'I'll say he died from his illness. Children die all the time.'

'You think that'll work?' I asked doubtfully.

Tunglo shrugged, 'Will you take him?'

'I could try to buy him.'

'If he says no, the chance will be lost. Look if you take him, you must keep him as a slave. It gives him some protection.'

I looked at Tunglo, 'This would make me a thief.'

'Maybe, I'm not sure Aelfric's birth was ever recorded. We were always separate from the other slaves. He might have slipped through the cracks.'

'Might.' I suddenly made up my mind, 'Alright, I'll take him. What have you told him?'

'He's to go with you.'

Great, I thought, poor kid.

'You know which way I'm going?'

Tunglo pointed.

I nodded, 'Bring him to the track where it meets the wood.'

Tunglo nodded, sighed, and walked off.

I met them by the wood, pulled Aelfric up behind me. He sobbed into my back as we rode away.

Chapter Fifteen

It was a short day's ride from Much Marcle to our destination which was a village called Hope. Being winter it was a short day, so, after a few mis-directions we found the stewards house in the late afternoon. It had been a strange ride, Aelfric, once he'd stopped crying, sat in sullen silence behind me. I had no idea what to say to him so I said nothing. We even ate our midday bread and cheese sat side by side without speaking. I made him wash his face in a stream before we arrived.

I'd been given a small horn as part of my travelling kit and, after dismounting, blew it outside the gate. Immediately a small pack of dogs burst out from under a granary building all barking and howling raucously. I eyed them warily and waited. Shortly after a door opened in the main building and a short chubby man with a belly that hung over his belt, walked out wiping his mouth. He started yelling at the dogs who then all bound around him, barking even more loudly.

'Yes, what do you want?' he shouted over the racket, looking me up and down.

'Are you the steward, Colbrand?'

'Whose asking?' he yelled.

'My name is Sar Nomansson. Earl Harold sent me,' I yelled back.

He looked at me doubtfully while pushing various dogs down, 'You're not what I was expecting.'

I pointedly looked him up and down, noticing his thick plain clothes. 'Could say the same about you.'

'Well, you're arrogant enough to be one of his men,' he said, stoney faced, 'You'd better come in.'

I handed the reins to Aelfric, while Colbrand pulled some dogs away from the gate. We walked in. Much to my surprise, once we were welcomed in, the dogs all calmed down and just milled around seeking attention which Aelfric was happy to give them with his free hand.

'Can my boy stable my horse?'

'Sure, here lad, go round behind the granary. There's a barn round there we keep the beasts in. You'll find an old man in there. He'll show you what's where. When you've brushed the horse down, go round the back of the hall. You'll find the servants there. They'll feed you.'

Aelfric nodded, 'I'll do that sir.'

I noticed his pallor had improved a bit. He'd be busy for a while with animals and food. I felt that was a good thing.

Colbrand and I walked into the hall. It was modest but warm, with a few carcasses still hanging in the smoke. It was clear that we'd caught him at his table.

Waving towards a large woman sat at the table in front of a large bowl of stew, he said, 'My wife, Siflead. This is Sar, says he's Harold's man. You remember? He's taking on Rwydin.'

I bowed politely.

'Hmm, good luck to you with that,' she said. 'Sit down. Eat.' She called out towards the back of the hall and soon after a harassed looking woman came out with a bowl of stew for me.

I sat down on the bench across from her. 'Good luck? Will I need it?'

Colbrand, who was spooning in his stew, chuckled, 'Put it this way. I've done my best, but they're, shall we say, different up there. I'll show you tomorrow.'

'You seem to be doing alright here,' I said.

'Yes, good ploughland here. This is my estate. I steward a couple of others nearby as well. We do alright eh, don't we love?'

She chuckled, 'We do my sweet, we do.'

A happy couple it seemed. Well-fed and thriving. I looked around, there were more stools, a loom in the corner, and various tools lying about.

'The children are out at the moment,' said Silflead, reading my mind, 'feeding the beasts.'

'You'll stay here tonight, we'll go up in the morning,' said Colbrand pushing a loaf and some cheese towards me. 'Here, eat. My wife makes a good cheese.'

I ate well and slept well, despite the arrival of more and more children as the night wore on. This felt like a good start.

I woke up relieved to be away from the pressures of Much Marcle's rival ladies and my responsibilities for the boys. I came round slowly, and after going out and dunging on the dung heap, country style, I joined everyone for a breakfast of barley porridge. A much longer table had been set out and people of all sorts sat around it eating heartily. Aelfric was at the far end with a couple of other slaves but all were being fed the same.

Colbrand gestured around, and, speaking with his mouth full said, 'Feed your workers well and they'll feed you well.'

I nodded, getting the lesson.

'How come you're not like the others? I mean, you don't look down on me.'

'Well, that would be a long story. Put it this way. I started with a lot less than this.'

'Rwydin then is your first estate?'

I liked this man, his fat wife, and his merry household, 'Yes, I've no idea what I'm doing.'

'You will be my neighbour. I've done the best I can, but here, I have a lot of good ploughland, enough woodland and my peasants have enough common land to keep them happy. Rwydin, has little ploughland but it makes up for that in other ways.'

'You're all being a bit mysterious.'

'Eat up, get your boy to saddle up and I'll take you up there.'

We walked the horses slowly southward, along a track, into some woods with Aelfric and some dogs running alongside.

'These woods are the boundary of our properties. Once we get through, we're on your land.'

We came out of the wood into a long narrow field, empty of everything but crows.

'This is good land, not a lot of it but rich, fertile soil,' Colbrand continued, 'The village is ahead of us.'

I looked ahead at another woodland, some cleared into a mass of stumps, above it all was a strange dark haze.

'Is the village on fire? Should we get a move on?' I asked.

Colbrand laughed out loud, 'Not exactly. You'll see.'

We entered the next wood into a smoky haze and soon came upon a clearing.

Aelfric started tugging at my leg, 'They're all black. Demons Sar, what's happening.'

He was right, the clearing was full of people, in black clothes with black faces with startlingly white eyes rheumed with red. An acrid smell filled the air. They were all raking apart the remains of a mound.

'Oi, who's in charge? Come over here,' yelled Colbrand.

'It's alright Aelfric. They're charcoal burners. You've seen them before.'

'Never a tribe of them,' said Aelfric.

One of the charcoal burners made his way over, 'Yeah, what do want steward?'

Colbrand squinted at him, 'Blethin, isn't?'

'Might be,' the man answered wiping his weeping eyes with the back of his hand.

'Welsh name,' I said, I asked him if he was Waelas in that tongue.

He looked at me vacantly.

'There's a few with Waelas names here,' said Colbrand, 'he pretends he is to scare the children, but he's as English as you and I. Well, me anyway. How come you speak their language.'

'Part of that long story,' I said.

'Hmm, full of surprises you are?' said Colbrand, and then, addressing the charcoal burner added, 'This man is your new lord, Blethin.'

'Don't look much like a lord to me,' said Blethin, spitting on the ground.

I could see Colbrand waiting to see how I dealt with this. As usual I was holding the reins in my left hand with my spear in my right, my small targe hanging on my back. Without a moment's pause I smacked Blethin around the head with the spear shaft. He fell to the ground.

Without looking at him I said, 'Let's ride on.'

Colbrand was quiet for a while then, 'Maybe you're going to do fine here,' he said. 'Maybe you will. You shouldn't be alone.'

'I'm hoping I won't be. I'm only here for a couple of days then I'll be away for a while.'

We rode on through two more clearings with groups of filthy people building or watching charcoal burns,

'Why so much charcoal?'

'Just through here.'

We rode through another long narrow field to a collection of huts. By them were more dirty people working around three strange tall pipes, about half the height of a man, which were pumping out visible heat waves. Surrounding all this were piles of grey and reddish ash, charcoal, and piles of reddish stones.

'Christ, this is like hell. What's going on here?' Aelfric was now so close to me that he was nearly tripping up the horse while the dogs were slinking along behind us, bellies to the ground.

'They're smelting iron ore,' said Colbrand, 'They dig it up out of the banks over there.' He waved vaguely. 'They follow it under the ground, dirty and dangerous but profitable. Though for all the work they put in not a lot comes out,'

'You should stop blaspheming Aelfric,' I said, while I tried to take it all in. 'Colbrand, I can't stay here for more than a night.

I need you to keep doing what you've been doing. I have to go somewhere.'

'Yes, I could do that. You'd better see the house. It's not in great shape. A couple of the older villagers take care of it but no one has lived in it for a while.'

We walked on by the iron workings towards a house on a rise. Its thatch was mossy and no smoke leaked through it. We left Aelfric holding the horses and went in. Inside it was dreary, cold and gloomy but the walls were intact and the door frames solid enough. There was even a pile of branches by the hearth with twigs and dried grass for kindling and tinder. Hanging from a rusty tripod was a pitted cookpot. I looked inside, it held a few wooden bowls, cups and spoons. All a bit soft looking but not rotten.

'What do you think?' said Colbrand, 'Needs a woman's touch really.'

I turned to see two figures silhouetted in the doorway.

'Who are these?' I asked.

'Ah, the villagers who look after the house.'

One, less dirty than the other, spoke, 'I'm Ailred, and this is my husband, Liofa.'

Colbrand looked at me.

'I'm Sar Nomansson. I serve Earl Harold of Wessex. I'll be taking over here.'

As I heard myself speak these words, for the first time, I began to feel this was real. I held land. I had status. I stood a little more upright. 'I'm staying the night here. Could you tell my boy where to stable my horse and feed it. Light this fire and find us something to eat. We'll need breakfast tomorrow as well.'

Ailred said, 'Anything else sir?'

'Yes, while I'm away I want the shutters off when the weather is fine. I want rushes ready to strew the floor. Would you have some sacks of straw we could sleep on?' I could get used to this I thought.

'We can do that, sir.'

She bustled in and took down a shutter which dispelled some of the gloom. Liofa went away, to show Aelfric where to go I supposed. Shortly he returned dancing a glowing coal form one hand to another, dumped it in the hearth and lit a pile of grass and kindling.

'How did you do that?' I asked.

'It's working with the iron sir. Toughens your hands. I'll go see to your boy. Should he lodge with us?'

'No, for tonight at least, he can stay with me.'

What was I going to do with Aelfric. Leave him among strangers? I was going to have to take him with me.

'Colbrand, could you lend me a pony for the boy?'

'I could, leave by mine in the morning. There's something else I need to show you.'

Shit, I thought and rushed out the door. 'Don't unsaddle the horse just yet, Aelfric.'

Colbrand rolled out after me, petted his dogs and mounted. I did likewise then I followed him as he rode off uphill for some distance over a swathe of rough pasture.

'Too stoney for the plough now, but if you ever got it cleared you could earn from this,' said Colbrand.

I was looking around, you could see for miles from here.

'Quite some view,' I said,

'Yes, that's why I brought you up here. Look Sar, I've been told that you're not just here to give you a place but also to keep an eye on the Waelas. From here you can see across to Wales and up towards Hereford. A single farm burns and you will know it. There are no fords across the river here but it is narrow and you can row across easily.'

'I'm also supposed to report if the English are burning Welsh farms,' I said, 'works both ways.'

'Here they're more likely to be crossing the river to fuck each other than fight,' laughed Colbrand, 'or swap a fine salmon for a bloom of your iron. That kind of thing.'

'Hmm, thanks for that. Handy to know.'

'Well,' said Colbrand, 'can't waste all day chatting. Got things to see to. Pick the pony up in the morning and we'll get together again when you get back.' With that he rode off.

I stayed for a while looking across the landscape. Then went back to my house.

Ailred fed us a bowl of stewed smoked eels and a chunk of bread that evening, not bad at all. We slept each side of the hearth and woke up to more barley porridge. I cut a penny in half and gave it to her asking for bread and cheese for the journey.

Her eyes grew wide, 'But it's your estate sir, you don't need to pay me.'

'I'm giving you this because I want you to make this place as homely as possible. Your husband can find someone to make some beds and paillasses. Let's say two beds, four paillasses, two child sized. Do you have the cloth?'

'Some, with this I can get the rest,' said Ailred, 'Do you have a wife?'

'Just do as I ask,' I said, not wanting to count any chickens.

'You know,' said Aelfric, 'It's not really her business. You need to get a lot haughtier if you're going to be lord of the manor.'

'Babes and suckling's,' I said, gently cuffing him over the head. 'How're you doing.'

Aelfric swallowed, teared up a little and declared that he was fine.

When we got to Colbrand's he was standing outside holding a very fine black stallion. After the dogs had quietened down a bit, I said to him.

'I could have sworn I asked you for a pony.'

'This my friend is for you. You can pay me later,'

'Talking of payment, don't I owe you for managing my estate?'

'I take my cut as I go along. I steward for three thegns as well as your manor.'

'You must be an honest man.'

'Sar, real world, every steward skims, every landowner knows this. It's accepted to a point. So, how do I put this, honest within limits. Now, what about this horse?'

I don't know a lot about horses apart from what Gyric says and things I overhear but he looked beautiful to me and, for a stallion, fairly calm.

'This is going to cost me a lot, isn't it, Colbrand?'

He smiled, 'We can talk about that when you get back. If you want to be taken seriously you need a fine horse and better clothes. Go inside Siflead has something for you.'

We did and she had. Both Aelfric and I were kitted out with new clothes. Wealthy farmer type of clothes rather than the finery housecarls like to wear but a lot newer than what we were wearing. As I buckled on my sword belt, I started to feel a whole lot better about this journey and the point of it.

'I guess I owe you too then, Siflead. Do I take that up with Colbrand?'

She smiled, 'Give me a couple of silver pennies now. It'll will be cheaper than dealing with my husband.'

I handed them over, beginning to understand why this couple were so cheerful. I didn't mind. I needed all the help I could get.

So off we went towards Glowcestre, me on a fine stallion while Aelfric had his first riding lesson on the horse I'd been loaned. He was getting saddle sore by the time we reached the town. Soon after, as we headed toward Cirenceaster, I had a bright idea. We could visit Fulk in Lundenburh. I reckoned he would remember me.

It took us a few days to get there, the poor boy had such a sore arse and thighs that we had stop often so he could lie on his front or sit with his backside in a stream. It was a carefree journey, staying in taverns or camping out in the woods. Aelfric kept his thoughts to himself but between his saddle soreness and his delight in the horse he began to cheer up and return to his constant chattering and desire for endless food.

Chapter Sixteen

To get to the land of the Sudfolc the best way is through Lundenburh. To get there you must either go north of the Thameses or south. If you go south, you can't cross the river until you get to Sudwerca where there's the only bridge into the town. Go north, and you spend your last night in Oxforda, where they will fleece you for your lodgings and food, and then fleece you again for stabling your horses. So, suitably fleeced we headed out to Lundenburh in the first light of dawn. Not only did we have to be in Lundenburh before dusk when the gates shut but I wanted to cross the town and find Fulk's fine house on the wharfs before it got dark.

Every town has a market but Lundenburh is more market than town. Even before you get to the city you pass through a massive market outside the walls with its own name: Lundenwic. Once through this, then you get to the gates of the city which has the largest walls I've seen anywhere. In theory the town is part of Mercia but, really, it rules itself.

Aelfric had not been here before so trying to handle my own horse through the crowds while keeping an eye on him on his while he gawped around at the sights. Somehow, I managed all this and we eventually found our way to Fulk's massive house overlooking his wharfs on the seaward side of the bridge. The street side of his house is walled, gated and guarded. The ground floor consists of stores and stables. After a brief argument with the guard, we were allowed entry. I left Aelfric rubbing down our horses and climbed the stairs to the second floor which was more sumptuous than most of Harold's houses or even that of the King's at Wincestre. There were even clothes on the floor.

'They're called carpets, Sar,' came a voice from across the room. It was Fulk, his massive bulk sat on the balcony where he liked to sit watching the loading or unloading of all the wide bellied knars moored at the jetties below.

'You remember me then?'

'How could I forget that rude skinny boy and his fierce desire for revenge. You went but you never came back.'

I walked up beside him. He was dressed in robes of linen with a top shirt of silk. Beside him on a small table were glasses of wine and bowls of sweetmeats.

'We had to go north to escape pursuit.'

Fulk waved a fat bejewelled hand, 'Don't worry, I know. I heard you acquitted yourself well in the raid.'

'Yes, I killed Oslaf's brother, Osric. Grim too avenged his brother. Those Frisians certainly knew their business.'

'Yes, better to employ and pay pirates than have them take my ships. And now your Earl owes me favours. Not that we would speak of that outside these walls. I heard that Grim Haldorson found his way back to Siward's side. Were you with him?'

'I was, and I joined Siward's army into Alba, sir.'

'It seems you have learned some manners since we last met,' said Fulk with a chuckle, 'and you arrived on a fine stallion. I'm guessing you might have quite a tale to tell. Have you come far?'

'From the Welsh borders.'

'Then you will stay here for two nights. Your horses and your boy can rest and we shall eat and drink while my friends and I hear your story. One thing though, before we have company what errand are you on.'

I explained as best I could.

Fulk laughed out loud, his many bellies wobbling along with his overlapping jowls. This man, this merchant, was everything a warrior or an Earl was not, but I knew from the past that his soft outside masked an acute mind and his power reached out across the seas.

'That was not what I expected,' he said, 'Gytha has sent you to find a wife.'

'Well, really to find my child.'

'No Sar, she wants you to find a wife. She knows you can't ever marry into the world of the nobility even though she knows they are nearly all parvenues.'

'Parvenues?'

'Late comers. The truth is Sar, that nearly all the old nobility were wiped out by Cnut. That's one of the reasons Leofric and his son Aelfgar have the sway they do. Their family represents a connection to a deeper past, one without the Danish connections. An older England than even the King's with his Norman mother.'

'Surely that would make it easier for me to climb?'

'Doesn't work like that. They all feel the need to appear blue blooded, separate from the herd. The Godwinson's mother comes from a way more prestigious family than Godwin. Just not an English one. Your friend Gyric, father's a Dane right? And his mother a well born Englishwoman.'

'That's true.'

'And he'll marry someone from a similar background.'

I shrugged.

'Gytha's a very wise woman. Wields power better than most men,' continued Fulk, 'so now she's setting up men like yourself who are tied to her family as her spies along the border and, most certainly, elsewhere as well.'

'I think it's Harold that has raised me,' I said.

'That is true, but Harold, for his mother, is only part of the picture. Stay on the right side of her and you can't go wrong.'

This fitted in with all I'd been learning recently. There was only one problem, Gytha didn't know Ymma.

* * *

That night I ate with Fulk and told him my story. I knew that Harold trusted him and that he knew of the blood feud Harold and I shared with Oslaf so I didn't have to hold back. Fulk rarely left his balcony overlooking the docks. His huge bulk makes that difficult. I even told him about having a share of Maelcolm's treasury.

'Growing money Sar, is my skill. For most people money is about acquiring land. That's what you'll be told. Get more land. And it's true, even for you, if you can accumulate enough land, you could be made a thegn, and then maybe your children could aspire to be accepted by the nobility.'

My head reeled at this. If I was to become a thegn it would be hard to deny me a place among the housecarls. Though it would still be up to Harold, and I wouldn't want to serve under anybody else.

'Thing is Sar, I don't own land anywhere. I'm not even an Englishman, yet I could buy half the country if I wanted. Even the land this house is built on I rent from an Alderman.'

'Why would you want to do that?'

'I'm free, Sar, anytime I find England too difficult, all I need to do sail on one of those boats moored below us. I'm welcome everywhere from Bruges to Hedeby and beyond and have contacts throughout Europe.'

'Does that mean you are one of Gytha's spies as well?'

'I forgot how quick you are. Let's just say I trade information as well as goods.'

'So how do you make so much money?'

'Mostly ships and cargoes. Or, more accurately, shares in ships and cargoes. Spreads the risk. Mostly wool to Flanders, your country has a lot of sheep, iron sometimes, wheat and barley at others, anything we have that someone else wants. I bring back Rhenish sword blades, silks, dyed cloth, slaves of all complexions. No ship I have a share in makes any journey empty. Invest with me Sar, and I will make you rich. For a substantial cut of course.' He raised a glass of fine wine and looked me straight in the eyes, 'I wouldn't cheat you Sar, I have no need to.'

'You know what I'd like to own one day Fulk, I'd like to own a ship.'

Fulk laughed out loud, 'Ships cost a fortune Sar, and then you need men to work it.'

I shrugged, 'Well, who knows, maybe one day. When I get my money, I'll try and get some to you. Or some iron, maybe? Do a trade?'

Fulk guffawed, 'You have iron?'

I told him what I'd seen on my estate.

'You do have iron. Where's the nearest port?'

'Proper port? Glowcestre, I think, though you could get a ship to the banks a few miles from my house.'

Fulk suddenly got serious, 'What would you want for it?'

'God, I don't know,' I answered bemused by this turn to reality, 'something I could trade with the Waelas, maybe.'

Fulk nodded, 'You're thinking, that's good. You will need to find a priest you can trust. Mostly, it's only priests that can write. Get yourself set up and send me a message. It's time to turn in. Tomorrow you can entertain a small company of my friend with your story minus the sensitive bits. Think you can do that?'

I could and I did.

The following day we set off again.

Aelfric was in a good mood and chattering away, 'Did you know there are no women in Fulk's household? Don't you think that's strange?'

'There's no women in a monastery either,' I said.

'That's different, they're monks.'

I laughed, 'I think a lot of them are there for the same reason.'

'Why's that then, Sar? Why's that?'

'People find a way,' I answered.

'Way? To do what, Sar?'

Saint Cuthbert help me I thought. It wasn't so long ago I had the same questions.

'Hard to say,' I answered, avoiding the question.

'They smelt a lot nicer than monks do anyway.'

That was true for sure. Fulk house was always clean and swept. No dogs either, I realised. A couple of cats. All noblemen kept dogs. Maybe it's because he was a foreigner. Living above the wharfs was a bit smelly but the were no shambles nearby or fishing vessels so there wasn't the usual stink except when the tide was right out. Fulk liked silks, fine food and wine. The only weapons in his home were those held by his guards at the gate. He could even read. He'd certainly given me a lot to think about. I let Aelfric chatter on. I knew we were in for a long day. I wanted to stay over in Colecestra so we could get to Belestede early enough to talk to Ymma. The closer we got the more nervous I became.

I made the poor boy get up early again the next morning. I knew I was being sharp but couldn't help myself. When we set off, he was nearly laying over his horse's neck trying to get a little more shut eye.

We got to Belestede in the middle of the morning. Even before we got to the village, I could see the place had changed. The wood in which Toki, Gyric and I had been ambushed was almost gone with some of the stumps piled up for burning. A group of peasants were chopping at roots while a team of oxen strained against their yoke trying to pull a large stump from the ground. They stopped and watched sullenly as we passed. At a guess, the oxen and the time was theirs. The land they were clearing belonged to the master.

Without the woodland the track to the house was wide open. The palisade had been repaired and the gates were new. It was nothing like the place I remembered. A new thatched roof was visible over the fence. I blew the horn and banged on the gate.

'Here Aelfric.' I said as I boosted him up to see over the gate. 'Is anyone coming?'

'Yes, there's a man coming. He don't look too happy though.'

I lifted him back down.

'Who's there,' shouted a gruff voice from the other side of the gate.

'Open the gate and you'll find out, won't you?' I answered.

'Gate stays shut until I know why you're here.'

This was stupid. 'I'm seeking the priest, Father Eoppa.'

'Dead.'

'What? How long?' I hadn't considered this possibility.

'Year, more. Who are you anyway?'

'Names Sar. I'm Earl Harold's man.'

'Not our Earl.'

Out of the corner of my eye I saw a head pop up above the palisade. Then a muffled conversation behind it. The gate slowly drew open. Amazing what a fine horse and decent clothes can achieve.

'Our master isn't here,' said a greasy looking man dressed in a leather jerkin.

Another similar looking bloke stood near him. Clearly the head I'd seen before. They both held sturdy wooden staffs.

'Does you master know you receive visitors like this?'

'Can't invite you in. Not allowed.'

'Eoppa's dead. That's sad. He was a kind man who cared for his flock.'

'How would you know that?'

'Lady Ealhild was my aunt.'

'She's dead too. The priest was cuckoo. Couldn't look after himself let alone his flock. We've got a new one now.'

This was probably true. Eoppa had been broken by the events that killed my aunt, my little cousins and many of her household. Events that had happened because of me. I shook those thoughts away.?'

'So can I see his housekeeper?'

They both started laughing and nudging each other in the ribs, 'The priest's whore you mean.'

I took a deep breath, 'She wasn't his whore.'

'Well, she had a kid and no husband, no father to be seen anywhere,'

I frowned. A kid, so she'd given birth and both had survived. I was a father.

The other one then opened his mouth. 'Dirty old bastard that priest, anyway. He was old enough to be her grandfather,' he said, beside himself laughing at his own wit.

I started to feel cold inside and that familiar icy calm descended. 'Hold my horse Aelfric,' I said handing over the reins.

Then the first looked directly at me and squinting slightly said, 'Looking at you. I'd say she was your whore first. Then the priests.' He turned to his mate, 'Look at his hair, just like that demon child.'

He stopped, looked at my face and grasped his staff in two hands. 'Now, you can't hit me for having a joke?'

'Can't I,' I said, and pushed the butt end of, my spear shaft over his staff and straight into his ugly face. He nose spouted blood and the staff slipped from his hands. As he fell, I managed to get a swipe in at his right temple. He went down like a stone. I felt a movement to my side.

'Watch out Sar,' cried Aelfric, but I'd already acted. I only carry a throwing spear, so the shaft was light compared to his staff which was descending rapidly towards my head. I couldn't block it so I ducked and twirled sideways and used my spear to knock his legs out from under him. He too lay down in the mud. I held the point of my spear against his throat. An unfair fight. Two village oiks against a trained warrior, but who cared.

I tickled his Adam's apple with the spear point. 'So, where did she go?'

'The freedwoman?'

'Yes, or did you think I meant Queen Eadgyth?'

'We hounded her out. The older villagers didn't want the child here. Said it was a demon whose father and grandfather had each brought destruction upon the village. Us incomers, well we didn't want the priest's bitch here anyway. She owned a horse. What peasant owns a horse?'

'A very small pack pony, you mean?' I said remembering that I'd left my little pony, Maeve with Ymma. 'You jealous prick. So where is she now?'

'She'll have gone to Gipeswic. She's been seen there once or twice.'

I reversed my spear and jabbed the butt end into his gut leaving him, flopping breathlessly, winded on the ground.

We mounted up and set off. Gipeswic wasn't far from here.

As we rode the horses through the ford beside the rickety old foot-bridge to the town, I began to wish I'd asked a few more questions. How was I going to find her?

Gipeswic is a middling kind of town but rich in its own way. It has a port which serves a lot of East Anglia with all the darkness and chaos that passing seamen bring. Between the port and the main town there is a large market place beyond which the better houses and taverns lay. Sprawling all around the outskirts of the town are clay pits, potter's sheds and the huge piles of peat and wood that the ships bring in to fuel the constantly smoking kilns. When the air was still the whole town choked. It was those potteries that the town was famous for. Their products were sought after by all the wealthy families of England and even some of Europe's.

I decided that we'd do better on foot so sought out a tavern in the better part of town with its own stables. After giving the tavern keeper a quick sighting of my fat purse, we sat down to eat. The food was good and filling. I sat thinking and, in the silence, Aelfric dozed off with his head on his arms. I called the bar keep over.

'Can I have a word?'

He looked around, 'Yeah, it's quiet now. Will be busy soon, midday, you know?'

'So, if a woman came to this town who's down on her luck. Where would she go?'

He grinned slyly, 'Oh if you want a bit of 'ow's yer father' you could have just said.'

'What?' Then I caught his meaning, why do people talk in riddles? 'No, I meant what I said, serious question.'

He sat on the settle, 'She young? Pretty?'

I took a swig of my ale and nodded.

'Liked her, did you?'

I shrugged and looked elsewhere.

'Hmm, you did. Sorry mate, but she's probably in a brothel if she's lucky. Or down at the docks if she's not.'

I shook my head. I just couldn't see Ymma doing that even as a slave she was proud. 'She's got a child, a toddler.'

'And?'

Yes, I wasn't that naïve. You do what you have to do for your kids. As I had that thought I flinched inside. I hadn't.

I thought some more, 'Look she had a pony, sturdy little pack pony.'

'If she sold it would support her for a while, I suppose. But then what?'

'She'd know that.'

'Why are you so keen to find her?'

I felt ashamed, 'The child is mine.'

'And the woman?'

'I ran away from her. Twice.'

'A woman, a pony and a small child. Hmm let's think it through.'

'She couldn't pay to keep the pony so she'd use the pony to pay for their keep.'

'You move stuff. No pack train would be interested in one woman, with a child, with no goods of her own and no collateral. She's likely still here.'

'Washerwoman?'

'They wouldn't be keen on the horse. Besides, those women are tough. Very hard to muscle in on their trade. They have all the fine houses locked down and everyone else does their own. She'll be doing something with the potteries. To and from the ships, or to and from the claypits, or moving fuel to the kilns, or finished goods to the warehouses.'

'Not many places to look then,' I said, feeling defeated.

The bar keep leant over and put his hand on my forearm. I tensed.

'No need to lose hope, son,' he said, 'You've got a horse. You can see a long way from the back of a horse.'

I choked a bit. I couldn't handle his kind words.

'Here' he said, getting up. 'I'll swap you some cut pennies for whole ones. Pass a couple of fourth parts out and you'll soon get word around.'

I did as he suggested then paid him more than enough for a place for us to sleep for the next few nights. Then I woke up the boy and we set off.

We started at the docks and worked our way through to the potteries. All the roads were teeming with horses and people. Everywhere we looked all the women wore shawls over drab clothes. Where the clay pits were, everybody and every beast was the colour of clay. All those around the kilns were almost as black as my charcoal burners. Horses are expensive beasts to buy and to keep but here there were more than enough for a small army. After a while I realised that this where horses came to die. Some had clearly been fine animals once but were now ending their lives being worked to death either dragging carts of all sizes or buckling under the weight of overloaded panniers.

In amongst all the bustle would be the odd ox cart slowly pushing through the throng. Each one was guarded by sturdy men with sturdy cudgels keeping the crowds away from the finished crockery loaded in baskets packed with straw to preserve their fragile, valuable loads. My heart sank, who was I even to try giving money to?

To make things worse, it started to rain. I managed to get us and our horses into a small alley. For a while we miserably watched the busy crowds while our horses shied from the dripping eaves we were sheltering under.

'What now, Sar?' said Aelfric, shivering now, rather than yawning.

'Search me,' I answered dejectedly, 'the bar keep suggested we use these cut pennies. But aside from the fact no one stays still long enough to talk to how do I know I'm not just giving money away?'

'Here, Sar, hold my horse,' said Aelfric, 'I've got an idea.'

I took hold of the reins and before I could protest at him telling me what to do, he shot off into the crowd. I waited and I waited. He was so long I was beginning to think he'd run away. A place like this an escaped slave boy could easily disappear, do odd jobs, or jump a ship.

Then, suddenly, he was back accompanied by a gang of dirty ragged children. I looked at their hungry faces and for a moment felt gratitude for my own hard upbringing.

'Here, give me a few of those cut pennies,' said Aelfric. I did so.

Aelfric addressed the children, 'You, you, and you,' he said, pointing at three of the taller kids. He then gave them each a quarter penny. Their eyes lit up.

'Now, get out a whole penny,' he said to me.

I held one up.

'Look at that. A whole penny to which ever one of you finds who we are looking for.'

They stared at him wide eyed, then, as if they were of one mind, they all disappeared into the crowds.

'That'll be the last we see of them,' I said.

'Want to bet?' said Aelfric, cheekily.

'I think I'll pass on that,' I answered, thinking how much I liked this lad. 'Won't those bigger kids just take their money and leave the rest to go hungry?'

'It's possible, but I think they all rely on each other to survive just like slave's children help each other when they can. Even slaves get fed. I'm not sure these do.'

We waited some more. We were both leaning on the horses to keep warm when the first children showed up. By their glum faces I could see that they'd had no success. They were, however, sharing a loaf between themselves. They whispered together while looking shyly sideways at me. Taking in my clothes, horse, slave boy and, of course, my sword. This was a day they'd remember for a while. More children arrived then, another two who were bouncing up and down in glee.

The taller one, a girl I guessed because of her ragged skirts, spoke up, 'We've found her. A pony, a woman, and a red headed little girl. Dark red, like yours.'

A girl, a daughter, then. I found a smile creeping across my face. I had a daughter.

'She's moving pugged clay from the pits to the potters.'

Pugged clay? What that was I had no idea. 'Can you take us there?'

She held out her hand, 'Where's the money?'

I held up the penny, 'Not until you take me to her?'

'Do you have more cut pennies?'

'Why?'

'If you give any of us a whole penny no one will believe we didn't steal it. Or they'll say that and steal if from us or worse.'

I showed her a handful of cut pennies. Carefully cut as they need to be to pass muster.

'There's more than a penny here. If you're right I'll share them out among you all. Does that work?'

As if by magic she produced a small knife. I could see by the shine across its blade that it had a keen edge. 'You'd better had mister. Or I'll hamstring that fine horse of yours.'

I believed her. She, or one of her friends, could do that and disappear forever into the crowd. I couldn't help but admire her. A true survivor. Just like me.

Chapter Seventeen

We followed the girl into the clay diggings. This was a world of constantly moving beasts and people, every one of them coloured grey. How on earth could you separate one person from another. The girl pointed, and there, perched on to the back of a pony, was a splash of dark red hair.

I stopped in my tracks, overwhelmed by strange feelings. Then I felt a tugging on my sleeve.

'Is that who you were looking for?' said the girl.

Distractedly I gave her the handful of cut pennies. She was quickly surrounded by a mass of excited children. I held my reins out to Aelfric and made my way into the slippery mass before me.

Beside the pony a shawled woman was yelling at a couple of men to load the pony's panniers evenly. It had to be Ymma.

I opened my mouth to speak and no words came out. I coughed and tried again, 'Ymma.'

'Who wants her?'

'It's me Ymma, Sar.'

She turned and looked me straight in the face, her grey eyes hard, 'I never expected to see you again. If you're not going to take us away from this misery then go away now.'

That wasn't what I expected. 'I've come to do just that,' I said.

The pony pricked up its ears and started trying to sidle round to face me. The men trying to load her panniers cursed, staggering to keep their footing. Maeve, my old pony, snickered excitedly and moved towards me. As it did so the child face turned towards mine, her eyes rounded in her white skinned, freckled face. A warm feeling rushed through me.

'I have a daughter then?'

'Not that you deserve her. You are taking us out of this then? You'll support her? Looking at that fine horse and your clothes you've done better than us.'

'Yes, I have.' I went to the pony who was snuffling at my clothes, 'Here Maeve, you remember me,' I said rubbing her nose and smiling shyly at my daughter who was just staring at me with no expression at all. 'Hello,' I said. She said nothing.

I saw that she was tied on to the pony's back with strips of cloth. I took out my knife, cut her free and lifted her down to the ground. She stood where I'd placed her and kept on staring.

'Here, you two, take these panniers off this pony?'

'We can't do that. How're we going to work today?' They both said in unison.

I wasn't in the mood for this. I showed them the top two inches of my sword blade, 'I don't fucking care. Do it.'

'I see you haven't changed,' said Ymma.

I sulked. Why am I always in the wrong?

Ymma picked up the little girl while I led Maeve to where Aelfric stood with the horses. He was chattering with the girl who'd led us here.

'What are you still doing here?' I asked, 'I've nothing else for you.'

'Nowhere else to be. That your kid, is it?'

'She is,' I said, feeling a small rush of pride. What was happening to me. 'How could you possibly tell?'

The girl opened her mouth to retort, then saw the joke and giggled.

I got curious, 'Nowhere else to be? Where's your family?'

'Dad was a sailor. He went to sea and never came back. Then one day my Mum left me and my little brother with a neighbour and she never came back either,' she said, very matter of fact.

'That's terrible,' said Ymma.

The girl replied, 'It was a long time ago. I don't really remember.'

'And your brother?' said Ymma.

'Oh, he stayed with the neighbour. He thinks they are his parents. They didn't have room for me as well so I've lived on the streets ever since.'

I had a bright idea, 'We're going to need a girl to fetch and carry and so on. I can feed and clothe you. Are you interested?'

'We, Sar, we're a long way from a 'we',' said Ymma.

More riddles.

The girl accepted straight away.

'God, Sar, you know nothing about this girl. She could be a runaway slave, or a thief?'

'Well,' I said, 'she'll be in good company then.

Ymma gave me a surprised look while the three children looked on rolling their eyes at each other.

'Let's get out of here,' I said and lifted the street girl up behind Aelfric, Ymma got on Maeve bareback and I lifted my daughter up to her.

'I don't know her name,' I said to Ymma.

'It's Inga, I named her after your mother. I don't know why.'

'Hello Inga,' I said, and was rewarded with a slight lifting of the corners of her mouth. Then to Ymma, 'Do you have lodgings, any belongings to get.'

'Nothing you can't replace,' she answered.

I mounted up and lead the way back into the town proper.

On the way back to the tavern it dawned on me that I'd left with just two of us and come back with a small household. I'd need to get a room, ask to stable another horse, feed everyone and probably other things I hadn't even thought of.

The tavern keeper sucked his teeth, ummed and aahed until I opened my purse and produced more coins.

As I handed them over Ymma said, 'Saint's alive, Sar, that's way more than needed.'

Then, turning on the tavern keeper she told him, 'We'll have hot water and soap. I want food for all of us here, in the room. Good food. Are you married? Good send your wife to me as soon as possible.'

The tavern keeper stared at Ymma's filthy clothes and at the rest of our motley crew and lifted his eyebrows. Then cupidity overtook caution and he agreed to everything.

No sooner had we been shown the room when Ymma ordered Aelfric and I out of it.

'Come Aelfric, let's see to the horses.'

It felt good to be fussing around my old pony. I was brushing her down while Aelfric was teasing matted lumps of clay from her fetlocks.

'It won't be just you and me, now Sar, will it?' said Aelfric.

I smiled, 'I don't think it will. Do you mind?'

'No,' he said, 'I think I'm going to like it. I like the girl anyway.'

'Which one?'

'Luka, she's a bit wild but funny.'

'That's her name, is it? What about Inga? The little one.'

'Your daughter?' I could see the smirk on his face without looking. 'She doesn't say much. Just stares.'

'True,' I nodded to myself, 'true.'

'What happens now then Sar?'

'Now, now I've got to get you all back to Rwydin after this,' I said, suddenly daunted by the responsibility.

We got all three horses fed, watered and groomed until they were fat, happy and gleaming. After that I figured we'd left the women long enough so we made our way back out to our room. I knocked, hesitantly, no answer. I put my ear to the door, lots of chattering going on, including the high tones of a toddler. She does speak then. I knocked again, more firmly.

The door flung open to reveal the broadly smiling face of the tavern keeper's wife. 'The ladies are waiting, sir,' she said, waving us in with a half curtsy.

We went into the room and I'm guessing our jaws dropped as the three strange females in the room all started laughing at us. The three of them were dressed in what were clearly used but clean, decent clothes. Their hair gleamed more than the horses' coats and the air even smelled of dried lavender.

I'd truly forgotten how pretty Ymma was. I'd only ever seen her with her hair cropped or her face lined with grief. Her long, dark brown hair partly hung over her soft grey eyes. My heart leapt in my chest. I could feel a goofy grin cover my face. I moved towards her.

Her hand went up, palm facing me, 'You can stop there Sar. Just because you believe you rescued me doesn't give you any rights over me. If you wanted them, you should never have freed me in the first place. We have a lot to talk about.'

I nodded, 'Fair enough,' I looked at the little girl, Inga. Her hair was coarse like mine but she looked, to me, closer to my sister Moira. Looks that people seemed to hate or adore, nothing in between. She looked a lot better for being clean.

She walked around me, then stopped in front of me staring at my face in that direct way only small children can.

'You look like me,' she said.

I took a chance. 'No,' I said, grinning, 'You look like me.'

She frowned for a moment, then laughed and wrapped her arms round my leg. Before I could respond she just as quickly let go and then occupied herself by trying to put her shoes on.

Ymma smiled, 'Good start. Let her come to you. Give her time.'

'Like getting to know a new dog,' I said, immediately wanting take these words back but Ymma just made a face and said nothing.

She then showed me a knife. I recognised it. 'This girl you brought had this. Not exactly an eating knife, is it?'

I looked at Luka who turned out to be blonde with legs and arms like sticks. I guessed she was about twelve.

'That's my knife,' she said, 'I want it back.'

'Ymma, give me the knife,' I said.

Ymma gave it me but instantly protested, 'You can't give her that. She could slit all out throats in our sleep.'

'So, you been sleeping behind armed guards have you, Ymma?' I said, and gave the knife to Luka, 'she needs this to feel safe.' I said this being fairly certain Ymma had one about her own person somewhere.

Luka snatched the knife from me and made it disappear. 'Why am I here,' she said, 'You've given me clothes and food is coming so what do you want from me?'

'You're to help Ymma and I with looking after things. We're moving into a new home, all of us,' I said.

'I'm not waiting on that slave boy.'

'What?'

'I'm a free person. I'm not waiting on a slave boy.'

'Bloody hell, can we agree to cross that bridge when we get there or do you want to leave now?'

I turned to see Aelfric's hurt face while Luka's had closed behind crossed arms.

'Fucking hell, I didn't ask for this.'

'I don't want that language around our daughter Sar.'

'Christ,' I said, wanting to run.

'And now, blasphemy,' said Ymma, sounding just like my aunt Ealhild. Ymma's onetime owner.

I took a deep breath, 'Let's all go and eat.'

As we ate everybody began to cheer up. Aelfric with his seemingly endless ability to let things go was happily chatting with Luka while Inga was stood upon the bench spooning barley and vegetable broth into herself with messy relish. Beneath her little dog that belonged to the inn ate everything that fell its way.

Ymma said, 'That boy is a slave then? Yours? I thought you didn't want to have slaves or was that only for the ones you abandoned pregnant with your child?'

'That's not quite how I remember it Ymma,' I said, 'Yes, he is a slave but not mine.'

'Oh, don't tell me you stole him?'

'Not exactly, his father wanted me to take him,' I said, very conscious that Aelfric's lugholes were twitching in our direction.

'You mean, his owner doesn't know.'

'He's been told he died.'

Ymma frowned, 'Do you know how old he is?'

I shook my head.

'He looks about the same age Godric would have been had he lived.'

Godric was my cousin, who, along with his sister Aebbe, had been murdered by Oslaf's mother's men when they raided my aunt's estate and burned it all down.

'Yes, I suppose so.' Then I had a bright idea. 'Aelfric, your name is now Godric, and you are my lost cousin.'

Aelfric looked at me and burst out wailing and sobbing. 'You've taken me from my Dad and everything I've ever known to drag me around the country and now you want to take my name that's the only thing I have from my mum,' he burst out in gasps between the sobs.

I was taken aback in no small way. I thought he would be pleased.

'I was trying to keep you safe,' I said.

'I was safe, until you came along,' he wailed.

'God, you men can be so bloody stupid,' said Ymma, as she rushed round the table to comfort the shaking boy.

Now who's swearing and blaspheming, I thought. I opened my mouth and then thought again and shut it. In the commotion I noticed that Luka had stolen Aelfric's bowl of food while Inga had put hers on the floor for the dog. At least the dog was happy.

That night we all crammed in the room and made the best of it. I couldn't sleep. I knew I had to have a talk with Aelfric, also only Aelfric and I had travelling cloaks and hoods. Maeve didn't have a saddle. We'd have to stay in taverns wherever we went as well as stable three horses. My purse was shrinking fast. I also wanted to get out of Gipeswic. Once I had killed a man in this town which was now, again, part of Aelfgar's Earldom. There was no way he'd be back here yet but Oslaf had been one of his followers. If someone wanted to please him I'd be a fine prize. We needed to leave. I decided we'd head for Waltham which was one of Harold's most favoured land holdings. I'd be known there.

I managed to get hold of a saddle the next morning that, with the help of some horsecloths, fitted well enough. It took three damp and uncomfortable days to get us all to Waltham. When we arrived the place was alive with builders who were expanding the abbey attached to Tovi's church of the Holy Cross. I made myself known and the monk's accommodated us and, after a chat with one of Harold's clerics, a leatherworker was told to make us hooded travelling cloaks. Travelling was easier after that though it took a long time to get anywhere. We'd forever be stopping for one reason or another. Small children are hard work though I was pleased to see that Luka helping Ymma willingly. I was learning to handle my stallion better as the days went on and sometimes one or the other of the children would ride up with me giving the other horses an easier time. The best moments were when Inga would sit tucked in front of me. She'd slowly loosened her tongue and would now chatter excitedly in odd words and little phrases. At these times Aelfric had to learn to ride carrying my spear. I also discovered that when I travelled with Ymma I paid the same or less, for all of us, than I had for Aelfric and I whenever we had to pay to stay anywhere.

I'd been instructed to return via Wincestre and go to Godwin's old house. Godwin being dead, Gytha still treated it as her own though it belonged to the Earl of Wessex, Harold. As we went in all our weapons had to be handed over and we were taken to that same room where, accidentally hidden behind the tapestries, I'd overheard family business I shouldn't have. That all seemed like such a long time ago.

Gytha was there but Harold's sons were not which, for now, avoided the problem of how to hide Aelfric. Ymma, Inga and I were taken to see her while the others were sent to the servant's quarters.

'There's no hiding whose child that is, is there?' said Gytha. 'Is this woman the mother then?

'This woman can speak for herself,' said Ymma.

I tensed fearing Gytha's reaction but she just chortled, 'Well some meek little woman would be no good for you Sar, you need keeping in order.'

I looked at these two women taking each other's measure. One, the most powerful woman in the Kingdom, the other a freed-woman of no status at all. They each seemed to be satisfied with what they saw. Meanwhile Inga, fearless it would seem, walked up beside Gytha and stroked one of her furs. Gytha indulged her with a wry smile.

'Those clothes will suit you to travel in as you have no escort but you'll need better ones to take up your new role. I'll send my women to you later. Now Sar, since you left, Bishop Wulfstan has died. I've pulled some strings and Leofgar will take over the diocese. He'll be invested towards the end of March. As you know, I hold your funds. You'll leave here with an escort of two of my warriors and you will equip yourself with a mail coat, byrnie, shield and a helmet from the stores here. I doubt your estate would have the craftsmen needed to make them for you. You'll need another horse to carry all that. One of your horses came from Harold's stable at Much Marcle. You can return both back there after you reach your estate,' said Gytha.

I opened my mouth to thank her but before I could she went on.

'I'll take what you owe me and hand over a large part of your wealth. You'll need to guard it carefully. I'd suggest that you deposit some, most, of it with the Benedictines at Glowcestre. It will be safe with them. Now, off you go.'

I left without saying a word.

* * *

We stayed a few days while our clothes and my mail were measured and finished. I'm not saying that the travelling was easy but my small household found a pattern that suited them all. Ymma kept everyone in order with a patience I couldn't find in myself. She remained cold with me but civil. Aelfric too, was much the same. I said no more about him taking Godric's name but I knew it could give him a chance for a better life.

Chapter Eighteen

When Gytha's cleric gave me my money it was in a brand-new cow hide bag. I could tell straight away that it was larger than before. Clearly after I'd spent so much it should have been smaller. For a moment, I thought that Gytha was doing me a favour. The feeling quickly passed when I opened the bag and saw that there were no longer any gold mancuses left in there. Just newly minted silver pennies. I had no idea how many pennies made up a mancus but it still looked like a great deal of money to me.

'That's a heavy looking bag you have there?' said Ymma, once we were on the road again.

'I'll show you the next time we rest.'

I did that and her jaw dropped.

'I've never seen so much money before,' she said. 'How did you get this?'

'I'm not meant to tell anyone. I will, but only when we are alone.'

'Sar,' began Ymma, 'I need to say something to you. I know you turned up on a fine horse and with a slave boy of your own but I didn't come with you for that reason. Well. Not exactly that reason.'

'I was surprised. I thought I'd have to argue. I know how fierce you can be. I know you don't think highly of me.'

She put her hands over Inga's ears, 'Sar, you were just a fucked-up kid.'

'So why bother with me then?'

'Then, I was a girl. I liked the wildness in you. You looked good to me too. Just as well when you look at Inga. By the way. How did you lose that finger?'

'Long story. What did you mean by 'not exactly?''

'The life we were living was terrible. I could have made it on my own but having to tie Inga on Maeve every day was heartbreaking. Nobody has time for a woman with a child and no man. Especially when you're young. They all think you're a whore even when you're clearly not working on your back. You get hassled all the time. And, yes Sar, like Luka, I carry a knife hidden in my skirts.'

'So, you are here because of Inga. Not because of me.'

She nodded, 'Also that you are her father, and you have the means to support us.'

This all made sense to me. Ymma owed me nothing. It was dawning on me as we travelled together that I hoped we could become something more. As I thought this Morwid flashed into my mind. Her beauty was stunning, and she could heal and make music. She was clever. We were tied together by the tragedies of our story but, the truth is, she frightened me. I would always be the needy one. While she, she needed no one. With Ymma, if I did things right, we could be together as equals. Maybe.

We talked about the money and decided not to leave it with the monks in Glowcestre. We'd bury it in Rwydin. We still went through the town and got ferried across the river a little further upstream. I told Gytha's men that we wouldn't need them from there.

Ymma asked me to tell them when we were close. Coming from another direction I wasn't too sure but as soon as I saw the sun lowering above a haze of smoke, I called a halt. Ymma and the girls disappeared into the woods and returned dressed in their finest clothes that Gytha had provided.

'I want no one here to know my story, or yours. Do you understand? Do you all understand? You, Luka, are my maid. Aelfric, you are Sar's cousin. We'll talk names later. Your hair has grown. If they saw you here with a cropped head before we'll say you had lice. Understand?' said Ymma in a tone that brooked no argument.

We rode in, dressed to impress. The villagers shouted at each other and by the time we reached the house there were a few dozen of them watching us go inside.

Next to me I could hear Ymma mutter, 'I left a place where everyone was grey, here everyone is black.'

'It's the charcoal and the smoke,' I said.

'A lot of mouths to feed,' said Ymma.

I thought this was an odd thing to say but then I remembered her whole childhood had been spent serving my aunt. She probably knew as much about running an estate as anyone, certainly more than I did.

We got inside and I shut the doors leaving the curious crowd outside. I looked around, Liofa and Ailred had clearly made an effort. There was one bed built, crudely out of stripped branches with a lattice of leather straps. I'd never slept on one but I'd seen them in wealthier homes. There were also some straw filled paillasses of sorts and the floor was strewn with rushes. The villagers must have seen us coming as there was already a fire burning in the hearth and enough fuel for the night.

All Aelfric and I wanted to do was lie down wait for some food and eat but Ymma immediately started bustling around.

'Aelfric, have you brought in all the saddle bags? Sar, where's your money? We need to bury it among our belongings until we can hide it properly. Luka, change back into your second-best clothes now and get Inga away from the fire. There's not even a single clothes chest here. What am I meant to do with these things Gytha provided?'

'Aelfric and I need to deal with the horses,' I said, escaping.

'Tell someone to bring us food.'

'There is a couple who have looked after the house. I expect she, Ailred is her name, is already cooking in her own house.'

'Make sure. I'll need to talk with her.'

It was strange watching Ymma taking on her new role. At times I could tell that she was mimicking my aunt's slightly imperious manner. What was a little unnerving is that her expectations weren't those of a down on her heels freedwoman but those of a landowners wife. I had a lot to live up to. And she wasn't even actually my wife.

I opened the door to find Liofa and Ailred hovering outside looking weirdly newly washed.

'Is everything alright, sir,' said Liofa.

'Yes, for now but I'm sure Ymma will want to discuss some changes with Ailred.'

'Ymma, that's your wife's name, sir? 'We could all see that the little girl is yours,' said Ailred, with a broad grin.

'Yes, that's her name,' I answered evasively. They need to believe that we were married in some form. Another thing to talk through with Ymma.

'She looks like a lovely little girl sir,' said Ailred.

I grinned, feeling stupidly proud, 'Yes, bit of a handful though.'

'They all are at that age,' said Ailred.

'Is that so?' I answered, doubtfully.

Ailred nodded happily, 'I'm preparing a meal to bring over. I hope that's alright?

'Of course, we've been travelling for days. We're all tired and hungry.'

Liofa helped us hump all the saddle bags into the house and then took himself off while Aelfric and I took the horses into the dilapidated shed we'd used as a stable.

'They need a paddock, Sar, really. A strong one to keep that horse of yours in.'

'Two of them will have to go back to Much Marcle but you are right.'

'You'll be going to Much Marcle?'

'I'll have to.'

'Do you think my father will still be there?' His voice trembled.

'He goes where Thurkill wants, and Thurkill goes where Harold wants so I think it's unlikely.' I took a deep breath, 'Tunglo wanted me to take you. He could have explained this but I think he found it too upsetting. He wanted you to have a better life than you would have had as a slave in Thurkill's household.'

I handed him a thick handful of straw and taking one myself started rubbing down my stallion. He needs a name I thought.

'I liked my life before. We did better than other slaves. Tunglo taught warriors how to fight. I liked that,' said Aelfric, his tone was defiant.

'He was worried about what would happen to you as he got older,' I said, feeling way out of my depth. 'If he slowed down or got wounded, you'd be just another slave boy. He wouldn't be able to look after you. Most slaves have a really hard life.'

'I just want my Dad,' wailed Aelfric, and throwing his bundle of straw on the ground he wrapped his arms around me and sobbed.

This, for me, was very strange, slowly I wrapped my arms around his small body and hugged him. I started to weep myself, not just for the small boy in my arms but also for the small boy in myself.

After a while, something changed and we drew apart. I turned my face away so he could not see my tears and wiped it with my hand while he wiped his wet face and snotty nose on his sleeve.

I crouched in front of him so our faces were almost level, 'Aelfric, I can see all this is very difficult for you but I want you to think about taking Godric's name.' As I said this his lips pursed stubbornly. 'Then we'll say that you are my cousin, and you won't be a slave at all. Your Dad said he'd say that you had died. Who's to know?'

Aelfric frowned, his eyes looking anywhere than in mine.

'Aelfric, all of us here are acting a part. Ymma's not a lady, Luka's not her maid. Well, I suppose she is now but you know what I mean. I grew up on the Welsh coast with no father, an English mother in a village of outcasts living in the crumbling ruins of old buildings. This place we've ended up in is a bit different from most villages don't you think?'

He snuffled and nodded, now looking at me closely.

'I think we can all make a home here. Be a little family, don't you think?'

I realised as I said this I was talking about my own hopes. Maybe this was what I wanted. With that thought came fear. For the first time since my mother was killed and my sister was enslaved, I had a lot to lose.

The boy had had enough for now. We finished sorting the horses and fed them some hay. I needed to get some grain from somewhere. That black horse of mine needed serious feeding. I had a lot to learn.

At night the girls and Ymma shared the bed while Aelfric and I slept on the rushes. From day one Ymma was a whirlwind of requests and demands. She was everywhere. She wanted a man with enough skills to build a room on the end of the house. The weaving shed was only being used to make rough woollen cloth. She had plans for that. Could we grow flax? Why isn't there a dairy? And most of all, could we move the iron smelting away from the house?

The last I could understand. Not only did it produce a lot of acrid smells the whole works is surrounded by messy stuff I learned was called slag. There were heaps of it everywhere. There were also heaps of charcoal under makeshift roofs and other heaps of the reddish rock. And in yet another filthy shed lay lumps of the iron they extracted called blooms. This was the reason there were so many more people here than the land could easily support. These blooms were traded with smiths for grains and other foodstuffs and needs. The long fields meant that a couple of the villagers owned oxen which together could pull the one plough. There was a small herd of pigs that would be run in the woods to the south as the season progressed. Beyond that lay the borders of the King's hunting forest. It seems Cnut had started this but Edward loved to hunt. Taking deer from those forests was strictly forbidden but if they came into my woodland, they were game for me.

The charcoal, the iron, and, I suspected, stealing deer were the obsessions of this strange village. When I watched the iron making,

I began to understand. The peculiar structures I'd seen were hollow pillars of clay a yard across. The were banked around with earth. At the bottom were holes that could be plugged or unplugged at the will of the ironmasters. Among all the men around these pillars there were two men who ran the show. They were ordering all the others around. Beside these two I felt like an immature boy, although, in law, I was their master.

I looked around, on one side a group of children and women were smashing the red rocks into smaller and smaller pieces until they were crushed into powder. This powder was then being scooped into wooden troughs like bakers used for dough. On another side charcoal workers were using handcarts to bring up loads of charcoal. Other people were slapping clay into any cracks in the hollow pillars. A huge man was inserting a fired clay tube about a foot above the bottom of the pillar and attaching a pair of bellows. Then one of the bosses pulled out a ceramic plug from the base and pushed in a bundle of dried reeds and grass. This was followed by a glowing piece of wood from nearby fire. At a signal from the other boss a boy threw in a few handfuls of charcoal. They watched patiently.

'It's warming, there's a draught,' said one to the other.

The other waved at the boy and more charcoal was added. More waiting. More charcoal. Then the huge man started plying the bellows. First slowly, then increasing his stroke as the fire roared. Then more charcoal. Then they started ladling in scoops of the red dust. The ceramic plug was put back in then more charcoal and dust. Then everyone. Apart from the man on the bellows seemed to relax.

One of the bosses turned to me, 'Takes a while now. It's usual that we have our ale now. It's hot, hard, dusty work. Ailred brews for us for now. The lady of the estate should take charge of that. Your missus.'

I nodded, 'We will learn your ways and who does what for who, I'm sure. Colbrand must know the ropes.'

The man spat on the floor, 'Colbrand does what's good for Colbrand.'

The other man looked me straight in the eye, 'Do right by us and we'll do right by you.'

I didn't think this was usually the way an estate was run but I liked the straight talk. 'I'm hearing you,' I said, carefully making no commitments.

The first man spoke again, 'We all had a good laugh when we heard how you dealt with that idiot Blethin. Charcoal burners.' He spat again.

Charcoal burners are generally regarded with suspicion by most people. Their isolated dirty lifestyle separated them from other people. It was interesting that that division still held here.

Ailred turned up with another huge man who was carrying a very large, two handled bowl of ale. The two bosses drank first then passed the bowl to me. I sensed a test. Would I join them. I paused. Should I? Would this lower or raise me in their estimation? I took the bowl. It was heavy being still very full. My wrists trembled as I lifted it to my lips. I drank. Not the best ale, hopefully Ymma could make better. All the same I smacked my lips. In the corner of my eye, I saw the two huge men change places so I passed it on to the man who'd been working the bellows. Everyone was watching me. As I passed the bowl, I could see small nods of approval. I'd got that right.

'I could use your names,' I said to the bosses.

'He's Gulli, I'm Hrut.'

'It's good to talk to you,' I said, and put out my hand.

They both shifted awkwardly. 'Bit dirty,' said Hrut as neither of them shook my hand.

An awkward moment. I smiled wryly and lowered my hand. I could drink with them but I was still the master and could not be one of them.

'So where does this red stone come from?

'The ore, walk over that way,' said Gulli pointing.

'Send for me if I'm not back before the smelt is finished,' I said and took off.

* * *

I walked in the direction indicated across another long narrow field. I heard footsteps running up behind me. Missing the spear in my hand I reached for the hilt of my sword. It wasn't there. I swirled round pulling the short seax from my belly sheath. It was Aelfric.

He drew up fast. His eyes opened with shock, then seeing the expression on my face he burst out laughing.

'Bit jumpy, aren't you?'

I felt a bit silly as I put the seax back. 'Guess I am, eh? Ymma let you go?'

Aelfric's eyes rolled around in his head, 'Should I have asked? I didn't think.'

'You want to come with me?'

'I do,' he said, 'We stick together, don't we.'

I laughed, put my arm over his shoulder, 'We do, little friend, we do.'

We walked along a track between the field and a scrubby hill. There was a real sense of spring in the air. Green shoots of grass, faint bumps suggesting ferns on their way, the chirruping of many small birds. I could not help smiling. Everything felt right with the world.

Soon we heard chopping sounds, and the clinking of rock on rock. Rounding a bend, we found a group of people surrounded by holes in the ground and another hole cut into the side of the hill. Among them was one man splitting a small tree trunk in quarters with wedges and a mallet. We waited until he finished then he chopped one of the lengths into yard long pieces. Taking three of them he dove into the hillside. I ducked down into a crouch and followed him in. In the dim light I saw him kick a flat stone into place. Then a younger man held one up to the roof. The first man placed the length of timber on the flat floor stone then stood it up while the second one punched the top of the timber against the upper stone until it was all wedged fast. It was clear this was to prevent the roof from collapsing.

We'd been seen.

'We have to follow the ore where it goes, young sirs. There's none left within easy diggings. The scowles round here are all cleaned out.'

'So how do you get it out.'

'When we have to, we lie on our sides and dig it out.'

'Can we get out of here,' said Aelfric, nervously.

I backed out with him along with the older man. I looked at the chopped ends of the timbers.

'You're the man who made the bed then?'

'I am sir. Never made one before.'

I'd never have guessed I thought but said, 'Thank you for that. Is there anyone who can make chests?'

'Making boards is beyond me.'

'Who builds the houses?'

'Him and I do that,' he said nodding towards the younger man. 'Everyone else helps.'

'I've got some work for you. Come to the house tomorrow. Bring your friend.'

'My son sir.'

'Bring him.'

As Aelfric and I walked back towards the house a small boy was running towards us.

'They're waiting for you sir. You should hurry.'

Aelfric looked up at me, 'Shall we run cousin. Bet I can beat you.'

He did. I let him. But he didn't need to know that.

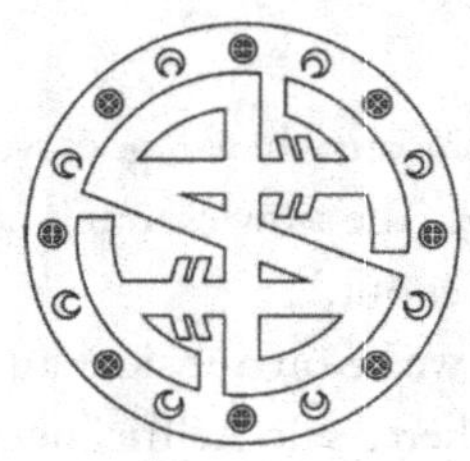

Chapter Nineteen

We pulled up, breathing heavily, where all the iron workers were crowded around the hot pillar. Liofa greeted us and pushed aside some of the crowd until I was next to Hrut while Gilla was crouched on the ground scooping a small gully at the base of the pillar by the ceramic plug.

'What do you think? Now?' said Gilla to Hrut.

Hrut nodded, then the two huge guys withdrew the bellows leaving a hole about a foot up. Gilla, his hand wrapped in a bit of old leather, pulled out the plug.

Everyone seemed to stop breathing. Gilla scraped into the hole with a bit of burnt stick. Then, like magic, a glowing red tongue of thick liquid oozed out.

I could feel my eyes widen, enthralled by the sight. I found myself crouched next Gilla. He looked sideways at me, 'You see it, don't you?'

I knew what he meant. I did see it. I was smitten.

Once again, everyone was looking at me keenly, then their faces became wreathed with smiles as they nudged each other chuckling.

'Look, the new master's an iron man.'

The flow had stopped and as the brightness dimmed a and little black flecks danced across the glowing surface. I put my hand over it to feel the heat.

'Oh sir, don't touch that. It's still very hot,' said someone.

Then another voice quipped, 'Though we have heard, sir. That you have a way with hot iron.'

They all started laughing uproariously. I could feel my white face grow red, of course they knew. I stood up and managed to laugh with them. There was something about the way they were laughing that made me think. It wasn't my innocence they were enjoying but the idea that I'd got away with something. I was among rogues. Likeable rogues but rogues all the same.

The ale cup went around again. Then Hrut picked up the still warm lump.

'We call this a bloom. It's still full of slaggy bits but the smiths we sell it onto will beat that out.'

Meanwhile Gilla was breaking out the clay around the hole from which the bloom had and scraping out the ashes and congealed lumps of slag. He quickly sorted through the still hot mass putting a few pieces in a separate pile.

'We'll put these through again. Sooner or later the flow won't happen and we let it burn for a while then break the furnace apart. Then we find a big lump of iron and slag. We grab it with tongs then beat some of the impurities out with those huge mallets you see over there.'

I looked at where he was facing. There were the two mallets beside a great stump with a blackened top.

'So, what happens after that?'

'We get more clay and start again. That's why we have three of them. The clay must be dry, then after a couple of firings it hardens, then in time, it cracks more and more. We patch them up until they're useless. Then we have to break them up.'

'The all this mess we're stood in is broken furnaces, slag and cinder,' I said looking at the dirty piles all around.

They all gazed around. I realised that they barely noticed them.

'So, you can build them again somewhere else. Away from the house.'

'Ay, we could do that.'

'And maybe tip all this mess on these muddy tracks we have going from place to place.'

'More work that sir.'

'Might make it easier after a while. Getting the full barrows and carts around.'

They all nodded, unconvinced.

Time to go I thought.

I went into the house to find Ymma and Ailred bustling around making food while Luka was wrapping Inga up by trying to get her hood over her head. The struggle had clearly been going on for some time.

As I walked in, Ymma lost her patience and, against the child's protests, she pulled the hood over Inga's head.

'Now that's that. You're going out for a walk. Luka, don't let her get away from you, she can run faster than you'd think. Sar, you're back?'

Why do people say that? Obviously, I was back else you wouldn't be able to ask me, I thought but I was bursting with all I'd seen. I opened my mouth to speak.

Ymma, without even looking at me said, 'I need a proper brewhouse and the weaving shed needs repairing. We must get some chests for our better clothes or they'll be ruined. A cat would be handy too.'

A cat, fucking hell. 'I've talked to them about moving the furnaces,' I said, pleased with now knowing what they're called, 'Watching that iron come out is amazing. They're a right bunch here, like three different tribes. Black ones that make charcoal, red ones that dig ore, and multicoloured ones who make the iron. There's two huge guys, maybe they're twins, lookalikes, then these older guys who run everything. Is there something to eat? Aelfric called me cousin. I think he might be coming round.'

Ymma ignored me, 'You need to get that horse back to wherever you got it. We don't have enough forage, let alone grains, to feed

Maeve, the other two, and that black beast of yours. You need to split up that money. Keep some out and hide the rest. Bury it under the hearth.'

'What if we're raided? That's the first place raiders look.'

'And you'd know that how?' she said, 'Oh, yes. Never mind. Stupid question.'

I always felt that Ymma was trying to make me feel like a felon. Talking about raids made me think. Why wasn't there a palisade or any defences at all around this place? Something else to ask Colbrand, or maybe Liofa.

'Food?' I said.

'Later, not long,' she said, 'and thanks for asking them to move those smelly pillars.'

'I'm going to get them to take away all that mess too. I've suggested they put it on all the rutted tracks. They didn't seem too happy. Tell you what though. They're a pack of rogues.'

I looked up at Ymma and caught her looking at me. We exchanged a smile. Whatever we were to each other, we were both here to make this place work.

'When you see that steward, we need to know who owes us what labour. There's probably a priest somewhere with it all written down. There's only one plough I hear. We have to know who we trade with or we'll starve. Inga and Luke could both use new shoes too.'

I memorised all this and decided to take myself off for a while until the food would be ready. I opened the door to see all the workmen walking off in different directions. Among them was Liofa.

'Liofa, what's happening?'

'Midday, they're off to eat.'

'Oh, yes, of course. Liofa does anyone round here make shoes?' as I spoke, I looked down at his boots. Above the layers of black and red grime they were clearly made of deerskin. 'Deerskin boots, Liofa? My deer?'

'From the woods. Sir,' answered Liofa shifting from side to side. 'We leave them alone here unless the crops are growing.'

'My woods?'

'Usually beyond them, Colbrand has been quite forceful about that. South of that. Each side of us is farmed.'

'The King's deer then?'

'I didn't say that sir.'

'No, you didn't. I think all the women in my household would love some deerskin boots.'

Liofa grinned slyly.

'Another thing, Liofa, no defences. You live near the Waelas. Don't you fear raiders?'

'This is the land between the rivers. There's the Afon Guoy between us and the Welsh, and the Safearn between us and the English.'

'Aren't you English then?'

'Well, I suppose. We're our own people in our minds. Mostly the world passes us by. If the Waelas raid they go for the rich settlements upstream where the river is easier to cross. You can get across near here but not in numbers. We have friends on both sides of the river. We'd know it was coming. Then we would disappear into the woods with our bows. Lots of us have hunting bows. As for the English, the King likes to hunt the boar and the deer so the woods are left alone. For him the wilder it is the better and that suits us just fine.'

I thought about his words. I'd rowed a longboat up the Guoy. I noticed Liofa used the Welsh name. It was true, for a lot of it, it ran fast and the steep banks and rocky gorges would make a hard landing for a raiding party of any size. The hills and the dense woodlands meant that most roads skirted the area to the north. Still, Colbrand's place was fenced, though maybe that was to stop his dogs wandering off.

I looked up to see Liofa still stood there.

'Is that it, sir?'

'Oh yea, sorry. Boots Liofa, remember, boots.'

He went off seemingly pleased. We'd made a deal. There's things I would turn a blind eye to, as long as I got my cut. I was learning fast. Luka came back running after Inga. I looked for the horse and found Aelfric and called his name.

'Aelfric,' I shouted.

A boy's voice called back. 'Aelfric, who's he? There's no Aelfric here. My name's Godric.'

'Come here cousin. It's time to eat.'

That afternoon I walked part of the estate with Hrut and Gilla. We decided to move the furnaces nearer to the ore diggings. The charcoal burners move about anyway. Apparently, the ore was once dug out nearer to our house than today and they'd just never moved the furnaces. That night Ymma and I dismantled the hearth, dug a deep pit under it and buried most of the money under some stones before we rebuilt it. We remade the fire and sat together beside it staring into the flames and chatted gently about the events of the day. I kept out a fat purse to take to Colbrand. I still had to pay for the horse and, hopefully, he could sell me some feed for them.

The next morning, I told Aelfric, now Godric, to run over to Hope and ask Colbrand if we could visit in the afternoon. If it was, he was to stay there, if not, to come straight back. Soon after he left, Liofa called by with some pieces of leather and a stick of charcoal and drew round the feet of Ymma, Luka and Inga.

'I'll take these to the shoemaker,' he said, rising to leave.

'Liofa,' I asked, 'do any of your hunting friends know the whereabouts of any of my own deer? It's still winter, just, and we could do with some meat here.'

'There's small groups of roe between here and the river. There's also some boar. Tricky though, one of them's a big bastard.'

I'd seen boar hunters setting out when I was with Harold after Godwin had settled with the King. Lot's of men and dogs. I had no idea how peasants would hunt a boar. It's not something anyone did in Caer Dydd.

'The boar can wait. Don't want anyone getting injured for my sake. The roe though, a buck carcass can go a long way. The hunter's presumably have an allotted share?'

'Oh, sir. I think the hunters have all the meat they need.'

This was a different world from most of the England I'd seen so far. For most villagers, meat was a rare treat, usually only as stock was culled before the winter or an old ox finally collapsed under the yoke. I had no idea when Ymma and the girls had last eaten meat.

'There's no mill here. Or a bread oven,' I stated.

'Most homes have their own quern. We make bannocks on the hearthstones. It's a long way to a mill and we'd have to pay the miller.'

Grinding wheat with a quern takes a lot of hard work and time. This was like my childhood home. Half the women spent half their time rocking back and forth turning the quern stones.

'You know,' said Liofa, 'we don't have much ploughland. By the time, the steward, or now you, and the church have taken their share there's not a lot left. We have to trade for more. Colbrand, does his job, takes his cut, but he doesn't understand what we do here. Why there's so many of us. We need a master who will fight for a good price from the smiths. Or better still a smith of our own. Finished iron is worth a lot more than the blooms we sell on.'

'So why hasn't that happened?'

'You need a master that cares. We can't bring people in. We do what we do because our fathers did it before us. Our iron is sold then we have to pay to buy tools or ploughshare edges and spade tips.'

'If we had our own smith we'd need even more charcoal,' I said, pleased with this insight.

'You could coppice more of your woodland.'

'Wouldn't that mean less deer?

Liofa pursed his lips, 'You have to keep them away while the new shoots grow but after that, they like the glades. It's not like there's swarms of them. Between all the villages around and the King the numbers stay steady. Especially of the red deer who do the most damage.'

'Then we'd need more charcoal burners.'

Liofa scoffed, 'Lazy fuckers can just work harder.'

'I noticed you iron workers spend quite a lot of time sitting around staring at the furnace, drinking ale.'

Liofa's face suddenly looked alarmed, 'I'll be off now then.'

As I watched him go, I thought about what he'd said. Most peasants don't want change. They've survived so far through fat years and lean. Sure, they'd like to do less work for their masters but if things change and their beans, wheat and barley don't grow, it's them that starve, not the masters. Here, it seemed, they'd welcome some changes.

As Godric hadn't returned, after our midday meal, we all dressed in our best and rode over to Colbrand's. We got there to find the gate opened and the dogs penned. Outside the door Colbrand and Silflead stood also dressed to the nines. Next to them, Godric was skipping from foot to foot with what looked like a large honey cake in his hand.

What's all the excitement? I thought. Then I realised it was about meeting my wife. We rode in and dismounted. Colbrand whistled and a boy came round from behind the house and he and Godric took the horses into a paddock. We were welcomed into the house to find the table laid with a substantial meal. There was nothing for it but to eat a second dinner, and delicious it was too.

Silflead and Ymma talked pleasantries about clothes and managing a household. I had a feeling she was sounding out Ymma and I could see Ymma doing a great impersonation of my aunt. I also learnt, to my surprise, that we'd met because she was a niece of my aunt's dead husband and was living with my aunt when I arrived. We should have thought about this before we came, I thought, feeling pleased I'd overheard before I said something different. Next moment I was faced with questions from Colbrand.

'Your boy says his names Godric,' said Colbrand, 'I could have sworn you called him Aelfric when you were here before.'

'My cousin, yes Godric is his name.'

Colbrand frowned, 'Usually my memory is good and there's nothing wrong with my hearing.'

Ymma saved me. 'It's a game they've been playing ever since Godric was small. Sar pretends not to know his name. Calls him different names all the time. The joke has worn a bit thin.'

Godric looked up and sniggered, 'Yes, sometimes he calls me Toad Fart.'

Ymma did not find this funny at all, 'No he doesn't, Godric, apologise to our hosts at once.'

Luka, meanwhile was practically choking trying to suppress her giggles while Inga, wanting some attention too, started banging her spoon on the table.

I snapped out, 'Ymma, is right, now apologise.' Where were Colbrand's children anyway I thought? Next time I'll come on my own.

To give him credit Godric stood up and apologised.

Colbrand wasn't letting it go, 'You know boy. I thought you were a slave boy when I last saw you.'

'Nits,' said Ymma, 'and head lice. He wouldn't comb his hair and Sar lost his patience and cut it all off.'

'Hmm,' said Colbrand, 'Proper discipline. Got to do what your guardians tell you boy.'

A serving woman came in with mugs of ale for us all. Colbrand helped himself to the largest mug and wished us all good health. I took a swig. This was much better ale than we had at our estate. I complimented Silflead on the ale and the awkwardness passed. As soon as the meal was over Ymma sent the children outside. While the women chatted Colbrand was very liberal with the ale. It was strong and I don't often drink much. By the time I had to pay for that horse I was sozzled. My purse was lightened by a huge amount. Trouble was, I had no idea what a horse like that was worth.

By the time we left I learnt from Ymma that we'd rescued Luka from a convent where she'd been left as an orphan and that the nuns had trained her. I got the impression that Silflead didn't think those nuns had done a very good job. What a lot of lies we had to remember.

When we left, I staggered out with Colbrand to catch the horses and saddle them up.

'He's a fine stallion, you have to admit,' said Colbrand and this, even I, could tell was true.

I slurred my agreement.

'Have you named him yet?'

Before I could speak, Inga's voice rang out, 'His names Sooty, 'cos he's black.'

Colbrand chortled, 'Sooty, you called him Sooty?'

Well, I wasn't going to deny my girl her moment in front of this man so I agreed. As we rode away, I realised what I'd done. Most of the warriors gave their horses names like Firebrand or Thunder. Now I rode a stallion called Sooty.

Chapter Twenty

We were riding back to Rwydin from Hope. My horse was restless under me, sensing my own unsteadiness. I still felt sozzled but the beginnings of a headache were forming behind my eyes and my mouth felt disgusting.

Ymma was not happy, she was giving Luka and Godric a severe scolding. 'We agreed that we were all playing our parts here. No one told either of you to pretend to be entitled rich kids.'

'What's entitled mean? Ymma, what's it mean?' said Godric.

'It means you don't make stupid jokes. Toad fart, what was that?'

Luka started giggling then suddenly I was laughing so hard I nearly fell off my horse. Godric was now so pleased with his joke he started making whoop-whoop sounds. Ymma was even more furious, but now with me.

'And I saw Colbrand and you drinking that strong ale. He drank a lot less than you. Did you know that? Did you?'

'You ever seen me drunk before? Eh? Just having a bit of a laugh with a mate. Alright?'

'Oh, yeah, and just what did you pay him for that horse?'

I struggled to think, 'I don't really know. Wasn't just for the horse. Some other things I can't rightly remember. Does it matter?'

'Of course it matters. How're we going to make a go of this if you throw money away?'

'You saw how much there is. So what if I spend it. It's mine anyway.'

'There it is. You've been longing to come out with that line, haven't you? Couldn't bloody wait. Could you?'

I thought for a moment, 'But it is mine, isn't it?' I went through hell to keep it.'

'You don't get it, do you? You are not just an 'I' now. You are a 'we.' You are responsible for us and for that whole village of dirty weirdo's we seem to have taken on.'

Even though I was pissed I knew she was talking sense, so, sulking, I took it out on Godric, 'Oi, Godric, you shouldn't have done that. Said that, I mean. Made me look a fool.'

'Stopped them asking anymore questions about my name though, didn't it?' said Godric, cheerfully.

Bloody kid was right. Clever little bastard. I hadn't even thought of that. Smart. Morosely, I didn't give him credit. 'Should learn when to keep quiet.'

'Leave the boy alone, Sar, leave him alone.'

'I was only sticking up for you Ymma.'

'No, you weren't. You were sulking. And, what's more. I can fight my own battles, thank you.'

Maybe Ymma was right about the money. Maybe Colbrand was having me over. I fumbled around trying to control the horse with one hand and untie my purse with the other. It didn't work. I fell off the horse. Now everyone but me was laughing. Inga, who'd slept against Ymma all through the argument, woke up to join in. That really stung.

It took me a while to catch that horse, by which time the others were well away. I realised that I was near the charcoal burners. I had a few words and they broached a casket of something strong. A mixture of fermented honey and hedge fruit, I think. I drank with them like they were old friends until I couldn't even hope to get back on that horse. Eventually I staggered home with the horse following me. When I got back to the house the woodworker and his mate were standing outside.

'What do you two want?' I said.

'You told us to meet you here. We've been waiting a long time. Your wife said you were on your way.'

'Well clearly I wasn't so you can fuck off now.'

They looked at me. The elder one spat on the ground looked at the other and walked off. Spitting on the ground seemed to be a common way of showing scorn in these parts. Fuck'em all, I thought and banged on the door which was fastened from the inside.

'Ymma, open the fucking door,' I shouted, 'open the door.'

The door opened a bit and Aelfric's face looked out.

'Aelfric, let me in. Get out of the way.'

'It's Godric now, remember. Your idea. You should sleep somewhere else Sar. You come in here like that and you'll spoil everything.'

I saw this boy looking at me and saw myself looking at my Step Da. He'd get drunk and want to fight everybody. Sometimes he got his wish and he'd crawl back bleeding and raise hell in our home until my mother threw him out. I suddenly sobered up and felt full of shame. I slunk off to the granary and, after a couple of failed attempts to get up to the platform it's built on, slid inside and fell into an unhappy troubled sleep.

I woke up in the night feeling dreadful, crept out, puked a bit, took a piss, and crept back in with my head full of troubling images. Something was bothering me but I just couldn't get a handle on it. I fell back asleep and this time the images were vivid. The faces of dead men, my mother's smashed in face, the blood spurting from Eardwulf's neck, Oslaf herding my sister onto the slave ship.

I woke up with a start feeling for my absent weapons. My heart pounded inside me before I remembered where I was. Oslaf, that's what was bothering me. If he wasn't dead, then where the fuck was he?

The cocks started crowing, dawn was approaching. My head pounding. I opened the granary door. I tensed, almost expecting to see him with his long white blond hair and his weird smile. Then I chuckled to myself, the hair wouldn't be there. I'd scalped the bastard. Whether he was alive or in hell, he'd won't be as pretty now.

I walked to the spring and drank deeply. For a moment the cold water made my pounding head feel like it would crack open. I thought for a while, then, realising that soon people would be coming up with their buckets and jugs for the days water, I knew I had to head home. I decided to do something my Step Da never did, I decided to say sorry whereas he would disappear for weeks or months then come back like nothing happened. I can only suppose my mother let him because he was the father of my half-siblings, Adaf and Elena. Or, maybe, she was lonely.

I followed through on my decision. The youngsters were fine about it and then proceeded in telling me how funny it was seeing me fall off my horse. Ymma, remained cold.

'Don't bother saying sorry to me. Go and see those woodworkers.'

I saw Ailred's face make a wry smile behind Ymma's back. The whole village would know before I could get down there.

'Do you want to eat before you go sir?' she said, grinning more broadly now.

My guts gurgled so loudly that it set the kids off giggling again while the bile rose on my gorge. I swallowed, shook my head, and left.

I got to the ore diggings to find them all crouched around a small fire. The older wood worker looked up at me and signalled the others to make a space.

'Heard you'd been slinking around like a whipped dog with your tail between your legs.' He paused, then looked me straight in the eye, 'Sir.'

Ouch. 'I'm sorry about yesterday, wasting your time,' I said, knowing this was not how master's behave but somehow knowing that, with these people having a fine horse and a long sword, would cut no ice.

The younger woodworker passed me a jug, 'Hair of the dog that bit you?'

'As long as it's not the stuff those charcoal burners drink.' I said.

'No, just small beer. Can't do what we do without a level head. Anyone turns up unsteady and my dad there, beats them with a pole. They don't do it again.'

They were father and son then, that made sense. I sat with them a while they ate their morning bread and cheese. When they returned to the work, I walked up to the top of the hill to see if any farms were burning in the distance. A bit of me wished there were. Then I could get back to the life I had. All I had to do then was keep my weapons sharp and deal with each day as it came.

I took my time up there gazing across the hills before heading back. When I walked up, there was an ox-cart outside with the beasts gently bellowing as Godric put a bundle of hay under each one's nose.

'Here Sar, come and help us with this,' said Ymma, wrestling with a chest on the back of the cart. 'Look, there's two of these. Old but serviceable. There's some earthenware dishes here, boards for whatever, even a wall hanging, it's a bit threadbare, but will serve. I want you to leave it under rocks in the stream for a few days, to get any bugs out. There's also sacks of grain and bundles of fodder.'

I helped hump everything inside the house that belonged there, then sent Godric to find Liofa to help me take the forage into the granary. Once that was done Godric and I took a pail of grain to the horses and shared it between them.

'I'm going to have to take these two over to Much Marcle,' I said to Godric about the two horse that weren't ours.

Godric got excited, 'Do you think my Dad will be there? I know lot's of people there. Harold's boys, oh, they'll be gone, won't they?'

'Oh Godric, Thurkill will have moved on and Tunglo is his slave. I can't risk taking you. Everyone knows you as the slave called Aelfric. I'm going to have to leave you here.'

Godric frowned, and in his usual fashion, let it go, 'But Sar, if you take these horses what will I ride when I'm your boy?'

'What do you mean?'

'Well, all the housecarls have a boy that helps with their horses and keeps their mail clean and so on. They all have one. You have mail now. You can't do it all yourself.'

I pursed my lips, 'Wouldn't really want to, either. You're still not coming to Much Marcle with me.'

'It's not that, Sar. I'll need a horse too.'

It was true, those lads usually did have ponies, which meant more work and more fodder and longer horse lines to guard but they not only helped the housecarls. They were the warriors of the future.

I shrugged, 'You can ride Maeve.'

'Maeve is too old, too slow and too Ymma's.'

'I was happy enough with her.'

'You didn't know any better. Besides, it's not like you bought her.'

I'd forgotten that I'd told him that story. He was right, and I knew it.

'Look Godric, you'll have to wait. My friend Gyric knows a lot about horses. Maybe he can help.'

'Won't be time. Talk to Fordraed.'

'You're a persistent little sod, aren't you?

Godric, grinning from ear to ear, agreed.

I set off the next morning, riding Sooty, while leading the other two horses. This took all the skill I could muster. I arrived at Much Marcle at dusk, exhausted and irritable. I took a few deep breaths before sounding my horn outside the gates. I knew I'd already been seen but custom had to be followed. The gates swung open and it was with great relief I handed the reins of all three horses to a pair of grooms who were waiting for me. One small reward of my new status.

Fordraed came out of the hall and welcomed me in.

'We've just sat down to eat, come join us young man.'

I followed him in and found everyone sat around long tables happily eating and drinking with Hildifryth sat at the top table with Fordraed's place beside her. The whole room felt easy unlike the tension that surrounded Gytha's reign here. I could see now why Hildifryth struggled so much to hold her tongue.

Fordraed sat down and made a space for me to sit next to him.

'Tuck in, young man, I can see that you're tired and hungry. I'd been wondering how long we'd wait before we saw you again.'

'Yes, I had to bring that horse back. I've brought another from Wincestre too.'

'Sar, we'd welcome you as a neighbour. You are only a long day's ride away.'

I smiled and toasted him, 'Thank you, Fordraed. I could use your counsel.'

Fordraed coughed and shifted uneasily, 'I would not have counselled you to ride away with that slave boy.'

I opened my mouth to speak. Fordraed held his hand up.

'Don't say anything Sar, let's not start our friendship with a lie. You were seen. I must tell you Thurkill is furious. He's lost his weapons master and his apprentice all at once. He says he will reckon with you in Hereford. You've committed a crime. He could have you hung. You're lucky he likes you but the fact that he likes you and you crossed him makes him even more angry.'

'I wasn't trying to cross him.'

'But you did, son, you did.'

Son, I thought, quite liked that. I'd felt so out of my depth recently I could use a steering ore. 'What do I need to do?' I asked, respectfully.

'You know you have to go to Hereford soon for Father Leofgar's investiture?'

I pulled a face, 'Yes, of course. Harold will want us all there for that.'

'He thinks highly of Leofgar, as you know?'

'I don't kn…' I started to say, when Fordraed raised a finger.

'Don't speak in front of a man loyal to his lord if you want your words to remain secret,' Fordraed cautioned.

I nodded and didn't finish the sentence, 'If Harold is there Thurkill will be there.' I thought some more, 'And what do you mean lost his weapons master? Tunglo was fine when I left.'

'One thing at a time. Thurkill is still a piratical Dane at heart. That's why he supported you keeping your ill-gotten gains.'

'Ill-gotten, they were.'

Fordraed raised his finger again. I stopped talking.

'Have you finished eating?

I nodded. Fordraed arose and headed for the door. I did the same and followed him outside. It was a dark night but Fordraed knew his own place so I followed behind him down to the slave quarters by the sound of his feet and the dark against dark shape of his body.

We got to the slave quarters and Fordraed pushed open the door. As he walked in all the slaves stood up clearly shocked by his late visit. Fordraed snapped his fingers.

'A rushlight now.'

Someone passed him one and he bent to light it at the pitifully small fire in the centre of the smoky room. He then walked to the shadowy end all the slaves shuffling out of his way. On the rush strewn floor lay a man with his face to the wall.

'There he is. That's Tunglo. He's decided to die. He was injured by one of the warriors he trains.'

'He said he was getting slower,' I said.

'Hmm, the man who wounded him said he as good as walked onto the sword. He said if hadn't changed his stroke he'd have killed your man here.'

'So how is that my fault?'

Fordraed looked at me, 'No words for your friend here then?'

'Doesn't look like he's listening,'

Fordraed shook his head, 'He changed after the boy left. Of course, we all thought he was mourning then it came out about you being seen riding away with a young boy up on your horse.'

'What now then?'

'That slave has decided to die. I've seen it before. His light has gone out,' said Fordraed in a thoughtful tone. 'It's rare but it happens. But that dying slave is yours. Your remedy for Thurkill is a very fat purse. A purse that you fill and you determine how full it should be.'

He turned to look at me raising the remains of the rushlight to eye level, 'You know that means you give him a fortune, right? A purse so heavy no one thinks to count it. And you apologise like you're pleading for your life. Which you may very well be.'

'Fucking hell,' I said, 'This getting rich is making a pauper out of me.'

Fordraed threw the stub of the rushlight into the fire and left me to it. I knelt down beside Tunglo and shook his shoulder. There was no resistance as I pulled him over on his back to see his open eyes staring into nothing.

'Christ Tunglo, what is this?'

'He's not spoken a word sir,' said a voice from the gloom, 'he has wound up his left side which was open to the ribs. We sewed him up and he didn't even wince.'

'Is the wound festering?'

'No sir, clean as a whistle. He's healing well,' said another voice.

'Funny you being a master now, sir. We remember when you were locked in the shed on Gytha's orders.' They all chuckled amongst themselves nudging each other.

'Fortune's wheel, eh?' I said.

'Not for us,' came another voice, filled with sadness, 'not for us.'

'You got that funny boy?'

'I have, but don't speak of it for his sake. He's a different person now,'

'He's free then sir.'

'He is, he is. But he stays with me.'

They all fell to whispering among themselves. Most of them it seemed were happy at Aelfric's good fortune.

I turned as Tunglo moved, turning his face back to the wall.

I sat beside him and deep into the night talked about Aelfric, about his changing his name, about him coming to Gipeswic with me, about him calling me Toad Fart and about the grief he was pushing down. One by one all those around me fell asleep and then, sometime later, I did so too.

I slept deep and long and opened my eyes to find all the slaves gone. I started as something moved behind me, then turned to find Tunglo sat against the wall. Seeing him in the daylight of the open door I was shocked to see how thin he was. I knelt in front of him and looked into his dull eyes in his withered face.

'Will you eat if I get you food?' I asked.

He coughed faintly and made some croaking sounds but no words came out. He gave up and just nodded.

I ran up to the house and hassled one of Hildifryth's serving women into giving me a loaf of bread and a jug of water. I went back to the slave shed as fast as I could without spilling things.

At first Tunglo couldn't eat so I held the jug up to his mouth and helped him drink. He drank some then vomited it back up retching so hard I feared his guts would follow. Then he waved at me and drank some more, sipping then swallowing. I tore open the loaf and dug out the soft inside. I fed him a little at a time and ate the crusts myself. Then I remembered that I'd heard if a starving man eats too much too quickly it can harm them, even kill them, so I took the rest of the loaf away and waited.

I was expecting some magic change but Tunglo just looked at me and lay back down and appeared to fall asleep. I left the jug and the remains of the loaf beside him and walked up to the house to find Fordraed. Eventually I found him about as far away from the house as you could get. He was down beside the woodlands watching his people leading horses to graze beside the trees. A couple of cursing men were leaning ladders up against holly trees and cutting down the topmost branches.

'We're running out of fodder. Some horse will graze the remains of the dead nettles and grasses left on the edge of woodlands when everywhere else is eaten to the ground. Also, some will eat the tops of the hollies. Did you know the leaves at the top are not spiky? What the horses turn down the cattle will eat in a hard year. Not that it's been that hard a year. It was the war with Gruffud that has eaten us out. Even Harold's great wealth can't buy fodder that isn't there.'

I didn't know that about the holly trees. Truly, I didn't know anything about what he was telling me but I would remember to tell Ymma about it later.

'When the new grass comes, I'll have a load of skinny horses stuffing themselves with the first flush. Then they'll all get tender swollen ankles and get sick. Best thing is to only let them on the grass for short sessions and feed them hay. But I'll have no hay left.'

'All sounds very complicated to me, Fordraed,' I said.

'Did you choose that horse of yours?'

'Not really, Coldbrand sold it to me.'

'Ah, I know Colbrand. He knows his horses and he's done you proud. That's a fine beast you have. Bet it cost you a pretty penny.'

'You said you knew Colbrand,' I answered, with a laugh.

Fordraed laughed too, 'I do. Always does well out of a deal does Colbrand. People complain about him but, the truth is, he always charges the best price he can get but he's not a swindler, just drives a hard bargain. That is a very fine horse. Still young, well trained, and beautiful. What did you call it?'

'Sooty.'

'Sooty!' Fordraed laughed so hard snot flew out of his nose and he ended up having a coughing fit, 'Sooty, ha ha ha.'

'My daughter named him,' I said, stiffly.

'How old is she, three?'

'About that,' I said.

'Daughters, eh? Drive their Dad's crazy.'

I felt part of something I never had before. Weird, father jokes. I loosened up and laughed alongside him.

'Maybe you can help me with something.' I said, 'I need a pony for my nephew.'

'A nephew as well as a daughter? You left here a single man with no family.'

I squirmed a little, 'The nephew…'

'Not my business,' said Fordraed, raising that finger again, 'Good to have family. As it happens, I do have something suitable. Not pretty but tough as nails. Going to squire you, is he?'

'Uh?'

'Your nephew, squire you, look after your mail and such.'

'Yes, that's his plan.'

'Your plan Sar, your plan. You'll also be taking responsibility for Tunglo's cart and pony. Getting on a bit that animal but you'll get a couple more years use out of her yet.'

'Really?'

'Yeah, slaves yours, or his body if he dies, and the pony and cart go with him. Thurkill took all the weapons and mail and left the useless stuff with me.'

'I think Tunglo might recover.'

Fordraed's eyebrows raised and he made an impressed face. 'Well, you might not know horses but it seems you know men. Is that why you never came back last night?'

I nodded, 'Not sure he's out of the woods but there's a good chance. I'd like to stay a couple more days if that's alright?'

'Of course, son, of course.'

There was that 'son' again. From some men it would annoy me, but from Fordraed it felt pretty good.

And so it was. In two days Tunglo improved enough to drive the cart with the new pony tied to the back. To Ymma's evident dismay I'd returned with as many horses as I'd left with and another mouth to feed. By the time we got home Godric was already asleep. When he found Tunglo in the house the next morning they were both so overwhelmed it brought tears to my eyes. That doesn't happen. I turned away, so no one would see.

Chapter Twenty-One

The most difficult thing about my return was explaining to Ymma what I would have to do to save my neck.

'I'm always in trouble with the Earl, or one of his family, and now Thurkill. Thurkill is not a man you cross.'

'But you did. Why?'

I shrugged unhappily, 'I liked the boy.'

'Enough to steal him from a powerful man who is, from what you tell me, your immediate commander. You're insane Sar.'

With hindsight this was hard to argue with. 'I couldn't have known what Tunglo would do.'

'True, if he had died as he had wished the boy's story might have never been told, but even that wasn't certain. Stupid, the both of you, stupid. And I suppose you realise that if you get hung, we lose all this. Your daughter will become what? We'll have to run again and build another life. Do you know how hard that was?'

'Fordraed says I have to pay Thurkill. A lot.'

'How much is a lot Sar?'

I shook my head, 'Many times more than they'd fetch in the market. Many times. I have no idea how much that is.'

'How much is your life worth then?'

I looked at her, 'Honestly Ymma. I've never thought further than the day in front of me since I was taken from my village.'

Her eyes glistened, 'You're still that hurt angry boy, aren't you?'

I squirmed and looked away. Who needs comments like that?

She continued, 'Well now Sar, your life is worth all of us.'

I looked around, everyone in the room was asleep. We took the money out again and made a plan. I'd need money for me and Godric to go to Hereford. Maybe I'd need money for fodder and lodgings, I wasn't sure. Before everything had been covered by Earl Harold when I was under his orders. Ymma would need money to buy in supplies until the estate could provide for us. Colbrand had kept the place turning over but there were no reserves and searching all the villager's homes for sacks of grain would both demean us and enrage them. We guessed at these sums and then I looked at what we were left with.

'When I got this money, it was a fortune even after we'd divided it up. Could never see it running out.'

'There's still a fortune there, Sar.'

'You don't know how these wealthy people behave Ymma. They'll go into battle wearing a jewelled belt that's worth more than this whole estate. Harold's whole banner is woven with precious stones. They give each other warships, and the busse-carls to fight in them.'

'Thurkill's not an Earl.'

'He's an Earl's right hand man, Ymma.'

'Perhaps you should take it all.'

'Then I'll be broke while everyone will think I'm rich.'

'It's your neck Sar, and our future.'

That night we slept together for the first time since our youthful secret meetings behind Ealhild's back. It was nice but not exciting. It's hard to be vigorous when you're trying not to wake sleeping children. We held each other afterwards until we fell asleep. Somehow, I'd earned Ymma's forgiveness.

The next day I walked a still weak Tunglo up the hill and told him to come every afternoon and if he saw large clouds of smoke rising to send a message to Colbrand. He would know what to do.

'I need you to protect my family Tunglo. I'm sure they are under no threat from the villagers but it won't hurt that they know she has a strong arm to enforce her will.'

He raised his arm. It trembled. 'It won't take long to recover Sar. Good food, a home. Staying in one place. That's new. I'll look after them. You keep an eye on my boy, yes?'

'You owe me Tunglo. I'm in a lot of trouble.'

'Nobody made you.'

I couldn't argue with that.

Godric and I set off in the middle of the night. I didn't want to go via Much Marcle with Godric because he was too well known there. I knew Hereford was northwards of us so I could use the north star as a guide as to which track to take. It was a typical March night with blustery showers scudding clouds across the starry sky. Once the sun had risen, we could ask our way and, as I'd hoped, we arrived in the middle of the afternoon.

I wasn't too worried about Godric here. He'd only ever been the weapons master's slave boy. With his hair grown and neatly cut while wearing good quality clothes it would take someone who knew him well to recognise him. For that reason, I told him to keep out of Thurkill's sight.

I only had to ask at the gate where the Earl was staying. Everyone always knew where Harold was. And where Harold was, Thurkill was. It was Thurkill you had to report to. The comings and goings of Harold's fighting men was not Harold's main concern. I sent Godric away with the horses to find where they were being kept and headed for the Earl's billets. To get there I had to pass by the Minster. None of the charred parts remained. The floor was completely cleared and workmen were erecting a temporary roof over part of the western end where more of the walls had survived. Feeling very aware of my last time in this town, I kept my dark red hair covered with my hood.

The only men allowed to bear arms near Harold were his house-carls but I was well enough known that I was treated as if I was one of them, so I kept my sword but left my spear at the door. I was expected to arrive any day soon so instructions had been left for me was to go to a side room and wait. I waited until evening by which time I was hungry and wondering where Godric would be, seeing him staggering about under the weight of my mail, our bags, and my helmet in my mind's eye.

The only bag that really mattered was the bag of money tied to my belt. I checked again to make sure it was there, though its weight was proof enough. I was sat on a stool by a small table when the door banged open. I jumped to my feet and, standing straight and tall, turned to face Thurkill.

I was expecting him to be furious but he looked distracted. I'd planned a dramatic gesture of getting on my knees and begging his forgiveness but it didn't go like that.

'Dealing with you again Sar, is not how I want to be spending my time. You have no idea what it takes to organise Harold's men and his security while liaising with all these pompous churchmen.'

I didn't know what to say so I said nothing.

'Well, what have you got to say for yourself then? Do you know we spend more time dealing with you than all Harold's other men put together. When you are actually here and not jaunting about in Ireland or fighting for our enemies that is.'

I was glad now that I hadn't knelt. It would have gained me no respect. I decided to cut to the chase.

'I did a stupid thing. I took your slave boy and caused your weapons master to give up. I hope that you will accept this compensation for my misdeeds.' With that I put the heavy purse on the table.

Thurkill glared at me in such a way that I shrank inside then he took the stool walked around the table and sat down. I swivelled on the spot so that I was always facing him.

'I could have you hanged. You know that?'

I realised that I was shaking, after Harold, and perhaps Faelen, there was only one man whose respect I most wanted. That man was Thurkill.

Thurkill looked at me, 'You know Sar, when we talked while sailing along the south coast, you were just a scared boy trying not to show it. You'd already killed, you'd helped turn the tide in the fight at Porloc and you'd warned us of the treachery of the Cornwaelas. You've tried to avenge the death of Beorn for your Earl, though we both know that your own desire for vengeance is your true motivation. This has given you a lot of leeway Sar, but there's lines you shouldn't cross.'

'I know, sir. I'm truly sorry sir.'

'Does that mean that you're going to give the boy back?'

That hadn't even occurred to me. I took a deep breath, 'He's a bit useless sir. It's probably better I keep him.'

Thurkill gave me a grim smile, 'Your loyalties Sar, might be the death of you. I'm not stupid yet you lie to me. Did Tunglo survive?'

Who knew what Thurkill knows. I decided to tell the truth. 'After I spent the night talking to him he started to eat. He's recovering slowly.'

'And his wound?'

'Nasty, he'll probably never be as quick again.' I knew how my own wounds pulled at times and my body holds back in a way it didn't used to.

'Did he do it on purpose?'

'Haven't asked him, sir.'

'I hear you found a long-lost nephew?'

'Yes sir, Godric sir, miracle really.'

'And the slave boy, Aelfric, run has he?'

I caught on, 'That's right sir. No one's seen him in weeks.'

Thurkill nodded, 'Well, pick up that purse and hand it to me then.'

I picked up the purse and put it in his hands. He carefully tipped it out on the table. Despite his stoney face I could see he was surprised.

'This must be all that you have left?'

'Not quite sir. I left some with my woman and have a little for expenses.'

'I can see that you're serious. Well, they're the most expensive slaves you'll ever purchase.'

'I'd give much, much more to get my sister back.'

'I seem to remember that your deal with Harold was to forget your family and make his household yours.'

'Not much choice.'

'No. Better stop talking before you say something stupid.'

Thurkill split the pile of coins into two. Took my purse and put one pile back in it.

'This remains between me, you and Fordraed, alright. Now go. Oh, and marry that woman.'

As soon as I got outside my stomach lurched and I puked up phlegm from my empty belly. Just as I was standing up, I saw Godric leading his pony up the street.

'I thought I told you to leave your horse in the lines.'

Godric paled, 'I couldn't carry everything Sar. And no one would help, so I came to find you. Sooty has been watered, groomed and fed.'

There was a rail outside one of the houses we were billeted in. Godric threw the reins over it and I helped him unload our belongings. I'd not been fair to the boy, there was too much for him to manage alone.

'You've done well, Godric. We're to stay here. If we take our stuff in, can you find it again if you take the pony back.'

Godric nodded unhappily. I noticed that he was near to tears.

'What's up with you?' I asked.

'I thought they might have hung you, and I would have to run. I was scared Sar.'

I crouched and put my hands on his shoulders. 'Why would you think that?'

'I heard you and Ymma talking,' he answered miserably.

'You can stop worrying now Godric, things went better than I expected. A lot better. Now wipe your face and let's get our stuff inside.'

We took out belongings in. Godric staggered under the weight of my mail shirt. I'd expected too much of him. It was dark by the time we'd found our place so I walked back down to the horse lines with him. I decided that we should eat in a tavern this night. I didn't want to deal with being social until I'd stopped shaking. Pissing myself on the end of a rope was not how I wished to go.

I found a tavern that looked prosperous and clean. Much as I like a rough pub, tonight I didn't want to get drunk, pay a woman, or brawl with other drinkers. Besides, Godric was with me, but really I just wanted to eat and get a little mellow before sleeping. The place was quite full, the upcoming ceremony had brought more people into the town from outlying settlements than usual. We found a small table in a corner. A girl came round and I ordered us food and ale. When the food came it was delicious, plentiful and the ale full bodied and strong. I stuck to the one jug and only allowed Godric a small cup or two from it. I didn't want him falling asleep on the table.

The place was warm and stuffy with all the people inside and the fire in the kitchen at the back. I pulled my hood off over my head and leant back against the wall behind me. I don't know about Godric but I must have dozed off myself.

I was woken roughly with a fat hand shaking my shoulder. I flew to my feet, my hand reaching for my sword. Quickly I realised where I was and pushed the inch I'd drawn back into the sheath. There, in front of me, leaping backwards in shock was the Ale-wife who'd accused me.

'You!' I said.

'You!' she said, 'I don't want you in my tavern.'

'You falsely accused me,' I said, sitting back down, 'You should be feeding me for free.'

'You're a priest killer. I don't know how you did it, but you are, whatever the iron said.'

'Leave the man alone, Bebbe. Leave him alone. He suffered enough for a crime only you seem the think he committed,' came a welcome voice from across the room.

An argument started and spread around the room. I'd had enough, I stood up and got on the table. 'Any of you want to test me again? You can either fight me or get a priest and ask him about God's decision. It's up to you.'

This place was not full of drunk troublemakers or soldiers so no one was willing to take up my offer to fight. As for the option of the priest, nobody wanted to be seen challenging a trial by ordeal for fear of facing one themselves.

I got down from the table in front of the silenced room and glared into the Ale-wife's face. As she recoiled, I could see fear come into her eyes.

'Shut your mouth or I'll fuck you up,' I hissed, my face in hers.

She looked shaken. Maybe it was the lack of support from her customers or a real fear of me. I felt sorry for her really. She was right. I was a priest killer.

'Get up Godric, we're leaving.'

While Godric got up, I took out my purse. As we left, I massively overpaid. The Ale-wife swept the coins into her apron, giving me a puzzled look as she did so. She stood for a moment, then made up her mind and called after us.

'Tell your friends they're welcome here. Bebbe's tavern. Tell them that.'

I laughed at that as we left. Then laughed again as I saw the confused look on Godric's face.

'Come on lad, let's go get some sleep.'

The next morning, we were called out of our billets to breakfast in the square in front of the Minster. As our rations were being handed out, I was delighted to hear a familiar voice call my name.

I turned, 'Gyric, I was hoping you'd be here. You're looking well, very well.'

'That my friend is because I'm now a married man.'

I congratulated him and embraced him, 'We have a lot to talk about. I'm with Ymma now. You remember Ymma?'

'Of course I remember Ymma. That's lovely. Is she well? And who's this?'

'Oh. this is Godric, Ealhild's son,'

'Godric is dead Sar. What's going on now? Never simple with you, is it Sar?'

I whispered, 'Please Gyric. Bear with me. I'm doing a good thing. Thurkill knows but I'm sworn to secrecy. I'll tell you of course, but not now.'

'Thurkill knows? Alright then, pleased to meet you Godric,' Gyric said, bending and shaking Godric's hand with a smile.

Godric beamed, 'You're Sar's friend. I'm happy to meet you too.'

'Are you squiring for Sar? I've a lad that does the same for me. My wife's brother's son.'

He put his fingers in his mouth and whistled, a trick I had never managed. 'Oi, Hriedar, come here.'

A grinning straw headed lad ran up. He looked like a typical boy from a landed family, muscly, well fed, well dressed and shod, short seax with a decorated hilt in a belly sheath suspended from a belt holding an eating knife, whetstone and purse.

'Hriedar, this is my old friend Sar, and this is, uh, Godric, his young cousin.'

Hreidar greeted us both politely. Godric started smiling and stuttering a greeting in return. I looked at him suddenly understanding his huge need for a friend, another boy.

'Excuse me a moment guys,' I said, pulling Godric aside. 'Godric,' I whispered to him, 'Remember you are Hreidar's equal. You are not a slave boy. You must not run around doing things for him, alright? He won't respect you for it.'

Godric's eyes grew wide, I was fairly sure he was taking my words in but he was fidgeting more than he was listening.'

'Go on boys, get your breakfast, we'll meet you back here after everyone has eaten,' said Gyric, sending them off. As they walked away he said to me, 'Does that sight remind you of anything?'

I looked at the two boys running off, already chattering happily and shook my head.

'Reminds me of you and I,' said Gyric.

'You mean when you brought me food when I was tied to a post on Fleet Holme beach?'

Gyric laughed, 'Well, not exactly that. More like two boys starting a friendship.'

Gyric always saw the bright side of things. 'Let's hope so Gyric, let's hope so,' I said watching them thoughtfully. In a way Gyric had a point. He and I came from very different worlds but I didn't have to begin with a lie. What if Hriedar, or any other of the squires, realises Godric had been a slave? There were more Wulfgeats than Gyrics among the landed Englishmen. Bloody hell, I was worrying about Ymma, and Inga and now Godric. I'd never worried about anyone except myself before. Except for Moira, my sister, who I needed to forget, but couldn't.

Gyric and I picked up the large bowls of barley pottage we were given for breakfast. Proper warrior food, thick and seasoned. After finding a place to sit out of the wind we spent a good while catching up with each other's lives since we last met. By the time we'd finished the boys had returned.

'I'll catch up with you later Gyric. Haven't seen to the horses yet. We have to be back here at noon according to the quartermaster to rehearse Leofgar's investiture.'

Gyric yawned a great pretend yawn and we both burst out laughing.

'See you later.'

We embraced, then Godric and I headed down to the horse lines.

'So, what's Hreidar like then, Godric?'

'Yeah, I like him. He's funny.'

'So how did you manage.'

'Oh, Sar, stop worrying. I just pretended I was Magnus.'

Chapter Twenty-Two

The next couple of days were spent rehearsing our roles for Leofgar's investiture. Then we played our part in the event itself. As Earl Harold's former chaplain there was even more than the usual pomp, accompanied by hours of monotonous prayer and chanting by choirs of priests and monks. Some of the singing was wonderful and you could forget your aching feet and stiff back. Mostly, for us soldiers, it involved a lot of standing around in brightly polished mail with warm bodies and cold feet. Leofgar clearly enjoyed it all. He had finally shaved off his moustache and, dressed in all his robes, looked like the magnate of the church he now was.

It was a relief when it was all over and all of Harold's men were relaxing and looking forward to either going home or joining Harold as he travelled around his estates or waited on the King. For me, my head was full of plans for my estate and my family. I'd swapped ideas with Gyric who had a much more conventional estate based around farming. Hreidar and Godric hit it off as I'd hoped, with Hreidar, to my surprise, following Godric's quick-witted. ways as they negotiated their way around the other boys. They moved around as a pair, with Godric always a pace in front of his taller friend.

Two days after the investiture we were paraded outside the town. Harold thanked us all for our service to his friend. He had a way of making you feel valued with a few words and a charming smile. Then he walked off and Thurkill spoke up.

'Sixteen of you are staying here to act as an escort when Bishop Leofgar needs to travel outside of the town until he employs his own guards.' He then proceeded to call out sixteen names which included Gyric, Wulfgeat and a man called Heofoc Hardhead, who was an older housecarl who would be commanding the detachment.

I gave Gyric a sympathetic look as I knew he wanted to return to his new wife. Thurkill then called out more lists of names for those who could leave and those who would be escorting Harold. My name hadn't been called which I assumed was because I wasn't a regular housecarl. Then, just as we were expecting to be dismissed, I heard Thurkill's last announcement.

'And, Sar, you are to remain here to act as a translator for Leofgar should he need to talk with any Waelas. Otherwise, you will act as one of his bodyguards.'

'Yes, sir,' I shouted, as my heart sank. Stay here. Serve Leofgar. Be his guard. Fucking hell.

Later that day we all had to attend on Leofgar. After we'd hung around for quite a while, buffeted by blustery showers, we were called into a fine house behind the Minster. It, like many other houses in the town, showed signs of recent repairs. It had a large hall and new tapestries hanging on the walls with religious themes. We were in the bishop's mansion.

Heofoc lined up the housecarls, then, both he and I uncertain of my role here, he put me on the end of the front row. Leofgar came in escorted by a couple of priests and took it upon himself to inspect us. He walked along the line with Heofoc, who was clearly irritated, by his side.

He made the odd condescending remark as he looked at each man in the front row. We were wearing our mail and carrying our helmets. Everyone wore a sword or carried an axe. We were without shields or spears.

He got to me. 'Ah, you, Harold's pet. We meet again. He said he'd leave you here to translate for me. Well, I wouldn't trust you just as much as I wouldn't trust any Waelas vermin to tell me the truth. Therefore, I have no use for you. In truth, I'd rather not even see you.'

You could feel the tension in the room. I might not be a housecarl but I was one of their companions. They didn't appreciate being inspected by a churchman and they didn't like me being demeaned. But we were under our Earl's orders.

I held my cool and asked, 'In that case Father, could I return to my estate?'

'Your estate, ha,' Leofgar scoffed, 'No, I don't think you can.'

'It's only a day's ride away. I could go and come back. I'd like them to know where I am.' Most of the other sixteen housecarls had estates inland and had arranged for messages to be passed on. Rwydin wasn't on the way to anywhere.

'No, that's not possible. On second thoughts I do want to see you. I want to see you outside the Minster, where those priests died, at Lauds every morning.'

I opened my mouth to speak, then decided against it. Lauds was at dawn. Thank God he was a Bishop not a monk, it could have been Matins, but still I wasn't pleased. All but three of us who were left as guards, returned to our billet.

I took Bebbe at her word and Bebbe's tavern became the haunt for all seventeen of us and our boy attendants. Gyric, Godric, Hriedar and I moved into a room in the tavern's loft. The food was good, the ale even better, so we all made the best of a bad job. Some nights Bebbe would amuse herself by trying to get me drunk enough to admit my part in the priest killings. It became a game amongst us to pass the jugs of ale she brought me between us every time she had to attend to other customers. I joked with her but carefully avoided getting drunk enough to give too much away. There's no way I wanted to face another ordeal.

Some nights the shire-reeve, Athelnoth's warriors would come and drink with us. Occasionally this would end in fist fights in the street outside, mostly good humoured but sometimes not. Then Heofoc would show us how he earned his name. He would steam into the fight and smash his forehead into the noses of any fighting drunk on either side. He could bellow louder than any ass and, sometimes with the help of one of Athelnoth's senior soldiers, would quell the fights. As Athelnoth's men were responsible for keeping the peace in Hereford there were never any consequences.

It wasn't long before we discovered another reason for Bebbe's wealth. Behind her tavern she had a long low building with many small rooms guarded by two or more burly bruisers. It was a brothel. I have to admit I visited it fairly often despite Gyric's scorn and my creeping feelings of guilt. I banished them by seeing a different girl every time. Nothing serious to see here. The biggest problem for me was getting up early enough every morning to be ignored by Leofgar. A bishop is a very powerful man, and the Church a very powerful institution, even Earl's showed them respect. There was no way I could defy his orders.

As the weather got warmer and the days longer, we spent less time in the tavern and more time training and riding out to the border with the Waelas. By the time May came around the feelings of guilt grew and I stopped seeing the girls and started to pine for my home and Ymma's company. This was nothing like anything I'd felt before. I spent more and more time with Gyric and put more effort into Godric. I realised that I felt better living like this than I did drinking and whoring.

Then one night I'm in Bebbe's quietly eating next to a table full of Athelnoth's men when I overheard these words; 'The priests are gathering stores. There's talk we might be going to teach the Waelas a lesson.' I couldn't hear the reply but I repeated what I'd heard to Gyric.

'You should know better than to pay heed to soldier's gossip,' was his response.

'Yeah, but if it's true I can't see Harold being happy. It would break the truce. We'd be fighting again.'

'Harold and Leofgar are close. If Leofgar were planning to attack the Waelas he would know.'

'You think? I was tasked to keep an eye out for signs of raids. You know, from my estate.'

'You told me, but it was Harold that left you here so he can't have been that worried.'

'No, maybe not. I guess I wasn't that important,' I said, feeling a bit flattened.

'What are you two sad fucks gossiping about?' It was Heofoc.

'Oh nothing,' I said.

'Tell him, Sar, tell him what you heard,' said Gyric.

So, I told him, 'Maybe just gossip,' I said as I finished.

Heofoc frowning said, 'Well he's clearly not gathering up an army. Takes time, lots of priests and carts. There has been a bit more traffic coming into the Bishop's yards than usual. It's probably nothing but I'll ask around.'

A couple of days later as I was training a felt a firm hand on my shoulder. I turned, saw Heofoc, sheathed my sword, nodded to my training partner, and stood straight, 'Sir.'

'Seems you were right. Leofgar is planning a raid.'

'Seriously, so he hasn't given up on his dreams of being a hero. A raid? Who with?'

'Athelnoth's men, a few warriors Leofgar himself has recruited.'

'Is that all?'

'And us.'

'What? We're going as well?'

'Leofgar is convinced that a heavily armed force of Englishmen on foot are a match for any bunch of Welsh savages.'

'Has he ever fought in a shield wall?'

'Not many have. Have you?'

'Not in the front rank, but close. Gyric has.'

For the first time ever Heofoc looked impressed. His eyebrows almost met his hairline.

Before he could ask, I said, 'We we're at the Battle of the Seven Sleepers.'

'What do you think then?'

'Look if the usually poorly armed Waelas fought head-to-head with a shield wall of mailed Saxons they'd lose.'

'Leofgar is right then?'

'They won't. I've both fought with the Waelas and against them. They won't fight head on. They might not fight at all.'

'Then we raid them, burn their towns and bring home riches and slaves,' said Heofoc.

'It won't work like that. How many towns did you see when we campaigned?'

'We didn't go in very far.'

'Why was that?'

Heofoc grunted, I think my tone was getting to him. 'Not sure how English you are Sar. You don't seem to have much faith in us.'

'Now you sound like Leofgar, sir,' I said.

I saw his head go back. I took two quick steps backwards before he could nut me.

'You should know your place, boy,' he said, and, turning on his heels, stalked off.

At times like this I didn't feel very English, or even Saxon as my mother called us. Only last year Gruffud had fought a much bigger country to a standstill which ended with King Edward ceding him territory. Now *we* were going to teach *them* a lesson with a raid. Arrogant fuckwits.

Maybe something I'd said had sunk in. Suddenly Heofoc had us running around in full gear, byrnie's, mail and armed with swords or axes, spears and shields. Which meant, after a week, that we could lumber along at about the speed of a startled ox.

I was sat next to Gyric, breathing heavily after training, 'So there's to be about ninety of us, eh? And, thank God we're not taking the boys.'

'Means we'll have to lead the ponies, look after all the gear and cook besides. A lot of the men won't be happy.'

'I'm just glad to get them out of harm's way. I'm going to send Godric home with what's left of my money and a message for

Colbrand. I'd like to send Hriedar with him. They can look out for each other.'

'You really think this won't go well, don't you?'

I nodded unhappily, 'I'm sure of it. I'm also sure that Harold would not want the truce broken.'

'Harold trusts Leofgar.'

'Gytha doesn't,' I said, 'but you never heard me say that. She thought she could promote him away from Harold to where he could do no harm.'

Gyric turned and looked at me hard, 'She told you that?'

'Good as,' I replied.

'She has that kind of power. To influence the church behind Harold's back?'

'You'd better believe it.'

Gyric looked thoughtful, 'Maybe a couple of the other boys could go with our two. I'll ask around. Would Ymma mind?'

'She'll be glad to get Godric back.'

'Wulfgeat has his younger brother with him. Is it alright with you if I ask him?'

I shrugged, 'Wulfgeat and I seem to get on fine these days. Not friends but not at odds either.'

'I noticed. He's even angry at Leofgar's treatment of you.'

I barely had time to get Godric and two other boys on their way before we got orders to march out. I'd told him to ride Sooty and lead his own pony. Gyric had done the same with his boy. I sensed he was starting to doubt the wisdom of this venture himself. The other two just took their own ponies. I was glad I wouldn't be there to see Ymma's face at all these extra mouths to feed. Then I realised I wasn't glad at all. I'd have given anything to be back there with her and Inga in the strange world we'd moved into.

The morning after next, instead of parading for Leofgar on my own, our whole party was lined up outside the minster. The force consisted of sixteen of Harold's men, Athelnoth had about eighty soldiers. There were also five warriors who'd been personally signed up as Leofgar's bodyguards and fifteen priests.

'Isn't one bishop enough?' I muttered to Gyric, 'Do we need all those priests?'

Gyric was about to mutter back when Athelnoth called us all to order.

'Your Bishop wishes to address you so shut up and pay attention.'

Leofgar mounted his horse with help from one of his priests, who then passed his ornate crozier up to him. He waved it in the air, vaguely making the sign of the cross over us. Then he began to speak, 'As most of you know, we are setting out on a raid into Wales. We want to revenge ourselves upon them for the treatment of our city, its people and the theft of the relics and treasures of our Minster. Most of all we would like information leading to the retrieval of those treasures. To this end we will need to take captives.'

He paused to let his words sink in, then continued, 'The Waelas are lightly armed savages without discipline. We will defeat them with our unbreakable shield wall. There will be no foolish forays on foot or horseback, indeed only my bannerman, Athelnoth and myself will be horsed. As for the rest of you, excepting my priests, half will be fully armed at any one time while the other half will lead the ponies carrying their mail and shields. This way no man should get too tired. If we are attacked the armed warriors can hold off the Waelas while the rest equip themselves.

'Know this all of you. God is on your side. It is the divine mission of the English to bring civilisation to its backsliding neighbours. These barbarians looted and burned our Minster. For this they must suffer. Our battle cry will be, 'God and Saint Ethelbert.'

With that Athelnoth, now also mounted, punched his fit in the air and shouted, 'God and Saint Ethelbert.'

This was our cue, we all drew swords or raised axes and, thrusting them into the air, shouted 'God and Saint Ethelbert' over and over again. Leofgar looked upon us, beaming, very satisfied with himself. Despite shaving his moustaches off after becoming a bishop, he clearly enjoyed his role as a military leader. When the shouting died down, we were led out through the town, past cheering crowds of townsfolk, to the meadows by the river. Here we were all fed a huge breakfast then determined who was to strip off their mail to lead the small herd of ponies ready laden with supplies.

Naturally Gyric and I paired off. As I helped him get out of his mail, I couldn't keep my mouth shut anymore.

'There's a lot wrong with Leofgar's plan, Gyric, a lot. It's a fool's errand. The sooner he realises that the better.'

Gyric shrugged, 'We've faced a lot worse than a walk into Wales Sar, a lot worse.'

I forced a laugh, 'Yeah, and here we are to tell the tale.'

Chapter Twenty-Three

On the first day we marched to the River Dore and headed north along the English bank. It was the early days of summer. Not hot, but warm enough to make you sweat hard and need to drink often. Ideal campaigning weather it wasn't. That night we camped near a ford. Spirits were high. We were on the move and most of the men either hadn't fought much before or had only been on hit and run raids so, in this body of heavily armed men, they felt invincible. I ate and drank with them and kept my misgivings to myself. Maybe Leofgar was right but with no throwing spears, archers, light troops or horsemen we could only fight Waelas warriors if they chose to attack us. King Gruffud would be furious that the truce was broken and, as soon as he heard, would gather his men. That would take a while, if his heart ruled his head, he might attack us with too few men. If his cunning ruled, what then?

Next morning we forded the river and marched on through an area of open farmland, mostly unploughed abandoned farms. The track was already growing over now the farmers could no longer sell their goods in Hereford. Then we came across some ploughlands that were sown, and the fields bright green with growing barley, peas or beans. A yoke of oxen and a few sheep grazed the fallow looked over by a couple of wary boys one of whom ran off as soon as he saw us. Shortly after we arrived at a small village to find its inhabitants had all gathered to wait for us. This surprised me, most villagers avoid armed men like the plague.

Leofgar called me to him. 'I need you to talk to these people. You are the only Welsh speaker here. Find out what this place is.'

'You trust me for this?'

'Just do as I ask.'

I approached the villagers and spoke to them in Welsh. An older man pushed his way forward.

'Most of us don't speak Welsh sir. We speak English and see ourselves as English,' he said, answering in that tongue.

'Yet you live in Wales, with the Waelas,' said Leofgar.

'We didn't choose the border, did we? My father and his father before him farmed here.'

'Bring that rude peasant to me,' commanded Leofgar.

Two of his own men went over and roughly dragged the man over to Leofgar. There was an audible gasp from the villagers and I noticed that some of the women were quietly slipping away with their children. After that, apart from the barking of village dogs, the place fell silent.

'Put him on his knees,' said Leofgar.

His men pushed the man down on his knees who protested, 'Why treat me like this? We were welcoming you.'

'Firstly, I am your bishop. You should address me as Your Excellency.'

'I'm sorry Your Excellency, but you are not my bishop. Bishop Tryferyn from Y Clas was my bishop until he died last year. Now our bishop is in Llandaf, we've been told, wherever that is.'

'What is this place?' asked Leofgar.

'Chewshope, Your Excellency.'

Leofgar signalled one of his priests, 'Is this true?'

The priest nodded, 'I believe so. The changes follow Gruffud ap Llewelyn's uniting the Waelas.'

Leofgar turned to the kneeling man, 'Is there a church there? Monks?'

'The church of Saint Cynidr, Your Excellency,' answered the man nervously.

'Are there treasures and relics there?'

'Our Saint is buried there. We are not wealthy. What treasures there are we see on his Saint's Day in April, Excellency.'

'And where are they kept?'

'I don't know. You'd need ask the priests.'

Leofgar nodded to another of his men who walked forward and punched the villager in his face.

The villagers began muttering angrily as blood spurted from the man's nose. Athelnoth spurred his horse up alongside Leofgar's.

'There's no need for this, Leofgar. These people aren't even Waelas.'

'But they stayed here, didn't they?'

The man on his knees cried out, 'Our farms are here. Our father's farmed here. We pay our rents and out tithes. We don't choose where the border lies. When Gruffud's men came through they plundered our grain and took some of our stock but otherwise left us alone. Why would we move?'

Athelnoth said to Leofgar, 'This is the nature of the borderlands. There were pockets of Welsh farmers near Hereford and English ones beyond them.'

'There's no Welsh ones there now are there?'

'There's no farms in the Archenfold now of any kind since the last war. That is everyone's loss. Hereford now gets no trade from the west.'

'And whose fault is that?' snapped Leofgar.

Athelnoth nodded, 'Gruffud's, and Aelfgar's, a Welsh king and an English earl. Definitely not this man's.'

A murmur of approval at Athelnoth's words ran through our ranks. God knows, we were all men used to violence but few of us approved of this kind of bullying. Well, bullying Englishmen at least. Athelnoth's men wanted revenge on the Waelas for the destruction of their town, Harold's men were largely indifferent. Leofgar, in my opinion, wanted to be a warrior priest, and, more importantly, to be seen to be one. So far, this wasn't happening.

Leofgar might have caught the mood, at any rate he told his men to let the man go. They did so reluctantly. Leofgar signalled us on. As we marched on, a gap appeared in the ranks between Leofgar's thugs and the other warriors.

Shortly after leaving the village the landscape began to change. The track ran through a valley criss-crossed by small woodlands. I was surprised that there were no orders to close up and take our shields off our backs.

Gyric wielded the long two-handed axe so did not carry a shield. These axemen fought in the wall behind a particular warrior who was trained to protect the axeman but also to give them space to attack at the right moments. Gyric's was a man named Ospak Oddman, for no other reason that it sounded good. I swung my shield onto my left side and encouraged Ospak to bear his on the right so that Gyric marched between us. I noticed some other soldiers swinging their shields off their backs. At least some of us were aware of the danger.

Sure enough, as we entered the second area of woodland a single arrow came whizzing between the trees striking a pony in the haunch. The poor animal screamed and reared, causing chaos among the other ponies. Now, messily, the mailed warriors made a wall down each side of the column. Before we could form, another arrow came from a different direction and wounded a man in the leg. Leofgar threw himself off his horse looking very confused while Athelnoth tried to bring order.

'Steady men, raise your shields, face out,' shouted Athelnoth.

By this point most of us were doing so while the unarmoured men started helping each other into their mail. Meanwhile the was still a commotion around the wounded horse.

'Either calm that animal or kill it,' commanded Athelnoth.

There was one last scream then silence. I stared into the woods. There was no movement, and no more arrows followed.

'I don't think there'll be any more arrows now, Gyric,' I said.

'What makes you think that?' said Gyric, who was now stood behind me and Ospak.

'I know this type of fighting. They've slowed us down without even revealing themselves or risking a man.'

'Why?' asked Gyric, before he answered his own question, 'I get it. They can get messengers out. All the time we lose is time they gain to get women and children away and assemble their warriors.'

As Ospak nodded along I saw Wulfgeat listening in and then talking to one of his companions. Soon the whole party would be aware of what I'd said.

Leofgar got back on his horse, a little shakily I thought. He and Athelnoth conferred then ordered everyone into mail. While the dead pony's load was taken off and spread among the other beasts, we all just stood around. If I was right about the purpose of this ambush it was working. The wounded man was lifted onto another pony which meant its load needed spreading out too. Eventually we headed off. More slowly this time.

We reached the settlement of Y Clas frustrated and angry in the late afternoon after being shot at two more times. Two bowmen had slowed down our column by the best part of a day. There had been no more casualties but everyone was far more alert and now all of us were wearing our mail all the time. Hot, sweaty, and tiring to wear but only a well shot arrow fired with full force will pierce mail hard enough to seriously injure a man.

Y Clas was deserted, most of it was north of the Afon Guoy which is fordable on foot at this point. Being soaked up to our thighs did not improve anyone's mood. We spread out through the town to find all the deserted houses empty of anything of value.

Leofgar headed straight for the church leaving his men outside with orders to guard it. I didn't bother searching the houses and, busying myself with the ponies, kept as far away from Leofgar as I could manage. It turned out there was a well on the north side of the village so, after leaning my spear and shield against one of the houses, I led some of the ponies up there and started to water them, after taking off their loads. To my surprise while I was there Wulfgeat came up leading more of the ponies.

As he helped me raise the bucket from the well, he spoke, 'Sar, you believe that we are on a fool's errand here, don't you?'

I tipped the bucket into the trough and, scratching the nearest pony behind the ears as he drank, I said, 'More than that Wulfgeat. I fear Leofgar's foolishness will get us all killed.'

'Most of the men are confident. We are well armed, well supplied and well trained. What have we to fear?'

'There's a lot of us Wulfgeat. How long do you think those provisions will last?'

'We can take them from the Waelas.'

'Was there a granary in the village? Was it laden with grain?'

Wulgeat scoffed, 'No, only the dried corpses of a few mice were left in there.'

'Exactly, the Waelas have few rich ploughlands compared to the English and even we run short of stores at this time of year. The new crops will be a while yet. What little they have will be easy to carry away.'

'Those bowmen,' said Wulfgeat,

'We have no lightly armed men we can send out as scouts. No horsemen so we can get to settlements before they know we're coming. True, scouts and horsemen can be ambushed,' I said, heading off Wulfgeat's objections, 'but we're going in blind, relying on Gruffud, or his vassals, to attack us on our terms.'

'They'll attack us, or we return unscathed and hopefully richer.'

'Oh, they'll attack us. The question is how and when.'

As I pulled the pony away from the trough, a voice called out, 'Nomansson! The bishop wants you in the church.'

It was one of Leofgar's men, the one who'd hit the village elder. He was a well-built stocky man with a pocked face and a slight cast in one eye, probably in his late thirties. There was a rail near the well so I wrapped the lead reins of the ponies I'd been leading around it and left them there.

'So,' I said, 'what's your name, and where are you from.'

'They call me Wolf,' he said, and baring his teeth at me he jerked his face towards mine and laughed.

I showed no reaction.

He turned to walk on, 'as for where I'm from. That's for me to know.'

Fucking twat, I thought.

Before going to the church, I retrieved my spear and shield. As I hefted the heavy war spear in my right and felt the absence of the throwing spear I usually carried. It bothered me that even if I saw an enemy I couldn't strike him until he came up close. All those skills I'd had to learn, wasted.

I got to the church to find two of Leofgar's men outside. I pushed past them and through the open door of the church. I paused for a moment to let my eyes accustom to the gloom. The church was small and empty except for an old altar in the chancel. This church had been around a good while. Its timbers were black and warped with age and the murals smudged by the bodies of generations of worshippers. A window each side of the chancel threw light down to the altar in front of which were Leofgar, one of his priests and the remaining two of his men. The four of them were standing over a young priest on his knees. As I approached them, I could see that his nose was bleeding and his bottom lip split.

'Strange way for a bishop to treat a priest, isn't it?' I said as I got close.

'It's not for you to comment on the actions of your superiors, boy. Something you seem to forget,' he said, turning to face me.

I held his gaze just long enough to see a flicker of uncertainty in his eyes. 'So, what am I doing here?'

'This excuse for a priest doesn't speak English and his Latin is so accented I can't understand a word.'

'You want me to translate. Why?'

'Saint Cynidr lived five hundred years ago. This pathetic town was the seat of a bishop. They must have accrued a lot of treasures and gifts over that time. Ask him where they are.'

I leant my shield against the wall and laid my spear on the floor then walked forward and standing over the young priest asked him, in Welsh, 'Do you know what he wants?'

He nodded, and, looking up at me with a mixture of blood and saliva dribbling down his chin, said, 'Yes, I could understand his Latin. He wants the church's treasures. I told him that we don't have any.'

'Bit stupid, don't you think?' I said waving towards the clean, cross shaped patch on the back wall. 'There's also round marks and wax stains on the altar. No font, so I guess you had a metal one and chalices. Every church has those.'

The priest hung his head and stared at the floor.

'What are you saying?' demanded Leofgar.

'I'm telling him that it's obvious he's lying. Clearly there's been a cross and candlesticks here at the very least.'

'He was lying to me then?'

I nodded. Leofgar made a sign and one of his men stepped in front of me and punched the kneeling priest in the side of the head, who slumped sideways onto the floor. The man leant forward to pull him up. As he did so I lifted my leg and slammed my foot, sole first, into his arse. His head slammed into the wall and he collapsed, stunned. Everyone else turned to face me, clearly shocked at the turn of events.

'That's one of my men you've just assaulted,' said Leofgar furious.

I stepped back and drew my sword, 'Do you want me to gut another?'

Leofgar's other man had barely got his hand on his sword hilt. I was still faster than most.

'Or slash his throat?'

One of the guards from outside crashed in, 'I heard a noise.'

'Stop right there or your friend dies,' I said so calm and quiet that the room stilled.

Leofgar spoke, 'What are you doing Nomansson?'

I laughed curtly, honestly, I had no idea why I was doing this, 'You're beating up a priest in God's house. Can't be right. Do you want to hold some hot iron?'

Leofgar blanched, 'Why then?'

'I felt sorry for him. God knows why he's even here.' I turned my head towards the Waelas priest, 'Why are you here anyway?' I asked him in his own tongue.

'There should always be a priest in the house of God to welcome the faithful or the sinner,' he replied.

I felt a lot less sorry for him now, idiot. I translated his answer to Leofgar who visibly squirmed, then changed the subject.

'Are we going to stand here all day?' he said.

My arm was getting a bit tired, holding a sword out at arms-length is hard work. I needed to do something before it started to tremble.

'You three,' I said, nodding towards the armed men, 'undo your sword belts and drop them to the floor.'

They hesitated, so I pushed the point of my sword against the man's Adam's apple. He dropped his as did the other man. The stunned one was getting to his feet, his head obviously still swimming. I swung the sword point in his direction. He quickly fumbled off his belt. I then ordered Leofgar's priest to pick them up and dump them in the far corner of the church.

'I will question this priest but no one will hit him.' I paused, 'Unless I ask then too. Alright?'

Everyone nodded. I repeated what I'd said to the Waelas priest who was sobbing noisily on the floor.

'No one kills him after either, alright?' I added.

Everyone nodded. I stared round, everybody's eyes shifted from mine.

'You men, and you, priest, get behind altar. I will question this man in my own way.'

All of them, except Leofgar, did as I told them. What the fuck was I doing? I wasn't making friends here. I placed my sword on the floor my side of the altar. They'd seen how fast I was. Now it was my turn to pull the Waelas priest back to his knees. I turned him so I could crouch in front of him and still keep an eye on everyone else.

I knelt in front of him and waited for his sobs to subside. His eyes came up to mine. By the saints, he wasn't much more than a child. So what? I wasn't much older. I spoke again in Welsh.

'So, where are they? The candlesticks, the cross, other things.'

'I don't know,' he said, 'no one tells me anything.'

I looked closely, behind the tears his face flushed red.

'Alright then. Which way did they go?'

He blushed again, 'I didn't see.'

'What's he saying,' asked Leofgar.

'He's saying that he doesn't know. I don't believe him,' I said. Then turning back to the priest, 'I don't believe you.'

He didn't answer, just stared sullenly at the floor.

'Put your hand out. Flat on the floor,' I said, gently.

He looked up at me, puzzled.

'Do it,' I shouted, my voice cracking like a whip, 'Do it?'

He put his hand out.

'Spread your fingers.'

He did so. Then I took my little throwing axe from out of my belt and grabbed his wrist with my left hand. One of Leofgar's men started to laugh.

He tugged back, his eyes wide with shock, but I was much stronger than him.

'God save me, I thought you were the good one.'

'Which finger?'

He started crying again. 'They went north?'

'Who did?'

'The rest of the priests and a couple of servants,' he said, blushing again.

I went back to English, 'He says the priests from here went north.'

'Ask him where they would be going. What town?' said Leofgar. 'No, more important, this was a bishopric. There would have been a lot more here somewhere. Gospels, croziers embroidered vestments and much more. Which was the bishop's house?'

I held the blade of the axe against the priest's forefinger and, while he winced, asked about the bishop's house. He gave me the directions straight away without a blush. I passed them on to Leofgar who told one of his men and his own priest to go and search the place. I knew for certain they were wasting their time.

'They won't find anything, will they?' I said.

'You didn't ask that.'

'So, where were they taken? When?'

'They were taken north too, after Bishop Tryferyn died.'

Again, the blushing. He clearly found lying difficult.

'You're a good Christian, aren't you? So why are you lying to me?'

I told Leofgar that the bishop's house would yield nothing. He snorted.

'Get the truth out of him before I put my own men back to the task. Cut off his finger,' he demanded.

'Your Excellency,' I said, 'Give me time. I'm doing better than your man anyway.' I turned back to Welsh, 'He wants me to take off your finger?'

The poor boy started snivelling again. 'Martyr me. I'm not afraid to die for my faith.'

I looked at the top of his tonsured head then grabbed him, gently, by his hairless chin and turned his face up to mine, 'Being martyred is one thing being tortured is another. Answer all his questions and I promise you I will try to get you out of here alive. There's no need to die for some earthly treasures.'

I thought my last line was truly inspired and then I had another bright idea.

'This town must be part of a princedom. Which one?'

'Brycheiniog, we had a king. Until last year when Gruffud ap Llewelyn decided otherwise.'

'And where was this King's seat?'

'Talgart,' he said, blushing again.

Why would lie about that? 'Is that north of here?'

He nodded vigorously, 'Yes. Yes.'

I could hear Leofgar tapping his foot impatiently.

'You need to stop lying. I've been to the north of this town. The only track from there goes northeast, back towards England. There's no road north past the well, is there?

He started sobbing again. I dropped his chin and picked back up the axe. 'Which way is Talgart. We will find out. Is that where all the townsfolk went?'

Suddenly he started babbling, 'The bishop's treasures went to Llandaf. I think our priests went to Talgart. Our people went in all directions as soon as we got the message. That's all I know. I swear, by Christ, that's all I know.

I believed him because of the blasphemy. I told Leofgar everything he'd said and tucked the axe back into my belt. Then I pushed the young priest down on the floor, 'Stay there and be quiet,'

'Where's Llandaf?' said Leofgar.

I knew that because it wasn't far from where I was reared. 'Long way south of here. Either over the hills or round back the way we came and south west from there. Long way.'

'And Talgart?'

'That can't be far. It's not north or east from here, so it must be westwards. He was lying about anyone going north.'

I picked up my sword and stood up. I held it up and spoke to everyone left in the room. 'I found out what you wanted. I'm sorry to have treated you all that way,' I lied. 'I wanted him to trust me. Seemed like the best way. No hard feelings, alright? Tell your mates.'

The nodded confusedly at me. I would need to watch my back.

I then turned to Leofgar, 'You've done with me?'

He nodded, 'Yes, but be ready. We'll be heading for Talgart once we've all eaten.'

I sheathed my sword and then yanked the young priest to his feet. I then picked up my shield and spear and using the butt of the spear's shaft roughly pushed him out of the door. I walked him to the edge of the town. There was one thing that bothered me.

'Why were you so keen to send us north?'

'I'm not telling you anymore. I thought you were going to be kind.'

'I was, I got you out of there without hitting you again, still able to walk and most of still alive.'

He stopped walking, 'I suppose I should be grateful.'

'Wouldn't hurt.'

'I wanted you to go north because there's a small army of deserters, both English and Welsh, commanded by a mad cripple. They raid and extort, stealing livestock and girls, then disappear northwards.'

'You hoped we'd kill each other, then?'

He nodded.

'So, not as green as you're cabbage looking?'

All of a sudden we were both sniggering.

'Go on,' I said, 'fuck off before I change my mind.'

He stumbled off, slowly quickening his pace until he disappeared into the scrubby woodlands on the other side of the town's fields.

Chapter Twenty-Four

'You think he doubled back and stole one of our ponies,' said Heofoc, laughing loudly, then choking as he tried to shovel food into his mouth at the same time.

'Yeah, the little sod, and after I tried so hard to save him from a beating,' I said.

'What made you do that then, Sar?' asked Wulfgeat.

I looked at him sharply, and deciding that it was a real question, gave him an evasive answer, 'The truth, I don't really know. He was so young, maybe. Also, I don't like Leofgar nor those men he's taken on.' Something inside my belly squirmed. Guilt, I think. Guilt, because I had murdered unarmed priests.

'Well, they don't like you now either do they?' chortled Waebheard. He was the other axeman among Harold's contingent. They're usually big men and Waebheard was no exception. His muscles had muscles. To swing a battleaxe you need a firm stance. Its weight can pull you off your feet if your opponent dodges an extended swing. Having legs like tree trunks helps.

'Don't worry, Sar, we'll all be watching your back,' said Teothic, a young warrior, not much older than Gyric or me.

'Even though your father came out of a burial mound,' said Heofoc, raising his cup towards me.

For a moment there was silence, then everyone burst out laughing and various hands slapped me on the back. I smiled uncomfortably. Happy, though, feeling accepted by these men felt good. Then it was time to move on.

It had been decided that Harold's men would form the vanguard for the next stage of the journey to Talgart. This meant we were fully armed and helmeted at all times but didn't have to lead ponies.

Soon after we'd waded back through the ford, I heard a horse coming up behind us. I tensed a little expecting some demand from Leofgar, but it was Athelnoth's voice that called out.

'Which one of you is Sar?'

For a moment I was surprised at this. Then I remembered that my helmet was covering my distinctive dark red hair. I stepped out of the marching ranks and, laying down my spear, took off my helmet.

'That would be me, sir,' I said.

Athelnoth dismounted, 'I want a word with you.'

I put my stupid face on, 'How can I help, sir?'

'You can help by learning when to keep your mouth shut.'

'Yes, sir.'

'Don't act stupid with me, man. I know a few things about you. Things I was told before your ordeal. You are one of the youngest men here but you've seen more of war than nearly all of us.'

Diw Sant knows where this was going. 'I believe that is so, sir,' I answered warily.

'Your grumbling is undermining the morale of this force. Now is your opportunity to grumble to me.'

'What do you mean?'

'You've complained about this raid. What then, in your opinion, are we doing so wrong?'

I held his gaze and decided that he meant what he said.

'For a start. I don't think we should be doing this raid at all. A truce was agreed with Gruffud. Terms were made and met, oaths made.'

'Do you think Gruffud cares about oaths?'

'Don't know, don't care. My Earl made an oath.'

'You saw what the Waelas did to our town, to our Minster. In fact, you had a part in it I'm told. If it was up to me, I'd have you hanged.'

'So did Earl Aelfgar, would you hang him too?'

'Careful, Sar. I have men and rope here. Here where Harold can't save you.'

'Oaths are important. If I hadn't been sworn to Harold, I'd be a very wealthy man in Ireland right now. Oaths matter.'

'Alright, you're loyal to your Earl. What else?'

'We don't have scouts, sir.'

'Hmm, I have raided into Wales before. What happens to scouts who get caught.'

'We hear them screaming in the night, and find their tortured bodies hung from trees.'

Athelnoth nodded, 'Is that a risk worth taking?'

'Good scouts rarely get caught. Bring hunters and poachers for the woods and fleet horsemen for the open areas. In fact, if all of us were like that we might get somewhere before the inhabitants have left.'

'Like when the Waelas raid us?'

I thought for a moment, 'Well, yes.'

'Bishop Leofgar wants to try another way. As I see it if the Waelas do attack we'd win. If they don't we can still get home safely.'

Maybe, I thought, 'They have no reason to attack us. They can throw things at us, slingshots, arrows, spears and darts. We have nothing to throw at them except what we pick up.'

'And you think our men can't work all that out for themselves?'

I shuffled, awkwardly, 'I suppose so.'

'Tell me then. How does your grumbling help?'

I was starting to feel more respect for Athelnoth, he had a point, morale matters.

'It doesn't, sir,' I said, hoping this would soon be over.

Athelnoth put his right hand on my left shoulder, 'Look Sar, you swore your oath to Harold and he chose to lend the services of you and your companions to the bishop. If you value your oath so much you should serve the Bishop Leofgar as you would your Earl, yet you create a scene and threaten his men. This sort of behaviour must stop. I want no feuds among the men. I've spoken to them and now I'm speaking to you. You understand?

'Yes, sir.'

Athelnoth mounted his horse, 'One last thing. Don't forget, there's plenty of trees and plenty of rope.'

He spurred his horse and rode up the column, nearly all of which had passed us by. As I strapped on my helmet, I heard the crackling of flames and saw clouds of smoke rising. Y Glas was burning. I picked up my spear and, after splashing through the ford, had to run the whole length of the column to rejoin my men. I arrived, hot and sweaty.

'What was that about?' said Gyric, as I marched alongside him my chest heaving.

'I've been told to shut my mouth and behave.'

'Shock, horror,' was his response.

I was still gulping in air. 'You know what Gyric? I don't want to be a housecarl anymore. I want out of this mail, to take off this fucking helmet, throw away this spear and shield and pickup my targe and a nice light throwing spear and rely on my speed and agility to get by.'

'Not so good in the shield wall.'

'Shield walls are not the only way to fight.' I said and added, 'The trees are thickening on the hillside to our left.'

'Eyes on your left lads,' shouted Heofoc. We all swung our shields from our backs onto our left arms.

'Sometimes, Sar, you could just trust your commander,' said Gyric, pointedly.

After only one mile's march we came to a large house surrounded by pasture grazed by a few sheep and oxen. We marched on until orders from behind us called a halt. Parties of men were ordered out from the main body to ransack the empty house and slaughter as many of the beasts that could be rounded up. This all takes time. Then it was decided that we might as well cook the meat right away so the house was smashed up and used for cooking fires. We all ate well for the second time that day. As we ate all I could see in my mind's eye was messengers running out across the whole country alerting the various leaders to our presence. Sooner or later, the word would reach Gruffud's court in the far north. If there's one thing I knew about Gruffud, he was not a merciful man. This time I kept my misgivings to myself.

We marched on very quickly finding ourselves surrounded by woodland again. On the right a river ran not far from us so we were able to see clearly through the trees and brambles, but on the left the woods were thickly cladding a steepening hillside. As we reached the first houses of what I guessed must be Talgart some of the tension left me.

Then behind us there was uproar. Screaming ponies and shouting men. We all lifted our shields and lowered our spears. Then we slowly paced our way backwards to the main force. Behind us I could hear Athelnoth's voice commanding men to come back. Angry shouts came from the English and war cries from the Waelas. Shortly afterwards a slingshot pebble cracked into my helmet. I reeled, thankful now for that heavy headpiece.

'Hold fast, and tighten up,' yelled Heofoc from behind me.

The shot was followed by arrows thudding into shields or ricochetting off from helmets. It was impossible to see the archers, only the odd shadowy movement in the trees. Then this was followed by the high-pitched squealing of a trumpet. Just as quickly as the tumult began it ended. A perfect ambush.

We soon learned that they had targeted the ponies and that three of them had been so seriously wounded they'd had to be killed. Much worse though, angered by the assault six men had tried to run into the wood to find and kill the archers. That's why Athelnoth had been shouting so loudly. Four of the men had obeyed. The other two never returned. One of the priests, only protected by his habit, was seriously wounded. The dead pony's loads were spread among the ones that had survived as was the load on the pony that now carried the priest. We'd be a lot slower now.

Shortly afterwards we marched into Talgart. This was a more substantial town with a market square. Here some of the residents must have waited to be sure we'd come this way. The odd bundle of belongings lay in the streets. Mainly bundles of clothes, cooking pots and the like. Things not worth picking up on a raid like this. Iron things, clothes and the like need more than overloaded ponies to carry them away. We were looking for things of real value. There were some tapestries in the one, very fine, house, more valuable, but with the same problem. Being summer the granaries were almost empty.

We stayed in those houses that night. Soon after dark the screaming started. It was so loud that we knew the torturers were not far. I looked around my companions in the dim light of the fire and as a mixture of anger, fear and despair overtook them, I made a decision.

I'd already taken off my mail with Gyric's help. Now I removed the byrnie leaving me in a brown tunic and leggings. I sneaked my little axe and my eating knife from my sword-belt and left it with the mail.

'I'm just of out for a piss, lads,' I said calmly, and without waiting for an answer slid out of the door.

Once outside I waited for my eyes to adjust to the gloom. There were pickets set up at the end of every street. There was enough of a moon to cast some dark shadows so I crept into them and moved silently past one of the pickets. He was fearfully looking out into the darkness surrounding the town. I could see he was agitated and sure enough he soon edged closer to the next picket along. I darted across the clear ground into the undergrowth.

The screams continued. Horrific, blood-curdling screams. Only those of one man though. I circled around the edge of the woods until I could locate the source of those screams. Staring up into the darkness under the trees I glimpsed a small red glow. I half crawled half crouched towards it, every move slow, quiet and steady. I bit my lip at one point as I crawled into a stand of nettles, indistinguishable in the dark. They say they grow where men have died bloody deaths. I winced at the stings and hoped that tonight it wouldn't be my blood they fed on.

I got closer. Four men in the glow of a small fire. One tied to a tree was being mocked and derided while one of the others was cutting pieces of skin from the tied man's chest. Despite the numerous bleeding patches on parts of his body I could see there were plenty more cuts to come. The man screamed again, then fainted. The torturer slapped his face, then taking out a flask tipped some liquid into his mouth. The man revived. Another patch of skin was taken. Another gurgling scream.

As I watched this demonic scene. I felt nothing as a coldness came over me. I shifted myself until I had I had clear view of the victim. Taking a deep breath, I took one or two false throws with the axe and then let it fly. It went over the torturers head and deep into the face of their victim. His screams stopped. The men looked frantically around. Two of them took off through the trees and disappeared. The third, the torturer turned, scanning around him, bloody knife in hand. He kicked the fire, which, instead of going out, set alight the dry leaf litter on the forest floor.

It flared up surprisingly fast. Suddenly the wood was full of leaping shadows and patches of red light. I saw the man's eyes widen with shock and fury as I was lit up by the glow. Did I run or fight? I wanted my axe back. I decided to fight.

I switched my knife into my right hand and picked up a dead branch on the floor with my left. The man, black haired and bearded, his wiry frame looked tough and he moved quickly. He stalked towards me, his face drew into a grin, teeth white in his face. I ran sideways into a dark patch and darted around a tree as he lashed out. More of the litter was burning now, spreading fast, filling the air with acrid smoke, leaping flames and flickering shadows. I came around the tree and hit him with the branch on his left elbow. A lucky hit. He was shaking his hand ruefully. I'd caught his funny bone. Not fatal but distracting.

We were now both facing each other in a clearing. I could see his eyes searching around. He wanted to be certain I was alone.

'Your friends have abandoned you,' I said to him in Welsh.

'You're a traitor,' he spat at me.

'Maybe in your eyes. So where are my English friends, eh?'

His eyes started darting around. He wasn't sure now. If he ran, would I stab him in the back or would he run into my friends in the dark. In that moment of hesitancy, I threw the branch into the shadows. His eyes leapt to the noise. I lunged at his chest. And missed. He'd caught the movement and moved. I was wide open. He lunged at me. I twisted sideways as he stabbed with all his force. His knife thudded into a tree. He panicked, and, as he frantically tried to free his knife, I stabbed him under his ribs and watched the life leave his eyes. There'd be more nettles in the wood next year.

The man's still twitching corpse fell to the floor and, as his hair sizzled and flared, I wrenched my axe out of his victim's face. I vaguely knew him from the tavern but he was no friend to anyone I knew well. He'd died because he was stupid. I hoped his stupid mate was already dead for his own sake.

I crept back into the town past pickets staring at the now burning hillside. Hard to believe that my life depended on these useless guards.

I quietly let myself back into our lodgings. We'd all sleep better now. As I wedged myself between the snoring bodies a voice spoke out.

'You've taken your bloody time. And why do you smell like a bonfire?'

'Go back to sleep, arsehole,' I said, and, lying down, did the same myself.

Chapter Twenty-Five

Gyric and I were stood next to the small strips of wheat and barley along the valley floor guarding the ponies while they grazed off the growing crops. We were one of many pairs of warriors posted along the field boundaries, looking out for attackers but unable to stop watching the woods burn on the other side of the valley. Being summer the foliage was green and lush but the understory burned vigorously, crackling and snapping as it sent wreaths of thick smoke up through the canopy.

'Who'd have thought kicking over that little fire would set off all this,' I said, smirking a little as I watched for Gyric's reaction.

His eyes moved from side to side, then they narrowed, the penny had dropped, 'What! That was you? You went out in the woods last night? On your own?'

Pretty fucking vehement I thought, taken slightly aback, 'Yes, couldn't sleep, you know, with all that noise going on.'

'Fucking hell, Sar, are you a fucking moron?' he shouted at me, his face reddening.

'Whoa, Gyric, swearing, eh? Not like you.'

'Christ's blood, yes, I'm swearing. If you'd have been caught there'd have been two men screaming in the night.'

Jesu Mawr, he was very angry. Blaspheming now, definitely not his style. I tried to dismiss it with bravado, 'Oh, there was only three of them.'

'Only fucking three! By all the Saints.' He slammed the butt of axe down so hard it stuck fast in the ground. Next, he's grunting hard trying to pull it out. He finally wrested it out then threw it into the field.

'Bloody hell Gyric, what's got into you. I snuck into the woods, no one saw me. Then I …'

'I don't want to know what you did. I don't want to fucking know,' he said storming up to me and shoving me in the chest with both hands.

I was so surprised that I fell backwards dropping my spear and letting go my shield as I did so. I sat up, trying to wipe my muddied hands on the green wheat stalks.

Gyric stood over me, 'Why Sar? Why do you do these idiot things?'

'The screaming was keeping me awake.'

'Same as for the rest of us. But do we go out in the night without a word to anyone?'

'If I'd said anything I'd have been stopped.'

'Ever thought to ask yourself why?'

I was puzzled, 'What do you mean?'

'Let me guess. In the woods one of the men who left the column, against his orders, was being tortured.'

I nodded. My turn for the penny to drop. I tried again to pass it off. 'We all got some sleep though, didn't we?'

Gyric looked at me, disgust on his face. Then he turned and stalked off to get his axe. I got to my feet. He stalked back then stood in front of me and shook the axe in my face. The sun glinted off the newly whetted edge.

'What is it with you? Why do you do these things? First the business in the church and now this. Why?'

I felt like a small boy in front of my mother, 'I don't know Gyric, I get a thought then I just do it.'

'Learn to count to ten you fucking idiot. Before you get yourself killed.'

'We're all going to die anyway. Be lucky if any of us get home.'

'You can keep thoughts like that to yourself as well.'

We lapsed into sullen silence until we were ordered to load up the ponies. Their loads were a lot lighter now. It's amazing how quickly men can eat through provisions but the loading wasn't helped by the arrival of a fierce summer squall. By the time we marched away into driving rain, the smoke had turned to steam, then into a faint mist above the trees.

We headed out on a different track headed north west. The tail end of our column had barely left Talgart when the vanguard, not us today, found itself in a small village. It had an equally small church into which Leofgar and his priests squeezed themselves and started praying. Hopefully for guidance. If God was on our side, he'd tell them we needed to head home.

We sat around, then sat around some more. The men were wary and watchful after the events of the day before. There was little chatter while many of us spent the time whetting our blades with the little stones we carried for the purpose. Then I heard it, a shrill but faint sound in the distance.

'Gyric, did you hear that?'

'Hear what?'

I stood up, 'Heofoc, did you hear that?'

He shook his head and looked at me sharply, 'Why?'

'I thought I heard a trumpet.'

Heofoc scoffed, 'Trumpet? Angels, was it? Waiting for you?'

'That's not funny. The Waelas use them, very shrill, talk to each other.'

Heofoc frowned, 'I heard they had a lot at Hereford. Frightened the horses, they say?'

'Hush everyone,' I said, making a palm's down motion with my hands.

Heofoc put his hand behind his ear. I could see he was about to mock me again when another faint sound came over almost lost beneath the pattering raindrops. His eyes widened.

'Was that the sound you meant?'

'You heard it? Yes, but that came from a different direction. It's war bands letting each other know they're coming.'

'War bands?'

'Yes, small groups don't use them.'

'Why not?'

'The Waelas are always fighting each other so you'd only announce yourself if you didn't fear ambush. But now, at least for a while, they're united under Gruffud. He's calling up his followers.'

'How far away are they?'

'Hard to say with the wind and all.'

Heofoc got to his feet, 'I'll go and talk to Athelnoth.'

He came back a little later, 'I spoke with Athelnoth and the bishop. They believe that if they gather up together, they will attack us openly. In which case they will fall upon our shield wall and we'll defeat them. If you look behind you, you can see Talgart is burning. This village will burn as we leave so that even if we gain no treasures, we will be punishing them for attacking our city.'

'So, we're waiting for them to assemble an overwhelming force to attack us?'

'Leofgar believes they will attack us before then, because no king can allow his people to keep suffering without trying to rescue them,' said Heofac.

'I think Leofgar does not understand Gruffud. Gruffud ap Llewellyn will let a thousand villages burn without giving a shit. What he won't want to do is let a truce breaking English force leave his country unhurt,' I said.

'How do you know all this?'

'Think about it. He brought both Aelfgar's forces and Irishmen in to fight his own countrymen in the south then set them against the English so he could pay those troops at no cost to himself. In what part of that do you see him caring for his people?'

Heofoc looked at me steadily, 'I'm beginning to see your point of view, but we're here as Leofgar's protectors. Those are my orders.'

That was that. Sure enough, a column of smoke was rising behind us and as we burnt the village we were leaving, more trumpets sounded in the distance.

By the time we headed out the morning was gone, the heavy showers continued broken by spells of sunshine so warm we steamed. We trekked just south of west on a well-used, so very muddy, track and soon found ourselves marching alongside yet another fast-flowing river running between steep wooded banks. Inevitably the column stretched out. As the vanguard rounded a bend it ran up against a few large trees felled across our path. We all stumbled to a halt. Then arrows started to fly from the woods and from across the river making us form up back-to-back along the narrow track, in two outward facing rows, with the priests and ponies between us.

Athelnoth's voice rang out, 'Axemen to the front of the column now.'

I felt Gyric leave my side, then Ospak closed up against me. We held our shields up with our spears levelled. It's not easy shooting arrows downhill accurately and the trees themselves, while giving the archers cover, limited the scope of their fire. Behind a shield, mailed and helmeted you are more than likely not going to get hurt. But, once again, a lot of the fire seemed to be directed against the ponies. While we hunkered down waiting for the axemen to clear the way I reflected on this. Normally the Waelas would covet those ponies. They're worth a lot over many years, yet no one had tried to steal them in the night or separate the warriors from them. Instead, they were killing them. Someone was directing this. Someone who knew what they were doing.

One of the wounded horses bolted into the river, dragging a warrior with him. By the time the warrior had let go he was floundering in the water. A flight of arrows pursued him. It takes a powerful bow to pierce mail from a distance but the poor guy was hit twice in the legs and could not regain his footing. Struggling against the weight of his mail in the fast-flowing waters he tumbled back the way we had come. Back in the column a priest gurgled his last while at least two more ponies had their throats cut to prevent the arrow maddened beasts from breaking up the column. If broken, many more of us of us would be lost.

At last, we started to move again. I had two arrows stuck in my shield and a cut on my face where a ricocheting arrow come from an unexpected direction. We stepped crabwise along the track to where the axemen had cut back many of the branches. The path wasn't completely cleared. We had to climb round, partially on the track but also on the slippery bank of the river. Two more men were lost here. Trying to keep your footing while holding a heavy shield and a war spear while fending off arrows is near impossible. Gyric and the other axemen were till hacking away protected by a wall of shields. Athelnoth was giving orders, I guessed that Leofgar was already through. Men were close to panicking. If we lost our nerve there would be a rout.

'Steady men, steady. Help each other. Form up once you are back on the track. Come on now. Shields up.' Athelnoth's voice was steady and calm. Fair play to him.

I slung my shield on my back and threw the heavy spear over the obstacle and with my right hand grabbing the cut ends of branches pulled Ospak along with me as he splashed and stumbled through the shallows. He had the wit to keep his shield high and we both passed the cut tree ends unscathed. Breathing heavily, we formed another defensive wall and waited for more of our companions to join us. At this point the arrows had stopped.

Heofoc came struggling round along with Wulfgeat.

'Christ, this is close work, where's Leofgar? Find him, Wulfgeat, and report back.'

While we all stood breathing heavily, Wulfgeat headed up the track. He quickly returned. The man was so fit he barely broke a sweat.

'It's alright, sir. The bishop is just ahead. They've formed a wall across the track and he's shouting for the Waelas to come and face us like men.'

I scoffed, 'Been listening to many manly ballads, that one. Glorious fights between stalwart foes, blah, blah, blah.'

'Shut your mouth Sar. He led the way past the ambush, waist deep in the river. Now turn and help your comrades move those trees.'

I nodded to Ospak, 'Let's get Gyric out of there.'

We returned to the fallen trees, with Wulgeat shielding me on one side and Ospak on the other, I started hacking at the smaller branches with my throwing axe.

I wasn't happy. 'I don't carry this around for cutting twigs,' I said, grunting as I cut and tore away the side branches. At least when the axemen got through to here, they'd be able to get to the main stems.

'Is that you moaning down there, Sar, you miserable cur.'

It was Gyric voice. He stood hacking at a thick branch, sweat pouring out from under his helmet. The branch cracked and split, tearing a wedge up to the main trunk. I ducked under the branch in front of me and cut into the still attached lower part. It was bouncing and would kick once I got through.

'Stand back, Gyric,' I shouted.

The split part cracked, severed and breaking away, bounced. As we leapt out of the way the main trunk, relieved of some of its weight, rocked back, a cut off side branch caught Ospak under the chin and he fell back stunned. As soon as the hidden archers saw him fall arrows thudded into the ground around him. Wulfgeat stepped forward and covered Ospak with his shield. This was a dangerous moment and Heofoc and the rest of Harold's men gathered into a tight bunch.

The felled tree had partially righted itself. After hacking through two more branches, we were able to toss the upper limbs of the tree into the river and start to lead the panicked ponies through. The rain of arrows had stopped. I guessed they'd run out, but they had done a lot of damage. While faint figures flitted off among the trees on both sides of the river, we assessed the damage. We'd lost ten men in all, eight warriors and two more priests. We'd also lost Athelnoth's horse and a dozen ponies, and with them half of the hard baked loaves and sacks of barley we relied on as our staple foods, had ended up in the river. Leofgar led a few short prayers as we slid the bodies of our dead into the water. Ideally, we would have stripped off their valuable mail to prevent it falling into our enemy's hands. With luck, the mail would rust before they could retrieve it.

We reformed into a marching column and set off at a rapid pace. We all wanted to get through this wooded pass in the hope of the road widening. Which it did, after a long steady uphill march. Once over the watershed we could see another village before us. We broadened the column and marched down on it. Again, the village proved to be deserted but clearly only recently. There were a few pigs roaming around or poking into the houses taking advantage of their owner's disappearance. They were soon despatched, along with any irritating stray dogs.

The village being surrounded by cleared fields felt a lot safer. We stayed to eat and to bind our wounds. Some of us half-heartedly sought loot in the emptied houses but there was little of value. By now, most of us had ceased to be surprised by this. Ospak, he was still trying.

'There's really no point in looting these villages is there?' he said, as he entered the house where Wulfgeat, Gyric, some other men and I, had a weaner pig turning on a spit we'd found over a hearth we'd fuelled from the beams of the next-door house.

'Mostly they are poor people,' I said, hacking away at a crisp forequarter 'that's why they raid each other and the English.'

'Me, I don't care if they've wealth or not. They burnt my home, and my Minster, two of my cousins disappeared at that time too. Slaves now, or dead. I just want to burn their villages and kill their men,' said one of Athelnoth's followers.

'Not that we've killed any yet,' grumbled another of them.

I stuffed the greasy pig meat into my mouth before I could say anything stupid. Delicious fat dribbled down my chin. For a moment I felt happy, full belly, good company, shame we'd no drink though. Adam's ale would have to do. For me, this wasn't my fight. I understood revenge but Hereford wasn't my city, and anyway, I'd played a part in its destruction.

Heofoc came crashing through the door, 'Is Sar in here? Ah, there you are. Come with me.'

I quickly cut another slice of pig, then followed him out, 'What's happening?'

'They've found some old guy laid up in one of the houses. Leofgar wants to talk to him.'

I followed him to another part of the village which was bigger than I'd thought. The house I was brought to was on the run-down fringe of the village. Outside, on the ground, sprawled a gnarly old man. Or maybe just worn out. Hard lives age people fast.

'Speak to him. Find out where we are?' demanded Leofgar.

I took that in for a moment. Our leader didn't know where we were. It seems this ill-thought-out raid doesn't even have a plan. I should have been surprised, but I wasn't.

I spoke to him in Welsh, 'Why are you still here, man?'

'Can't walk, you traitorous cunt,' he answered, spitting at me.

I took the bait, 'Gruffud was never my king, nor yours till recently.'

'Well, he is now, you shit.'

'I'm fucking English. What's your excuse?'

'You don't sound English. Any Welsh king is better than a two-faced mongrel like you.'

Weirdly, that stung. I don't have a drop of Welsh blood in my veins but I did spend my childhood in a Welsh settlement. Sort of Welsh anyway, outcasts, runaways and the like scratching a living on the shore of the Safearn Sea.

'This man here is a bishop. God's,' I couldn't think of the right word so I used an English one, 'emissary on earth. He wants to know where this is.'

'Ha, lost is he? I don't care if he's Satan's left bollock. I'm not going to tell you.'

I tell you the truth. I was upset about the losses we'd taken and I had no feeling left in me for this old fool. I got my little axe out from my belt and ran my thumb along the blade. It was bent and chipped slightly from hacking at that tree. I would need to attend to it when I got a moment. For now, it would serve its purpose.

He pulled himself up a little, his eyes wide, 'What are you going to do with that?'

'I'm going to start by cutting your toes off, and then I'll work my way up until you tell me what we want to know?'

'I don't care, can't walk anyway. Do you think I'd still be here if I could?'

I looked at one of Leofgar's thugs, 'Grab his left leg and hold his foot still.'

He pulled on the old man's leg. There was something wrong with it. It wouldn't straighten out.

'Hmm, still feel it though, can't you?' I said, and chopped his big toe off, and a bit of the one next to it for good measure.'

He yowled and then scrambled backwards until he was half leant up against the hovel's wall. 'You cut my fucking toe off! Jesu, fuck, fuck.'

'Told you I would.'

Leofgar was getting impatient, though he seemed to approve of my methods.

His man grabbed the old man's other leg. I raised the axe.

'I'll tell you. You are in Brecheniauic, named after a prince, Brychan. Lived here centuries ago when your Saxon ancestors were still living in mud huts in a Friesian bog and worshipping logs.'

I enjoyed this and translated it word for word. There was some truth in this according to my Step-Da. The Saxons had been pagans long after the Waelas had received Christ's teachings. I knew Leofgar wouldn't like to be reminded of it.

I chuckled to myself as I saw the annoyed look on his face. He'd been owned by an old Waelas peasant.

'What else does he know? Why has everyone left? How do they know before we get there?'

Stupid questions mostly. I asked them anyway.

The old man cackled as he tried to staunch the bleeding with mud from the street, 'Because you travel like snails. Plenty of time to pack up and hide in the hills.'

'I hear the trumpets,' I said to him in his own language.

'Then you know. No harm in telling you. The tribes are gathering. You're all going to die here.' He started cackling some more, and pointing from one man to another, 'You, you are going to die, and you, and you, you and you too.'

His cackling jibes stopped abruptly as Wolf hacked his sword into the man's neck.

I translated his words, we all exchanged looks as shivers ran down our spines.

Chapter Twenty-Six

Before nightfall we'd turned the town into a small fort by breaking down houses in the centre and using their timbers to barricade the streets. We split the night into two watches. I was in the first so I was sleeping fitfully as the sun began to rise.

'Get up, all of you, get up,' shouted Heofoc, as he kicked us all awake in turn. Help each other get your mail on.'

I buried my head under my mail and tried to wriggle it over my byrnie, 'Fuck's sake, Gyric, Ospak, give me a hand.' I found the arm holes and punched them up the sleeves, short ones on mine, thank Christ. Suddenly I felt tugging and finally got my head through the collar. 'Phew, thanks guys,' I said, and helped Ospak and Gyric don their own suits.

I was already sweating as I buckled on my sword belt, tucked in the axe and blackjack, grabbed my spear and shield, and headed towards Heofoc's bellows.

'Come on men. You're all too slow,'

We all looked wildly around for threats.

Heofoc lined up us housecarls. 'Alright lads, the enemy has surrounded us. They are all around the town. Lots of them, but they're keeping their distance. Now our task is to be Leofgar's body-guard. From this moment on that is your only job. Everything else is down to Athelnoth.'

With that Leofgar came out of a nearby house, pale but composed. 'Heofoc, where are they?'

'Any direction you choose, excellency,' said Heofoc.

This town was at a crossroads, streets ran off in five directions. Leofgar mounted his horse and headed back to the road we came in on. We formed up and followed. As we got to the end of the street Athelnoth's men pulled aside. We crammed into the gap and there they were. All along the edge of the cultivated ground was a line of Waelas warriors. Some on the rugged ponies they ride. Tough little beasts, not so different from our pack ponies but trained to be ridden. Most though were on foot. Very few wore mail of any kind, boiled leather caps and tunics sufficed. Some carried light shields, I guessed hide stretched over wickerwork. Only good for deflection but much lighter than our linden boards. The men with shields carried two of three throwing spears while other carried bows. A swarm of boys had slings dangling from their wrists. At the sight of the bishop howls of derision bridged the gap between them and us.

'It's like this on all sides, bishop,' said Heofoc to Leofgar. 'Maybe a couple of hundred of them.'

'Could we beat them?'

'In the open, with our flanks covered, perhaps. It takes a lot to break a shield wall.'

'As I thought. Let us challenge them to fight like men. Where's your Welsh speaker?'

'Sar, come here.'

'Here we go, I thought. Next thing, one of the priests and I are walking out between the two forces. I'd unbuckled my belt and left my spear and shield behind but kept my helmet on. The helmet with its nose guard would make me hard to recognise. There was a possibility that one of the Waelas might know who I am. The priest carried a processional cross. My mind flew back to the beach at Porloc when I'd carried the cross for the monk, Aethelric. That was when I was a wide-eyed boy still reeling from seeing my mother murdered and the destruction of everything I had ever known, with no idea what to expect next. It all felt so long ago.

The priest walked nervously by my side, 'Do you think they'll kill us?'

'They might, though they usually respect priests.'

'Oh yes, like they did at the Minster?'

I gave him a sideways look. He clearly knew who I was, 'I heard that was the Irish Vikings, not that I could be certain. You know, not being there.'

He took a deep breath and holding the cross up higher he began to pray. We kept walking until we were about halfway between the lines. A couple of arrows thudded into the ground as we came into range before I heard them commanded to hold fire.

We stopped and waited. A couple of riders raced along their front and out of sight. They soon returned with another rider on a larger horse. Even at a distance I could see a gold circlet in his hair. They drew up in front of us then two of the riders cantered towards us and as they got close lowered their spears to out chest level.

'Just hold steady,' I said to the priest, 'You'll be fine.'

And he was, but maybe I wasn't. The next moment both spear-points were prodding me in the chest.

'Hey,' I said in Welsh, 'I'm just the messenger.'

One of the riders turned his head and shouted back, 'It speaks like a human being. Says he's just the messenger.'

The man on the larger horse rode up. Well-dressed but not extravagantly so. Nice horse. Under thirty I guessed. Probably a local princeling of some kind.

'You speak Welsh,' he said, not really a question but I answered anyway.

'Yes, sir. I speak it well. I have a message from my bishop.'

'You're from the south by your accent.'

I looked up into his face, maybe he was nearer twenty than thirty. Dark haired, little curly. A neatly trimmed beard surrounded what appeared to be a genial smile. I found myself smiling back. A charmer, like Harold, probably a lady's man like him also. A charming smile covering a cunning mind perhaps. Like Harold's.

I chose not to answer that, 'My bishop challenges you and your troops to fight like men. Face to face, in the field.'

'I'm sure he does. Tell him Seisyll ap Cynan says he can ask again in a week's time.'

'Seisyll? Same name as Gruffud's grandfather. You related?'

'Not close enough to be a threat,' he laughed. 'To him, anyway. But to Bishop Leofgar, and you? Definitely,' he said, neatly turning the subject. 'Your King and mine agreed a truce. You've broken it.'

'Yes, not my choice. I'm Earl Harold's man. I'm sure he wouldn't have wanted this.'

He laughed again, 'Well, Harold's man. You are here, in Wales. Harold's desires won't change your fate.'

With that he turned his horse and spurred back to his own lines.

I took his message back to Leofgar.

'What does he mean, ask again in a week?' he said, angrily.

'I think he means just that. We've heard the trumpets in the hills. Gruffud is gathering his forces,' said Athelnoth.

'We should head back to England as fast as we can,' I said.

'No one asked you,' said Leofgar. 'For all we know you are on their side,' he added, spite and frustration clear in his tone.

Fuck him, I thought, I'm going to have my say, 'We should free the ponies, then fight our way back through the valley moving as fast as we can. The forces we know about are all up here. Once through we should jettison our shields, maybe even our war spears, and march straight for Hereford.'

'That's madness,' said Athelnoth. 'What would we eat?'

'It's easy enough to go a couple of days without food, and this is Wales, there's water everywhere. We should run.'

'We'd be disgraced,' said Leofgar, uncertainly.

'Better disgraced than dead,' I said.

'How would we fight them if we are attacked,' said Heofoc.

'We still have our mail. We're all trained swordsmen.'

'No shields against arrows, slingshots and throwing spears,' said Heofoc.

'Difficult, true, but if we could move fast enough, we might not have to fight at all. Or at least only against small war bands.'

'I'm not sure about that. Our shield wall is the best defence,' said Athelnoth.

I opened my mouth to speak further. Heofoc butted in, 'We've heard you Sar, now return to your troop.'

I did as I was told.

Not long after this we were formed back up into a marching column. Thicker this time, almost square shaped as the open ground allowed us. We didn't head back as I'd wish but marched westward. To prove a point I supposed, Leofgar ordered the town burnt. Once again, our departure was signalled by the crackling of burning buildings and the acrid smell of smouldering thatch. Our wounded were slung over the pony's backs. The remaining priests tried to support them. We were moving more slowly now, tired men, tired ponies all of us hungry as our shrinking provisions meant shortened rations. Weirdly not one arrow or slingshot pursued us as the Waelas forces melted away in front of us.

'If Leofgar didn't know where we were, how does he know where we are going?' I said, talking out of the side of my mouth to Gyric.

'No idea, perhaps he's seeking another way home. Don't think any of us want to fight our way back through that valley.'

'There was a track heading south east from that last town. Why didn't we try that? At least it was back towards England.'

Gyric sighed wearily, 'Does it matter Sar? Things are as they are.'

One of the wounded men kept slipping down the pony he was tied to so as we came to another wooded hill it was decided we'd make him a stretcher from some cut boughs and a horse blanket. Poor fellow looked done in and was starting to get feverish. We all knew he was going to die and so did he. As we marched on, we could hear his stifled sobs under the words of the priest's prayers.

We followed two more bends in the river by which time another of the wounded men was becoming delirious. Some of us warriors looked at each other knowing that the kindest thing to do would be to help them into the next world. We also knew that no priest would allow that. For them that would be a great sin.

Then we came upon a tributary river joining the one we were following. The recent rains had turned them into torrents. There was no way to go, other than north or back the way we'd come, without trying to wade through the wild waters. What there was though, were banks and several stone walls. We marched in amongst them and it became clear that we were in the remains of an old Roman fort. After hacking down the hawthorns that were growing in and around these walls and using them to block the collapsed gatehouses and other gaps in the surrounding earth banks, we laid down the wounded and settled while our leaders discussed what to do next.

The day dragged on as we sat under sullen cloudy skies. After some heated discussion it was decided to slaughter one of the ponies and enough dead wood was gathered to make cooking fires under our cauldrons. The pony meat was thrown into boil with some of the remaining barley and the little salt we still carried.

'I don't like this. Eating horsemeat is forbidden. It's wrong. It can only bring us more misfortune,' complained Ospak.

'You'd rather go hungry?' said Heofoc, 'You're soldiers. You'll eat what you're given.'

'Besides,' said Wulfgeat, 'the priests have blessed it. Said something about necessary exemptions.'

'Ha' I laughed sardonically, 'A priest can always find a way to avoid going hungry.'

'You saved a few of them from that problem, didn't you?' came a voice from a group of Athelnoth's men around another fire.

I stood up, furious, 'I was proven innocent. You take that back. We're only here because you fuckers ran from the Waelas on your horses.'

Next thing I knew me and that man were wrestling on the ground while a small brawl raged around us as some of Harold's housecarls fought with Athelnoth's men. This fight was nasty but short as Heofoc waded in clubbing us randomly with a chunky branch for the firewood pile.

'For God's sake. Keep your anger for the Waelas. Who's in the middle of this?'

As the brawlers drew apart that left me and the other man on the ground.

Heofoc swiped me hard across the back then kicked me a couple of times as I tried to get up. 'You, of course, now get to your meal before I fucking kill you. You'll be on the picket tonight.' He glared around at us, 'If any of you has a blade in your hand I will hang you now.'

Luckily no one did. As we drew apart there were a few eating knives lying about on the floor so, as no one was bleeding, Heofoc turned his back as their owners grabbed them up. We all returned to our meals shamefaced and sullen.

'You shouldn't have done that, Sar,' said Gyric, 'we need to stay united.'

'Yes, yes, I know.'

Then Heofoc came back, 'We're staying here to take care of the wounded. There's a well here, enough dead wood to make fires. Two out of every ten of you will be on the banks as pickets and look outs. I'm guessing that when this was still a fort, God knows how long ago, the scrubby woodland you can see now would have been cut back, so use your ears as well as your eyes.'

Gyric and I looked at each other, 'to look after the wounded?' I said.

'More like wait for them to die,' said he.

We both shuddered, remembering the aftermath of the battle in Alba.

'Yes, and that could take some time.' I said.

'If the Waelas give us that,' he answered.

Almost as if Gyric had made a signal, a small volley of arrows plummeted into the camp. They stuck practically upright into the ground, startling the ponies and lightly wounding another priest.

'Christ's blood, they must be firing straight up above us,' Ospak shouted.

'All of you to the wall and line up behind it.'

We grabbed up our shields and war spears and did as we were ordered. From the western side of the oblong, we could here shouts that they'd seen movement. By now the clearing skies had revealed a lowering sun into which we all squinted.

'Eyes forward,' said Heofoc.

As we obeyed, we could hear Athelnoth's voice ordering his men to stay at their posts. 'No, you can't go after them. Have you learned nothing?'

Some of us moved the wounded against the walls of the roofless buildings and leant their shields over them as best we could. It felt like a small mercy, most of them were feverish now. The priest prayers and feeble ministrations were of little help. Then we heard screams from the western wall. I guessed what had happened. Angry or excited, some men had climbed the bank lighting themselves up in the sun's rays. Easy targets.

Sure enough, not long after that three wounded men were brought into the buildings with five shields. So, two more were dead. Two of the wounded had arrows in their legs. I knew that the arrows would have their flights cut off and then be hammered on through the leg. Painful. You can't pull out a barbed arrow. The third must have dropped his shield. An arrow was stuck in his guts, right through his mail. He was due to die a horrible death. I could see in his eyes that he knew this.

With a shock I realised that this was the man I had fought with only a short while before.

'I'm sorry,' I said, 'I should not have accused you of cowardice.'

He spoke to me through gritted teeth, 'Hardly matters now, does it?'

With that beads of sweat burst out across his forehead and he bent double over the arrow

'Priest, come here. Help this man,' I shouted.

He reached up and grabbed my arm, 'You know I am beyond earthly help. That priest might confess me but I want something from you.'

'Yes, anything,' I said, my guilt speaking.

'When it gets too dark to see clearly. Come and finish me off.'

Tears sprang to my eyes. I patted him on the shoulder and as he began to writhe again, I nodded.

Later that night, just before I was due for guard duty, I snuck in through the twilight of a clear summer's night to find him deep in the shadows of a wall. He was delirious by now, tossing and turning while screaming at visions. No shield lay over him, so I took out my eating knife, lay across him, and, punching it through his mail, I searched for his heart. It was quick, he gurgled something softly, a woman's name I think, then he quieted and his feverish motions stopped. I scanned the room to check that I hadn't been seen, then slowly stood up and left.

I felt sad and weary as I went to my post. Twice now I had mercy killed one of my own countrymen in the space of a few months. I knew a lot of my companions would not have done this seeing it as murder. For me it felt right but it also felt so very, very wrong.

While I peered over the earth bank, which had a disintegrating stone wall along its ridge, a couple more volleys of arrows descended into the fort. This time though, our precautions worked. They either thudded into shields or mostly into the bare tussocky ground.

Even when they were firing, I could see no movement to the front of me. I didn't think they'd actually attack. I knew, and they must have known, that the moment they topped that bank they'd receive a war spear in the groin or gut. I reckoned that, apart from the few bowmen, the rest of them were enjoying a quiet night's sleep while I and the other pickets leant on our spears desperately trying to keep our tired eyes open.

I heard a noise behind me and turned and said, 'Ah thank God, I really need to sleep,' only to find a spear point at my throat. The centre man of a group of three, was on the other end of the spear. I could tell by their shields they were Leofgar's men.

The man with the spear against my throat spoke, 'By the way you speak you are the translator that gave us all that trouble.'

I didn't deny it, 'Wolf? Is that you?'

'No noise mind, not a fucking peep,' said one of his companions.

I relaxed a little, they hadn't sought me out then. If they'd been out to kill me, they'd have stabbed me in the back. Carrying my shield and spear meant I could not make hand gestures so I whispered. 'I'll keep quiet as long as you're not looking for a fight.'

Wolf, I'm certain that was who it was from his voice, then said, 'No we don't want a fight. We just want to get out from here.'

'Aren't you sworn to protect Leofgar?' I whispered back.

'Yes, but we signed up for parading about Hereford, not this. As to this we thought we'd just march around, steal some stuff, maybe a bit of legal raping, then back to the Minster with some money and some stories for the pub.'

'So, what changed?'

'You know yourself. You've made it clear you think this is a fool's errand and it looks like you were right. Now, stay silent and let us pass.'

So, they're deserting I thought. Well, I was told to guard the fort from people trying to get in, not seeking to get out. I silently stood aside and watched them climb over the bank. I didn't wish them luck.

Chapter Twenty-Seven

I was relieved soon afterwards and breakfasted on cold boiled pony and water. The water tasted good. Then I collapsed into a deep dreamless sleep under my shield. I was woken roughly by a boot in my ribs.

'You need to get up. The bishop wants you now.' It was one of Leofgar's remaining men.

'Fucking hell,' I said, 'What's going on?'

'You'll see soon enough. Come on.'

I got up, put on my helmet, and twisted about until my mail shook itself back into shape on my body. I noticed it was already beginning to rust, it badly needed burnishing and greasing. I then buckled on my sword belt and tried to gather my scattered wits. Then I grabbed my shield and spear and followed the man to the southern side of the encampment.

'Ah, there you are,' said Heofoc as he hustled me towards the bank through groups of our soldiers all trying to get a view of what was happening.

When I got to the bank, I could see a small bush attached to a spear waving above the track we had followed into the fort. The bush on a pole was widely understood as a sign of truce.

Under the bush stood Seisyll and an older burly man I had seen before, just out of the range you could throw a light spear.

'That's one of Gruffud's brothers,' I said to Heofoc.

'Who is it? You've seen him before,' this was Athelnoth who was stood beside Leofgar to my right.

'Yes, I'm pretty certain it's one of Gruffud's brothers, or perhaps half-brother. I don't know for sure.'

'A powerful man, then. Close to the throne,' said Leofgar, 'A man I could talk to as an equal.'

'If you say so,' I answered, looking at Leofgar. My God, he had pulled his vestments over his mail. They were so stretched he looked like a fat man in a too small shirt. As he put on his mitre and one of his priests passed him his crozier, I realised that at least one of our ponies had been carrying Leofgar's ornamental trappings.

The same priest who had walked out with me before spoke to me, 'Drop your shield and spear and come with me.'

I leant my weapons against the bank and joined the priest as he climbed to the top. I tensed, for a moment expecting to receive a flight of arrows. It didn't come. I looked at the priest, clearly, he'd had the same thought, he was shaking like an aspen.

'Repeat what I'm about to say,' he said.

I nodded

'I am here representing the Leofgar Bishop of Hereford. Who are you, and who do you represent?'

As he spoke a line of men appeared all along our southern front. Some on ponies but most on foot. All of them were armed. Just behind the two leaders was a group of better armed men, a few mailed and helmeted like ourselves. Some of the Waelas nobility I guessed. As they appeared shouts arose from all sides. We were once again surrounded.

As I repeated the priest's words in Welsh the burly man stepped forward. 'You can tell your bishop that my name doesn't matter. He won't need it in hell.'

When I translated his words the priest blanched, just the thought of a bishop in hell shocked him. 'Go on,' I said, 'Tell your master.'

He did so. Leofgar leant forward as another of his priests placed his mitre on his head, then, with the man's assistance, he climbed the bank next to me.

I looked at him, a bit surprised at this act of courage. As he drew himself up I realised that he believed his holy robes would protect him. There may have been some truth in this.

'What do you want me to say?'

'Offer them the opportunity to fight like men, like you did before.'

'You're not asking them to fight like men. You are asking them to fight like Englishmen.'

'You are not here for your opinion. Now do as I ask,' said Leofgar sharply.

I shouted Leofgar's pointless offer across the open space then I translated the answer back to Leofgar.

'He says Seisyll told you to ask again in a week. It's only been a day. Meanwhile I have another message for you.'

Leofgar was about to say something when there was a noisy tumult among the Waelas as a naked man, hands bound, was brought to the burly war leader.

'By Cuthbert's bones, that's Wolf,' came a voice from behind me.

'How? Did they come into our camp and snatch him up,' came another.

'Not just him, though, is it? What about the other two who disappeared in the night?'

I guessed this was Leofgar's remaining two thugs. I decided to keep what I knew to myself. Let them wonder.

The burly man shouted, 'He tells us he's one of your men, Bishop. We found him and two others sneaking through the bushes. Once we caught them, they said they were trying to join us. Even your own men are deserting you, Bishop of the blighted Hereford.'

As I translated these words to Leofgar, the burly man clutched Wolf's hair in his left fist and forced him to his knees.

'We've decided to honour him by treating him like an English Aetheling,' he shouted as he drew a knife from his belt. 'Translate my words traitor, and be sure, we have a worse fate for you.'

I shuddered and did as he asked. The burly man waited then, once I had finished, with two quick stabs he blinded the sobbing Wolf in both eyes.

'Is that not how your King's elder brother was treated,' he shouted as the shock rippled through our ranks. 'Left to die on a beach, wasn't he? Well, we are kinder than that. We are going to leave him in the beauty of our wonderful country.' Then watching as Wolf screamed and writhed in agony, he cut the ties binding Wolf's hands and shouted, 'But, oh dear, he can't see it can he, Bishop?'

He then kicked Wolf to his feet and pushed him away. Wolf staggered about his hands before him pleading for help. He was ignored. Even in his pain he must have known that a deserter had nowhere to go.

Leofgar, visibly shaken, shouted that the man would go to hell and burn for eternity. I translated. The man laughed loudly, 'But long after you, truce breaker, long after you.'

With that he turned on his heels and vanished among his men. Then the enemy withdrew some distance and lit campfires on every side. Wolf continued to stagger around, his hands either in front of him or clutching at his sightless eye sockets. He pleaded for help. He got none.

After this Leofgar became very keen to have Harold's house-carls in close attendance, which was, after all, why we'd been left in Hereford. This meant we could hear Athelnoth, Leofgar, Heofoc and the priests arguing about what to do next. Go north, go back, leave the wounded, stay here until they died, and so on. They argued through the day while the odd flight of arrows descended into the camp keeping us all alert and nervous. We used the last of the firewood to boil more horseflesh, now without barley or salt.

While we ate, I heard Ospak asking Wulfgeat about the way Wolf had been blinded.

'You don't know?' said Wulfgeat, 'Our King's brother was left to die after being blinded during the war with Harold Harefoot.'

'Yes, the King always thought Godwin was responsible, if not for blinding him but for handing him over,' added Gyric.

'Yes,' said Heofoc, suddenly appearing among us, 'and it's something we don't talk about either. Your lord being Godwin's son. And that is an order.'

'Christ,' said Ospak, 'Wish I hadn't asked.'

We stayed there another day and a night, plagued occasionally by further arrows while the number of campfires around us increased. We were now chewing on raw meat while at least two men had the shits. If the bloody flux entered the camp we'd be in even more trouble. Another uneasy night followed then, just before dawn, we were formed up into a column, took down the thorn barricades and marched out.

'They'll have to fight us or let us pass. You'll be pleased to know, lads, that we are heading home,' Heofoc said to us before we left. Leofgar and Athelnoth still rode their horses while the bannerman's had been lost to a stray arrow and the cooking pot. The severely wounded that still survived were being carried on stretchers. This meant we could only move as fast as two stretcher bearers staggering along on a muddy track.

The Waelas soon saw what we were doing and those in front of us dismantled their camps and gave way before our levelled spears. They shouted and jeered at us from a few yards away, confident that they could run before we could get to them. This was humiliating. Then every time the column stretched or broke around trees or rocks, they'd shower us with arrows and slingshots, causing more casualties. Wounds rather than deaths, which hampered our progress all the more. Then as we entered Brecheniauice the Waelas all disappeared.

We stopped again while our leaders discussed whether to take a broader trackway to the south-east. For fear it would lead us further into the mountains it was decided to face the devil we knew. None of us really wanted to face that valley again and at last it was decided to abandon any wounded unable to walk. Being clustered around Leofgar and none of the more severely wounded being our housecarls, I don't know their fate. I hoped someone would be merciful enough to end their days before the Waelas found them. We marched out to the north-east even more subdued than we had been when we arrived.

As we marched into the valley we were ambushed repeatedly. There were no large trees felled this time but we met small barricades from which we would be fired upon while more arrows flew in from the sides. Hunkered down behind our shields we had to force our way through. Even Leofgar couldn't ride here. Up on his horse he made a clear target and the panicked beasts had to be led along the track. As we were clustered around the bishop and his banner many of the arrows flew our way. With so many arrows stuck in our shields they got more and more unwieldy. Our progress was slow and men began to drop. Now, we just forged on. If you went down, you stayed behind. With wild whoops the Waelas finished them off.

In the end we could not manage the horses and ponies so we stabbed them in the throats and left them bleeding out on the track. The priests, unmailed and shield less, all went down before we broke out from the woods. We were close to panic. Heofoc and Athelnoth somehow kept us all united. If we'd broken, we'd all have perished.

As we came into clearer ground the attacks ceased and for a few blissful miles we were left in peace. What could have been a morning's march took most of the day. By the time we reached Y Clas everyone was wide eyed with the horror we'd been through while our limbs trembled with exhaustion. We could not march any further. Totally spent and demoralised we forded the river and camped in the burnt ruins of the town. Somehow the bannerman, clearly a stalwart soul, had kept the heavily embroidered piece still hanging from its crossbar aloft the whole day. The gold wire cross on its blue background with the silver wire stars stitched into its borders remained a thing of beauty. As we gathered beneath it, I took a hurried count, there were less than sixty of us left and many of them limped or bled. All those men dead and we'd not directly fought with a single one of our enemies.

It was very close to midsummer by now and the nights were short. I wasn't on guard duty that night but still got little sleep. My aching and battered body could not find any comfort on the wet ground or in the ashes of the houses. Every time I began to doze the sound of trumpets would awaken me. I could feel my mother trying to come to me in my sleep, then I'd be woken again. I didn't need her to tell me that I was up shit creek.

Chapter Twenty-Eight

We were paraded before dawn. Some of us were sick, wounded or both. All of us were still well armed but all of us were tired and hungry.

'Do you think we should have carried on through the night?' I said to Gyric.

'And fight through another wood?'

He was right. I wasn't sure I could have marched another step. Our column would have broken up.

'To go back the way we came would mean fording the river with the enemy on the other bank,' I said.

'Yes, and I don't expect that war leader will behave like Byrhtnoth and let us across,' said Wulfgeat.

I said 'Who?'

'Battle of Maldon, you must have heard the songs,' said Ospak.

'Nah,' I said, 'What about it?'

'Earldoman Byrhtnoth let the Danes across the water to fight honourably. Then his force was defeated.'

'Pretty stupid, then,' I said, 'Never heard the Danes were so honourable anyway.'

There were sharp intakes of breath all round. Now I'd managed to offend everyone. Those who were all English would revere the valiant losers while the Danes and half Danes among us, like Gyric, would feel insulted. What was it Gyric said? Count to ten. Too late now. In for a penny in for a mancus.

'No Waelas would be that dumb,' I added.

Now there were angry mutterings but as it was among the house-carls they were used to me by now. They'd settle the score later.

We were marched to the ford and, as expected, there was a massive force on the opposite bank. Our leaders conferred again and we were marched alongside the river to where a bend encircled us on three sides. Behind us was a marshy bank dropping into the river, thick with alders hanging into the waters below, their branches heavy with weed and debris that had floated down in the recent rains. Inside the bend was a fallow field of scrubby grass and grazed off crops. Firm enough and level. We formed up along the fourth side. We were our own fortress now, behind our wall of shields.

Forty men were allotted to the front row. One of them was me. We were on the left flank under Leofgar's banner while the centre and right were covered by Athelnoth's men. Our section, being heavily influenced by Harold's Danish heritage, had the three remaining axemen. They, for now, stood in the second row along with the shaky and wounded. I was standing with Wulfgeat to my left, Ospak on my right, Gyric stood behind and between Ospak and I. Teothic too was behind us, he had a nasty gash in his face and an arrow had partially penetrated the mail on his sword arm. He could barely lift it above shoulder height.

We heard the Waelas cross the ford to our right while another huge force assembled before us hollering and jeering. A group of horsemen pushed their way through. Two of them we'd seen before. Another was the brother I'd seen in Caerleon. Leading them was the grizzled old bastard, Gruffud, the first king of all Wales.

'That's the King of the Waelas,' I said, rather pointlessly.

Gruffud began to speak in his own language. His words were then translated by another man I'd seen before, Rhys Sais of Faelor. A border lord on the Welsh side from up by the Deva River, wherever that was. His lands had been added to extensively by the terms of the truce.

'You, the Bishop of Hereford, broke your king's truce. I, the King of all the Cymry and he agreed on peace. Now, you, a churchman who should believe in peace, have forced war back upon our lands. You were impatient to fight. You were told a week. We have decided to compromise. Today is your day. If you wish to surrender, I will only take the heads of Bishop Leofgar and the Reeve Athelnoth. The rest of you will be allowed to live as slaves for the rest of your days,' Rhys shouted, repeating Gruffud's words.

There was a pause to let his words sink in. Then Rhys cried out again, 'If you don't, you will all die here today or be enslaved at our mercy.'

We, the housecarls, all reacted with defiance by shouting Harold's war cry, 'Holy Cross, Holy Cross.' Athelnoth's men bellowed out theirs.

I looked at the massive force arrayed against us and knew that this was the day we died. I thought of Inga and Ymma, even Godric, and tears rolled down my face. I heard a voice from behind me, it was Gyric.

'You know Sar. You never asked my wife's name,' he said.

'I didn't, did I?' I said, 'I'm sorry.'

'I don't think I'll see her again,' he said, 'her name is Mildrith. If you survive this tell her my last thoughts were of her.'

I thought of Ymma and my little girl, our new home, and the chance of happiness it stood for. I thought of Gyric and the smile on his face when he told me he was married. I thought of Gytha's plan to promote Leofgar somewhere where he could do no harm. Well, that worked out well, didn't it? At first, I felt dreadfully sad, then I felt furious.

As we weren't being attacked at that moment, I turned to him and whispered, 'If we are still standing when the shield wall breaks, fight backwards to the bank and slide out of sight. I have an idea. I don't want to die for Leofgar's idiotic fucking vanity.'

'Our duty is to protect him. Those are our orders. I won't be disgraced.'

'Alright, 'I said, impatiently, 'if Leofgar has fallen, do as I said.'

The fight didn't start for some time. Despite our hunger and weariness, we were still a formidable force for our, mostly lightly armed, foe to assault. We were subjected to volleys of arrows and slingshots making our already splintering shields unwieldy. We stood spears butts on the floor with their points in the sky as we weathered the storm. A couple of men received arrows in their feet or cuts from them glancing off their shins. A few more were unlucky enough to have an arrow pass between their shield rim and the brow of their helmet and get struck in an eye or cheek. Ospak was swearing to himself, getting louder and louder while Gyric muttered prayers. I could hear Heofoc marching about behind us.

'Steady lads, this is what you trained for. We're not done yet. And if we are, we'll take a lot of them with us,' he shouted. 'Hold fast and look out for the man on each side of you.'

The Waelas got closer and threw a volley of spears at us. We hunkered down and the front row levelled their war spears. A spear thudded into my shield. It stuck for a moment then dropped to the ground. I kicked it away a piece. I didn't want that underfoot. Another flew by my ear. I heard Teothic cry out.

'I've got it,' he said, placing his war spear on the ground and running for the Welsh spear, he threw it back.

I saw it strike a Waelas man right in his chest. At last, we'd done some damage. Our enemy was steeling themselves to attack. They could have waited longer and worn us all out for a couple more days. I'm guessing the strident voices of the hotheads and glory seekers had finally won over the more cautious types. We stayed silent, let them come.

The clamour from their side rose to a crescendo. Blades were beaten on shields, the names of saints were bellowed out and the trumpets' shrill cries rose to an even higher pitch. Then with a roar they were upon us.

Weary we might have been but we were ready for this. This is what every free born Englishman trained for. The spear and the shield. The companion on each side. Our faith in the shield wall.

And for that first attack that faith was merited. We thrust, we stabbed, we warded off all blows, as they tried to fight their way past our spear points. Their back rows pushed their front rows onto our spears. Our front rows thrust forward. Our second row thrust downward. The noise was shattering. I pushed my spear into one man and in the corner of my eye saw another come between Ospak's spear and my own. Then I heard Gyric yell in my ear.

'Open.'

Ospak and I stepped apart and Gyric hacked down with his axe onto that man's head. It split to his chin and he fell to the ground. Gyric wrenched his axe from out of the man's skull and swung it into the leg of another man. He was wide eyed and red faced, already battle crazy.

I shouted as loud as I could, 'Step back, Gyric step back.'

It's not like I had a hand free to pull him back but thankfully he heard me. He made one more swing and missed his target. Recovering himself he stepped back and Ospak and I closed together. The enemy were beyond our spear points. Their ferocity spent for the moment they fell back. Our shield wall had held.

In front of us was a row of dead and wounded men. I stepped forward and pushed my spear point into the throat of one screaming man. He was wearing a boiled leather breastplate and his arms were encased in rawhide. One of them was bent awkwardly, broken bones white through the shattered flesh. A club lay on the floor beside him.

'Well done lads, well done. You, and you, get to the river and fill the flasks,' said Heofoc.

I suddenly realised how thirsty I was. I had my own leather flask slung across my chest. With a start I realised it was empty, gashed open by a blade I hadn't even seen. I turned to find Teothic passing me his own.

I drank deeply, 'God, thanks. I needed that.'

He was grinning but his eyes were wide and staring.

'You're alright, Teothic, you're going to be fine,' I said gently. 'Now go to the river and fill that up.'

'But hurry yourself man,' shouted Heofoc. 'You'll be needed again before long.'

He was wrong there. We were made to wait. While we waited the Gruffud organised his troops. Our leader, Leofgar, made encouraging noises though, by his ashen features, we could see that he was clearly shaken. There was no organising for him to do, so he, still dressed in his vestments, waved his crozier about, and marched up and down behind us with his one remaining henchman who now carried his banner. It would have been better if they'd have taken up a spear each and joined the front rank.

I watched as Gruffud brought together a group of his better armoured men. Possibly fifteen of them with mail shirts, wooden shields, and metal helmets. Even from this distance I could see he'd set up a group of younger men behind them. They each carried throwing spears. I knew what was to come. He then positioned them all opposite where Athelnoth's men and our own joined. Now this was clever.

I looked up to see the tip of my spear trembling in the air. Puzzled, I followed the shaft down to my hand. It was clenched so tightly around the shaft that my knuckles had gone white. I breathed slowly in and out and let my hands relax. They'd grip hard enough when the time came.

And come it did. This time there was only a flurry of arrows. I supposed they'd already used most of them. Then they advanced towards us. Slowly this time. Then the heavily armed men attacked after the men behind them first threw a tight volley of spears. Our men were either handicapped by spears in their shields or were confused by orders coming from either side of their rear. The line fell into disorder just as the mailed Waelas came upon them.

A few of the mailed warriors had long spears with which they engaged our men, distracting them enough to allow their fellows to hack at spear shafts of the men in front. Our side fought back hard. Men went down on either side. In front of us the Waelas kept their distance, shouting abuse and throwing the odd spear while boys darted in and out of their ranks slingshotting stones at us. I'm trying to watch them while my eyes kept flitting to my right to see what was going on. There was a pause, while everyone caught their breath, then the line stretched and gaps appeared in our ranks. The men in front of us attacked, we held them back briefly then the ranks to our right broke. Our shield wall was breached, overwhelmed by the sheer numbers of our foe. With men fighting in small groups or singly all around my heavy war spear was a burden rather than a help. I threw it blindly towards a group of Waelas and drew my sword.

I found Gyric was still with me, Ospak too. Gyric's axe was swiping in all directions blood flying from its blade. There was a groan as Leofgar's banner fell. In amongst the chaos, I caught a glimpse of Wulfgeat, true to his heritage, defending the bishop. Who, to be fair to him, was fighting manfully using his crozier like a pole-axe until a spear was pushed into his back. Wulfgeat killed the man holding it then was bludgeoned from behind before falling under a swarm of assailants.

I heard Teothic cry out as he tried to lift his arm to fend off an arrow. I turned to see him struck in the throat. I heard Heofoc bellowing defiant curses which abruptly ended. I lashed about me with my sword and stepped slowly backwards towards the bank. My shield had become useless, stuck with a spear, and beginning to shatter. I let it go.

'Are you with me Gyric,' I yelled, 'Leofgar is down.'

He grunted as he fought. There's no fighting man to man in this situation. If you're sure the thing in front of you isn't your own man you slash at it. Ospak lost all control and rushed out in front of Gyric and I and was instantly set upon by a screaming horde.

'Now, Gyric, now.'

I stepped backwards and slid out of sight, catching myself a nasty blow on an alder root. Dropping my sword, I pulled myself back up to the edge and grabbing Gyric's foot I pulled him over the edge of the bank. He crashed down beside me dropping his axe as he fell.

'Come,' I said as I crept down into the water among the alders draped over the river. 'Come on.'

He followed me in. I could see that part of him did not want to stop fighting. To die on his feet. A hero.

'No one will know Gyric, you can die as bravely as you like but no one will sing songs for you. Come.'

He shook himself and looked at his blood-spattered body and his empty hands.

'My axe,' he said, looking dazed, 'I must get my axe.'

I sheathed my sword and took off its belt. 'Leave it. It can only get you killed. We must get deeper into the water. Under the branches.'

Luckily, it being summer, the leaves were thick upon the boughs. So thick it was almost dark.

'Gyric,' I shouted, he'd started to head back up the bank, 'Leave your axe. You won't be needing it. Now, help me.'

He did as he was told. I took off my helmet and threw it in the river and messed up my hair. 'Help me get this mail off,' I said.

Gyric looked puzzled.

'Just do it,' I said urgently as the water seeped into my clothes. 'Now take off your helmet and help me.'

I leant forward as he pulled the mail over my head. Then I hacked away at the leather laces of my byrnie. I realised I was bleeding from a gash on my forearm and that I had been stabbed in my thigh. Not deep, but it was starting to feel sore. I knew how my body ached that I was covered in bruises that would stiffen later. Gyric looked unharmed. A miracle, but it wouldn't do. I smeared my blood into his hair, he needed to look wounded. Before I let my mail sink into the water, I tore off the leather trim from around its bottom edge.

'Now, Gyric, we wait.'

By now the tumult above us had ceased. All our comrades must be dead or taken. We crouched in the river covered by the trees while shapes occasionally moved along the top of the bank. Soon afterwards we could hear sounds of celebration. I crept up the bank and peered over the edge. It was a macabre sight, watching the gleeful victors wrestling off the accoutrements of the dead.

'We'll have to wait further,' I said to Gyric, my teeth chattering. Thank the saints its summertime I thought as I slid back into the water until only my face was showing. We lay there for a time until the sun past the zenith. My stomach was churning with hunger and I was so tired that I was struggling to stay awake. I looked over at Gyric.

'You alright?' I whispered.

He nodded, 'Hungry, cold, very wet. I suppose you have a plan.'

'I do. Look I don't think we can just hope to sneak our way back. I have an idea. Not sure you're going to like it.'

I told him. He didn't.

Chapter Twenty-Nine

We climbed out of the water once the shouting above us had calmed down. I didn't want any man, still battle-crazed, cutting Gyric, now my captive, into pieces. We wrapped his sword belt and the sword his father had given him in my byrnie and buried it in a scooped out hollow under the bank.

I crept up the bank and peered over the edge. The field was a lot quieter now. There were still a few men, and some women, stripping the bodies of the dead and collecting fallen weapons. Once Gyric got to the top I tied his hands in front of him with the leather strip.

We'd decided that he should limp and stagger so as to look injured, maybe still stunned from an earlier blow. From now on I would only speak Welsh. We were both shivering from our long immersion in the water.

'Hey,' I shouted to a nearby scavenger, 'Look what I found in the water. Got totally soaked getting the fucker out.'

The man looked up, 'You might have found the only survivor. You keeping him?'

'Yeah, could really use a strong slave where I live. Might sell him, though. We'll see.'

As I spoke, I cuffed Gyric across the head to look convincing. If we were the only survivor, in a way, that would be good for us. Last thing I needed was to be recognised and called out.

'Any men from the south camped near here friend?' I said, knowing my accent would give away my roots.

He pointed, 'Over there somewhere past the ford I think.'

I picked up a broken spear and prodded Gyric along in front of me and headed off in the direction the man had pointed. Once I'd gone far enough, I veered off. The last thing I wanted was to meet other southerners. Only last year I'd been fighting against them with the Irish and although most of the time my hair was stained black, I didn't want to take any chances. I saw the smoke of a nearby fire. We cautiously headed that way past a woman keening over a body in the grass. Many Waelas had died that day. Our defeat had come at a cost, even after their tactics of wearing us down.

She saw Gyric and, leaping to her feet, started slapping his face and kicking his shins.

'You, English scum, you killed my man,' she both screamed and sobbed at the same time. 'No one asked you to come into our land burning and killing.'

I didn't fail to notice the irony of this but now I needed her to stop before she encouraged any vengeful actions from nearby warriors. I pushed Gyric to his knees and threw my arms around her.

She went limp and sobbed against my chest. This is the side of war no soldier really wants to deal with. I let her cry, then reassured her that I would make my captive's life a living hell until he died. She quieted. I held her out at arms-length,

'Now, go grieve your man. There will be others grieving with you both here and in the land of the Angles.'

I don't think my words helped much but she returned to the dead man and started pulling him about, scolding him for abandoning her. Grief takes many forms.

Crows were already on the field, picking at the dead bodies, while kites, ravens and buzzards circled above. The Waelas would pick up the bodies of their dead while all my companions would be left to the scavenging beasts of the air and the night.

Back in Y Clas I saw a large group of men and a few women sat around a fire on the track to the well. I prodded Gyric in front of me.

'Hey, fellas, look what I found lying in the river,' I shouted merrily.

A lot of faces turned my way, suspicion in their eyes.

One of them spoke, a heavyset man with bushy eyebrows, 'You're not one of us. Where's your own people?'

I laughed, 'Don't know, my friend. I saw this lad here. I prodded Gyric with the spear point, 'lying face down in the river. Had to drag him out from under the alders. Got fucking soaked. Probably saved his life. Thought he was dead. I was trying to drag his mail off when he started spluttering.'

The man stared at me longer. I knew from his first answer that he didn't come from the south. The Waelas have fought each other for so long that everyone is an enemy until you know otherwise.

'Oh, my people. I guess I was so long in the river they'd moved on by the time I got this sad fuck up the bank. Hey, I'm bloody wet and hungry, thirsty too. Tell you what. Give me a space by your fire, some food and drink and I'll give you his mail shirt. Oh, and a bit of rope as well would be handy.'

The man had some authority within this group and, on his signal, we were let in.

'You going to let him sit by the fire too,' said another of the band.

'Yeah, suppose so, that's why I need the rope. Do we have a bargain? I need a couple of you to watch him while I untie his hands and we get that shirt off his back.'

I pushed Gyric roughly to the ground.

'Get off me you bastard,' he said.

I looked around, 'Any of you hear that? Don't know what he said but it didn't sound friendly.'

There was some laughter. I then punched Gyric, hard, in the face. His nose spurted blood. There was more laughter, mocking this time.

'Hey, be careful there. You'll spoil his good looks.'

I laughed too. 'He doesn't need to be pretty to work my land,' I said, and hit him again.

Gyric glared at me, furious. Now, I felt, we both looked the part. He was roughly manhandled as his mail was pulled off him. Then I retied his hands with the leather trim I'd used before.

'Where's his sword belt?' said the heavyset man.

'Oh, that's what I'm wearing. I'm keeping this. Look, the sheath is very plain but the sword is a fine one.' I answered, there was no way I was losing Oslaf's sword. 'Right, does anyone have some rope.'

One of the women got up and walked over to a couple of pack ponies tethered behind their camp and returned with a couple of yards of rope. I cut a short length off and used it to hobble Gyric's ankles. I used the rest to put a loop around Gyric's neck with a long tail I could keep in my hand. Then my guts audibly growled.

'Well, that's him sorted out. Now let me sit close to the fire while you feed us.'

There was some muttering and for a moment I thought I was about to be double-crossed.

'Come on fellas. We're all on the same side now.'

Apart from a pair of bodies laid out near the ponies they were all satisfied by their victory. Shortly after that I was eating and drinking and laughing along with them. I managed to feed Gyric too on the basis that he was no good to me dead.

Everyone mellowed after we'd eaten and drank and people started moving from one campsite to another to exchange stories and loot. I joined in here or there but was so tired that I put my feet towards the fire and after making a big show of tying Gyric's rope to my left arm I began to doze.

It had started to get dark when I was woken by a round of cheers as a larger group of men rode up to our camp and dismounted. I sat up as a voice said, 'Hey, we' heard you've got a captive.'

I know that voice I thought. I was not wrong. I looked round to find that I was staring into the face of Seisyll ap Cynan.

'I've been told you have a captive,' he said.

My mind turned over furiously. Had I been wearing my helmet? I was sure I had. Had my hair been showing. Maybe a little had poked out at the back. No choice but to bluff it out.

'I do, sir,' I said respectfully, he was clearly of a higher status than anyone else here.

He smiled at me, 'Where did you find him? I've only heard of one other captive. In the final assault no one was taking prisoners.'

So, I told Seisyll the same story I'd told the others but embellished it a bit as people do. I made a big joke of getting my prisoner up the bank while trying not to slide back down myself.

Seisyll looked at me wryly, 'You're a chatty young man, aren't you?'

'I suppose I can be,' I said, regretting now that I'd let my nerves get to me.

'You're from the south right?'

'Oh yes sir. Caer Dydd. By the Sefearn Sea,' I said. If you're going to lie, stick close to the truth.

'Never heard of it.' He was looking at me very closely now. 'I feel that I've heard your voice before. Why would that be?'

'Don't know, sir. Doesn't seem likely.'

'At least one of those Englishmen spoke Welsh. What's your name?'

'Muirchu,' I said, cursing myself. I'd not even thought to give myself a name. I knew exactly what the next question would be.

'That's not a Welsh name. Are you not of the Cymry?'

I was thinking fast. God knows why I'd blurted out Muirchu's name. The first man who'd taught me to fight before he died on the field at Porloc.

'Ah, no. It's Irish, there's a lot of mixing goes on in those coastal towns.' Forgive me Mother I thought. 'My Ma, she had a lot of friends,' I said with an embarrassed laugh.

His eyes narrowed, then there was a stir at the edge of the camp and a great hairy shape, pushed everyone aside, scattered burning cinders everywhere, and bowled me to the floor.

For a moment I lashed out, then I realised.

'Fucking hell Sib, let me up,' I grabbed thick chunks of his fur before throwing my arms around the great big, grey hunting dog, completely overjoyed.

Seisyll got to his feet, 'Clearly this dog knows you. Where is its owner? Somebody needs to control this beast.'

And there they were, Maelcolm and his woman Bruni. Not that she was really anyone's woman. Dressed in a bloodstained tunic and trousers and carrying a light shield and a throwing spear, she stood there like a vision from a nightmare. With her brown skin, long plaited hair, and with two long wicked looking knives in her belt, she was like no other woman here.

I got to my feet, trying to calm Sib's exuberance. He was so big he could put his paws on your shoulders and lick your face.

'You two can vouch for this Muirchu then, can you?'

Maelcolm looked at Seisyll, whose choice of words had saved me from another tortured explanation.

'Oh yes, we know this Muirchu from when we came over with the Irish.'

Maelcolm was a Strathwaelas from up in the far north beyond the old wall. They spoke Welsh too. After we'd come from Ireland he and Bruni had decided to stay here.

Seisyll must have known them, or known of them, as he addressed Maelcolm as an equal and took his word. I now knew that, for now, Gyric and I were safe. Gyric had met Maelcolm before in very different circumstances. If he did recognise him he wasn't letting on. Sib had stuck himself to me making strange whimpering noises and constantly pushing his head under my arm seeking more attention. I'd missed him more than I'd known.

'We have our own camp not far from here. Why don't you come and join us,' said Maelcolm.

I untied Gyric's rope from my arm and dragged him to his feet. Sib looked puzzled and after growling at Gyric licked his face.

'Get away from him,' I commanded the dog, who obeyed.

'Looks like he's still your dog, then. . ...Muirchu,' said Bruni.

Bruni, Maelcolm and I all spoke passable Irish so we spoke in that language so we could talk unhindered.

We approached their camp and a few men got up to acknowledge their arrival.

'You have a following then?' I said to Maelcolm.

'Yes, we hold a couple of cantrefs from Gruffud,' said Maelcolm, 'the men come with them. Bit like your fyrd.'

A cantref is like an English hundred. A land area that supports a hundred households.

'I think your money goes a lot further in Wales then. I only have part of a hundred,'

I said.

'Probably does, but don't forget we had two shares,' chipped in Bruni.

I smiled, these people were my friends, 'So, life has got a lot better for you then Bruni?'

She smiled broadly, 'It's a lot better than being a slave, or slave on the run. It's good though I'm not called Bruni anymore.'

I looked at her questioningly.

'Yes, Bruni was a name given to me because of my skin. My girlhood name is strange to everyone and makes for too many questions. My name now is simply Gwen.'

I smiled at her, looking over her wild appearance, 'Yes, Gwen, sweet Gwen. It suits you.'

Two days later we were in Maelcolm's and Gwen's comfortable home. It lay in a valley floor, near a stream like nearly every other place I'd seen in Wales. The house was small but comfortable with a byre attached to one end. There was a small ploughed field of barley, just beginning to yellow, and a smithy. Smithies were meeting places because at any time of year there was a fire. If you were passing you stopped to gossip. A good place for a landowner to get the news. The blacksmith and his family lived in a small hut by the forge. They told me that all their other families lived scattered here and there in the surrounding hills. There was no village. The land was hard so two houses together was considered a hamlet.

'No priest then?' I said.

'Oh, there is. Not too far away. He comes and holds a Sunday Mass at the forge to make sure the locals don't believe the smith has magic powers,' said Maelcolm.

Gwen, as I must now learn to call her had vanished into the house and returned soon after. She wore a pale-yellow dress and with a brown shawl covering her hair she looked like any normal Waelas woman.

'Welcome to my home,' she said, in her attractively accented Welsh.

I tied Gyric to one of the posts holding up the roof over the forge and went on in. Once inside a serving girl of theirs cleaned and bound the wound on my arm. I wiped off the wound in my thigh and thought no more about it. All three of us were aching from the fight and the long walk here. Shortly after that food was brought to us and a bowl taken out to Gyric. None of us spoke much all being weary to the bone. The same girl brought in a sheaf of old straw and spread it in a corner. I gratefully collapsed onto it and was soon in a deep sleep.

The next morning, I didn't feel great. I put it down to the last few weeks, and losing a battle. Everyone was already up and about when I rose. I went out to find Gyric pumping a bellows at the smithy. The smith had wasted no time putting him to work. I felt sad for him as my story meant that I couldn't be heard speaking English. Maelcolm spoke English because of his time at the King's court but would have little to say to a slave. Gyric was in for a lonely time.

I greeted Gwen, by her new name. She got her girl to get me a breakfast and I sat down on a settle against the wall of their house. I looked in my bowl but, strangely did not feel hungry. Setting the bowl on the floor suddenly felt sweaty and a little faint.

Next thing I'm on the floor, 'Ugh, what just happened?'

'You fainted. I turned and you were just lying on the ground, 'said Gwen. 'You there, Phelip, Phelip Hammer, bring some water.'

A man with massive forearms and a leather apron lifted my head up and poured water into my mouth. So Phelip is the smith I thought. I drank the water then vomited it back up. Every part of my body started trembling and sweat began to pour out of me.

'He has a fever,' said Gwen. 'Let's get him inside. No, not in the house. Put him in the lean to.'

I was vaguely aware of Gyric taking my legs while the smith lifted my body. They got me to the door of the lean to when Gwen told them to put me down.

'Let me look at your wounds in the light,' she said.

I shakily held out my arm and she tore of the wrappings.

'This probably should have been sewn up but it looks alright. Do you have any other wounds?'

'My legs a bit sore, here,' I said, pointing at my thigh, 'throbbing.' It was only a small wound. Whatever it was that struck me pierced my mail.'

Gwen ripped at my clothes around the tear and drew in a sharp gasp.

'Jesu Mawr,' she cursed, as she saw it. Even in my distress I chuckled at how quickly she'd adopted our ways.

'Does this hurt,' she said, poking at my leg.

A foul smell followed as my thigh felt like it was bursting. I threw up again.

'Sar, no Muirchu, there's puss welling out from the wound and the thigh is all red and swollen. I fear that you are in for a rough time. Phelip, get your son to bring the pony down off the hill and find Maelcolm. Then tell him to ride for the priest. He knows a little healing. Oh, but first, get him in the shed.'

I was laid in the lean to, feeling very strange. I was shaking uncontrollably and my teeth were chattering. Now we were on our own she called me by my name.

'Sar, you might lose your wits, get delirious. The priest is a kind man but you mustn't speak English. Remember no English.'

I nodded. 'I'll try,' I said weakly, then I think I must have passed out.

Chapter Thirty

I was in that lean to for weeks. The door, facing south, was left open most of the time and in between bouts of fever and the visits of the priest I spent days watching the beam of light cross the room. At one point I realised that I was naked under cow hides. Sib spent whole days with his big head lying on my chest. Gwen would drag him out when the priest arrived. Poultices were heated and tied onto my wound and many prayers were said. I must have fouled myself, as Gyric was brought in to turn me and scrape the straw out from under me and replace it. He would whisper encouraging words to me in English and treat me tenderly if no one was around. All I could do was smile faintly and pat his hand. Then, almost as quickly as it had come upon me, I started to feel a bit better and started drinking watered down milk, then curds, then meat broth and slowly I began to recover. Eventually I could be carried outside and led against the wall. To my great surprise they were reaping the barley. Summer was nearly gone.

Still too weak to walk I was sunning myself with the dog at my feet, when Gwen came and sat next to me. Sib stretched out luxuriously, sunshine, and his favourite two people, he was a happy dog. I looked at Gwen and, with a start of surprise, I realised that her belly was swelling.

'You're carrying a child?' I said.

She smiled a quiet smile and caressed her belly, 'Yes, it's quickened for a while now. Feel here.'

She placed my hand on her lump and I could feel a bulge move under my palm. I couldn't help but smile myself.

'You must be pleased. I have a little girl myself and a wife, not officially, but like one. And land, and a home. I need to get back there.' I was so weak I could not hold back the tears.

'They'll wait for you my friend,' said Gwen, 'They'll wait.'

I changed the subject, 'I bet Maelcolm is delighted too. By the way. I've not seen him. Is he not around?'

'When your bishop raided us, it started a whole new conflict. Fighting has been raging all up and down the frontier. It's a loss to everyone as once again we will fight to a draw. Maelcolm is with the king.'

'Is Aelfgar fighting alongside him again?' I asked.

'If he has men in the fight, it's not openly. Gruffud has all the tribes under his banner now. We lose men but the English lose more.'

'I should be with my Earl,' I said. 'My oath is to him.'

'You'd be about as much use to him as a falling leaf in a storm.'

It was true. I was as weak as a kitten but without their sharp little claws.

'You know Bruni, sorry, I mean Gwen. I wonder what would have happened if we'd met in that fight by the river. There's no way I could kill you.'

'Nor I you, Sar. Oh, sorry, I mean Muirchu,' she teased. 'I've both loved and hated you, but we are closer than siblings.'

I thought of my sister, and tears came into my eyes as I doubted her words. I'd shared my mother's womb with Moira and our hardscrabble childhood. Nothing would ever come close.

'You would not have known me. Helmeted and mailed, we all look the same,' I said, not needing to voice my thoughts.

She laughed merrily, 'Ha, I'd have known your gangly carcass anywhere. And would have swerved away.'

'Where's Gyric? What's he been doing?'

'He's playing the slave resigned to his fate. It's not always easy.

Men visit the smithy and bait him. They try to make him angry knowing that if he fights them, he'll be put to death.'

'Really, hmm, that can't be easy. He's a proud man and a fierce warrior. How does he deal with that?'

'He drops to his knees and prays in his own language. He acts like he doesn't understand his persecutors words but I suspect he has learned more than he lets on.'

'He prays. Yes, that sounds like Gyric. Just as well it wasn't me. I can't manage myself. I'd have been dead inside a week.'

Gwen laughed again, then her face fell and turned to mine with tears in her eyes.

'I'm sure he'll be back, Gwen. Maelcolm is nothing if not a survivor,' I said, feeling fond and protective of her. I'd never seen her so vulnerable.

Thank the Lord, I was right. Maelcolm returned with his small war band after the equinox. The campaigning season was nearly over. He was riding a new horse, a little larger than the tough little ponies they bred around here. He was leading the pony he had ridden away on. As he dismounted Gwen greeted him with a cup of mead in her hand. They greeted each other tenderly and talked quietly. The horses were set free to roam as they did around here. The new one looked befuddled for a moment, then wandered off after the pony. I was walking about now, stronger than I was but a long way from fit. I stayed out of the way.

Maelcolm's weary looking men stayed for a drink around the smithy furnace. A couple asked the smith to repair weapons for them. I sat on a stump while Gyric plied the bellows and listened in. There was no tone of triumph but there was one of relief.

Phelip asked for the news.

'The kings are making another truce,' said one man.

'Luckily for us Maelcolm had no desire to be there when the kings met,' said another.

I bet he didn't I thought. Be difficult if any of King Edward's court recognised him.

'I'd have liked to see the English king. They say he dresses in long robes covered in gold thread and precious stones and his household is almost as magnificent,' replied the first man.

I knew this to be true. King Edward was a vain man and his wife, Eadgyth, my Earl's sister, liked him to dress as a European monarch. The English court lived well and dressed better, much given to sumptuous display.

Another man chimed in, 'I'm just happy to be going back to my homestead with all four limbs.'

There was a murmur of agreement. 'Where are they to meet?' asked Phelip as he hammered a heated blade back into shape.

'A place called Aust,' another voice replied.

'No idea where that is,' said Phelip, as he quenched the blade in his trough.

'I do,' I said, 'It's on the English side of the Safearn Sea. Small place, people cross the river there if the winds are calm and the tide out.'

'You know it?'

'More like I know of it,' I said, 'My home is not far on the other side of the water.' I felt a strange pang of sadness for the boy who belonged nowhere. Then I remembered this wasn't true anymore. I had a new home and a family of my own. I needed to get back before I was declared dead and my lands given to someone else. Who would take my family in?

Maelcolm, Gyric and I were sat on the hillside above the homestead chewing on crusts and supping watered ale. There was a chilly wind and a light rain but we were all sweating from sword and spear practice. I was a lot fitter now but still tired easily. We took Gyric under the pretence of him carrying our food and spare weapons. I was back to carrying a couple of light spears and, until I could retrieve my targe, a light wicker shield. Apart from my fine sword I looked like any other

Waelas fighting farmer. We only ever let Gyric spar with an untipped spear shaft and always play a defensive role. There're not many people in these parts but somehow, in the countryside, someone always knows your business. Still, it saved Gyric from feeling quite so alone and when we had clear surroundings we would talk quietly in English.

'There's something I've been keeping from you, Sar,' said Maelcolm. 'Something you are not going to want to hear.'

I stiffened, 'What? Why have you not spoken before?'

'To be honest, Sar. None of us were sure that you would live.'

'So, whatever it is, Gwen knows too?'

'She does, but I told her not to speak in case you started raging at her,' said Maelcolm.

Gyric spoke, 'Well, you'd better tell him before he starts raging anyway.'

Maelcolm took a deep breath, 'Sar, I need to tell you that we're almost certain Oslaf still lives.'

I felt a surge of shame, rage and hatred course through my veins and jumping to my feet, swore, 'I knew it. I fucking knew it. How the fuck did he survive what I did to him? How the fuck?'

I couldn't stay still. I started stomping around, kicking at tussocks, then seizing one of my spears I threw it into the distance, not marking where it fell.

Maelcolm and Gyric calmly sat and watched until I stopped performing and, breathing heavily, squatted back down.

'What do you mean, 'I knew it'?' asked Maelcolm.

I told him about the excursion up the valley when I was meant to be showing Harold where Oslaf fell.

'His body was nowhere to be seen. Christ, Maelcolm, I'd stabbed over and over, then I'd scalped that white hair from his fucking head. How could he possibly still be alive?'

'I don't know Sar. Gwen and I were with you. We saw him face down in the water, we saw his body go over the fall. You were punching your knife through his mail. Can you remember a killing strike. Under the armpit, neck, groin?'

I shook my head. I'd gone over my actions a thousand time. I'd stabbed him until he stopped moving, then I'd stabbed him again. Did I see the dark blood flow? We were in the water. I shook my head again.

Maelcolm paused, then spoke again, 'Thing is. There's a band of brigands to the east of here. They've been around for some time. Surprisingly well armed and provisioned they carry out small raids each side of the border, apparently for women and cattle.'

'So why doesn't Gruffud burn them out?'

'Well, the answer to that question is worth a full purse. The story is they are a mixed bunch of Welsh and English deserters and they are led by a mad Englishman who is horrifically scarred and walks with a long staff. They say his body is twisted and so is his mind.'

'It has to be him but I still don't get how he survived,' I said.

'I've heard it said that very cold water can slow the bleeding and keep a body from dying. That water was cold, very cold.'

I scoffed, 'Even so, really? He was a mess.'

'Well, something happened, didn't it? Gwen and I think, well,' he paused again, 'do you remember how two of his men deserted him before the fight? Maybe they came back.'

'Why would they do that?'

'God, I don't know. Do you think I have all the answers Sar. Get a grip. To steal perhaps, or they thought better of their cowardice. Whatever, maybe they returned, or maybe some wandering shepherd or monk found him, or an angel came down. We don't know. But you didn't find his body and now there's these stories.'

'East of here, did you say?

'Yes, Fforest Glud, it's near the border. Strange place, wild, kept for hunting but no one wants to live there anyway. They say the last dragon in Wales lives there. It's kept in by a ring of churches.'

'But east of here? So, that's north of Y Clas?'

Maelcolm thought for a minute, then nodded.

I jumped to my feet, 'That fucking young priest. Jesu, he was a clever little bastard.'

'The priest whose fingers you nearly cut off?' said Gyric.

'Yes, that one. Stole the pony. Don't you see? He was trying to send our raiding party northwards. Kill two birds with one stone.'

Gyric laughed, while Maelcolm looked puzzled. After we told him the tale, we all sat our arses back down.

Gyric sighed, 'Pity we didn't do what he suggested. Perhaps our friends would still be alive and Oslaf, he might now be dead.'

We all fell silent. Gyric face was lined with tears. I realised he was grieving for his fellow housecarls. Me, not so much. Open that door and who knows what else would follow?

'I still don't understand why they've been left to cause a nuisance,' I said, to break the silence.

'You know, the forest is near the Mercian border and has no great use for Gruffud. The Earl of Mercia is Leofric, Aelfgar's father. Each of them has a force they can direct at an insubordinate subject but deny they have a part in it,' said Maelcolm, 'Anyway, that's what Gwen thinks.'

'Sound likely,' I said, 'Gruffud is known for not tolerating opposition and English Earls aren't above underhand tricks.'

We walked back to the homestead. Gwen took one look at my face and said, 'you've told him then.' It was a statement not a question.

'He has, we need to leave,' I said, 'I'll get fitter walking home.'

Gwen nodded, 'You'll stay another day. I will find an old cloak for your friend and something better for you. You can take that English horse Maelcolm brought home. It's not tough enough to winter in the hills and we've not the feed for it here. I'll get the girl to double bake some bread for the journey.'

I agreed, double baked bread can break your teeth but it lasts longer. The cloaks too, would be a blessing. With only our tunics and leggings it would have been a cold journey home.

We left with Gyric, hands tied, walking alongside me with a rope around his neck tied to the pommel of my saddle tree. We were followed by long plaintive howls from Sib, he still felt like my dog, but was not really my dog anymore. The more Gwen's belly had swelled, the more protective he had become. Visitors feared to get near her. he was spending more and more time shut, howling, in the lean to. It was hard letting him go again.

Mostly I walked alongside the horse trying to build up my endurance, only mounting when I was to weary to walk. Gyric's hair had been roughly cropped, his beard was unkempt, and he was still dirty from the forge. He was, if anything, more muscular than when we'd arrived. When I had to ask directions, no one questioned his status.

'We're going south then,' said Gyric, when we were certain no one was nearby. 'Did wonder if you'd be dragging us over to this Glud place, full of rage and seeking your revenge.'

'You know what Gyric? I counted to ten,' I said, chuckling, 'No, seriously, I want Oslaf's head but I'm not rushing in. Got more important things on my mind. I need to get home and we need to report to Harold too. They'll be thinking we're dead.'

'You've changed, Sar, well, you still do stupid things, but you've changed.'

'You know, I think it's having a family. Not sure I like it. Too much to lose. Makes me fearful in a way I've not felt before. When my mother was killed and my sister sold, all I had to live for was my revenge. Then I had an aunt and cousins and they were taken too. I've been hard and mad ever since. Things are different now.'

Gyric spoke, 'If my hands weren't tied, I'd give you a hug right now.'

'Nope, wouldn't be having that. You can keep your hugs to yourself.'

'Never thanked you for saving me in that fight. We were done for.'

'No need. Must've have been hard spending most of your time tied to a post. Never thanked you for wiping my arse.'

Gyric laughed, 'Yeah learnt a lot about holding my breath, and patience, and ironworking. What do you think? Shall we risk going back to Y Clas?'

'Got to get your sword. Do you remember facing Grim when we'd lost our weapons in Jorvik?'

We laughed together at the memory. Truth was, ever since I met Gyric on Fleet Holm I'd had something of value to lose. I just couldn't see it.

We got to Y Clas early in the afternoon. There was some bustling where people were finishing rebuilding their homes and chanting could be heard from the chapel. I thought about bursting in and surprising that young priest but thought better of it. Instead, we circled around the town and waited for dusk. Where the battle had been fought a few old sheep were penned behind some hurdles. Their destiny to die before winter took its grip. They bleated and shifted uneasily. We froze but no one came. We then crept under the riverbank, slipping and sliding until we were as wet and muddy as we'd been before. Then I found the spot. We were just in time. The river had continued to scour the bank and the remains of my byrnie were hanging out of the earthen bank. I gave it a tug and the bundle fell into my arms. I quickly unfolded it to check that all its contents were still there. Above us we could hear a group of villagers chatting while the sheep bleated loudly.

'Let's wade down the river to the ford. No sense in being seen now. In our state a few peasants could finish us off,' whispered Gyric.

'I left the fucking horse tied up in the woods,' I hissed back.

'Fuck the fucking horse,' said Gyric, with a grin.

'Now you're speaking my language,' I said, smothering a laugh.

We forded the river then veered off the path and into the woods. We lit no fire, and after soaking some bread, we filled our stomachs and slept under the trees. With no fire and no horse, the chances of being found were near zero.

When I woke up Gyric was squatting beside me with his father's sword in his hand.

'Look,' he said, putting his whetstone on the ground, 'Almost as good as it was when we buried it. The silver wire on the hilt has blackened as has the silver chasing on the scabbard. The leather of the scabbard itself and the belt are covered in mould but it's only surface deep, there's a fine stone missing but that might have gone beforehand. I can get that replaced.'

I watched him wiping his cloak along the blade then holding it up to the rising sun and watching the play of light along its newly sharpened edge with a broad smile on his face. I wished I could get pleasure from such simple things.

'We need to avoid the next village too,' I said, 'We'd not be popular there if we were to be recognised. 'To be honest, I don't want to be seen in Hereford either. What if we were the only ones who came back?'

'What not one more visit to Bebbe's tavern? Never understood why you brought us all there after she falsely accused you.'

I looked at Gyric and felt sad. There'll always be at least one guilty secret I'd have to keep from him.

'No, not ever. I feel bad about those girls in the back. You won't say anything will you?'

Gyric grinned again, 'No, Sar, I think you can learn. I'll keep my own counsel. That's between you and your priest.'

We waded the Dore the next evening, then crossed the next river above Hereford through the ford it was named for, rather than over the bridge, after dark. Then ran around the town to warm up. When we got too tired, we crept into another wood and tried to light a fire. I had a flint but could not get enough spark to light the moss I'd gathered. I'm usually good at this but that night we spent shivering violently under a pile of leaves.

Chapter Thirty-One

It was just after first light when we made our shivering way to Much Marcle. The lack of a fire meant that our wet clothes hadn't dried. I felt weak and was leaning on Gyric's shoulder. Maybe I should've gone back for the horse. What's done is done.

'Wulfgeat's brother. Can you remember his name?'

Gyric frowned, 'You know, I can't. I should.'

'No reason you should really. What will we tell him?'

Gyric heaved a sigh, 'That his brother died a hero surrounded by enemy dead.'

'He'll know that he hasn't come back. Everyone will think we're dead too, you know.'

'Yes. You were sick for a long time and now it's November,' said Gyric, 'That last fight was about a week before midsummer. Unless some men were captured and ransomed, there's no one left but us.

'That boy will be heartbroken. He adored Wulfgeat. He was his hero, I do remember that,' I said.

'He's had months to get used to it. But he will want to know how he died. A lot of people will have questions,' said Gyric. 'I'm guessing that you can't say where you've been?'

'Jesu Mawr, no. I don't think I even told Harold that Maelcolm had come from Ireland. I can't remember for sure.'

'That's the trouble with lies, you have to remember them all,' said the always honest Gyric, pointedly.

I turned all this over in my mind. I figured Harold was unlikely to be at Much Marcle but that Fordraed would know where he was or would be. We'd have to find him or at least report to Thurkill. Until now it had seemed simple. Get home, find Harold, get on with our lives. Now, I realised that I'd have to explain how we'd survived, where we'd been and above all tell anyone who wanted to know, what had happened to Leofgar, Athelnoth and all those men. Perhaps I should've stayed in Wales.

'You're sworn to Harold and you have a family now,' said Gyric, as if he'd read my mind, 'You always knew you were coming back. As did I.'

By the time we reached Much Marcle I was staggering. Clearly. I hadn't recovered as well as I'd thought. The cold of the previous night had never left my bones. Once we were within shouting distance of the gatehouse, Gyric let me slide to the ground. I felt like a whipped dog.

'Who goes there?' came a cry from the gatehouse.

'Earl Harold's men. Sar and Gyric seeking our lord and needing help,' shouted Gyric through cupped hands.

'You don't look like the Earl's men. You look like vagabonds. Where's your mail and shields? And you're on foot.'

As I heard this, I realised how we must look dressed in the cast-off clothes of Waelas men. Gyric's hair still too short, mine too long, though presently covered by a hood. We looked like peasants, or disgraced fighting men. For the first time I got a taste of the shame Gyric had been, and probably, still was, feeling. Heroic tales would have had us fight to the death. Well; I'm no fucking hero.

'Tell him to ask Fordraed and Hildifryth who we are,' I said to Gyric. He cupped his hands again and did so.

'You know our master's name,' the voice shouted back. This was followed by some noises from behind the gate. In my mind's eye I could see the gatekeepers arguing with each other before one of them ran to the house. While I imagined the messengers every pace, I struggled back on to my feet.

The voice cried out again, 'You're to show me your hair. I've been told you must show me your hair.'

I chuckled to myself as I pulled my hood back.

The gate swung open wide enough to let a man through.

'There's no mistaking you, is there Sar,' said a cheerful deep voice. It was Fordraed. 'Help this man into the house,' he said, ordering one of his gatekeepers. I recognised the man but couldn't remember his name.

'Shall I lock him in the shed again, sir?' he said.

'For God's sake man, no. Take them to the room behind the hall while I go and find Hildifryth,' said Fordraed. 'Oh, and you and the other gatekeeper, keep this to yourself.'

I was half carried into the homestead with my arms across Gyric's and the gatekeeper's shoulders, then across the yard, through the hall and into the back room. The gatekeeper stirred up the ashes in the still warm hearth, dropped a few twigs on them and quickly blew them alight.

'Here, I'll feed the fire, you go and get us some water, or better still ale,' said Gyric. The man hesitated then opened his mouth to protest.

'Now!' roared Gyric. The man shut his mouth and scuttled out.

I laid down alongside the hearth, shivering violently. I feared my fever was returning. The next voice I was conscious of hearing was Hildifryth's,

'Here, boy, drink this this.'

A gentle hand lifted the back of my head and dribbled warm mead into my mouth. Its tangy sweetness coursed through me, then I spluttered and choked.

'Lean him up against the wall and make him keep sipping this,' she said to Gyric, 'and drink some yourself. You both look perished.'

She left the room while Gyric followed her instructions. Before long she was back with a bowl of barley pottage for each of us. I felt well enough to feed myself now my hands had stopped shaking. She went outside and I could hear her exchanging whispers with someone then Fordraed strode in.

'Your arrival here is quite a surprise. Gruffuth told our king that you'd all been wiped out to the last man.' He sat down on a stool and stared at us, and, frowning, stared at each of us in turn. 'That was before midsummer. Where, then, have you two been?'

Gyric told him the tale. How we escaped the battle and how I pretended to be a Waelas and that we'd stayed with someone I knew.

'You stayed with a friend in Wales? What? How come you have friends in Wales, Sar?'

'Well, I fought with and against the Waelas with the Irish, sir,' I said, 'we found them, well they found us, really, by chance.'

'What friend?'

'I'd rather not say, sir. Earl Harold knows about him. He's from Strathclyde. That's all I can say.' I said, saying a little too much. The more I thought about it the more certain I was that I hadn't told Harold that Maelcolm was in Wales. Another bridge to cross when the time comes.

'Hmm, well Harold's not here.'

'No,' said Gyric, 'but we thought you might know where he is.'

'Well, I do and I don't,' said Fordraed, 'He's somewhere in Europe. The emperor died so now we could send a mission to Hungary to seek the Atheling. Harold has gone to Europe.'

'Overseas then?' I said.

Gyric sniggered into his bowl.

I blushed, then let it go. I was so, so tired. In the warm glow of the fire, I dozed off.

I awoke to find Fordraed, Gyric and Hildifryth huddled together lit up only by the red glow of the fire. As I stirred, they turned to face me.

'Sar, we've been talking and we think that Leofgar's exploits do not resound to anyone's honour,' said Fordraed.

'Won't disagree with you there. It was a fool's errand from the start,' I said.

Gyric spoke then, 'Your views don't matter now Sar. There's no point in saying I told you so.'

'But I …'

Fordraed raised his hand, 'Gyric is right. What's more important is that your return will raise a lot of questions which will be hard to answer. We have decided to invent a story that explains your absence and late return.'

'And leaves the fate of the bishop's raid clouded in mystery,' said Hildifryth.

I frowned, 'More secrets.'

Gyric said, 'We can tell Harold or Thurkill privately and ask them. When the time comes.'

Hildifryth chipped in, 'Much as I struggle with Gytha, she is wise and powerful. I'd tell her the story and take her advice.'

I could tell her about Oslaf's whereabouts too I thought to myself.

'Where would we find her? Bosham? Wincestre?' I said.

'I can't tell you that. But what I do know is that the king will be at Glowecestre for Christ's Mass. She is likely to be there. Or, if not, some of her son's will be, and, of course, her daughter, the queen. One of them will know,' said Hildifryth.

I winced at the idea of facing Earl Tostig's hostile glare, but Hildifryth was right. I could probably approach one of the more friendly brothers. Glowecestre wasn't too far from my home.

'You are to say you were wounded in the first encounter in the woods. Gyric stayed to look after you but then you were captured. Your wound festered, as indeed your later wound did.'

'They'd have killed me,' I said, 'I'd have been of no use.'

'Invent something. You speak their language, maybe they thought it was worth saving you to use you later. Something like that,' said Gyric.

'Yes, that might work, and when the long nights drew in, we managed to escape in the dark,' I said, thinking quickly.

Gyric squirmed, 'We'll have to lie to our boys, and not tell Wulfgeat's brother that we witnessed Wulfgeat's end.'

'We'll have to lie to everyone, Gyric, until it's all forgotten.'

'It's settled then,' said Fordraed, 'Gyric, your father, Scalpi, is with Harold so I suggest you head home as soon as possible to your grieving mother. You have a boy at Sar's homestead, yes?'

Gyric nodded.

'You go there, get him, and you take Wulfgeat's brother back to his family. No one seemed to know where he could be found. His mother will be none too pleased with you.'

'You can stay here another day to recover then I'm lending you a man and some horses to get you home,' added Hildifryth.

And so it was. Two days later we bypassed Colbrand's place and headed to my home. Even through my tired eyes I could see improvements had been made. The furnaces were gone and the tracks potholes filled with the remains. There was new thatch on the house and we seemed to have gained a forge. There was a bustle of activity which suddenly halted as we rode in. I was shocked that we had got so near before the alarm was raised then I remembered, the war was over.

Godric was the first to recognise us and he and the two boys ran towards us shouting gleefully. Tunglo then appeared, a pair of tongs in his hand, from the forge. He took one look at us then rushed into the house to be followed out by Ymma and Inga. As I dismounted Inga flew at me and threw her arms around my legs.

'Daddy's home,' she cried, 'Daddy's home.'

As I bent to cuddle Inga I looked over her head at Ymma who was stood there with both hands covering her mouth. She fell to her knees and as her hands came away, she spoke.

'By the Virgin Mary, you're alive. We'd been told that you'd all died. I've been expecting us all to have to leave.' She burst into tears, 'You're back. Oh Sar, how I've missed you.'

I unclamped Inga's arms from my legs and picked her up.

'My you've got heavier. What have they been feeding you? Stones.'

She giggled, 'No, Daddy, that would be stupid.'

I laughed at this and with my other arm lifted Ymma from off her knees and embraced her too. By now it seemed the whole village was here, the red ones, the black ones, and all the shades in between. The smoky acrid smell of my people. I was home.

That night, after we had all eaten, all the dwellers from the main hall were sent to sleep with different households in the village. Ymma and I were alone. I told her the whole sad story and the tale we had to tell instead. As I told her, I, for the first time in months, felt truly safe.

'It was terrible, Ymma, horrific, I've seen slaughter before but that whole time, knowing it would end badly and not being able to stop it. It was just bloody awful.'

That night, in Ymma's arms, I cried myself to sleep.

Historical Notes

My last book, *Blood on the Water,* dealt with the events leading up to the start of this one. Again, my main source of information is the Anglo-Saxon Chronical as well as the many learned scholars who have enquired into this era.

The central event of this tale is Bishop Leofgar's truce breaking raid into Wales. This did happen. We know that his and Athelnoth's forces were wiped out at Glasbury on Wye 'eight days before midsummer.' There may have been survivors but the chronicle isn't clear, nor do we have any information about that raid. All the events of the raid in this book are products of my imagination.

We do know that Leofgar was criticised for his warrior like presentation by other churchmen. He was, before becoming a bishop, Harold's chaplain. Glasbury is not far into Wales. Did Leofgar's force get beaten before it had gone very far? This would have meant a small force that could be defeated by another small force. This seems unlikely to me. Peace had been declared by both Kings so it is likely that the Welsh fighting men were mostly back in their villages and farms. It also seemed unlikely that Leofgar and Athelnoth would have had a small, lightly armed raiding party as both men were important figures in their society. This is why I chose my imaginary force to push further into Wales. And why I chose the Welsh to respond in the way I have described.

The whole Englishmen relying on their shield wall as the only way to fight is probably an over-egged pudding but Ralph of Mantes was heavily criticised for his mounted attack on the Welsh. I've portrayed Leofgar as the type of Englishman who adhered to rigid tried and tested tactics much as post-Napoleonic Englishmen might have blustered about the 'thin red line' when it was past its sell by date. We know that Harold used different tactics at other times (I'll be writing about them in later volumes) but we also know that the shield wall was significant at Hastings.

That said there does seem to have been a conservative attitude to the use of bows by the English as, perhaps, a weapon that a serious warrior despised. I have assumed that the Welsh did not feel the same way. I also, do not think they would have arrived at the powerful longbow as we know it from later medieval times, or the bowmen who practiced for many hours, or the arrowheads designed specifically for war. I imagine that lots of Welsh fighting farmers would have had hunting bows that they would have taken to war.

There is some controversy about whether a byrnie was the padded jacket alone or whether the mail shirt was stitched on to it making it one garment. I have chosen to see them as two separate garments on the flimsy grounds that I once read that a mail shirt was cleaned of rust and polished by shaking it in a bag of sand. An impossible feat if stitched to a padded jacket. My personal view is that students of this period rely too much on the accuracy of the Bayeaux Tapestry.

Before my hero's ordeal the practice of corsned is mentioned. This was the practice of giving the suspected criminal a morsel of consecrated bread, or possibly bread and cheese, which they had to swallow cleanly to prove innocence. Choking signified guilt. I suspect that many criminals of our day would have no trouble with this but in a time of very real belief in an interventionist God this would have had some success in separating the sheep from the goats. A dry mouth is a symptom of fear.

It was tempting to have Sar face an ordeal by fighting but at this time it was not part of English jurisprudence. It was introduced later under the Norman kings.

One last point; the adventures of the exiled Aethelings deserve much more attention than I have given them here or will in the next book. There are different versions of their story concerning where they were when. If you are interested go do some research. It is a story worthy of a fairy tale.

This period of our history is overcast by the events of the Norman Conquest but, for me, the twilight of our ancient Saxon culture was a fascinating time. This book covers part of the only time there was a King of all the Welsh and a King of all the English. Sar was present during these events and will be there to witness what follows. Hopefully you will join me in his next adventure.

Simon Phelps

COMING SOON

Book 4

– Into the Wolf's Lair

Chapter 1

Mul the Stealthy pointed his hand back to me palm down. I crouched even lower and crept up next to him.

'Sar, there's something ahead of us. Up there in the valley floor,' he mouthed.

We'd been stalking slowly along the valley side through woodland thick with falling trees whose size had been their undoing. Below us a small river ran made its noisy way south. We'd been circling the area for a day and a night since leaving our horses with our Waelas guide at the church at Llanfihangel Nant Melan. At this point our guide had refused to come any further.

'The last dragon in Wales lives in these parts,' he'd said, in his own language.

Having been brought up in Wales I spoke it too, 'but you know there's outlaws living in Fforest Glud.'

'Don't care where the heathens are. This church is one of the four built to keep the dragon in. I will go no further.'

We knew when we were beaten so had set out to find tracks into the area. So far, we had found none. Mul was the hunter from Earl Harold's estate at Much Marcle. He could track a summer breeze through the grass. We knew that whole raiding parties went from here, but how?

We were wading through a stream to continue our search when Mul stopped suddenly, 'They go up a river. That's how they do it.'

So that's what we decided to do. We'd already waded through a much larger flow than the one we were crossing so we carefully made our way back. Everything we did had to be slow and careful. To be caught would end our purpose. For good at the hands of my mortal enemy, Oslaf.

Mul, as always, was carrying his hunting bow and a quiver of arrows. Me, I was back in the outfit of my mail free days. A dark tunic, my small targe on my back and carrying a pair of throwing spears. My very dark red hair had grown long again and was now plaited into three long thick strands. In my sword belt, a blackjack, a small throwing axe and the sword I'd taken from Oslaf the day I thought I'd killed him. We'd buried our bags under some leaves at the foot of the valley and both of us had smeared our hands and faces with mud.

The wind shifted, and with it came the smell of smoke.

Mul sniffed, 'Campfires, dry wood and roasting meat.'

I grinned at him, 'If you say so. Like you can really do that.'

He grinned back, shrugged, and carefully stretched all his limbs. I'm guessing he was in his forties now. His face was lined but his eyes were still keen.

He was right about the fires though. As we crept on, we could see below us a rough palisade built on both sides of the water. Behind that lay the first fire in the level bottom of the valley. Being summer, the river was not in spate, nor likely to be. Below us I could see a roof, roughly thatched with branches of alder and hazel.

'They look pretty well set in. They've even built huts,' I whispered to Mul.

As we carried on up the valley we saw more huts, tents and fires then a cleared space surrounded by logs laid horizontally on the ground.

'Meeting place? Where are the horses? They must have horses,' I said.

This had to be true. To bring provisions into a place like this you'd need pack ponies at the very least. We moved on up the valley.

The thick foliage helped keep us covered but the steepness of the valley side meant every step had to be taken with care. The sound of running water grew as we progressed until it became a thunderous roar. No one would hear us now.

'There must be a waterfall near,' said Mul.

I nodded, still trying to count the buildings and fires below through the trees without showing myself.

'There must be a good few of them here,' I said, 'but with them all along the valley floor I've no idea of how many.'

'There's a lot of people moving about. Some are definitely women, some probably slaves doing the dirty work. There's some armed men, but no sign of pickets. We carried on. If Oslaf was here, he was inside or his blond, almost white hair covered. Then, with a chuckle, I remembered, most of that hair was gone. I'd scalped him. I guessed that he wasn't so pretty now. Thing is, he should've been dead.

As we went further up the valley, we realised that the trees were thinning out behind us just before we got our first sight of the waterfall. It was breathtaking cautiously I moved until I could see through the trees to the top of the fall. With a start I pulled my head back. There was a man, outlined against the sky, right above the falls.

'There's a lookout up there. He must be able to see down the whole length of the valley. If the trees were bare, he'd see everything.'

Mul nodded, and having more sense than to look for himself, asked, 'Have you seen enough?'

We made our way back down. I'd learned a thing or two. This place would be hard to attack but not impossible. They were over-confident and had only protected themselves against an attack from the river. Another thing I knew? To charge downhill on a camp like this risked losing our footing and arriving like a bunch of kids doing roly-polies.

We were not far from where we'd entered the river when I snagged my sword hilt in a thorn bush. I was cursing myself for having brought the sword, which was a foolish vanity for a scout, when I heard a hiss from behind. I turned to see Mul firing an arrow into the throat of a startled man leading a loaded pony. Behind him was another man heavily burdened with a pack. I snatched a spear from the ground where I'd laid it while I tried to untangle myself and threw it at him. My hasty throw meant my aim was poor and the spear pierced the man in the thigh. He let on one loud yell before Mul was on him, hand over the screaming man's mouth as he pulled a knife across his throat. The first body lay in the water, face down, twitching as his life drained away. A few moments later the other man stopped thrashing about and, when Mul took his hand away, gurgled as he choked on his own blood. It was soon over.

I tore myself free from the bush and rushed down to calm the pony. Luckily, like many pack ponies, it was completely unperturbed by the commotion going on around him. Casually it helped itself to some hazel leaves from a nearby tree that leaned over the water. We both froze, waiting to see if anyone was following the two men.

Nothing. All was quiet. I burst into action and, after quickly wrapping the pony's lead rein around an overhanging branch, started dragging the first body up into the woods.

'For Christ's sake, Mul, help me here,' I said.

Mul was staring about wildly, his face pale and his hands shaking. I let go of the body and grabbed Mul's shoulders and shook him roughly.

'Mul, I need your help. What the fuck is up with you?' I hissed into his face.

He came to with a start and, staring at me, asked, 'What? What shall I do?'

'Help me here. We have to hide these bodies.'

We pulled the first body up the hill and concealed it as best we could by pushing it under some brambles before shovelling old leaves over the drag marks. As we walked back down Mul started retching, then was violently sick. I cut the back pack from the other man's body then started dragging it in a different direction. Mul came and helped until we'd hidden it too.

I felt angry with Mul, though his quick actions had probably saved our bacon. He looked at the mess we'd made and spoke for the first time.

'Any decent tracker could see something had happened here.'

'Only if they look for it,' I answered as I dragged the pack up into the woods too, 'By the time the bodies start stinking or scavenging animals drag them out we'll be long gone. 'So, where do they keep you?' I said to the pony, as I gently stroked its muzzle. My first horse had been a pack pony. I'd called it Maeve after Earl Harold's ship, *Maeve's Lover.* I had an idea.

'Let's turn this pony back down the river and see where it goes,' I said to Mul.

We followed it down the river on a very loose rein, and, sure enough, when it came to a tributary stream, the pony turned into it and made its way uphill. A few hundred paces up it left the stream and joined a clearly well used track thick with hoofprints. We followed the trail, I was holding the pony tighter now, while Mul scouted ahead. The trees thinned until we came to open grassland rising steeply uphill. Mul made a halt sign, while the pony whinnied, smelling, I assumed, his friends somewhere ahead.

Mul turned, 'I've seen enough. There's signs of a herd up there. There'll be men to herd them too.'

'We must keep the pony. If it returns, they'll seek its drivers. Better they think they ran off or something,' I said, tugging the reluctant pony around.

We silently retraced our steps for many miles until we returned to the well-used trails of normal folk. Mul was very quiet. He always was a man who said little, now he was saying nothing.

I pressed him, 'What happened back there Mul? You were fantastic, never seen such a quick shot, so accurate. You shut him up straight away, and then when I mishit the second man you were on him like a demon. Then you just fell to pieces. What happened?'

Mul stopped walking and looked at me, his eyes shifting, his unease was clear. 'Sar, I've never killed a man before. Taken a human life. Now I've killed two, one so close I could feel his heart stop beating,' he said. His eyes filled with tears.

For a moment I was shocked. Then I thought, why would he have? He wasn't a housecarl and even if he'd been called up in the fyrd, he still might never have fought.

'But you've killed hundreds of animals in your time,' I said.

'That's different.'

'But they are innocent creatures. You can bet your life those two weren't, I said, struggling to understand.

'God created animals to serve us. Their lives are taken to feed us or to stop them stealing our crops. Killing men is murder. You've killed men. I know you have. Didn't you shake and tremble at first?'

Now he was saying too much. 'The first man I killed, I was crazy with rage. He'd just killed my mother by smashing her head into a doorpost. Then, well, all hell kicked off and I didn't have time to feel anything.'

Mul's eyebrows almost met his hairline, 'My God, how old were you?'

My face went red, 'I don't know. Maybe thirteen or fourteen.' I always felt stupid not knowing my age.

'And how many summers since?'

I coloured up again, 'Maybe five or six. A lot has happened since then.'

Mul looked at me steadily, 'I always thought you must be older than you looked. Seems I was wrong. And you've killed more men since then?'

I nodded, 'Yes many.'

'How does that make you feel?'

'I don't feel anything.'

'Nothing at all?'

'No,' I said, 'Nothing.'

'Sar, you do know that makes you the strange one? Not me.'

I shuffled awkwardly while my guts felt like they were twisting inside me. My friend Gyric's father, Scalpi, had said I was a cold killer. A man who didn't need to work himself up to kill like most men did. Made me just like my enemy Oslaf, the son of my mother's killer, the man I hated above all living men. The man who'd sold my sister into slavery and carved the long scar down my jawline. I felt ashamed, then I felt angry.

'So what if I don't feel anything. I'm sure I'm not alone in that,' I said, forcefully spitting on the ground.

'You're ridden by the nightmare though, aren't you?'

I was taken aback, 'How the hell do you know that?'

'People talk. Last year when you stayed at Much Marcle you'd shout and cry in your sleep. You're not the first warrior to do that. What do you see?'

Truth was, I do get nightmares. When I got home from Bishop Leofgar's ill-fated raid into Wales they'd started up with a vengeance. My mother's ruined face demanding I avenge the deaths of her sister, her family and the fate of our village and the reproachful faces of the men I had killed. Many of them. The farmhand on the walls of Hereford, the man I'd pushed under the waves with an oar, the Hutha horse thief, Osric, Oslaf's brother, and more. It had got so bad that Ymma had told me that I had to sleep in the granary as my waking up at night shouting and seizing my weapons was frightening everyone. They'd only stopped after I'd seen Gytha, Earl Harold's powerful mother, and been given a new mission. I had a feeling that everyone was relieved to see me go. Except, perhaps, my little girl Inga.

'I don't see anything I want to tell you,' I said, rudely, to Mul.

We took the pony back to the church where we'd left our guide and our horses then spent a few more days scouting in the hills above the camp we'd found. Most of the hills were grazed bare by wild cattle and deer. Lot's of them, all left alone under the dragon's protection. By sticking to the wooded edges or sneaking through the grass we could keep an eye on the horse herd and its herdsmen. Every once in a while, men would take ponies away or lead them back. One time about a dozen men came and saddled up horses and rode off carrying shields and spears.

'A raiding party, by the looks of it,' I said to Mul, 'Let's get gone before they return.'

We rejoined our guide and began our ride home to Maelcolm and Gwen's homestead in Trecoed. Mul was uneasy about this, he didn't like being the only non-Welsh speaker in a homestead of people he saw as the enemy.

It was a long ride so the sun was dropping behind the hills when we arrived. Even as we approached, I knew by the smell of burning and the lack of voices or the hammering of hammer on iron from the forge that something was wrong. Very wrong.

About the Author

Simon's love of history and historical novels goes all the way back to his childhood when he discovered the novels of Rosemary Sutcliff and Mary Renault in junior school. Since then, he's led an interesting and varied life. At the tail end of a not very successful education he, aged 17, had an accident while changing scenery overnight for a local theatre. This left him permanently wheelchair bound.

Three years after this he co-founded a commune aimed at self-sufficient living which is where he first became involved in animal husbandry. After its anarchic nature became its own undoing, he went on to work on a city farm in Bristol, before buying a smallholding. Eventually living the life of a medieval peasant lost its appeal and he decided to get an education by completing an Access course. Then he studied the public under-standing of science before going on to do a master's degree in the History of Science, Medicine and Technology. Then, in another abrupt change of direction, he retrained as a counsellor and then as a counselling supervisor.

This has resulted in a character who knows how to skin a goat, ferret for rabbits, grow vegetables, write learned essays on science history and dissertations on 18th century electrical medicine and help traumatised people heal. During all this he has been married twice and has helped raise his own children, step-children and grandchildren. He believes this mixture of experiences informs his writing, his characters and the adventures they have.

After retiring from his counselling career, he now travels when he can and writes historical novels both to entertain people and in the hope of encouraging his readers to share his own love of history and the doings of our ancestors.

9 781916 764064